BAD
WOLF

Center Point
Large Print

Also by Nele Neuhaus and available from
Center Point Large Print:

Snow White Must Die

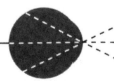

**This Large Print Book carries the
Seal of Approval of N.A.V.H.**

BAD WOLF

NELE NEUHAUS

Translated by Steven T. Murray

CENTER POINT LARGE PRINT
THORNDIKE, MAINE

This Center Point Large Print edition is
published in the year 2014 by arrangement with
St. Martin's Press.

Originally published by Ullstein Buchverlag GmbH
in Germany under the title *Böser Wolf.*

This is a work of fiction.
All of the characters, organizations, and events
portrayed in this novel are either products of the
author's imagination or are used fictitiously.

The text of this Large Print edition is unabridged.
In other aspects, this book may vary
from the original edition.
Printed in the United States of America
on permanent paper.
Set in 16-point Times New Roman type.

ISBN: 978-1-62899-040-9

Library of Congress Cataloging-in-Publication Data

Neuhaus, Nele.
  [Böser Wolf. English]
  Bad wolf / Nele Neuhaus ; translated by Steven T. Murray. — Center
Point Large Print edition.
     pages ; cm
  ISBN 978-1-62899-040-9 (library binding : alk. paper)
  I. Murray, Steven T., translator. II. Title.
  PT2714.E95B6713 2014b
  833´.92—dc23
                                                                    2013046972

For Matthias
Heaven is a place on earth with you.

BAD
WOLF

Prologue

He set down the shopping bag and put away his purchases in the tiny refrigerator. The ice cream, her favorite flavor of Häagen-Dazs, had almost melted, but he knew that was exactly the way she liked it, so creamy and rich with the crunchy bits of cookies. It had been weeks since he'd seen her. Although it was hard for him, he never pressured her. He knew he really shouldn't rush her; he had to be patient. She had to want to come to him on her own. Yesterday, she had finally gotten in touch, sending a text message. And soon she would be here. The anticipation made his heart beat faster.

He looked around the trailer, which he'd given a good cleaning the night before. He glanced at the clock over the narrow kitchen counter. Already twenty past six. He had to hurry, because he didn't want her to see him like this, all sweaty and unshaven. After work, he'd stopped at the barbershop for a quick trim, but the rancid smell of the lunch stand still clung to every pore. He tore off his clothes, which were reeking of sweat and deep-fry oil, stuffed them into the empty shopping bag, and jumped into the minishower next to the kitchen. Even though it was cramped and the water pressure was low, he preferred the confines of his trailer to the unhygienic public bathrooms at the trailer park, which weren't cleaned very often.

He soaped up from head to toe, shaved carefully, and then brushed his teeth. Sometimes he had to force himself to do these things because it was so tempting to let himself go and sink into self-pity and lethargy. Maybe that's what would have happened if she hadn't been around.

A couple of minutes later, he slipped into fresh underwear and a clean polo shirt, then took a pair of jeans out of the dresser. Finally, he strapped his watch to his wrist. A couple of months ago, a pawnbroker at the train station had offered him 150 euros for it—an outrageously paltry sum, considering that thirteen years ago he'd paid eleven thousand D-marks for this masterpiece from a Swiss watch company. He was keeping this watch. It was the last reminder of his former life. One more look in the mirror and then he opened the door and stepped out of the trailer.

His heart skipped a beat when he saw her sitting outside on the rickety garden chair. He'd been looking forward to this moment for days and weeks. He stood there, allowing the sight of her to sink in completely.

How beautiful she was, how tender and delicate! A sweet little angel with soft blond hair falling over her shoulders; he knew what it felt like and how it smelled. She was wearing a sleeveless dress that revealed her lightly tanned skin and the fragile vertebrae of her neck. She had a rapt expression on her face as she busily thumbed a text on her cell phone, and she didn't notice him. He didn't want to frighten her, so he cleared his throat. She looked up and her eyes met his. Her smile began at the corners of her mouth and then spread over her whole face. She jumped to her feet.

He had to swallow hard as she came over and stopped right in front of him. The look of trust in her dark eyes gave his heart a pang. Good God, how sweet she was! She was the only reason why he hadn't thrown himself in front of a train long ago, or in some other affordable way had put a premature end to his miserable life.

"Hello, sweetie," he said hoarsely, putting his hand on her shoulder—only briefly. Her skin felt silky and warm. At first, he always felt shy about touching her.

"Where did you tell your mother you were going?"

"She and my stepdad went to some party tonight, at the firehouse, I think," she replied, sticking her cell into her red backpack. "I told her I was going to Jessie's place."

"Good."

With a glance, he made sure that no curious neighbor or chance passerby was watching them.

He was tingling inside with excitement, and his knees felt weak.

"I bought you your favorite ice cream," he said softly. "Shall we go inside?"

Thursday, June 10, 2010

She felt like she was tipping over backward. As soon as she opened her eyes, everything started spinning around. And she felt sick. No, not sick; she felt ghastly. She could smell the vomit. Alina groaned and tried to raise her head. Where was she? What had happened, and where was everybody else?

They had all been sitting together under the tree, Mart beside her, with his arm around her shoulders. It felt good. She laughed, and he kissed her. Katharina and Mia kept on complaining about the mosquitoes, and they'd been drinking this sweet stuff—vodka and Red Bull.

Alina sat up with an effort. Her head was pounding. She opened her eyes and was shocked to see the sun was about to set. How late was it anyway? And where was her cell phone? She couldn't remember how she'd gotten here, or where exactly she was. The past few hours were a blank, a total blackout.

"Mart? Mia? Where are you?"

She crawled over to the trunk of the huge weeping willow. It took all her strength to get to her feet and look around. Her knees felt as soft as butter, everything was spinning around her, and she couldn't see clearly. She'd probably lost her contact lenses when she was throwing up. And she'd certainly done a lot of that. The taste in her mouth was disgusting, and she could feel vomit on her face. The dry leaves crackled under her bare feet. She looked down. Her shoes were gone, too.

"Shit, shit, shit," she muttered, fighting to hold back the tears. She was going to be in big trouble if she showed up at home looking like this.

From a distance, she could hear voices and laughter drifting toward her, along with the aroma of grilled meat, which made her feel even more nauseated. At least she hadn't landed somewhere out in the boonies; there were other people close by.

Alina let go of the tree trunk and took a couple of tentative steps. Everything around her was spinning round like a carousel, but she forced herself to keep walking. What a bunch of assholes they all were. Some friends! They'd just let her lie here drunk, with no shoes and no phone. Maybe fat Katharina and that stupid cow Mia were having a good laugh at her expense. She was really going to let them have it when she saw them tomorrow at school. And she would never speak to Mart again in her life.

At that moment, Alina happened to look at the steep bank leading down to the river and stopped short. There was somebody lying down there, in the stinging nettles, right next to the water. Dark hair, a yellow T-shirt—it was Alex. Damn, how had he gotten down there? What had happened? Cursing, Alina made her way down the bank. The nettles stung her bare calves, and she stepped on something sharp.

"Alex!" She squatted down next to him and shook his shoulder. He stank of vomit, too, and was groaning softly. "Hey, wake up!"

She waved away the mosquitoes that kept buzzing around her face.

"Alex! Wake up! Come on!" She tugged on his legs, but he was as heavy as lead and didn't budge.

On the river, a motorboat passed by. The wake sloshed up on shore, making the water gurgle in the reeds and lap against Alex's legs. Alina gasped in terror. Right in front of her eyes, a pale hand emerged from the water and seemed to reach out for her.

She recoiled and uttered a frightened cry. Among the reeds—not six feet away from Alex—Mia was lying in the water. Alina thought she could see her face just below the surface. In the diffuse half-light of dusk, she could see long blond hair and wide-open, dead eyes that seemed to be looking straight at her.

As if paralyzed, Alina stared at the gruesome sight, her mind reeling in confusion. What the hell had happened here? Another wave rolled in, Mia's body moved, and her arm stuck out of the dark water as pale as a ghost, as if she were begging for help.

Alina was shaking all over, even though it was still intolerably hot. Her stomach rebelled, and she staggered, turning around to throw up in the nettles. But instead of vodka and Red Bull, only bitter gall came up. Sobbing desperately, she crawled up the steep bank on all fours, scratching her hands and knees on the stubbled slope. Oh, if only she were home in her room, in bed, safe and sound! All she wanted was to get away from this horrible place and forget everything she'd seen.

Pia Kirchhoff was typing into her PC the final report on the investigation into the death of Veronika Meissner. Since early morning, the sun had been baking the flat roof of the building where the offices of Kommissariat 11 of the Criminal Police were located, and the readout on the digital weather station sitting on the window-sill next to Kai Ostermann's desk showed it was eighty-eight degrees. Room temperature. Outside, it was probably a good five degrees hotter. Schools had canceled lessons because of the heat. Although the doors and windows were open wide, there was no hint of a breeze to bring any relief. Pia's forearm stuck to the desktop as soon as she leaned on it. She sighed and pressed PRINT, then added the report to the slim folder. All that was missing was the autopsy report, but where had she put it? Pia got up and searched through her out-box, eager to be done with this case at last. Since yesterday, she'd been holding down the fort alone at K-11. Her colleague Kai Ostermann, with whom she shared the office, was attending a course at the National Criminal Police office in Wiesbaden. Kathrin Fachinger and Cem Altunay were taking part in a nationwide seminar in Düsseldorf, and the boss had been on vacation since Monday at an undisclosed location. Commissioner Nicola Engel had granted Pia some time off when she was promoted to detective superintendent, but that, too, had fallen by the wayside because the department was so short-staffed. Pia didn't really mind. She hated for anyone to make a fuss over her; the change in her rank was no more than an administrative formality.

"So where's that damn report?" she muttered in annoyance. It was almost five already, and she was planning to go to her class reunion in Königstein at seven. The construction work they were doing on her farmhouse, the Birkenhof, often left her no time for any social life, but she was looking forward to seeing the girls from her old school after twenty-five years.

A knock at her open door made her spin around. "Hello, Pia."

Pia couldn't believe her eyes. It was her former colleague Frank Behnke, but he was totally transformed. He had changed his usual look—

17

jeans, T-shirt, and worn cowboy boots—for a light gray suit with shirt and tie. He wore his hair a little longer than before, and his face no longer looked as haggard, which was an improvement.

"Hello, Frank," she replied, amazed. "Long time no see."

"But you did recognize me," he said with a grin, shoving his hands into his pants pockets and giving her the once-over. "You're looking good. I heard you stumbled up another rung of the career ladder. I suppose you'll be taking over from the old man soon, eh?"

As always, Frank Behnke lost no time pushing her buttons, and he did it effortlessly. Her polite query as to how things were going for him stuck in her throat.

"I didn't 'stumble up' the career ladder, no way. My rank was changed, that's all," she responded coolly. "And to whom are you referring as 'the old man'? You mean Bodenstein?"

Behnke just shrugged it off with a grin and kept on chewing his gum. That was one thing he hadn't managed to give up.

After his inglorious departure from K-11 two years earlier, he'd lodged a complaint about his suspension and been lucky enough to be reinstated. At any rate, he'd been transferred to the National Criminal Police office in Wiesbaden, and nobody at the Regional Criminal Unit in Hofheim had been sorry to see him go.

He slipped past her and sat down in Ostermann's chair.

"Everybody flew the coop, I see."

Pia muttered to herself as she kept on looking for that autopsy report.

"To what do I owe the honor of this visit?" she then asked.

Behnke clasped his hands behind his head.

"Well, what a shame that you're the only one here I can share my happy news with," he said. "But the others will find out soon enough."

"What is it?" Pia gave him a suspicious look.

"I got fed up with working the streets. I've done that shit long enough," he replied without taking his eyes off her. "The Special Assignment Unit, K-11, all that's behind me now. I always got the best evaluations, so they forgave me my minor indiscretion."

Minor indiscretion! Behnke had punched their colleague Kathrin Fachinger in a fit of uncontrolled rage and committed enough other transgressions to warrant a suspension.

"I was having personal problems back then," he went on. "That was taken into account. At the State Police office, I passed a couple of additional qualifications, and now I'm at K-134, the Office of Internal Affairs, responsible for investigating and bringing charges against police personnel and preventing corruption."

Pia couldn't believe her ears. Frank Behnke as

an Internal Affairs investigator? That was utterly absurd.

"Along with my colleagues from the other federal states, in the past few months we've developed a strategic concept that will go into effect on July first nationwide. Improvement of services and professional oversight within subordinate departments, sensitivity training for personnel, and so on . . ." He crossed one leg over the other and jiggled his foot. "Dr. Engel is a competent manager, but occasionally we get reports from the individual investigative offices about transgressions committed by colleagues. I can vividly recall certain incidents in this very office that were quite disturbing: failure to administer punishments in the office, not following up on misdemeanors, unauthorized IT queries, passing internal documents to third parties . . . just to mention a few examples."

Pia abruptly stopped searching for the autopsy report.

"What are you getting at?"

Behnke's smile turned malicious, and his eyes took on an unpleasant glint. Pia had a bad feeling about all this. As always, he was enjoying demonstrating his superiority and power with regard to his opponent, a character trait of his that she despised. As a colleague, with his envy and perpetually rotten temper, Behnke had been a veritable torment, but as a representative of internal investigations, he could be a disaster.

"You, of all people, should know best." He stood up and came around the desk to stand close to her. "But you're the obvious favorite of the old man."

"I have no idea what you're talking about," Pia replied icily.

"Oh, don't you? Really?" Behnke moved so close that it made her uncomfortable, but she resisted the urge to step back. "Starting Monday, I'm going to start an authorized internal investigation in this building, and I probably won't have to dig very deep to bring a few corpses to light."

Pia was shivering despite the tropical heat in the office, but she remained outwardly calm, even though she was boiling inside; she even managed to smile. Frank Behnke was an unforgiving and petty person who forgot nothing. Old frustrations were still eating at him and seemed to have multiplied tenfold in recent years. And he was contemplating revenge for the injustice and humiliation he imagined he'd suffered. It wouldn't be smart to make an enemy of him, but Pia's anger was stronger than her good sense.

"Well then," she said sarcastically, resuming her search. "I wish you much success in your new job as . . . a cadaver dog."

Behnke turned to go.

"Your name isn't on my list yet. But that could change at any time. Have a nice weekend."

Pia didn't react to the unambiguous threat his words implied. She waited until he was gone, then grabbed her cell and punched the hot key for Bodenstein. The call went through, but nobody picked up. Damn. She was sure that her boss hadn't the slightest idea what a nasty surprise was waiting for him here. She knew pretty much what Behnke was insinuating. And it could have very unpleasant consequences for Oliver von Bodenstein.

The deposit on three returnable bottles was enough for a pack of noodles. Five more would buy veggies to go with it. That was the currency he dealt in these days.

Before, in his former life, he hadn't paid any attention to collecting the deposit, but had blithely tossed empty bottles into trash cans. That was exactly the sort of person who ensured his basic needs today. He'd received twelve and a half euros from the kiosk owner for the two bags of empty bottles. He got paid six euros an hour under the table by the greedy cheapskate for standing all day in this tin box at the edge of an industrial zone in Fechenheim, grilling hot dogs and burgers and deep-frying potatoes. If the cash register didn't add up perfectly, the amount was docked from his pay. Today, everything had come out even, and he hadn't had to beg for his money like he usually did. Fatso was in a good mood and had paid him what he was owed for the past five days.

Combined with the money from collecting bottles, he had about three hundred euros in his wallet: a small fortune. That was why, feeling suddenly flush, he'd splurged not only on a haircut but also a shave from the Turkish barber across from the train station. After a visit to Aldi, he had enough left to pay the rent on his trailer space for two months in advance.

He parked his rickety motor scooter next to the trailer, pulled the helmet off his head, and took the shopping bag out of the carrier.

The heat was driving him crazy. It didn't even cool off at night. In the morning, he would wake up soaked with sweat. In the miserable lunch stand of thin corrugated iron, it could get up to 140 degrees, and the stifling humidity made the stench of sweat and rancid fat settle in his hair and pores.

The dilapidated trailer in the RV park in Schwanheim was supposed to have been a temporary solution, back when he still believed he could make a go of it and restore his financial situation. But nothing in his life had turned out to be as long-lasting as this temporary arrangement—he'd already been living here for seven years.

He unzipped the awning, which must have been dark green decades ago, before the weather had faded it to a nondescript pale gray. A puff of hot air gusted toward him. Inside the trailer, it was several degrees hotter than outside, with a stifling and stuffy smell. No matter how much he scrubbed and aired out the place, the odors had settled into the upholstery and every nook and cranny. Even after seven years, it still filled him with disgust, but for him there was no other option.

Ever since his plunge into the abyss, and as a convicted criminal, he belonged to the under-class, even among the residents of the slum on the outskirts of the metropolis. Nobody wandered in here on vacation or to admire the glitzy skyline of Frankfurt, the concrete and glass symbols of big money across the river. His neighbors were mostly blamelessly impoverished retirees or failures like himself who had landed on the down escalator. Alcohol often played a leading role in the story of their lives, which were depressingly similar. As for himself, he drank no more than one beer in the evening, he didn't smoke, and he paid attention to his weight and grooming. He didn't bother with the Hartz IV law of 2005, which combined unemployment insurance with social welfare, because he couldn't stand the thought of having to show up as a supplicant and kowtow to the bigoted whims of indifferent bureaucrats.

A tiny scrap of self-esteem was the last thing he

possessed. If he lost that, he might as well kill himself.

"Hello?"

A voice outside the awning made him turn around. A man was standing behind the half-desiccated hedge that divided the property of his tiny plot from the neighbor's.

"What do you want?"

The man came closer, hesitated. His piggy little eyes flicked angrily from left to right.

"Somebody told me you would help anyone who was having trouble with the authorities." The high-pitched falsetto was a grotesque contrast to the massive figure of the man. Sweat was beading on his balding head, and the smell of garlic overpowered the even less pleasant body odors.

"Oh, really? Who says that?"

"Rosi, from the kiosk. She told me, 'Go see Doc. He'll help you.'" The sweating hunk of lard glanced around again, as if he was afraid to be seen there. Then he took a roll of bills out of his pocket. Hundreds, even a couple of five hundreds. "I'll pay you well."

"Come on in."

Right off, the guy seemed kind of disagreeable, but that didn't matter. He couldn't be picky about his clientele, his address was not in any phone book, and he certainly didn't have a Web site. Still, there were limits to what he'd do, no matter how much money was offered, and people knew that. With his previous conviction and the probation that was still in force, he couldn't get involved in anything that might send him back to the slammer. But word on the street was that he'd already helped tavern owners and operators of lunch stands who had come into conflict with official regulations, desperate pensioners who'd been bilked on promotional shopping trips or by door-to-door salesmen, unemployed people or immigrants who couldn't understand the complex bureaucracy in Germany, and young people who were seduced early by the temptations of a life on credit and had fallen into the debt trap. Anyone who asked for help knew that he worked only for cash.

He had long since gotten over any feelings of sympathy. He was no Robin Hood; he was a mercenary. For cash in advance, he would fill out official forms on the scratched-up Formica table in his trailer, translate complicated bureaucratic German into understandable everyday language, and offer legal advice for any situation in order to augment his income.

"What's the problem?" he asked his visitor, who cast an appraising glance at the obvious indicators of poverty and seemed to gain confidence.

"Man, it's sure hot in here. Have you got a beer or a glass of water?"

"No." He made no effort to be friendly.

Long gone were the days of mahogany-veneer

conference tables in air-conditioned rooms, trays holding little bottles of water and fruit juice, and glasses arrayed upside down.

With a snort, the fat man pulled out some rolled-up papers from the inside pocket of his greasy leather vest and handed them over. Recycled paper, small print. The tax office.

He unfolded the papers, which were damp with sweat, smoothed them out, and scanned the text.

"Three hundred," he demanded without looking up. Rolls of cash stuffed in pants pockets always signified illegal earnings. The sweaty fat man could afford to pay a bit more than the usual rate he charged seniors and the unemployed.

"What?" the new client protested, as anticipated. "For a few pages?"

"If you can find someone to do it cheaper, be my guest."

The fat man muttered something unintelligible, then reluctantly peeled off three banknotes and laid them on the table.

"Do I at least get a receipt?"

"Sure. My secretary will make it out later and give it to your chauffeur," he replied. "Now have a seat. I'll need some information from you."

Traffic was backed up at Baseler Platz leading to the Friedensbrücke. For a couple of weeks now, the city had been one big construction zone, and

Hanna was annoyed that she'd forgotten all about that and driven into downtown instead of taking the route via the Frankfurter Kreuz and Niederrad to Sachsenhausen. As she drove along at a snail's pace behind a bunch of rusty pickup trucks with Lithuanian license plates crossing the bridge over the Main River, Hanna replayed the unsatisfying conversation with Norman that morning. She was still pissed off about his stupidity and his lies. It had been hard for her to fire him with no notice after eleven years, but he'd left her no choice. Before he stomped off in a huff, he'd fired off a series of nasty curses and issued several vile threats.

Hanna's smartphone hummed, and she grabbed it and opened her mail app. Her assistant had sent her an e-mail. The header said "Catastrophe!!!" Instead of a message, there was a link to FOCUS online. Hanna clicked the link with her thumb, and her stomach lurched when she read the headline.

Hanna Heartless, it said in bold letters, and beside it was a rather unflattering photo of her. Her pulse began to race and she felt her right hand trembling uncontrollably. She gripped her phone harder. *All she cares about is profit. The guests on her TV show have to sign a nondisclosure agreement before they're allowed to speak. And whatever they say is scripted in advance by Hanna Herzmann, 46. Bricklayer Armin V., 52,* *wanted to speak during the show about his hassle with his landlord (the topic was "My Landlord Wants to Evict Me"), but with the cameras rolling, he was labeled a transient renter by the moderator. When he protested after the broadcast, he discovered another side of the supposedly sympathetic Hanna Herzmann, and of her lawyer. Now Armin V. is unemployed and homeless after his landlord finally succeeded in evicting him. Something similar happened to Bettina B., 34. The single mother was a guest on Hanna Herzmann's program in January (topic: "When Fathers Hit the Road"). Contrary to preliminary arrangements, Bettina B. was portrayed as an overtaxed mother and alcoholic. For her, too, the broadcast had unpleasant consequences: She received a visit from Child Welfare.*

"Shit," Hanna muttered. Once something was on the Internet, it was impossible to delete. She bit her lip and thought hard.

Unfortunately, the article was close to the truth. Hanna had a real knack for finding interesting topics, and she wasn't afraid to ask embarrassing questions and stir up dirt. In doing so, she basically couldn't care less about the people and their often tragic fates. She secretly had nothing but contempt for most of them and their urge to bare all in return for fifteen minutes of fame. Hanna managed to coax the most intimate secrets out of people in front of the camera, and she was a master at pretending to be sympathetic and interested.

Besides, the true story was often insufficient, so a little dramatization was necessary. And that had been Norman's job. He had cynically called the show *Pimp My Boring Life* and was happy to distort reality, regardless of how painful it might prove to be. Whether that was morally acceptable or not wasn't Hanna's concern; in the end, the show's success in the ratings validated his tactics. Of course, the letters of complaint from disgruntled guests filled several file folders. They often didn't understand until later, when they were subjected to public mockery, what sort of embarrassing things they'd said in front of a television audience. As a matter of fact, complaints arose only seldom, and that was due to the polished, absolutely airtight legal contracts that each person who wanted to speak on her broadcast had to sign in advance.

A car honked behind her, startling Hanna out of her reverie. The traffic was moving again. She raised her hand in apology and stepped on the gas. Ten minutes later, she turned down Hedderichstrasse and then into the back courtyard of the building where her company was located. She put her smartphone in her shoulder bag and stepped out of the car. In the city, it was always several degrees warmer than out in the Taunus region; the heat built up between the buildings until it felt like a sauna. Hanna fled into the air-conditioned foyer and stepped into an elevator. On the way to the sixth floor, she leaned against the cool wall and took a critical look at herself in the mirrored surface.

In the first weeks after her breakup with Vinzenz, she had looked terribly harried and exhausted, and the girls in Makeup had had to muster all their professional skill to make her look the way the television viewers expected. But now Hanna found her appearance quite passable, at least in the dim light of the elevator. She'd colored her hair to cover the first silver strands, not out of vanity, but from a sheer instinct for self-preservation. The TV business was unforgiving: men could have gray hair, but for women, that would mean eventual banishment to the afternoon cultural and cooking shows.

Hanna had hardly stepped out of the elevator on the sixth floor when Jan Niemöller appeared out of nowhere. In spite of the tropical weather outdoors, the manager of Herzmann Productions was wearing a black shirt, black jeans, and even a scarf around his neck.

"All hell has broken loose!" Niemöller trotted along beside her excitedly, waving his skinny arms. "The phones are ringing off the hook, and nobody can reach you. And how come I have to hear from Norman that you fired him with no notice? Why didn't you tell me? First you give

Julia the boot, now Norman—who do you think is going to do the work?"

"Meike is going to fill in for Julia during the summer; that's already been set up. And we're going to be working with an independent producer."

"And you don't even ask me about it?"

Hanna looked Niemöller up and down.

"Hiring and firing is my job. I took you on to deal with the business stuff so I wouldn't have to worry about it."

"Oh, so that's how you see it?" He was insulted, of course.

Hanna knew that Jan Niemöller was secretly in love with her, or, rather, with all the glory surrounding her, which also spilled over onto him as her associate. But she viewed him solely as a business partner—as a man, he was not her type. Besides, he'd been acting so possessive lately that she needed to put him in his place.

"That's not just the way I see it; that's the way it *is*," she said with a tad more coolness. "I appreciate your opinion, but I'm the one making the decisions."

Niemöller opened his mouth to protest, but Hanna cut him off with a wave of her hand.

"The network hates this sort of publicity. We're no longer in a very strong position. With the shitty ratings in recent months, I had no choice but to kick Norman out. If they take us off the air, all of you can go scrambling for another job. Do you get it?"

Irina Zydek, Hanna's assistant, appeared in the hallway.

"Hanna, Matern has called you three times. And almost every newspaper and TV news desk, except for Al Jazeera." Her voice had an anxious undertone.

The rest of the staff appeared in the doorways of their offices, and their concern was palpable. The news had obviously gotten around that she'd fired Norman without notice.

"We're meeting in half an hour in the conference room," Hanna said as she walked by. First, she had to call Wolfgang Matern back. She couldn't afford any trouble with the network at the moment.

She stepped into her office at the end of the corridor; it was flooded with light. She dropped her shoulder bag on one of the visitors' chairs and sat down behind her desk. As her computer booted up, she leafed quickly through the call-back messages that Irina had written on yellow Post-its, then picked up the phone. She never liked to put off unpleasant tasks for long. She hit the speed-dial number for Wolfgang Matern and took a deep breath. He picked up in a matter of seconds.

"It's Hanna Heartless," she said.

"Good to hear you've still got a sense of humor," the CEO of Antenne Pro replied.

"I've just fired my producer without notice because I learned that for years he's been doctoring the bios of my guests if he found the truth too boring."

"You mean you didn't know that?"

"No!" She put all the indignation she could into this lie. "I'm stunned. I couldn't check out every story, so I had to depend on him. That is—or was—his job."

"Please tell me that it won't turn into a bloodbath," said Matern.

"Of course not." Hanna leaned back in her chair. "I already have an idea for how we can turn this thing around."

"What is it?"

"We'll admit everything and apologize to the guests."

There was a moment's silence.

"Retreat disguised as an advance," Wolfgang Matern said at last. "That's precisely why I admire you. You don't run and hide. Let's talk about it tomorrow over lunch, okay?"

Hanna could almost hear his smile, and a weight lifted off her heart. Sometimes her spontaneous ideas were the best.

The Airbus had not yet come to a stop when people started undoing their safety belts and getting up, ignoring the instructions to remain seated until the plane reached the gate. Bodenstein stayed in his seat. He had no desire to stand in the jammed aisle and get jostled by the other passengers. A glance at his watch assured him that he had plenty of time. The plane had landed precisely at 8:42 P.M. after a forty-five-minute flight.

Ever since this afternoon, he'd had the feeling that he was finally putting his life in order after two turbulent, chaotic years. He'd made the right decision to attend the trial of Annika Sommerfeld in Potsdam and draw a line of finality under the whole matter. He felt that a load had been lifted off his shoulders. He'd been carrying it around since last summer—no, actually from that day in November two years ago when he'd been forced to acknowledge that Cosima was cheating on him. The breakup of his marriage and the fling with Annika had thrown him for a complete loop emotionally and caused serious damage to his self-esteem. In the end, his private misery had affected his ability to concentrate on his work and led him to make mistakes that he never would have made before. Although in the past few weeks and months, he had also recognized that his marriage to Cosima had not been nearly as perfect as he'd convinced himself it was during their twenty-year relationship. Far too often he'd backed down and acted against his will for the sake of harmony, the children, and outward appearances. Now that was all in the past.

The queue in the aisle finally began to move.

Bodenstein stood up, retrieved his bag from the overhead compartment, and followed his fellow passengers toward the exit.

From Gate A49, it was a real hike to the terminal exit. At one point, he followed the wrong sign, as he often did in this gigantic airport, and ended up in the departure hall. He took the escalator down to the arrivals level and stepped outside into the warm evening air. A few minutes before nine. Inka was supposed to pick him up at nine. Bodenstein crossed the taxi lane and stood in the short-term parking area. He spotted her black Land Rover in the distance and smiled in spite of himself. Whenever Cosima had promised to pick him up somewhere, she would always show up at least fifteen minutes late, making him very annoyed. Things were different with Inka.

The SUV pulled up next to him and he opened the back door, heaved his roller bag onto the seat, and then climbed in the front.

"Hi." She was smiling. "Have a good flight?"

"Hello." Bodenstein was smiling, too, as he fastened his seat belt. "Yes, wonderful. Thanks for picking me up."

"No problem. Anytime."

She put on the left-turn blinker, glanced over her shoulder, and merged back into the line of slow-moving cars.

Bodenstein hadn't told anyone why he'd gone to Potsdam, not even Inka, although in recent months she'd become a good friend. He leaned back against the headrest. The episode with Annika Sommerfeld had undoubtedly had one positive result. He had finally begun to think about himself, which had proved to be a painful process of self-realization. He had come to understand that very seldom had he done what he really wanted to do. He'd always yielded to Cosima's wishes and demands, because of his basic good nature, because it was easier, or maybe because he felt a sense of responsibility, but none of that mattered. The end result was that he'd turned into a boring yes-man, a henpecked husband, and with that he'd lost all his sex appeal. No wonder that Cosima, who hated routine and boredom more than anything, had fallen into an affair.

"By the way, I got the key to the house," said Inka. "If you like, you could take another look at it tonight."

"Oh, that's a good idea." Bodenstein looked at her. "But first you have to drive me home so I can pick up my car."

"I can drive you home afterward; otherwise, it'll be too late. They haven't turned on the electricity yet."

"If it's not too much trouble."

"No problem." She grinned. "I'm off tonight."

"Well then, I'll gladly take you up on that offer."

Dr. Inka Hansen was a veterinarian and worked at an animal clinic in the Ruppertshain district of Kelkheim with two colleagues. Through her job, she had found out everything about the house. It was half of a duplex, and the builder had run out of money. For six months, construction had been stopped, and the house had gone on the market at a relatively reasonable price.

Half an hour later, they had reached the construction site and teetered their way across a plank to the front door. Inka opened it and they went inside.

"The stone floor has been laid, and all the wiring is done. But that's it," said Inka as she strolled through the rooms on the ground floor.

Then they went up the stairs to the second floor.

"Wow!" Bodenstein exclaimed. "The view is spectacular." In the distance they could see the glittering lights of downtown Frankfurt to the left and the brightly illuminated airport to the right.

"And nobody can build in front of it to block the view," Inka declared. "In the daytime, you can see all the way up the hill to Schloss Bodenstein."

Life certainly took strange detours sometimes. He'd been fourteen years old when he fell in love with Inka Hansen, the daughter of the horse veterinarian from Ruppertshain. But he'd never worked up the courage to tell her. And so it ended in misunderstandings, which had driven him to study far away. There he had met Nicola, and then

Cosima. He'd stopped thinking about Inka until they happened to meet during a murder investigation five years ago. Back then, he had still believed that his marriage to Cosima would last forever, and he probably would have lost contact with Inka if her daughter and his son hadn't fallen in love with each other. The past year, the two had gotten married, and at the wedding he, as the father of the groom, had been seated next to her, the mother of the bride. They'd had a good conversation, then kept in touch by phone and went out to eat a few times. Over several months, a genuine friendship had developed, and the phone calls and dinners soon turned into a regular habit. Bodenstein liked being with Inka; she was easy to talk to and a good friend. Inka was a strong, self-confident woman, who placed great value on her freedom and independence.

Bodenstein was happy with his life now, except for his housing situation. He couldn't stay in the carriage house at the Bodenstein ancestral estate forever.

In the vanishing daylight, they inspected the whole house, and Bodenstein was warming to the idea of moving to Ruppertshain so he could be closer to his youngest daughter. For the past few months, Cosima had also lived in Ruppertshain. She had rented an apartment in the Zauberberg, the former TB sanatorium, where she also had her office. After months of accusations, counter-accusations, and insults, Cosima and Oliver now got along better than ever before. They shared custody of Sophia, which was the top priority for Oliver. He would have his youngest daughter to himself every other weekend, and sometimes during the week as well, when Cosima had deadlines to meet.

"This is really ideal," he said enthusiastically when they'd finished the tour. "Sophia could have her own room, and when she's a little older, she can come over here alone or even ride her bike to my parents' place."

"I thought of that, too," Inka replied. "Shall I put you in touch with the seller?"

"Yes, I'd appreciate that," Bodenstein said with a nod.

Inka closed the front door and led the way across the plank toward the street. The night was hazy, and the heat of the day was still palpable between the houses. The scent of charcoal and grilled meat was in the air, and they heard voices and laughter from one of the backyards. "Just imagine," he said, "if all goes well, we could wind up being neighbors."

"Would you like that?" Inka asked.

As she stood next to her car, she turned around to look at him. In the light of the streetlamps, her natural blond hair shone like honey. Bodenstein admired once more her classic facial features, her high cheekbones and lovely lips. Neither the years nor the hard work as a veterinarian had diminished her beauty. He once again wondered why she'd never had a husband or a steady boyfriend.

"Sure." He walked around the car to the passenger side and got in. "That would be wonderful. Why don't we grab a quick pizza at Merlin's? I'm as hungry as a bear."

Inka got in behind the wheel.

"Okay," she replied after a brief hesitation, and put the key in the ignition.

For the third time, Pia drove around the narrow cobblestone streets of the old town in Königstein, looking in vain for a parking spot as she cursed the size of her SUV. In front of her, a minivan pulled out of a spot, and she skillfully backed into the space. After one last look in the rearview mirror, she grabbed her bag and got out. She had never been to a class reunion and was honestly eager to see the girls from her old school. As she walked past the ice-cream shop, her eyes fell on a lattice fence with the gaping hole of a construction site behind it. This was where the building had stood in which she'd found the corpse of Robert Watkowiak two years before. The fact that there had been a dead man in the house certainly hadn't helped the real estate agent sell the property.

Pia went down the pedestrian street and turned right at the bookstore, heading toward Villa

Borgnis in the direction of the spa park. Pia could hear laughter and the babble of voices drowning out the splashing of the fountain surrounded by a border of flowers. She turned the corner and had to smile. The same flock of chickens as in the old days!

"Piiiiia!" a red-haired woman called shrilly, coming toward her with arms outstretched. "How wonderful to see you."

A big hug and kisses left and right.

Sylvia's face was radiant as she pushed her toward the crowd, and the next moment Pia was surrounded by familiar faces, astonished to see how little her friends had changed over the years. Someone put a glass of Aperol spritz in her hand. Kisses, smiles, effusive embraces, genuine joy at seeing one another again. Sylvia gave a witty speech, which kept getting interrupted by laughter and whistles, and finished by saying she hoped everyone present would have a lot of fun. As thanks from the class of 1986, Yvonne and Kristina gave her a big bouquet and a gift certificate for a wellness weekend, and Pia had to stifle a grin. Typical gifts from well-to-do women of a certain age. But they came from the heart, and Sylvia was moved to tears.

Pia sipped her cocktail and made a face. This sweet stuff was not exactly her favorite drink, but it was totally in at the moment, having regrettably supplanted good old Prosecco in popularity.

"Pia?"

She turned around to see a dark-haired woman in whose adult features she recognized the fifteen-year-old girl she once knew.

"Emma!" she cried in disbelief. "I had no idea you'd be here, too! How great to see you."

"I'm glad I decided to come. I confirmed at the last minute."

They gazed at each other, then laughed and shared a big hug.

"Hey!" Pia's eyes now fell on the round belly of her old childhood friend. "You're pregnant!"

"Yep, imagine. At forty-three."

"That's no big deal these days," replied Pia.

"I have a daughter, Louisa, who's five. And I actually thought that would be it. But when it rains, it pours." Emma took her by the arm. "And you? Do you have kids?"

Pia felt the familiar pang that this question always provoked.

"No," she replied breezily. "But I've got horses and dogs."

"At least you can lock them up at night some-where."

They both grinned.

"Wow, I never thought we'd ever see each other again," said Pia, changing the subject. "A couple of years ago, I ran into Miriam. Somehow, every-one always comes back to the beautiful Taunus."

"Yep, even me." Emma let go of her arm.

"Excuse me for sitting down for a moment. This heat is really getting to me."

With a sigh, she sank onto a chair, and Pia sat down beside her.

"Miriam, you, and I," said Emma. "We were truly the Terrible Trio. Our parents had their hands full with us. How's Miri doing?"

"Good." Pia took another sip of the orange-colored stuff. In this warm weather, her mouth had dried out from talking so much. "Last year she married my ex."

"Are you kidding?" Emma opened her eyes wide. "And . . . you—I mean, that must be pretty tough for you, isn't it?"

"Oh no, no. I'm fine with it. Henning and I get along better than ever, and we still work together occasionally. Anyway, I'm not alone."

Pia leaned back and looked out across the terrace. It felt like being on a class outing in the old days. The girls who'd been friends back then had quickly found one another again. Behind the tall cedars, the tower of the ruined fortress was glowing in the light from the spotlights against the dark blue backdrop of the evening sky, and the first stars were faintly glimmering. A peaceful, carefree evening. Pia was happy she'd come. She didn't do enough socializing in her free time.

"Tell me about yourself," Pia said. "What are you doing these days?"

"I got a teaching degree, but after two years

at an elementary school in Berlin, I joined the German Development Service and went abroad."

"As a teacher?" Pia asked.

"At first, yes. But then I wanted to go into crisis areas. Really do some good. So I joined Doctors Worldwide. As a logistics tech. Then I was really in my element."

"What did you do there?"

"Organization. Transporting medicines and health-care supplies. I was responsible for communications technology, plus the housing and welfare of staff members. Customs clearance, route planning, the motor pool, the maintenance and daily operation of the camps, project security, and contact with personnel back in Germany."

"Wow. That sounds exciting."

"Yes, it certainly was. Usually, we'd find catastrophic conditions, zero infrastructure, corrupt officials, and tribes at each other's throats. In Ethiopia six years ago, I also met my husband. He's a physician with Doctors Worldwide."

"So why did you come back here?"

Emma patted her belly.

"Last winter, when I found out I was pregnant, Florian—that's my husband—insisted that I return to Germany with Louisa. After all, a pregnancy at my age is risky. I'm staying with his parents in Falkenstein. Maybe you've heard of my father-in-law: Dr. Josef Finkbeiner. Many years ago, he founded the Sonnenkinder Association."

"Of course I've heard of it," said Pia with a nod. "Helping single mothers and their children."

"Precisely. A really fantastic cause," Emma declared. "Once the baby is born, I won't be able to do much else. At the moment, I'm helping out a little at the organization, planning the big celebration for my father-in-law's eightieth birthday in early July."

"And is your husband still in some disaster zone?"

"No. Three weeks ago, he came back from Haiti and is now giving speeches all over Germany for DW. I don't see a lot of him, but at least he's home on weekends."

A waiter came over with a tray, and Emma and Pia each took a glass of mineral water.

"Hey, it's really great to see you again." With a smile, Pia raised her glass. "Miri will be glad to hear that you're back in Germany, too."

"The three of us should get together. Maybe chat about old times."

"Good idea. Here, I'll give you my card." As Pia rummaged in her shoulder bag for a business card, she felt her cell phone vibrating.

"Excuse me a moment," she said, handing Emma her card. "I have to take this."

"Your husband?" Emma asked.

"No. My job."

Today was Pia's day off, but if murder was suspected and her colleagues belonged to a different Kripo unit, she was the one they'd call. It was as she'd feared: A girl had been found dead in Eddersheim.

"I'm on my way," she said to the officer on duty, who was already at the scene. "Half an hour. Text me the exact address."

"You're with the Criminal Police?" Emma asked in astonishment as she held up the card. "Detective Superintendent Pia Kirchhoff."

"As of today, *chief* detective superintendent." Pia gave her a wry smile.

"What do they want you for at this time of day?"

"They found a body. And unfortunately, I'm on call."

"You work in Homicide?" Emma stared at her in surprise. "Jeez, that's exciting. Do you carry a revolver, too?"

"A pistol. And it's not really that exciting. Mostly frustrating." Pia grimaced and stood up. "Well, at least I'll spare myself the big good-bye with everybody. If anyone asks about me . . ."

She shrugged. Emma also got up.

"You know what? Why don't you come to our summer party? Then at least we'll get to see each other again. And if Miriam feels like it, bring her along, too, okay? I'd really love to see both of you."

"I'd love to come." Pia gave her friend a hug. "See you soon."

She managed to escape unnoticed. Ten after ten!

Crap. A dead girl. It was going to be a long night, and since she was the only one on call in her department, the unpleasant task of notifying the parents would fall to her. Facing the disbelief and despair of the victim's family members was the worst part of her job.

As she walked down the pedestrian street to her car, her cell phone rang again and the display lit up. The duty officer had texted her the address: *Mönchhofstrasse in Hattersheim-Eddersheim. By the locks.* Pia got into her car, turned on the ignition, and rolled down the windows to let in some fresh air. She typed the address into her GPS, fastened her seat belt, and drove off.

Calculating route, the friendly female computer voice informed her. *The route is in the direction displayed.*

Distance: 22.7 kilometers. Arrival time: 22:43.

Hanna turned down the little cul-de-sac at the edge of the woods. Her house stood at the end. The exterior floodlights, which were activated by a motion detector, bathed the house in bright light. She braked to a stop. She hoped she wouldn't find Vinzenz waiting there, or even Norman. But then she saw a bright red Mini with Munich plates parked in front of the double garage door and gave a sigh. Meike had apparently arrived a day early. She parked next to Meike's car and climbed out.

"Hi, Meike!" she called, smiling, although she wasn't exactly in a cheerful mood. First the ugly argument with Norman, then the conversation with Wolfgang Matern. At seven o'clock, Hanna had had a crisis meeting with the whole team in the conference room. Then she and Jan had met with a female freelance producer who chain-smoked for an hour and a half in a dim, stuffy lounge full of suits in a side street off Goethestrasse and kept making outrageous demands. A total waste of time.

"Hi, Hanna." Meike got up from the top step. Two suitcases and a carryall stood by the front door.

"Why didn't you call and tell me you were arriving today?"

"I tried about twenty times," said Meike reproachfully. "Why'd you turn off your cell?"

"Oh, there were so many hassles today. I must have turned it off at some point. But you could have called the office."

She kissed her daughter on the cheek, prompting a grimace. Then she opened the front door and helped Meike take in the bags.

Moving from Berlin to Munich seemed to have done Meike good. Since Hanna had last seen her, she'd put on a little weight. Her hair was washed and her style of clothes had normalized a bit. Maybe she was finally about to give up the late-puberty look of a homeless squatter.

"You're looking good," she said.

"You sure aren't," replied Meike with a critical glance. "You're really looking old."

"Thanks for the compliment."

Hanna kicked off her shoes and went to the kitchen to get an ice-cold beer from the fridge.

Her relationship with Meike had always been complicated, and considering this initial exchange, Hanna was no longer sure it had been a good idea to ask her daughter to fill in as a production assistant during her summer vacation. She had never paid any attention to what other people said about her, but Meike's hostility was causing her more and more concern. On the phone, her daughter had immediately made it clear that she wasn't taking the job as a favor, but for purely financial reasons. Still, Hanna was looking forward to having Meike stay with her over the summer. She hadn't yet gotten used to being alone.

The toilet flushed and Meike reappeared in the kitchen.

"Are you hungry?" Hanna asked.

"No. I already ate."

Exhausted, Hanna sat down on one of the kitchen chairs, stretched out her legs, and wiggled her aching toes. Hallux rigidus in both her big toes, the price of wearing heels for thirty years. Walking in shoes with heels more than an inch and a half high was becoming more and more of a torment, but she couldn't resort to wearing tennis shoes.

"If you want a cold beer, there are a couple of bottles in the fridge."

"I'd rather make some green tea. Have you started drinking again?" Meike ran water into the kettle, took a mug out of the cupboard, and looked in drawers until she found the tea. "Maybe that's why Vinzenz left. How is it that you manage to scare off every guy?"

Hanna didn't react to her daughter's jibes. She was too tired to get into the sort of argument that Meike used to provoke on a daily basis. She knew that the worst of the hostility would taper off after a couple of hours, so she tried to ignore her comments for the time being.

Meike was a child of divorce. Her father, a notorious smart-ass and nitpicker, had moved out when she was only six. Since then, he had spoiled her on every other weekend and successfully incited her animosity toward her mother. His brainwashing was still working eighteen years later.

"I liked Vinzenz," said Meike, crossing her much too skinny arms over her meager breasts. "He was witty."

She had been a completely normal kid, but as a teenager she'd put on almost two hundred pounds as a result of overeating because of emotional problems. Then at sixteen, she'd practically stopped eating altogether, and a couple of years ago, her anorexia had landed her in a clinic for eating disorders. At five seven, she had weighed only eighty-six pounds, and for a long time Hanna had been expecting a call telling her that her daughter was dead.

"I used to like him, too." Hanna finished her beer. "But we grew apart."

"No wonder he decided to leave." Meike gave a contemptuous snort. "Next to you, nobody has any room to breathe. You're like a tank, rolling over everybody with utter disregard for the consequences."

Hanna sighed. She felt no anger at the hurtful words, only deep sadness. She would never be able to feel real affection for this young woman, who had deliberately tried to starve herself to death. And it was Hanna's own fault. During Meike's childhood and youth, her own career had been more important than her daughter, and that's why she had yielded the field almost without a fight and with a feeling of relief. Meike had not seen through the perfidious little power play of her father, and for years she had idolized him without reservation. Meike had no clue that he had used his daughter to exact revenge on Hanna. And Hanna took care not to mention the topic.

"So that's the way you see me," she said softly.

"Everybody does," Meike snapped back. "You never care about anyone but yourself."

"That's not true," Hanna countered. "For you, I've—"

"Oh, give me a break!" Meike rolled her eyes. "You haven't done shit for me! All you ever cared about was your job and your boyfriends."

The teakettle began to whistle. Meike turned off the burner, poured water into the cup, and dropped in the tea bag. Her abrupt movements betrayed the inner tension she was feeling. Hanna would have liked to put her arm around her daughter, say something nice to her, talk and laugh with her, ask her about her life, but she didn't do it because she was afraid of being rejected.

"I made up the bed in your old room upstairs. There are clean towels in the bathroom," she said instead, putting the empty bottle in the recycling bin. "Please excuse me. I've had a trying day."

"No problem." Meike didn't even look at her. "When do I have to show up tomorrow?"

"Is ten o'clock all right for you?"

"Sure, that's fine. Good night."

"Good night." Hanna stopped herself from adding her daughter's childhood nickname, "Mimi." Meike wouldn't appreciate hearing that from her mother. "I'm glad you're here."

No reply. But no insult, either. That was progress at least.

"What's going on here?" Pia ducked underneath the crime-scene tape after making her way through an excited crowd.

"There was a summer party over there in the

53

sports club tonight," her uniformed colleague explained.

"I see." Pia looked around.

Looking up ahead, she could see fire engines and two ambulances with mutely flashing blue lights. Next to them were a patrol car, two plain-clothes cars, and Henning's silver Mercedes station wagon. Behind them, a section of the woods was brightly lit. She went around the beach volleyball court and glanced briefly into the open side door of one of the ambulances, in which a dark-haired young woman was being treated.

"She discovered the body," explained one of the EMTs. "She's in shock and has a blood-alcohol content of point twenty percent. The doc is down by the river tending to the other boozer."

"What happened? Did she drink herself into a coma?"

"I don't know." The medic shrugged. "The young lady here is twenty-three, according to her driver's license. Actually a bit old for this sort of thing."

"Which way do I have to go?"

"Along the path down to the river. They've probably gotten the gate open by now."

"Thanks." Pia continued on. The path ran alongside the soccer field. The floodlights had been turned on, and the crowd of rubberneckers on the other side of the chain-link fence was even bigger than up front by the crime-scene tape. Pia was having a hard time walking in her unusually high heels. The glaring lights from the fire department and rescue vehicles were blinding her, so she couldn't see where she was going. Firemen holding their cutting torches stood in front of an open iron gate.

Two EMTs came toward her in the darkness, carrying a stretcher, and the emergency doctor ran alongside them, holding an IV in the air.

"Good evening, Ms. Kirchhoff," he said. They knew each other from similar incidents at similarly ungodly hours.

"Good evening." Pia cast a glance at the boy on the stretcher. "What's with him?"

"Found him passed out next to the corpse. Very drunk. We're trying to wake him up."

"Okay. I'll see you later." She teetered along the path as curious bystanders gaped at her from behind the fence of the stadium. She silently cursed her decision to wear high heels today.

A few yards farther on, she encountered two uniformed officers and her colleague Ehrenberg from the break-in department, who'd been on call today and had phoned her.

"Good evening," Pia said. "Could all of you please make sure to clear the people out of the stadium? I don't want to see any photos or videos of a corpse showing up on Facebook or YouTube."

"Sure thing."

"Thanks." Ehrenberg briefed Pia on the situation before she moved on, thinking enviously about her colleagues, who were now enjoying a pleasant weekend. She could hear excited voices in the distance, which gave her a hint as to what was going on. Another fifty yards and she had reached the brightly illuminated scene on the bank of the river. At the foot of a steep slope stood Pia's ex-husband, Dr. Henning Kirchhoff, with Christian Kröger, head of crime-scene investigations at Hofheim police HQ. Dressed in white protective overalls and under the harsh light of the floodlights that had been set up, they looked like two Martians on a riverside stage who were calling each other names like "dilettante" and "bungler," one with corrosive arrogance, the other with hot-blooded rage.

Directly beyond the reeds, a boat from the river police heaved to and turned a glaring spotlight on the bank, bathing it in light bright as day.

Three colleagues from the evidence team were following the heated argument from a suitable distance with a mixture of resignation and patience.

"Hey, Ms. Chief Superintendent. Nice dress," one of them remarked with an appreciative whistle. "And great legs."

"Thanks. What's going on over there?" asked Pia.

"Same old, same old. The boss is claiming that

the doc is deliberately destroying evidence," said another officer, raising his camera. "At least we already got our photos."

Pia made her way down the slope, hoping that she wouldn't stumble in front of everybody and land in the stinging nettles, which grew abundantly on both sides of the narrow path.

"I can't believe it!" Kröger shouted heatedly when he caught sight of her. "Now *you're* tramping right through the DNA evidence! First Ehrenberg, the smart-aleck detective, then the damned corpse slicer, then the emergency doc, and now you, too! Why can't everybody be more careful? How are we supposed to do our work properly?"

His question was entirely justified. The spot where they were both standing measured no more than fifty square feet.

"Good evening, gentlemen." Pia paid no attention to Kröger's outburst; she was used to it. He was a perfectionist and preferred to have every crime scene or discovery site all to himself for a few hours before anyone else contaminated it.

"Hi, Pia," Henning greeted her. "Are you a witness to the slanderous statements that this person has once again heaped on me in the most unprofessional manner?"

"I'm not interested in any problems of cooperation you two may be having," Pia snapped. "What happened here?"

Kröger glanced up, his eyes widening as he stared at her with an expression of amazement.

"Is this the first time you've ever seen a woman in a dress?" Pia barked at him. Without jeans and sensible shoes, she felt out of place and oddly vulnerable.

"No, but . . . you, yes." The appreciative look in his eyes might have flattered her at some other time, but right now it pissed her off.

"Have you had a good look? Then tell me what we have here." Pia snapped her fingers in front of his face. "Well?"

Kröger cleared his throat. "Uh . . . yes. Hmm. Here's the situation: The unconscious boy was lying on his stomach, precisely where our colleague the medical examiner is standing now. His left leg was in the water. The girl is exactly where we found her."

The body of the young girl was caught between the reeds and the weeds on the riverbank. She was floating on her back, her eyes wide open. One arm was sticking out of the water. With each gentle wave, she seemed to move.

Pia looked at the gruesome scene in the cold glare of the floodlights. For a moment, the horror of the deed threatened to overwhelm her. Why should a person so young have to die before she'd even had a chance to live?

"A short distance away, underneath a weeping willow, we found vodka bottles and Red Bull cans. Also a few articles of clothing, shoes, a cell phone, and quite a lot of vomit," said Christian Kröger. "It looks to me as though a group of young people got unauthorized access to this off-limits area so they could get drunk undisturbed. And somehow things got out of control."

"What about the boy?" Pia asked.

Henning had already examined the unconscious youth before he was taken away in the ambulance.

"The kid had been boozing a lot," he replied. "And threw up. His pants were unzipped."

"And what do you conclude from that?"

"Possibly he wanted to relieve himself. But then he fell down the riverbank. He has fresh scratches on his hands and forearms, presumably from trying to break his fall."

Pia took a step to one side to make room for Kröger's people. Two of them hauled the girl's corpse out of the water.

"She hardly weighs a thing. Just skin and bones," said one of the men.

Pia squatted down next to the dead girl. She was wearing a bright-colored top with spaghetti straps and a denim miniskirt that had hiked up and was bunched around her waist. There wasn't enough light, but to Pia, it looked like the girl's pale, bony body was covered with dark spots and welts.

"Henning? Are those bruises?" Pia pointed to the belly and upper thighs of the dead girl.

"Hmm. Could be." Henning shone his flashlight on the body and frowned. "Yes, bruises and lacerations."

He inspected first her left, then her right hand.

"Kröger?" he called.

"What is it?"

"May I turn her over?"

"Go ahead."

Henning handed Pia the flashlight and with his gloved hands turned the girl over onto her stomach.

"Good God!" Pia blurted out. "What is *that?*"

The lower portion of the girl's back and her buttocks were completely shredded; her backbone, ribs, and one side of her pelvis shone white through the darker muscle tissue.

"Wounds from a boat propeller," Henning pronounced with a look at Pia. "The girl didn't die tonight or in this location. She's been in the water longer than that, and the formation of skin maceration on her hands is already fairly advanced. Her body was probably washed up here on the current."

Pia stood up.

"You mean that she had nothing to do with the other teenagers?"

"I'm only the medical examiner," said Henning. "Figuring it out is your job. The fact is that the girl did not die tonight."

Pia rubbed her bare upper arms and shuddered,

although it was not cold in the least. She looked around, trying to get a picture of what might have happened here.

"I'm going to try to find out something about the young woman who discovered the body," she said. "Please take the body to the forensics lab. I hope the DA will grant authorization for an autopsy ASAP."

"Here, let me give you a hand." Kröger gallantly offered her his arm to help her up the slope, and she took it.

"Thanks." Pia flashed him a quick smile when she reached the top. "But don't make a habit of it."

"Absolutely not," he said with a grin. "Only when you're negotiating rough terrain in a cocktail dress and inappropriate footwear."

"You hang out with Henning too much." Pia grinned, too. "I can tell by your choice of words."

"He may be an arrogant bastard, but his vocabulary is unbelievable. I learn something new every time we go out on a call."

"Then you could probably write off your emergency calls as continuing education. See you later."

Kröger waved good-bye and made his way back down the slope.

"Oh, Pia?" he called. She turned around.

"If you're cold, there's a fleece in my car."

Pia nodded and made her way to the ambulance.

• • •

Spending the evening in the company of old classmates and the unexpected encounter with Pia had done Emma good. Elated and in an excellent frame of mind, she opened the dark green Gregorian front door of her in-laws' big villa. She and Florian and Louisa had the entire second floor to themselves. Having grown up in a faceless neighborhood of row houses in Niederhöchstadt, Emma had fallen in love at first sight with the big house of weathered red brick with its oriel windows, little towers, and white-mullioned windows. She loved the high ceilings with their plaster ornamentation, the glassed-in bookcases, the pattern of the parquet floors, the elaborate carving of the banisters. It was charming. Florian's mother called the style of the house "rococo," but Florian had disparagingly dubbed it "wedding cake–style." He found it kitschy and overly ornate, and to Emma's great regret, he had no intention of living in the house on a permanent basis. She could easily have stayed on forever.

The villa stood on the edge of a huge park that extended all the way to the woods. Right next door was the residence of the Sonnenkinder Association. Before Florian's father had founded the group in the late sixties, it had been an old folks home. Later, the building across the street had been added, in which the administration, the kindergarten, and the classrooms were located today. Farther back in the park stood three bungalows with their own driveways, in which close associates of Emma's father-in-law lived with their families. The house in the middle had actually been built for Florian, but he had preferred to leave home, so now it was rented out.

Emma had slipped off her shoes as soon as she got in the car. Her ankles and feet swelled up every day in this heat wave, and in the afternoon it was almost unbearable to wear shoes. The wooden steps creaked under her weight. Behind the milky-glass triptych of panes in the front door she could see a glimmer of light. She quietly opened the door and tiptoed inside. Florian was sitting at the kitchen table in front of his laptop. He was so lost in concentration that he didn't notice her come in. Emma stood in the doorway for a moment, observing the sharp contours of his profile. Even after six years, she still found the sight of him fascinating.

In the beginning, there had been no love lost between them when they first met at the camp in Ethiopia—she was the technical leader of the project, he her medical counterpart. From the first instant, they had done nothing but argue. Nothing happened fast enough for him, and she was angered by his arrogance and pushiness. It was no simple task to transport medicines and technical gear hundreds of miles on the country road. Yet they were working for the same cause, and although she had been terribly annoyed by him, as a doctor he had impressed her deeply. He worked on behalf of his patients until he was utterly exhausted, sometimes seventy-two hours at a stretch, and in emergencies he was quick to improvise so that he could help and heal.

Dr. Florian Finkbeiner never did anything halfway; he was a doctor through and through, and he loved his profession. Anytime he could not save a human life, he regarded it as a personal defeat. It was the contradictory nature of his personality that slowly but surely had cast its spell over Emma: on one side the sympathetic humanitarian and on the other the worrywart doubter who could sound almost cynical. Sometimes he sank into a deep melancholy that bordered on depression, but he could also be witty, charming, and downright entertaining. Besides, he was probably the best-looking man she had ever met.

Emma's colleague had given her a warning when she admitted that she'd fallen in love with Florian. "Keep away from him if you don't want to make yourself unhappy," she'd said. "He lugs the problems of the whole world around with him." Then she added mockingly that maybe he was exactly the right man for someone like Emma, with her need to help everyone. Emma had immediately suppressed the doubt that these words aroused in her. She would always have to share Florian with his job and his patients, but what was left over for her was enough. Her heart overflowed with tenderness when she saw him sitting there. The curly dark hair, the shadow on his cheeks and chin, the warm dark eyes, the sensitive mouth, the tender skin on his throat.

"Hello," she said softly. He gave a start and turned to stare at her, then slammed his laptop shut.

"Good God, Emmi! Do you have to sneak up on me like that?" he blurted out.

"Sorry." She flicked on the ceiling light. The halogen lamp bathed the kitchen in a gleaming white glow. "I didn't mean to."

"Louisa's been whining all evening," he said, getting up. "She didn't want to eat, said she had a stomachache. Then I read her a couple of stories, and finally she fell asleep."

He took Emma in his arms and kissed her on the cheek.

"How was the reunion? Did you have fun?" he asked, placing a hand on her stomach. He hadn't done that in a long time. Just a little more than five weeks and this pregnancy, which had not had the most fortuitous start, would be over. Florian hadn't wanted a second child—and she actually hadn't, either, but somehow it had happened.

"Yes, it was really interesting to see everybody after such a long time. In some ways, they've hardly changed at all." Emma smiled. "And I met my best friend from those days. I haven't seen her since we graduated."

"That sounds great." Florian smiled, too, then cast a glance at the kitchen clock above the doorway. "Is it okay if I go over to Ralf's for a beer?"

"Of course. You deserve it after an evening of putting up with Louisa."

"I won't be late." He kissed her again on the cheek, then put on his loafers, which were standing next to the door. "See you in a while."

"Okay, see you. Have fun."

The door closed behind him, and the light went on in the stairwell. Emma heaved a sigh. The first few weeks after he got back from Haiti, Florian had acted strange, but now he seemed more like himself. Emma was familiar with his dark phases, when he acted cold and introverted. They usually passed after a couple of days, but this time it had taken a lot longer. Even though it was his idea to stay in Falkenstein until the baby was born, it had to feel odd for him to be suddenly back in Germany, living in his parents' house—the house he had fled almost twenty-five years ago.

Emma opened the fridge, got out a bottle of mineral water, and poured herself a glass. Then she sat down at the kitchen table. After all the years of their gypsy lifestyle, which had taken them to the most remote places on earth, she found the idea of finally settling in and putting down roots very tempting. Next year, Louisa would be going to school, and that would be the end of living in some camp somewhere. Florian was an excellent surgeon, and any clinic in Germany should be glad to take him on. Besides, at forty-six he was no spring chicken. Most of his bosses, as he had mentioned recently in a discussion of this very topic, were younger than he was. But he couldn't imagine having to face on a daily basis the degenerate and overfed victims of the affluent society at a hospital. He had made this statement with the same vehemence that he used to describe his own goals, and Emma understood that nothing would change his mind.

She yawned. Time for bed. Emma put her glass in the dishwasher and turned off the light. On the way to the bathroom, she looked in on Louisa, who was sleeping soundly and peacefully, surrounded by her stuffed animals. Emma's gaze fell on the book that Florian had been reading to the little girl, and she had to smile. Who knows how long he had to read out loud, she thought. Louisa was crazy about fantasy stories and fairy tales. She knew them all by heart: Hansel and Gretel, Rapunzel, Snow White and Rose Red, and Puss in Boots. Emma gently closed the door. Florian would get used to his new life soon enough. Someday they would have their own house and be like a real family.

• • •

The soccer field was empty now, but sensation-seeking onlookers still crowded in behind the fence blocking off the sluiceway, and members of the press had arrived by now, as well. Pia tried one more time to reach her boss. No luck. His cell was turned on, but he didn't pick up. She did get through to Detective Superintendent Kai Ostermann, who picked up at once.

"Sorry for bothering you," Pia said. "We just retrieved a body from the river in Eddersheim, near the locks. I could use your help."

"No problem," Kai replied, without a word about the late hour. "What do you want me to do?"

"I need a warrant for an autopsy, tomorrow morning early. And maybe you could check the list of missing persons. A girl between fourteen and sixteen years old. Blond, very thin, dark brown eyes. Henning thinks she's been dead for a few days."

"Got it. I'll drive over to the office right away."

"Oh, and please try to reach the boss." Pia ended the call and sent Bodenstein a text. He'd been away for four days now, but last week he'd told her that he'd be back Thursday night.

"Ms. Kirchhoff!" called a man with a camera marked *Hessen TV* on his shoulder. "Can we get a couple of shots?"

From force of habit, Pia wanted to say no, but after thinking a moment, she changed her mind. A spot on TV might be very helpful in clearing up the identity of the dead girl.

"Sure, go ahead," said Pia. She asked one of the patrol officers standing at the cordon to accompany the camera people and reporters to the site where the body had been found. HR, SAT1, RTL Hessen, Antenne Pro, Rhein-Main TV. All of them would rather listen to the police channels than to music on the radio.

One of the ambulances had left with the dead-drunk kid, and a hearse had pulled up.

Pia knocked on the side door of the other ambulance, and it was opened at once.

"Could I talk to the young woman?" she asked.

The EMT nodded. "She's still in shock, but we've got her stabilized." Pia climbed into the vehicle and sat down next to the young woman on the folding seat. She had a pale but pretty childlike face with wide eyes, in which Pia saw fear and horror. What she had just experienced was going to haunt her for the rest of her life.

"Hello," said Pia in a friendly voice. "I'm Pia Kirchhoff from Kripo in Hofheim. Would you please tell me your name?"

"A . . . Alina Hindemith."

She smelled unpleasantly of alcohol and vomit.

"She just told me her name was Sabrina," the assistant EMT interjected. "And her ID says—"

Pia cut him off. "Would you mind leaving us alone?"

"I . . . I can explain everything," whispered the young woman, staring at the ceiling of the ambulance. "It . . . it was stupid of me, but . . . but I borrowed my big sister's ID. We . . . we look a lot alike."

Pia sighed. Unfortunately, this trick worked in almost every supermarket in Germany.

"I . . . I used it to buy some booze. Vodka and slivovitz." She started to cry. "My parents are going to kill me when they hear about it."

"How old are you, Alina?"

"Fif . . . fifteen."

Fifteen years old with a blood-alcohol content of .20 percent. A brilliant achievement.

"Can you remember what happened?"

"We climbed over the gate. Mart and Diego knew the place and said nobody would bother us there. And then . . . then we just sort of sat around and . . . and drank."

"Who else was with you?"

The girl glanced at Pia and then frowned. She seemed to be having trouble remembering.

"Mart and Diego and . . . and me. And Katharina and Alex . . . and . . ." Alina's voice tracked off and she looked at Pia in terror. "Mia! I . . . I don't know exactly what happened. I . . . I blacked out. But then I saw Mia lying in the water. Oh God, oh God! And Alex was so drunk, I couldn't wake him up!"

Her face contorted, and then the tears streamed down.

Pia let her cry for a moment. The girl from the river couldn't be Mia, who'd been drinking with Alina and her friends. Henning was seldom mistaken, and the wounds from an outboard motor corroborated the fact that the dead girl had been in the river a long time. Pia's cell rang; it was Kai Ostermann. Unfortunately, all he could tell her was that so far his queries had produced no results. Pia thanked him and ended the call.

She asked the girl for the last name and address of the unconscious boy, then for his parents' phone number. After jotting them down, she climbed out of the ambulance and spoke briefly with the EMT.

"She's stable, so we can let her go home," he said. "Tomorrow, she'll probably have a huge hangover, but there's nothing to be done about that."

"What about the boy?"

"He's already on his way to Höchst. I'm afraid he's got more than just a pounding head in store for him."

"Good evening, Ms. Kirchhoff," somebody said. Pia turned around, to see a dark-haired man with a three-day stubble, who was wearing faded jeans, a T-shirt, and well-worn moccasins. He seemed vaguely familiar. It took a few seconds before she recognized Dr. Frey, the state attorney.

"Uh . . . hello, Dr. Frey," she stammered in

astonishment, almost blurting out "What on earth happened to you?" She'd never seen him wear anything but a three-piece suit and tie, and he was always clean-shaven, his hair slicked back with gel. He looked her over with the same mixture of curiosity and amazement.

"I was at a class reunion when Dispatch called," she said with a hint of embarrassment.

"And I was at a backyard barbecue with friends and family." Even the SA seemed to consider it necessary to justify his unusual attire. "They told me about the discovery of the body, and since I was in Flörsheim anyway, I volunteered to handle the case."

"Ah, that's . . . that's good." Pia was still a bit confused by this unexpected metamorphosis of the SA; she couldn't have imagined that he had friends or would enjoy a relaxing evening barbecuing. He smelled slightly of alcohol with a hint of peppermint. Apparently, he wasn't completely immune to worldly pleasures. It was a whole new side of this notorious Calvinist noted for his iron discipline and workaholic tendencies. In her eyes, he existed only in his office or a courtroom.

"Are you going to call the parents of the two drunk kids?" The EMT slammed the side door of the ambulance shut.

"Sure, I'll take care of it," said Pia.

"They told me you're in charge of the

investigation." State Attorney Frey took her arm and pulled her aside so that the ambulance could move past.

"Yes, that's right," Pia said with a nod. "My boss is still on vacation."

"Hmm. So what exactly happened here?"

Pia briefly explained the situation. "I considered it proper to grant the press access to the site where the body was found," she said, concluding her account. "My colleague could find no record of any missing person's report that might be linked to the victim. Perhaps the public can assist in identifying the dead girl."

The SA frowned but then nodded in agreement. "Clearing up a fatality. It's always preferable to resolve a homicide as rapidly as possible," he replied. "I'll take a look at the case. We'll probably be seeing each other later."

Pia waited until he had vanished in the darkness, then tapped in the phone number that the girl had given her. A light breeze had come up, and she shivered. The reporters returned.

"Do you think we could get another brief statement from you?"

"Just a moment." Pia walked away a few yards toward the riverbank so she could talk in private. An extremely alert male voice answered. "Good evening, Mr. Hindemith. My name is Pia Kirchhoff, from Kripo Hofheim. It's about your daughter Alina. Don't worry, she's fine, but I'd like to ask you to come to Eddersheim. To the locks. You can't miss it."

The men from the undertakers came down the footpath carrying a body bag on a stretcher. The cameras started flashing at once. Pia went over to Kröger's vehicle, which, as usual, was unlocked, grabbed the fleece jacket from the backseat, and slipped it on. Then she gathered her hair into a ponytail, using an elastic to hold it in place. Now she felt more like herself and ready to face the TV cameras.

Since early in the evening, people had been grilling and drinking all over the trailer park. During the summer months, the social life of the residents took place mostly outdoors, and the later it got, the more the noise and alcohol levels rose. Laughter, yelling, music—nobody took anyone else into consideration, and occasionally trivial incidents would escalate to loud and even physical arguments between neighbors who even when sober couldn't stand one another. Usually, the trailer park operator managed to mediate the squabbles, but the hot weather had stirred up animosities to such a degree that the police had been called in several times over the past week to prevent anyone from being injured or killed.

It had been years now since he had been invited by anyone, because he had consistently refused every invitation. The last thing he needed was some sort of camaraderie with the other residents of the trailer park. Given his history, it was clearly better if no one knew who he really was or why he was living here. The leaseholder was the only person he had ever told his real name, and he doubted that the man would remember him. There was no official lease agreement for the trailer. Not wanting to draw attention, he always paid the rent on time and in cash. His official address was a box at the Schwanheim post office. Here, at the trailer park, he didn't exist. And that's the way he liked it.

Years ago, he had made it a habit to go for a walk while people were partying and getting drunk. The noise didn't bother him, but ever since he'd started working at the lunch stand, he could hardly tolerate the smell of grilled meat and sausages that wafted over to him. So he'd walked a ways along the bank of the Main River, and he'd sat on a bench for a while. Normally, the slowly flowing river calmed him, but today the monotonous lapping of the water had put him in an agonizing state of heightened awareness, which made him even more cognizant of the wretchedness of his life and his total lack of prospects. To escape the senseless replay of his thoughts, he'd started jogging along the river, all the way to Goldstein and back.

Total physical exhaustion was normally the best way to put a stop to these bitter thoughts. But this time, it hadn't worked. Maybe it was because of the unbearable heat. A cold shower had brought only temporary relief; half an hour later, he was again drenched in sweat, tossing and turning in bed. A shrill ringtone suddenly came from his cell phone, which was in its charging stand on the table. Who could it be at this hour? he wondered. He stood up and glanced at the display, then took the call.

"Sorry to disturb you again so late," said a rough bass voice. "Turn on the TV. It's on every channel."

Before he could reply, the caller hung up. He grabbed the remote and switched on the tiny TV at the foot of his bed.

Seconds later, he saw the serious face of a blond woman on the screen. Blue lights were flashing behind her, and black water glinted between the trees illuminated by floodlights.

". . . of a young girl was found," he heard the woman say. "According to preliminary estimates, the body had been in the water for several days. We hope to obtain additional information from the autopsy."

He froze.

Two men were loading a stretcher with a body bag on it into the hearse, and behind them two figures clad in protective overalls were carrying a plastic bag. Then the camera panned over to the sluiceway.

"Not far from the locks at Eddersheim, the body

of a young girl was discovered today floating in the Main," said the voiceover. "The identity of the girl is unknown, and the police are hoping for tips from the public. This is reminiscent of a similar case from a few years ago."

An older man blinked under the bright lights.

"Yep, I remember there was a girl found in the river once before. It was over there in Höchst, at the Wörthspitze. To this day, they don't know who the poor girl was. If I remember rightly, it was around ten years ago, and then . . ."

He turned off the TV and stood there in the dark. He was breathing hard, as if he'd been running.

"Nine," he whispered in a strained voice. "It was nine years ago."

Fear crept like goose bumps all over his body. His probation officer knew that he lived here. So it would be no problem for the police and the SA's office to locate him. What was going to happen now? Would they remember him?

All trace of fatigue had left him, and his thoughts were coming thick and fast. There was no hope of going to sleep. He switched on the light and took the cleaning bucket and a bottle of bleach from the cabinet next to the kitchen unit. They were going to come here, search through everything, and they'd find her DNA in his trailer! No way could he let that happen, because if he violated probation, he'd have to go straight back to the joint.

• • •

Pia closed the front door carefully, making sure that the dogs weren't going to break out in a chorus of welcoming barks and wake Christoph. But no dog awaited her on the enclosed porch; instead, she smelled the aroma of roast meat and saw that a light was on in the kitchen. She set her shoulder bag and car keys on the hall cabinet. The four dogs were sitting in the kitchen, watching Christoph's every movement with synchronized adoration. He was standing at the stove, dressed in shorts, the T-shirt he wore to bed, and an apron, holding two meat forks in his hands. The fan on the stove was on high.

"Hi," Pia said in astonishment. "Are you awake or sleepwalking?"

The dogs turned their heads only briefly and wagged their tails; then they went back to watching what was happening on the stove, which was much more interesting.

"Hey, sweetie," said Christoph with a grin. "I was almost asleep when I remembered that I'd left the roulades in the fridge. And I promised Lilly that I'd make roulades for a homecoming dinner."

Pia had to smile. She went over and gave him a kiss.

"In all of Germany, could there be another man who would get up at one-thirty in the morning to roast roulades when the temperature is almost eighty degrees? Unbelievable."

"I've even filled them," Christoph said, not without pride. "Mustard, cucumbers, bacon, onions. A promise is a promise."

Pia took off Kröger's fleece jacket and hung it over the back of a chair before plopping down onto the seat.

"How was your class reunion?" Christoph asked. "Must have been fun if you could stand being there so long."

"Oh, the reunion." Pia had totally forgotten about it. The laughing and chattering women on the terrace of the Villa Borgnis beneath the velvety black sky filled with stars seemed to her like a harmless idyllic short film before the horror flick called reality. And in this particular reality, a teenager had died.

She kicked off the sling-back heels, which were now candidates for the garbage can after she'd tramped through the underbrush.

"Yes, it was quite nice. But unfortunately, I had to leave and go to work."

"Work?" Christoph turned and raised his eyebrows. He knew what nighttime work meant in Pia's profession. It was seldom benign. "Bad?"

"Yep." She leaned her elbows on the table and rubbed her face. "Really bad. A dead girl, and two teenagers who drank themselves into a coma."

Christoph didn't bother with a cliché like "Oh God, I'm sorry." Instead, he asked, "Do you want something to drink?"

"Yeah, a nice cold beer would hit the spot about now, even though I was once again reminded this evening that alcohol doesn't solve any problems, only creates them."

She was about to get up, but Christoph shook his head.

"Stay there. I'll get it for you."

He put down the meat forks, covered the roasts, and turned down the temperature of the gas oven. Then he took two bottles of beer out of the fridge and opened them.

"Glass?"

"No. Not necessary."

Christoph handed Pia a bottle and sat down next to her at the table.

"Thanks." She took a big swig. "I'm afraid you'll have to pick up Lilly by yourself tomorrow. Since there's nobody else at the office, I'll have to go to the autopsy. Sorry."

The next day, Christoph's seven-year-old granddaughter was arriving from Australia to stay at Birkenhof for four weeks. When Pia learned of the plan a couple of weeks before, she hadn't been especially enthusiastic. She and Christoph both had full-time jobs, and they couldn't leave a small child alone in the house. What upset her most was the selfishness of Lilly's mother, Anna, Christoph's second-eldest daughter. Anna's companion and father of the little girl was a marine biologist, and he'd taken over the leadership of a research expedition in Antarctica that spring. Anna wanted to go with him, but it was impossible to take a school-age child along. At that time, Christoph had turned down her request to take care of Lilly, saying that she was the mother and was responsible for her daughter, so she would have to forgo the trip. Anna had begged desperately, until Christoph and Pia finally agreed on a compromise. They would take care of the girl during the two weeks of Australian winter vacation. Anna was the only one of Christoph's three daughters whom Pia didn't particularly like, and she wasn't surprised when the two weeks turned into four. Anna had pulled one of her tricks with Lilly's school and arranged a leave of absence for her daughter. Typical. So once again, she'd been successful at getting her way.

"That's no problem." He reached out and stroked Pia's cheek. "What happened?"

"It's all a bit mysterious." She took another swallow of beer. "A sixteen-year-old boy who's in a coma after an orgy of drinking, and a young girl we fished out of the Main. She must have been in the river for a long time, because her body had been run over and partially shredded by the screws of an outboard motor."

"Sounds horrible."

"It was, believe me. We have no idea who the girl is. There's no missing person's report that fits her description."

For a while, they sat at the kitchen table, drinking beer without talking. That was one of the many traits that Pia loved about Christoph. Not only did she find it easy to talk to him but they could also sit in silence without feeling uncomfortable. He always knew when she wanted to talk about something or when she simply needed his silent company.

"It's already two o'clock." Pia got up. "I think I'll jump in the shower and then go to bed."

"I'll be finished here soon." Christoph stood up, too. "I just have to clean up the kitchen."

Pia grabbed his wrist, and he stopped and looked at her.

"Thank you," she said quietly.

"What for?"

"For being you."

He smiled. She loved the way he smiled.

"That's all I have to give," he whispered, wrapping his arms around her. She snuggled up to him and felt his lips on her hair. And for a moment, everything was all right.

"We're going to Uncle Richard's, just you and me," said Papa, motioning her over. "Then you can ride the pony and open your presents."

Oh yes, she wanted to ride the pony! And all by herself with Papa, without Mama and her brothers and sisters! She was happy and excited. She'd been to Uncle Richard's only a couple of times with Papa, but it was strange that she couldn't quite remember the house or the ponies. She was looking forward to it immensely, because Papa was also taking along the lovely new dress that she had tried on but never worn until now.

She looked at herself in the mirror, touched her fingertips to the little red hood on her head, and laughed. The dress was a real dirndl, with a short skirt and apron. Papa had plaited her hair into two braids, and she really looked exactly like Little Red Riding Hood in her fairy-tale book.

He always brought presents—it was a secret that she and Papa shared, because he never brought anything for the others. Only for her. She was his favorite. Mama had gone away with her siblings, so Papa had her all to himself.

"Did you bring something for me?" she asked curiously, because the big paper shopping bag was still bulging.

"Of course." He gave her a conspiratorial smile. "Here, do you want to take a look?"

She nodded eagerly. He took another dress out of the paper bag. It was red, and the material felt cool and very soft under her fingers.

"A princess dress for my little princess," he said. "And I bought you some matching shoes, too. Red ones."

"Oh, awesome! Can I peek?"

"No, later. We have to go. Uncle Richard is waiting for us."

She let him pick her up, snuggling close. She loved his deep voice and the scent of pipe tobacco on his clothes.

A little later, they were sitting in his car. They drove for quite a while, and she got excited whenever she saw something she recognized. It was a game that she always played with Papa when they were together on a secret outing. That's what he called it, because she couldn't tell her siblings, or they'd be jealous.

Finally, the road came to an end after passing through the woods to a clearing where there was a big wooden house with a porch and green shutters.

"That looks just like the one in my fairy-tale book!" she cried excitedly, and she was delighted to see the ponies in the meadow in front of the house.

"Can I take a ride now?" She was fidgeting on the seat.

"Of course." Papa laughed and parked the Mercedes next to a couple of other cars. There was always something going on at Uncle Richard's, and that made her happy, too, because they were all friends of Papa and had brought presents and candy for her.

She got out of the car and ran over to the ponies, who let her pet them. Uncle Richard came out and asked which pony she wanted to ride. She liked the white one the best. His name was Fluff; she remembered that now. How sad that she knew the pony's name but couldn't remember anything about what the house looked like inside.

After half an hour, they went inside. Papa's and Uncle Richard's friends were there. They all said a cheerful hello and admired her dirndl and red hood. She turned around to show it off and laughed.

"Okay, now take off the dirndl." Papa put the shopping bag on the table and took out the dress. Uncle Richard set her on his lap and helped her put on the dress and the genuine silk stockings, the kind that Mama wore. The others laughed because she was so clumsy attaching the garters, which were fastened to a belt. That was fun!

But the most beautiful thing was the dress—a real princess dress in red. And the red shoes to go with it, with high heels.

She looked at herself in the mirror and felt so proud. Papa was proud, too; he led her through the living room and up the stairs, as if they were at a wedding. Uncle Richard led the way and opened a door. She was amazed to see in the room a genuine princess bed with a canopy.

"What are we going to play now?" she asked.

"Something that's a lot of fun," replied Papa.

"We're going to change our clothes, too. Just wait here."

She nodded, then climbed onto the bed and began hopping around. They had all admired her beautiful dress and were so nice to her. The door opened, and she uttered a frightened cry when she saw the wolf. But then she had to laugh. It wasn't a real wolf after all; it was only Papa, who had put on a costume. How lovely it was that she was the only one to share this secret with Papa. Too bad she could never remember anything afterward. That was really sad.

Friday, June 11, 2010

Hanna Herzmann had not slept well. She'd had one nightmare after another, and in one of them Vinzenz had been on her TV show, making her look like a fool with the cameras running. Then Norman had threatened her, and in her dream he suddenly turned into that man who'd been stalking her for months, until he was picked up by the police and sentenced to two years in prison as a repeat offender.

She finally got up at five-thirty and rinsed off the sticky sweat of anxiety in the shower. Now she was sitting at her computer with a cup of coffee. As she'd feared, the Web was full of the crazy story.

Damn! Hanna massaged the bridge of her nose. It wasn't too late for damage control, but it would have to be done fast, before more unhappy guests on her show started encouraging people to do the same thing as Armin V. and Bettina B. Unimaginable what the consequences might be. Even if her broadcast wasn't yet under threat, station management wasn't going to back her up forever. It was too early to call Wolfgang, so she decided to go for a run and come up with some new ideas. She always thought better when she was running. She put on her exercise clothes, pulled her hair into a ponytail, and slipped on her running shoes. In the past, she had run every day, but now that her foot problems had grown worse, she ran only occasionally.

The air was still fresh and clear. Hanna did some deep-breathing exercises and stretches on the front steps, then turned on her iPod and looked for the music she wanted to hear. She walked down the street to the corner by the parking lot, then turned into the woods and began to run. Every step hurt like hell, but she gritted her teeth and forced herself to keep running. After only a few hundred yards she had a stitch in her side, but she kept on going in spite of it. She wasn't going to give up. Hanna Herzmann never gave up. All her life, she'd regarded any head-winds or problems as nothing but a challenge and incentive, never as a reason to stick her head in the sand. Pain was purely a mental matter, and she wasn't going to let it affect her. If she were a different sort of person, she never would have chosen such a career for herself, or been so successful. Ambition, persistence, endurance— these qualities always got her through hard times.

Fourteen years ago, with her investigative reporting program *In Depth*, Hanna had developed a completely new, revolutionary format that had caused a furor (as well as dream ratings) in the German television world. The concept was simple and inspired: a wide-ranging mixture of explosive and topical reportage that had an impact on people in the state of Hessen, including personal stories, human drama, garnished with prominent guests—all in ninety minutes of prime time. There had never been anything like it on TV before. Success brought out the copycats, but no show with a similar focus was as popular as hers. And her media presence had a number of thoroughly lucrative side effects: She was one of the most recognizable faces on TV and was always in demand. If the money was right, she was willing to moderate gala broadcasts and award shows. She also developed ideas and concepts for other formats, and was well paid for her efforts. Ten years ago, she had founded Herzmann Productions, and she now produced the show herself.

The flip side of her professional success was her

screwed-up private life. Obviously, there was no man who could stand to play second fiddle to her fame. Meike's words from last night shot through Hanna's mind. Was it true? Was she really a tank running right over everyone else?

"And what if I am?" she murmured with a trace of spite. That's the way she was. She didn't need a man in her life.

At the first crossing in the woods, she decided to take the longer path and turned to the right. Her breathing was steady now and her gait looser. She had found her running rhythm and could hardly feel the pain. From experience, she knew that it would soon disappear entirely; just a couple minutes more before her body began producing the endorphins that would switch off the pain and fatigue. Now she could focus her thoughts on her problem and enjoy the nature surrounding her: the tangy smell that the forest exuded only in the early-morning hours, the springy ground, which was so much more pleasant to run on than asphalt. It was a little past seven when she reached the edge of the woods and saw the white dome of the Baha'i temple gleaming in the sun, which was already high in the sky. Although she hadn't run recently, she wasn't yet out of breath. She wasn't entirely out of shape. It would take her another twenty minutes to go back through the woods to the community of weekend cabins. She was bathed in sweat as she resumed her pace, but this time it was more pleasant, real athletic sweat, not the anxious sweat of last night. And she had also figured out a strategy that she could discuss with Wolfgang at lunch. Hanna removed her earbuds and rummaged in the pocket of her jacket for her house key. As she ran past, she glanced at her car, which she hadn't put back in the garage last night, but left parked next to Meike's Mini.

What was *that?*

Hanna couldn't believe her eyes. All four tires on her black Porsche Panamera were flat! She wiped the sweat from her brow with her sleeve and went over to take a look. One flat tire could be a coincidence, but not all four. As she examined the car more closely, she saw something even worse. She stopped short. Her heart began to race, her knees went weak, and she felt tears welling up in her eyes, tears of helpless rage. Somebody had scratched a single word into the gleaming black lacquer of the hood. Just one word, brutal and unequivocal, in big sloppy letters: CUNT.

Bodenstein set a cup under the spigot of the coffee machine and pressed the button. The grinder churned, and seconds later an exquisite aroma was spreading through the tiny kitchen.

Inka had driven him home shortly after midnight. As they were eating pizza, he'd done most of the talking, but he didn't realize this until she dropped him off at the parking lot in front of the carriage house. After they had taken a look at the house, Inka had been more laconic than ever, and Bodenstein asked himself whether he'd said or done anything that might have made her mad. Hadn't he adequately thanked her for picking him up at the airport and giving him a key to the house? In his euphoria over the liberated feeling with which he'd returned from Potsdam, he'd spent the whole evening talking only about himself and his mental state. That wasn't like him at all. Bodenstein decided to call Inka later to apologize.

He finished his coffee and squeezed into the tiny, windowless bathroom. After the almost luxurious facilities in the hotel in Potsdam, it seemed darker and more cramped than ever.

It was high time to arrange a proper place to live, with his own furniture, a decent bathroom, and a kitchen with more than just two hot plates. He'd had enough of the two rooms in the carriage house, with their low ceilings and the tiny windows that were hardly bigger than fortress embrasures, and the door frames, barely high enough for dwarfs, on which he was always hitting his head. He was also fed up with being a guest in the house of his parents and his brother, and he knew that his sister-in-law was looking for a more desirable tenant for the carriage house than some relative who only wanted to split the costs. She kept asking bluntly when he intended to move out, and lately she had even brought potential tenants by to look the place over.

In the meager light of the forty-watt bulb above the mirror, Bodenstein shaved as best he could. To tell the truth, the house that he had looked at yesterday with Inka had haunted his dreams all night long. This morning, half-asleep, he had started furnishing it in his mind. Sophia would have her own room close to his, and finally he could have visitors again. The house in Kelkheim was as good as sold; it was due to close with the buyers next week. With his half of the proceeds, he was sure he could afford to buy the duplex in Ruppertshain.

There was some sort of commotion outside, and he heard voices. A second cup of coffee raised his spirits. He set the cup in the sink, grabbed his jacket, and took the car keys from the hook by the front door. In the parking lot, city workers from Kelkheim were unloading barriers from their orange truck. It occurred to him that tonight there was going to be a jazz concert in the courtyard. The town regularly rented out the historic estate for cultural events, and Bodenstein's parents were happy to have the extra income. Bodenstein locked the front door and nodded to the workers on his way to the car. Someone honked behind him, and he turned around. Marie-Louise, his talented sister-in-law, pulled in next to him.

"Good morning!" she called. "I've tried to call

you a zillion times. Rosalie got invited to the Concours des Jeunes Chefs Rôtisseurs in Frankfurt! Actually, she wanted to tell you herself, but she couldn't reach you. What's wrong with your cell phone?"

Rosalie, Bodenstein's older daughter, had decided two years ago not to take her university entrance exams, but instead to start an apprenticeship to become a chef. At first, he and Cosima had thought that the main reason for this decision was that Rosalie was secretly in love with a celebrity chef. They were sure that after a couple of months under the thumb of that strict Frenchman, she'd throw in the towel. But Rosalie had talent, and she'd tackled the job with enthusiasm. She had completed her apprenticeship with flying colors. The invitation to the cooking contest of the Chaîne des Rôtisseurs was a great honor and a validation of her achievement.

"I haven't had any reception all morning." Bodenstein held up his smartphone with a shrug. "It's funny, really."

"Well, I don't understand a thing about those gizmos," said Marie-Louise.

"But I do!" Her eight-year-old son leaned forward from the backseat, waving his hand out the window. "Give it to me; I'll show you."

Bodenstein handed his cell to his youngest nephew with a hint of amusement, but his grin vanished five seconds later.

"It's not working because you've got it in airplane mode, Uncle Ollie," the precocious whippersnapper told him, sliding things around on the touch screen. "See, this is the airplane icon here. Now it's working okay."

"Oh . . . thanks, Jonas," Bodenstein stammered.

The boy nodded to him from the backseat. Marie-Louise laughed, unable to hide her glee.

"Call Rosalie!" she yelled then, and stepped on the gas.

Bodenstein felt quite stupid. He was not a frequent flier, and the day before he'd used the airplane mode on his iPhone for the first time, and only because the man sitting next to him in the plane had shown him how to do it. On the flight to Berlin, he had simply turned off the phone.

As he was heading toward his car, his cell emitted a veritable cacophony of tones; a dozen text messages came in, requests for callbacks, notices of missed calls, and then the phone started ringing.

Pia Kirchhoff. He took the call.

"Good morning, Pia," he said. "I just discovered that you tried to reach me yesterday. Is—"

"Haven't you seen the news yet?" she asked, abruptly interrupting him, a clear indication that she was under a lot of pressure. "Last night, we pulled a dead girl out of the Main near the Eddersheim locks. Are you coming in to the office today?"

"Yes, of course. I'm on my way now," he replied, getting into the car. He briefly considered calling Inka from the car but then decided to take her a bouquet of flowers that evening and thank her in person.

Driving a car got harder every day. If things kept up like this, Emma soon wouldn't be able to fit behind the steering wheel with her big belly, and her feet wouldn't be able to reach the gas pedal or the brake. She turned left onto Wiesbadener Strasse and glanced in the rearview mirror. Louisa was staring out the window. During the whole trip, she hadn't made a peep.

"Do you still have a stomachache?" Emma asked her with concern.

The little girl shook her head. Normally, she babbled like a waterfall. Something was definitely wrong. Was she having problems in kindergarten? Trouble with the other kids?

A couple of minutes later, they pulled up in front of the day-care center and got out. Louisa was able to undo her seat belt herself and get out of the car on her own, and she was very proud of this. In her condition, Emma was glad that she didn't have to lift her daughter out of the car.

"What's the matter?" Emma stopped at the door of the day-care center, squatted down, and gave Louisa a searching look. This morning, she had been listless and offered no protest when Emma put the green T-shirt on her, although she really didn't like it because, she said, it was scratchy.

"Nothing," said the girl, avoiding her mother's eyes.

There was no point in pressuring her. Emma decided to phone the day-care teacher later and ask her to keep an eye on Louisa.

"Well then, have a good time today, sweetie," she said, and kissed her daughter on the cheek. Louisa dutifully kissed her back and then vanished through the open door to her group, without her usual enthusiasm.

Deep in thought, Emma drove back toward Falkenstein, put the car in the garage, and decided to take a walk around the sprawling grounds and the scattered buildings that belonged to the Sonnenkinder Association. Near her in-laws' villa, at the heart of it all, stood the administration building; it had seminar rooms, a birthing center, a nursery for the younger children, and day-care facilities for the older children whose mothers were at work during the day. A short distance away was the residence hall for mothers and children, formerly an old folks home. There were various other buildings, the vegetable garden, the workshop, housekeeping, and, at the other end of the park, the three bungalows that formed the rear boundary of the gigantic estate.

In the early morning, the air was still cool and fresh, and Emma felt the need for some exercise.

She strolled along the path, which wound through the park in the shadow of ancient oaks, beeches, and cedars, through carefully mown, dazzling green lawns and blooming rhododendrons, to the administration building. She loved the luxuriance of nature, the scent that wafted from the nearby forest on warm summer evenings. Although she'd been living here for six months now, she still enjoyed the sight of all that green, taking it in with all of her senses—a refreshing treat for the eyes compared to the barren, dry landscapes in which she'd lived and worked over the past twenty years. Florian, on the other hand, found the fecundity of nature disturbing. Recently, he'd reproached his father, saying that the waste of water was downright obscene. Upset by the criticism, Josef had replied that the water for sprinkling the lawns came from rainwater cisterns.

Every conversation between Florian and his parents turned into a controversy after only a few sentences. Even the most harmless subject provoked long discussions that usually ended with him getting up and walking out.

Emma found his behavior unpleasant. She'd discovered an opinionated side of her husband that she didn't like at all. He wouldn't admit it to her, but she could see that he didn't feel comfortable in his parents' house, in his childhood world. She would have liked to know why, because she found her in-laws to be friendly, unassuming hosts who never interfered or showed up unannounced.

"Good morning!" someone called behind her, and she turned around. A bearded man with a ponytail came bicycling along the path and now stopped beside her.

"Hello, Mr. Grasser." Emma raised her hand in greeting.

Her in-laws called Helmut Grasser the caretaker, but actually he was much more. He was a true jack-of-all-trades and always in a good mood. If her in-laws had to go somewhere, he acted as their chauffeur; he put up shelves and changed lightbulbs. He was also responsible for the maintenance of the buildings and was in charge of keeping up the park and vegetation. Along with his mother, Helga, who worked in the kitchen, he lived in the middle bungalows of the three.

"So, is the TV still working?" he asked, and his dark eyes, wreathed with laugh lines, flashed merrily.

"Oh, it's so embarrassing." Emma gave an awkward laugh. The day before yesterday, she had phoned Grasser and asked him to take a look at her television set, which was on the blink. It turned out she had merely pressed the wrong channel on the remote control; that's all it was. Grasser probably thought she was a real dunce.

"Better embarrassed than a broken TV. This

afternoon I want to change the faucet in the kitchen. Will around two o'clock be all right?"

"Yes, of course." Emma nodded, pleased.

"Great. I'll see you later, then." Grasser smiled and set off on his bike.

Just as Emma passed the administration building and was about to turn toward the villa, Corinna Wiesner, the head of administration of Sonnenkinder, came out of the glass door, a cell phone at her ear, and walked rapidly toward her. She looked preoccupied, but when she caught sight of Emma, she smiled and ended the call.

"This party is getting on my last nerve," she called cheerfully, putting away her phone. "Good morning. How are you? You look a little tired."

"Good morning, Corinna," said Emma. "Well, I didn't get much sleep last night. We had a class reunion."

"Oh, yes, that's right. So? Was it fun?"

"Yes. I enjoyed it."

Corinna was a bundle of energy and had an unshakable composure and a memory like a computer. She was never in a bad mood, even though as head of administration she had a mountain of responsibilities: She had to worry about the staff, purchasing, organization, cooperation with the social and youth authorities. And she knew every single resident in the mothers' residence hall and every child in the shelter. Corinna always had time to lend an ear. In addition, she had four kids of her own. The youngest was two years older than Louisa. Emma was always astounded at how Corinna managed the workload, seemingly without ever resting. She and her husband, Ralf, were themselves products of the Sonnenkinder; Ralf had been a foster child of Emma's in-laws, and Corinna had been adopted by them as an infant. They were both among Florian's best and oldest friends.

"Well, it doesn't look to me as though you had such a fun evening." Corinna put her arm around Emma's shoulders. "Hey, what's wrong?"

"I'm a bit worried about Louisa," Emma admitted. "She's been acting strange for a few days now. She says she has a stomachache and seems very listless."

"Hmm. Have you taken her to the pediatrician?"

"Florian examined her but couldn't find anything specific."

Corinna frowned.

"You should keep an eye on her," she advised. "But you're doing all right, aren't you?"

"Well, yes . . . but I wish the baby would come soon. This heat is hard to take. The past few weeks have been difficult, but at least Florian is starting to feel better."

A while ago, she had talked to Corinna about the change in Florian's behavior, and Corinna had advised her to be patient. For a grown man, it's never easy to return to his parents' house, she said, and especially not for someone who had spent years in conflict areas. After all that stress, he had suddenly landed in a world of great abundance.

"Glad to hear it." Corinna smiled. "Maybe we'll have a chance to get together for a barbecue before the baby arrives. I haven't seen Flori in ages, even though he lives less than half a mile away."

Her cell phone rang, and she glanced at the display.

"Oh, excuse me, I have to take this. I'll see you later at Josef and Renate's. We have to go over the guest list for the reception and party."

Bemused, Emma watched her go, noting the way she strode over to her mother's house. Why did she say she hadn't seen Florian in ages? Hadn't he been over at their house just last night, having a beer with Ralf?

In a marriage like theirs, when they were so often apart and sometimes for long periods of time, trust had to take top priority. Emma trusted her husband, and jealousy was foreign to her. She never doubted his word. But suddenly, a tiny flame of mistrust flickered up inside her and settled in her mind. The suspicion that he might have lied to her aroused an oddly empty feeling in her.

Emma slowly continued on.

There had to be a simple explanation for why Corinna hadn't seen Florian yesterday. After all, it was already very late when Florian left the house. Maybe Corinna had gone straight to bed after a hard day at work.

Yes, that certainly seemed plausible. Because why would Florian lie to her?

He hung up the phone and stared at the TV screen, which displayed a shot of red-and-white police crime-scene tape, grim-looking officers in front of it, assigned to keep curiosity seekers from entering the crime scene. The evidence team was still working, searching for relevant clues, but they wouldn't find any there. Not in Eddersheim. The locks were only a mile or so downstream from here. He knew where it was.

Cut.

The Frankfurt Forensic Medicine Lab on Kennedyallee. Standing in front, a female reporter was speaking into the camera with a serious expression on her face. Dissolve to a photo of the dead girl, and he swallowed hard. So pretty, so blond, and so . . . dead. A tender young face with high cheekbones and full lips that would never laugh again. In the forensics lab, they had obviously gone to a lot of trouble. She didn't really look dead—more like she was sleeping. Seconds later, she was staring out from the TV screen, her eyes almost reproachful. His heart jumped in fright before he realized that it was a facial reconstruction, a computer-generated animation, but the effect was incredibly realistic.

He reached for the remote and turned the sound back on.

". . . estimated her age at around fifteen or sixteen. The girl was dressed in a denim miniskirt and yellow top with spaghetti straps, size four, from H&M. Does anyone recognize this girl? Or can you provide information on where she was living in recent days or weeks? Any police department will welcome useful tips from the public."

He was somewhat surprised that the police were already asking the public for help so soon after the body had been found. Obviously, the cops had no idea who the girl was. They were depending on Inspector Coincidence.

Unfortunately—as he knew from the phone call he'd just received—it was fairly certain there would be no single useful tip that would lead to solving the case. Every busybody would feel obligated to call the police to claim they had seen the girl somewhere, and the cops would then have to check out hundreds of useless leads. What an absolutely senseless waste of time. A squandering of important resources!

He was about to turn off the TV and get to work, when the face of a man came on the screen. The sight gave him a start. A flood of long-suppressed emotions shot through him. He started shaking.

"You filthy pig," he muttered, feeling the familiar helpless rage and the old bitterness rise up. His hand clenched the remote so hard that the battery lid popped off and the batteries fell out. He didn't even notice.

"We are in the very early stages of the investigation," said State Attorney Markus Maria Frey. "Until the results of the autopsy are in, we cannot say whether we're dealing with an accident, a suicide, or even a murder."

The angular chin, dark hair combed straight back, revealing the first strands of gray, the empathetic, cultivated voice and the brown eyes, which inspired confidence and seemed so friendly. But that was his trick. "Don Maria," as he was known internally at the Frankfurt state attorney's office, was a man with two personas: With wit and eloquence, he would turn on the charm for those who might prove useful, trying to wrap them around his little finger, but he could also be entirely different.

He had often looked into those eyes, deep into that black soul that was consumed by ambition. Frey was a ruthless power freak—arrogant and craving admiration. So it was not surprising that he'd snatched the investigation for himself. The case promised to attract huge attention, and Frey was addicted to being in the spotlight.

The cell phone rang again, and he took the call.

It was his boss from the fast-food stand, and his voice was seething with anger.

"Have you even looked at the clock, you lazy bum?" Fatty squawked. "Seven o'clock means seven o'clock, and not eight or ten! You'd better be here in ten minutes or you can—"

His decision had been made for him the instant that State Attorney Frey came on the TV screen. He could always find another job like the one in the fast-food stand. Right now, something else had priority.

"Kiss my ass," he said, interrupting the fat creep. "Find yourself some other idiot."

Then he punched off the call.

There was a lot to do. He had to prepare himself for the arrival of the police. Sooner or later, they'd appear, ready to toss all his belongings and turn the trailer upside down. No surprise, now that Don Maria had taken over. And the man had a memory like an elephant, especially for things that affected him personally.

He knelt down and pulled a cardboard box out from under the corner bench. Carefully, he set it on the table and raised the lid. On top lay a plastic sleeve containing a photo. He took it out and looked at it reverently. How old was she when that photo was taken? Six? Seven?

Tenderly, he stroked the sweet face of the child with his thumb and finally kissed it before he stowed the photo in a drawer underneath a pile of underwear. Longing stabbed him like a knife. He took a deep breath. Then he closed the box, stuck it under his arm, and left the trailer.

Bodenstein and Pia left the ready room on the ground floor of the Regional Criminal Police station, which had almost overnight been converted into the headquarters of the Special Commission. It was the only large room in the building. Under the aegis of Chief Commissioner Nierhoff, it had been the site of many spectacular press conferences; Dr. Nicola Engel's predecessor particularly enjoyed talking to the media. During the whole turbulent discussion, Pia had been trying to remember what it was she wanted to tell her boss. It was important, she knew that, but she couldn't put her finger on it.

"Engel was fantastic today," said Pia as they closed the security gate behind them and walked across the parking lot.

"Yep, today she was certainly in fine form," Bodenstein confirmed.

Shortly before nine o'clock, a young, overeager representative from the Frankfurt SA's office had made a dramatic entrance worthy of a movie. Along with two colleagues, he'd burst into the conference room, flamboyantly taken the floor, and confronted Pia in front of all the officers of the "Mermaid" Special Commission because, in his view, she had been too rash in going to the press and revealing too much information. Clearly overstepping his authority, he had even demanded that he and his office should take charge of the investigation. Before Pia could say a word, Dr. Engel had stepped in. Recalling how she put the little shit in his place with a few cool words, Pia had to smirk.

Dr. Nicola Engel was a petite woman. She seemed almost girlish in her white linen suit among all the men and uniforms, maybe even delicate, but that impression was deceptive. People were always making the fatal mistake of underestimating her, and the young SA gofer was one of those arrogant types of men who underestimated women as a matter of course. Nicola Engel might follow along with a discussion in silence, but when she finally spoke, her words would hit home with the unfailing precision of a computer-guided intercontinental ballistic missile, usually with similar annihilating effect.

The SA rep had beat a hasty retreat after he realized the total failure of his mission, although not before ordering Pia to Frankfurt for the autopsy, which she was planning to attend anyway.

Despite all initial misgivings on the part of her colleagues, in the past two years Dr. Nicola Engel had developed into a good department head with a strict but fair leadership style. She always stood up for her team and never let internal problems leak out to the public. Within the Hofheim Kripo unit, her authority was undisputed; everyone treated her with respect, because, unlike her predecessor, she had no time for politics, and consequently paid more attention to actual police work.

"Engel is really good," said Pia, handing Bodenstein the keys to one of the squad cars. "Could you drive? I have to call Alina Hindemith."

Bodenstein nodded.

As part of the discussion, he and Ostermann and Pia had spoken to the younger officers who had been called to the site of the riverside booze party yesterday. From the girl who'd discovered the body, Pia had obtained the names of the other kids who'd been drinking and had ordered all four of them to come to the station, along with their parents. Two girls, two boys, meek and very upset, but only marginally helpful. None of them had noticed the dead girl in the reeds; they all claimed not to remember what had actually happened. All four were lying.

"I'm telling you that they all took off when they saw that the girl was dead," Pia said, searching in her bag for Alina's phone number. "And I'm fairly sure that they left their friend behind, just like Alina did."

"By doing that, in the worst-case scenario they may have made themselves accessories if their friend dies." Bodenstein stopped at the off-ramp and put on his left-turn blinker. Since he had no air conditioning, they were driving with the windows down until the stuffy heat became tolerable. "I'm sure their parents drummed into them what they should say."

"I think so, too," Pia agreed. They hadn't received any good news from the hospital in Höchst. Sixteen-year-old Alexander still couldn't speak and was on a respirator. The doctors thought he might have suffered brain damage from lack of oxygen.

Even considering the amount of alcohol involved, it was no minor offense to leave an unconscious individual to his fate—especially if he was a friend. They probably hadn't all been as dead drunk as they claimed, because then they wouldn't have been able to climb over the tall gate so easily.

Since early morning, the phones in Dispatch had been ringing off the hook. As always, when the public was asked for assistance, a large number of nutcases also called in, claiming they'd seen the dead girl in the most unlikely places. It was unproductive work following up on all the claims, but there could always be a real tip among them—and then it would be worth their while. Yesterday evening, the reporters had mentioned the cold case of another girl found dead in the Main River back in 2001, and now the press was harping on that. In order to placate the public and to quell the burgeoning criticism of the work the police were doing, a swift resolution of the investigation was needed, no matter what the cost. That was Pia's argument for informing the public early on—and Nicola Engel had approved it, just as State Attorney Frey had done last night.

Bodenstein turned off the A66, heading for Frankfurt, while Pia tried in vain to reach Alina. Her father pretended she wasn't home.

"All this lying pisses me off," Pia grumbled. "If it were their kid lying unconscious in the ICU, they sure would light a fire under our asses."

"Even worse, I find it highly questionable when parents set an example for their children by showing them how simple it is to shake off all responsibility for their actions," Bodenstein said. "This instant reflex to palm off all blame onto someone else is an indication of the complete collapse of morals in our society."

A call came in from Ostermann.

"Tell me, Pia, where did you put the file on Veronika Meissner? I have the autopsy report on my desk and don't want to leave it floating around here."

At first glance, Kai Ostermann might look like a somewhat chaotic nerd, with his nickel-framed glasses, ponytail, and sloppy clothes, but that was misleading. He was undoubtedly the most disciplined and orderly person Pia had ever met.

"I was looking for that report yesterday," she

replied. "The case file must be underneath my desk."

At that moment, she remembered what she'd wanted to tell Bodenstein so urgently.

"By the way, you know who showed up at my office yesterday?" she said to Bodenstein after she'd finished talking to Ostermann. "The best way is via Frankfurter Kreuz and past the stadium. If we go through town, we won't get there in time."

"No idea." Bodenstein put on his blinker. "Who?"

"Frank Behnke. In a suit and tie. And even more offensive than before."

"Oh yeah?"

"Now he's with the State Criminal Division. In Internal Affairs!" said Pia. "Starting on Monday, he's going to do an investigation of our department. Apparently, there have been complaints and accusations of irregularities."

"Do tell." Bodenstein shook his head.

"Not following up on criminal offenses, unauthorized access to data. Oliver, he's got *you* in his sights. He's out to get back at you for humiliating him during the Snow White case."

"And what did *I* do to him then?" Bodenstein asked. "He was behaving despicably. And he has only his own actions to blame for the investigation and his suspension, not me."

"He doesn't seem to see it that way. You know what he's like, that vindictive jerk."

111

"It doesn't matter." Bodenstein shrugged. "My conscience is clear."

Pia sucked on her lower lip for a moment. Then she said, "I'm still afraid of what he might do. Do you remember the first case we worked together?"

"Of course. What are you getting at?"

"The case with Friedhelm Döring. The castration. A charge of aggravated bodily harm was brought against the veterinarian, the lawyer, and the pharmacist."

"Yeah, but not as a favor," Bodenstein countered in consternation. "We had sent Spusi to the operating room of the veterinary clinic, but there were no viable leads, not a single piece of evidence. I can't torture suspects to make them talk!"

Pia could see that her boss was getting more and more annoyed the longer he thought about this charge.

"I just wanted to alert you to this in advance, so you'll be prepared," she said. "I'm actually rather sure that's exactly what Behnke is going to start with."

"Thanks," said Bodenstein with a grim smile. "I'm afraid you're right. But he'd better be careful not to lean too far out the window. Because, by God, he's no innocent lamb."

"How do you mean?" Now Pia was curious. She recalled the tension that had clearly existed from the first day between Behnke and Dr. Engel. Back then, rumors were flying that their mutual dislike had something to do with an old case in which they'd been involved during their time with the Frankfurt Homicide Commission. During an arrest, a contact man for the Frankfurt police had been shot to death.

"An old case," replied Bodenstein evasively. "Long ago, but still under the statute of limitations. Behnke is going to need to pull his socks up if he tries to piss on me."

"Crap!" Hanna muttered when the green light changed to red right in front of her. Somebody had just snatched the last available spot in the Junghofstrasse parking garage. She glanced in the rearview mirror, shifted into reverse, and turned the Mini that Meike had lent her toward the exit. Luckily, nobody was behind her and the exit was wide enough for this maneuver. It was already ten minutes before noon. She had a lunch appointment with Wolfgang in KUBU. In a plastic sleeve lying next to her on the passenger seat was the battle plan for damage control that she had worked out this morning.

She turned right onto Junghofstrasse and then onto Neue Mainzer at the corner. Just before the Hilton, she veered right, toward the stock exchange, and actually spied a parking place on the left side of the street between a delivery van and a black limousine. She put on the blinker, stepped on the gas, and moved over to the left. She assiduously ignored the wild honking and gesticulations of the driver behind her, who had to stop short to avoid plowing into the Mini. Courtesy and consideration were uncalled for in the inner-city war for free parking spots. The slot would have been too small for her own car, but the Mini slipped into it with no problem.

Hanna got out, sticking the briefcase under her arm. That morning, she'd had the Porsche Panamera picked up and taken to the shop. The owner of the shop had called her an hour later and asked whether she didn't want to file a police report against an unknown person for property damage.

"I'll think it over," she replied, agreeing that the vandalized hood and the four slashed tires should be set aside as evidence. In her mind, Hanna saw again the large letters on her car's hood spelling out CUNT. Who had done it? Norman? Vinzenz? Who else knew where she lived? All morning, she had banned this worrying thought from her head, but now it pushed to the foreground again.

Hanna decided to take a shortcut but regretted it seconds later, because restaurant row was packed to the gills. All the seats underneath the big awnings were taken in front of all the cafés and restaurants. People who worked in the surrounding buildings and stores were using their lunch hour to take a sunbath; there were teenagers with hardly any clothes on, mothers with strollers, and senior citizens who ambled along the shopping mile at a pace much slower than the usual Frankfurt rush. The heat was slowing down the whole city.

Hanna adapted her gait to match. She had left her high heels and suit at home today, and instead she was wearing white jeans, a T-shirt, and comfortable sneakers. She crossed Neue Mainzer with a throng of Japanese tourists and entered the terrace of KUBU from Opernplatz. Ninety percent of the midday crowd consisted of businessmen from the nearby bank towers; a smaller number of women in professional attire and a few tourists made up the minority. Wolfgang was sitting at a table at the edge of the terrace in the shade of a plane tree and studying the menu.

When she reached the table, he looked up and smiled, delighted to see her.

"Hello, Hanna." He got up, kissed her on both cheeks, and courteously pulled out a chair for her. "I've taken the liberty of ordering a bottle of mineral water. And some bread."

"Thank you. A very good idea. I'm famished." She reached for the menu and scanned the daily specials. "I'll take today's special, wild leek foam soup and sole."

"Sounds good. I'll have the same." Wolfgang closed his menu, and seconds later the server appeared and took their order. Two specials and a bottle of Pinot Grigio.

Wolfgang rested his elbows on the table, clasped his hands, and gave her a searching look. "I'm really curious to hear what you've come up with."

Hanna poured some olive oil into the little dish, strewed coarse salt and pepper over it, and then dunked a piece of French bread into the oil. In all the excitement this morning, she'd had no time for breakfast, and her stomach was growling. Low blood sugar was threatening to put her in a foul mood.

"We're going on the offensive," she explained as she chewed, putting her handbag in her lap and taking out the plastic sleeve. "We've gotten in contact with the people who complained about us. Tomorrow morning, I'll be meeting with the man in Bremen, and with the woman in Dortmund in the afternoon. They were both extremely responsive."

"Well, that sounds very good." Wolfgang nodded. "Our board and the shareholders' reps are pretty nervous. We can't afford any bad publicity right now."

"I know." Hanna swept a strand of hair from her brow and took a sip of water. Here in the shade, the temperature was still tolerable. Wolfgang removed his tie, rolled it up, and put it in an inside pocket of his jacket, which he'd hung over the back of the chair. Hanna explained her strategy to him in brief sentences as he listened attentively.

By the time the soup was served, they'd agreed to try to limit the damage.

"And how are things with you otherwise?" Wolfgang asked. "You look a little tired."

"It's all taking a toll on me, I have to admit. This thing with Norman and the whole mess. And last night, Meike was perfectly rotten toward me, as usual. I don't think we're ever going to get along."

With Wolfgang, she could be frank and didn't have to pretend. They'd known each other now for half an eternity. He had witnessed her meteoric rise from news anchor at Hessen Radio to idolized TV star, and if she had to make an appearance somewhere and didn't have a man at her side, he was always available as an escort. She had no secrets from Wolfgang. He was the first person she told when she got pregnant—even before Meike's father. Wolfgang had been her witness at her wedding and was Meike's god-father; he listened to her patiently when she had trouble with her love life and was happy for her when things were going well. He was without a doubt her best friend.

"And if that wasn't enough, last night some-body slashed all four of my tires and dented the hood of my car." She said this in a deliberately light tone of voice, as if it didn't particularly

117

bother her. Once she granted the demons of fear a place in her life, they would have the upper hand.

"What did you say?" Wolfgang was truly shocked. "Who would do such a thing? Did you call the police?"

"No. Not yet." Hanna wiped her plate with a piece of bread and shook her head. "It was probably just some jealous idiot who couldn't stand the sight of a Porsche Panamera."

"You shouldn't take it so lightly, Hanna. It worries me that you live alone in that big house by the woods. What about the surveillance cameras?"

"I need to have them replaced," she said. "At the moment, they're only for show."

The waitress came and poured white wine and took away the soup plates. Wolfgang waited until she left, then put his hand on Hanna's. "If there's anything I can do, if I can help in any way . . . you know you only have to say the word."

"Thank you," Hanna said with a smile. "I know."

All of a sudden, it occurred to her how happy she would be with Wolfgang if he weren't married or seriously involved. It wasn't because of his looks. He was no Adonis, of course, but he was attractive enough. The years had treated him kindly, unlike most men she knew, and lent his soft, youthful features a rugged masculinity that suited him. His hair was graying at the temples, and the laugh lines at his eyes were deeper now, but that suited him, too.

A few years ago, he'd had a girlfriend, a boring, pale attorney, whom he seemed to be pretty serious about, but she'd found no favor in the eyes of Wolfgang's father. Eventually, the relationship fell apart. Wolfgang never talked about it, but he hadn't had a steady girlfriend since.

The sole was served. At KUBU, the meals didn't take long; people knew that the patrons who came for a business lunch didn't have a lot of time.

Hanna picked up her napkin.

"I'm not going to let myself be buffaloed," she said forcefully. "Now we just have to salvage the situation as far as my show is concerned. Do you think my strategy will work?"

"I think so," replied Wolfgang. "You can be very convincing, even when you aren't convinced about something yourself."

"Precisely!" Hanna grabbed her wineglass and held it up for a toast. "Here's to resolving yet another minor mess."

He clinked glasses with her. The apprehension in his eyes had given way to quiet disappointment. But Hanna didn't notice.

Bodenstein couldn't find a parking place anywhere near the Institute for Forensic Medicine on Kennedyallee. He parked on Eschenbachstrasse, so they had to walk a couple of hundred yards. Pia's decision to go public with the case had provoked a good deal of media interest. There was a crowd of reporters on the sidewalk, and they pounced on anyone going in or out of the institute. One reporter recognized Kirchhoff and Bodenstein, and they were instantly surrounded. From the shouted questions, Pia gathered that they must have heard a rumor from somewhere that last night there had been another young victim of the phenomenon of "coma drinking," and now the pack of reporters was greedy for details. For a brief moment, she wavered. Did the press guys have more current information from the hospital than she did? Had Alexander died?

"Why didn't you tell us that two people died?" one young man shouted, louder than the others, sticking his microphone in Pia's face like a weapon. "What are the police trying to pull?"

This wasn't the first time in her life that she was astonished by the aggressive and excitable behavior of some reporters. Did they think they'd find out more if they shouted louder?

"There is no second fatality," replied Bodenstein for Pia, shoving the mike aside. "Now let us through."

It took a couple of minutes for them to fight their way to the entrance of the institute. Inside the building, it was cool and almost reverentially quiet; somewhere a computer keyboard was clacking. The doors to the lecture hall at the front of the wood-paneled lobby were standing open. Pia heard a voice and glanced into the spacious room. The rows of seats were empty, but State Attorney Dr. Markus Maria Frey was walking back and forth as he talked on the phone. He was once again impeccably dressed in a three-piece suit, with his hair parted meticulously. When he saw Pia, he ended his call and put away his cell phone. His annoyed expression faded.

"I must apologize for the behavior of my young colleague this morning," he said, extending his hand first to Pia, then to Bodenstein. "Mr. Tanouti is a bit overzealous."

"No problem," replied Pia. She was somewhat surprised to see Dr. Frey here, because it was unusual for him to attend an autopsy at the institute.

"I assume that Commissioner Engel probably gave him a taste of his own medicine." A smile passed over the SA's face, but he turned serious at once. "Is there anything to this rumor of a second fatality?"

"Fortunately, no," said Bodenstein. "My colleague called the hospital only half an hour ago. The boy who was found near the body is still in critical condition, but he's alive."

As they descended the stairs to the basement of the institute, the SA's phone rang again, and he stayed behind.

Autopsy room 1 was too small to accommodate all the spectators. Henning Kirchhoff and his boss, Professor Thomas Kronlage, were conducting the autopsy together, supported by two postmortem assistants. The state attorney's office had immediately sent over three representatives, including the zealous hothead from this morning. A police photographer whose name Pia couldn't recall completed the group.

"Standing room only," Henning's colleague Ronnie Böhme whispered to Pia as she and Bodenstein squeezed past the autopsy table.

"This is not a forensics lecture for lawyers," Henning complained to State Attorney Frey. They knew each other well, since the pathologist was often called upon to serve as an expert witness for the prosecutor's office or for the court. "Do we really need four of you standing around and getting in the way?"

The representatives from the SA's office put their heads together, and then two of them left the room with scarcely concealed relief. Frey and the overzealous Merzad Tanouti remained.

"That's better," grumbled Henning.

For everyone present, the autopsy of such a young person was bound to have a powerful emotional impact. The mood was tense, and even Henning refrained from his usual cynicism. When the victim was a child or teenager, everyone present felt a genuine sadness. It wasn't the first court-ordered autopsy for either Bodenstein or the staff from the SA's office, and Pia had spent countless evenings and weekends in this room or in autopsy room 2, next door, when she was still married to Henning. In order to have any time with her husband at all, there had often been no option but to come to his workplace, since his attitude toward his job bordered on obsession.

Pia had seen corpses in every stage of decomposition and in every possible or impossible condition—and smelled them: floaters, burn victims, skeletons, crash victims, and those who had died as the result of an accident or a horrendous suicide. Often she and Henning had stood by the autopsy table and discussed everyday topics; sometimes they'd even argued. And the detailed forays into forensic medicine under the guidance of a teacher as strict as Henning had sharpened Pia's handling of crime-scene investigations.

This didn't mean that Pia felt unmoved whenever she was called to a murder scene or the location where a body had been found. There were situations and circumstances so extreme or gruesome that sometimes she had to summon all her strength to maintain a professional demeanor. Like most of her colleagues, Pia did not see her job as a crusade against crime in the world. One of the reasons she loved doing her job, no matter how frustrating and depressing it could often be, was that she felt she was showing respect to the deceased by clearing up the circumstances of their deaths. She was restoring at least a small part of their human dignity. Because there was nothing as undignified as a nameless corpse, a person robbed of identity, who was buried somewhere or just left on the ground like a piece of garbage. No fate could be sadder than lying dead for weeks or even a month inside an apartment without being missed by anybody.

It was these cases, fortunately rare, that made Pia sense the true purpose of her work. And she knew that it was the same for many of her colleagues. And yet some of them shied away from forensic medicine, so in the past Pia had often volunteered to take over the task. As soon as a body lay here on the shiny stainless-steel dissection table under the glaring fluorescent light, it lost all power to terrify her. There was nothing sinister or mysterious about an autopsy; the court-ordered dissection followed a strict protocol, which began with the external post-mortem examination.

Riding the motor scooter was like traveling halfway around the world. Although his butt burned like fire after an hour and a half on the plastic seat, he enjoyed the ride. The warm wind caressed his face; the sunshine on his bare arms did him good. He felt young. For many years, he'd had no time or opportunity to take a trip on his scooter. It must have been twenty years ago that he took off with his best buddy, the one he remembered so fondly. They had actually made it all the way to the North Sea on the 80cc motor-bikes, keeping to country roads. At night, they'd slept in a tent, or sometimes out under the clear starry sky when they were too lazy to pitch the tent.

Of course, they didn't have much money, but they were freer than they'd ever been before, or would be ever again. That summer, he met Britta on the beach at St. Peter-Ording and fell in love at first sight. She was from Bad Homburg, and after vacation they'd gotten together again. He was a law student and had just passed his first state exam; she had recently finished her training as a retail and wholesale buyer and was working in a department store in the women's outerwear department.

Less than six months later, they got married. Their parents splurged to give them a dream wedding. Registry office, church, a coach with four white horses. A reception with two hundred guests at the Bad Homburg Castle. Wedding pictures in the park beneath the mighty cedars. Honeymoon on Crete. After passing the second state exam, he got a job with one of the best law firms in Frankfurt, specializing in business and tax law. His salary was good enough for them to buy a lot and build their dream house. Then their daughter was born, and he was crazy about her. Later, they also had a son. Everything was perfect. On summer evenings they barbecued outdoors with friends, in the wintertime they went skiing in Kitzbühel, and they traveled to beaches in Majorca or Sylt in the summer. He'd been promoted and made partner—at the young age of thirty—and began focusing on criminal law. His clients were no longer tax evaders or misguided CEOs; now they were murderers, kidnappers, blackmailers, rapists, and drug dealers. His in-laws weren't pleased, but for Britta, it didn't make any difference. He made more money than the husbands of her friends, and she could afford to buy whatever she wanted.

Yes, life had been great, even though he had to work eighty hours a week. Success had intoxicated him; he was the most famous defense attorney in Germany. He moved with ease in the circles of his prominent clients, and was invited to birthday parties and weddings. Without batting an eye, he had billed a thousand D-marks per hour, and to his clients, he was worth every penny.

But all that was long gone. Instead of driving a Maserati Quattroporte and a Porsche 911 Turbo, he was now relegated to an ancient motor scooter. The villa with gardens, pool, and every imaginable luxury had been replaced by a trailer. But even though the outward appearance of life had changed, the man inside him had remained the same, with all his secret wishes, dreams, and longings. Most of the time, he succeeded in controlling them, but not always. Sometimes his inner urge was stronger than any sense of reason.

He had left behind the last buildings of Langensebold. Now there were only two miles to go. The estate wasn't easy to find, which was precisely the intention of its residents. Back then, they had searched for a long time before they found a suitable property: a run-down farm with extensive grounds behind a stretch of woods, not visible from any road. It was years since he'd been there, and he was impressed when he saw what they'd made of it. He stopped the scooter by a spike-topped wrought-iron gate seven feet high. The motion-activated cameras spotted him at once, zooming in on him. The property had been converted into an impregnable fortress, surrounded by a fence that was covered with an opaque façade. He took off his helmet.

"*Benvenuto, Dottore Avvocato,*" a voice croaked from the speaker. "You're just in time for dinner. We're behind the barn."

The double gate swung slowly open, and he drove through. Where once cowsheds and pigsties had stood along with tons of old manure, he now saw a junkyard. The carefully renovated barn contained the workshop. On the paved forecourt stood rows of Harley-Davidsons gleaming with chrome; beside them, his miserable motor scooter looked like a poor relative. On the other side, two Staffordshire bull terriers were barking in a big kennel behind confidence-inspiring, solid-looking fence posts.

He stuck the cardboard box under his arm and went around to the back of the barn. Maybe he would have been shocked if he hadn't known what to expect. Steaks were cooking on a big suspended grill, and at least a thousand years' worth of prison time was sitting at the tables and benches. One of the men, a beefy giant with a carefully trimmed beard and wearing a head scarf, got up from his spot in the shade and came over to him.

"*Avvocato*," he said in a gruff bass voice, giving him a quick hug with his muscular arms, which were tattooed from shoulder to fingertips. "Welcome."

"Hey, Bernd." He grinned. "Great to see you again. It must be ten years since the last time I was here."

"It's your own fault for not stopping by. The business is going really well."

"You always were a gifted gearhead."

"Whatever. And I've got a couple of really good boys." Bernd Prinzler lit himself a cigarette. "Have you already eaten?"

"Thanks, but I'm not hungry." The mere smell of grilled meat turned his stomach. Besides, he hadn't rattled thirty miles along a country road to come here and eat. The tense anticipation that he'd only barely managed to keep under control since Bernd's phone call last night now flared up, making his heart beat faster. He'd been waiting so long for this! "On the phone, you said you had something new for me?"

"Yep. A lot. It'll blow your mind." The giant squinted his eyes. "I bet you can't wait, eh?"

"Honestly, no," he admitted. "I've had to wait long enough already."

"Well, come on, then." Bernd put his arm around his shoulders. "I just have to go and pick up the kids at school. But I'm sure you'll be able to manage on your own."

"Ninety-one and a quarter pounds at a height of five six," said Professor Kronlage. "That is massive undernourishment."

The emaciated body of the girl was covered with scars, old ones and relatively fresh ones. In the glare of the fluorescent lights, they were clearly visible: the burns, bruises, scratches, and hematomas—shocking evidence of the years of abuse that the girl must have suffered.

A young woman came into the room.

"The photos," was all she said as she shoved brusquely past Bodenstein and Pia without greeting them. She sat down at the computer on a little table by the wall and started typing. A moment later, the skeleton of the dead girl appeared on the screen. The days when black-and-white X-rays were clipped to light boxes were long gone.

Kronlage and Kirchhoff interrupted their external examination of the body and stepped over to the computer to analyze what they saw there: broken bones in the face, ribs, and extremities. And like the external injuries, some were old and healed, but some were fresh. They counted twenty-four fractures.

Pia shuddered at the thought of the horrible martyrdom this girl must have endured. But more important to the forensic physicians than the fractures were the various indicators of the age of the skeleton. Fusing of the cranial growth sutures and of the long bones enabled a preliminary estimate of the victim's age.

"She was at least fourteen, but no more than sixteen years old," Henning Kirchhoff said at last. "We'll be able to be more precise very soon."

"In any case, the child was abused over a period of years," Professor Kronlage added. "Also, the abnormal pallor of the skin and the almost complete lack of vitamin D in the blood, as reported by the laboratory, are striking."

"Striking in what way?" asked the young lawyer.

"Vitamin D is not actually a vitamin, but a neuroregulatory steroid hormone." Kronlage peered over the top of his half-moon glasses. "The human body creates the hormone whenever the skin is exposed to sunlight. Nowadays, vitamin D deficiency is nearing epidemic proportions world-wide, because dermatologists and health authorities have been stirring up hysteria about skin cancer and advising people to stay out of the sun or to use sunblock with an SPF of thirty or higher. Which means that—"

"What has that got to do with the dead girl?" Tanouti asked him impatiently, interrupting.

"Just listen," Kronlage chided him.

Tanouti silently accepted the rebuke and merely shrugged.

"A value of fifteen to eighteen nanograms per milliliter of blood, as was determined in a large-scale screening in the USA after the winter months, is considered a sizable deficiency. The optimum is fifty to sixty-five nanograms per milliliter of blood," the professor went on. "Only four nanograms per milliliter was measured in the blood serum of this girl."

"So? What do we conclude from that?" Tanouti's voice sounded even more impatient.

"I have no idea what *you* conclude from it, young man," Kronlage replied calmly. "For me, this fact, combined with the skin pallor and the porous bone structure evident in the X-rays, supports the assumption that the girl had not been exposed to sunlight for a very long time. This may mean that the girl was held captive."

For a moment, the room was totally quiet. Then a cell phone rang.

"Excuse me," said State Attorney Frey, and left the room.

The general condition of the girl was very poor; her body was extremely undernourished and dehydrated, her teeth were full of cavities, and she had apparently never been to a dentist. That eliminated the possibility of determining her identity from dental records.

The external examination was concluded; now the actual autopsy would begin. With a scalpel, Kronlage cut the scalp from one ear to the other, folded the skin forward and then left it to an assistant to open the cranium with an oscillating saw in order to remove the brain. At the same time, Henning was opening the chest and abdominal cavities with a single vertical incision from neck to pubis. The ribs and breastbone were separated with the saw, and the organs that were removed were placed on a small metal tray above the dissection table and examined immediately. Tissue samples were also taken. Condition, size, shape, color, and weight of each organ was determined and logged.

"What have we here?" Henning asked himself, ignoring the onlookers. He had cut open the stomach to take samples of its contents.

"What's that?" Pia asked.

"Looks like . . . fabric." Henning smoothed out

the oily scrap with two pair of pincettes and then held the scrap up to the bright light. "It's been pretty well damaged by the stomach acid. Well, maybe the lab can make something out of it."

Ronnie Böhme held out an evidence bag and made a note of the finding.

The minutes passed and turned into hours. The chief state attorney had left. The pathologists were working, focused and meticulous. Henning, who was responsible for the report, spoke the findings into the microphone he wore around his neck. It was four in the afternoon by the time Böhme placed the organs back inside the body and sewed up the incisions. The autopsy was completed.

"The cause of death was clearly drowning," Henning summed up in his closing comments. "There were also serious internal injuries caused by kicks or blows to the abdomen, chest, extremities, and head, which sooner or later would also have resulted in death. Ruptures of the spleen, lungs, liver, and rectum. In addition, the massive injuries to the vagina and anus indicate that the girl was sexually assaulted shortly before her death."

Bodenstein listened in silence and with a stony expression. Now and then, he nodded, but he asked no questions. Kirchhoff looked at him.

"Well, I'm sorry, Bodenstein," he said. "We can rule out suicide. But whether the injuries were due to an accident or the result of murder is your job to find out."

"Why do you rule out suicide?" Pia asked.

"Because—" Henning began, but he got no further.

Tanouti broke in. He suddenly seemed to be in a hurry. "Dr. Kirchhoff, I want the autopsy report from you on my desk first thing tomorrow morning."

"That goes without saying, Mr. Tanouti. Tomorrow morning, it will be in your mailbox." Henning smiled with exaggerated charm. "Shall I type it up myself?"

"If you like." Tanouti was so blinded by his own importance that he didn't even notice how in a matter of seconds he'd become the most unpopular member of the state attorney's office. "So we can announce to the press that the girl in the river died of drowning."

"I didn't say that." Henning peeled the latex gloves from his hands and tossed them in the wastebasket next to the washbasin.

"Excuse me?" The young man took a step back into the autopsy room. "But you just said that the girl obviously drowned."

"Yes, that's true. But you interrupted me before I could explain why I've ruled out suicide. In fact, she did not drown in the Main."

Pia gave her ex-husband a baffled look.

"When someone drowns in fresh water, the lung tissue is so severely overinflated that the water pours out when the chest cavity is opened. We call

134

this phenomenon emphysema aquosum. But here, that was not the case. Instead, a pulmonary edema had formed."

"And what is that in plain German?" snapped Tanouti in annoyance. "I don't need a lesson in forensic medicine. Just give me the facts!"

Henning cast a disparaging look in his direction. He had an ironic gleam in his eye. Tanouti had spoiled any chance of ever being on good terms with the pathologist.

"A more detailed knowledge of the field of forensics is never a drawback," he said with a sardonic smile. "Especially if someone wants to make a name for himself in the tempest of flashing cameras from the press."

The young attorney flushed and took a step toward Henning, but he had to beat a hasty retreat because Böhme shoved the gurney with the body of the dead girl right up against him.

"For example, a pulmonary edema can form in salt water." Henning took off his glasses and polished them calmly with a paper towel. Then he held the glasses up to the light and squinted at the lenses to see whether they were clean. "Or by drowning in chlorinated water, such as in a swimming pool."

Pia exchanged a quick glance with her boss. That was really an extremely important detail, and typical of Henning that he'd left it until the end.

"The girl drowned in chlorinated water," he said at last. "In the next few days, a precise analysis of the water sample taken from the lungs will be done by the lab. Now you'll have to excuse me. Pia, Bodenstein, Mr. Tanouti, have a pleasant day. I have to type up the autopsy report." He winked at Pia and left the room.

"What an arrogant idiot," grumbled the young attorney; then he left as well.

"Well, everyone eventually meets his match," Bodenstein commented drily.

"And in that guy's case, it happened twice today," said Pia. "First Engel and now Henning. That should be plenty for one day."

When Emma arrived with Louisa from child care, the table on the terrace had already been set for coffee. Her in-laws were sitting in comfortable rattan chairs in the shade of the pergola, which was covered with ivy and blooming wisteria. They were playing Scrabble.

"Hello, Renate! Hello, Josef!" Emma called. "We're back."

"Just in time for tea and cakes." Renate Finkbeiner put down her reading glasses and smiled.

"And just in time to witness my three to two victory," Josef Finkbeiner added. "QUAGGA. That makes forty-eight points. I win."

"What kind of a word is that?" Renate protested

with feigned indignation. "You just made that up."

"No, I didn't. A quagga is an extinct type of zebra. Just admit that today I was simply better." Josef Finkbeiner laughed, leaned over, and kissed his wife on the cheek. Then he shoved back his chair and spread his arms wide. "Come over here to Grandpa, princess. I've filled up the wading pool extra high for you. Why don't you go put on your bathing suit?"

"Sounds great," said Emma, who wished she could stretch out full length in the wading pool herself. Usually, she was immune to heat waves, but these temperatures, combined with the high humidity, were absolutely unbearable.

Louisa happily allowed her grandfather to pick her up.

"Shall we get your bathing suit?" Emma asked.

"Naw." Louisa squirmed out of her grandfather's arms and climbed onto one of the easy chairs. Her eyes were fixed on the table. "Wanna have cake."

"All right, then." Renate Finkbeiner laughed and lifted the cover she'd put over the cake to keep the bugs off. "Which would you rather have? Strawberry tart or cream-cheese cake?"

"Cream cheese!" Louisa shouted, eyes sparkling. "With extra cream!"

Emma's mother-in-law cut slices of cream-cheese cake for both Louisa and Emma and put them on plates. Then she poured Emma a cup of

Darjeeling. Louisa shoveled the cake into her mouth in record time.

"Want another one," she demanded, her mouth still full.

"What's the magic word?" asked her grandpa, who had put away the Scrabble game.

"Plee-eez," murmured Louisa with a mischievous grin.

"But just a little piece," Emma admonished.

"No! A big one!" Louisa countered, and a morsel of cake fell out of her mouth.

"Now now, what sort of way is that to behave, princess?" Josef Finkbeiner shook his head disapprovingly. "Well-behaved little girls don't talk with their mouths full."

Louisa gave him a dubious look, not quite sure whether he was being serious or joking. But he was looking at her sternly as she gulped down the last bite of cake.

"Please, dear Grandma," said Louisa, holding out her plate. "Another piece of cheesecake, please."

Emma didn't say a word as her daughter gave Josef a beseeching look.

He nodded and winked at the child. Louisa's face instantly lit up, and Emma felt a tiny stab that felt like jealousy.

No matter how hard she tried, she'd found no way to draw close to her daughter. Since they'd been living here, it had become even harder, and she often felt completely shut out. Louisa simply didn't respect her. And yet she obeyed Josef and Florian without protest—even happily complying with their wishes. What was the reason for that? Did Emma lack the voice of authority? What was she doing wrong? Corinna thought it was normal for girls to side with their father and rub their mother the wrong way, especially at Louisa's age. Emma had read the same thing in various parenting manuals, but it was still painful.

"Now I think I'll leave the ladies to their tea." Josef Finkbeiner got up, tucked the box with the Scrabble game under his arm, and hinted at a bow, which made Louisa laugh loudly. "Renate, Emma, princess—I wish you a pleasant afternoon."

"Grandpa, will you read me something?" Louisa called.

"Today I can't, unfortunately," replied Josef. "I have to go somewhere right now. But tomorrow I will."

"Okay," Louisa accepted his explanation without further comment.

If Emma had refused like that, Louisa would have thrown a fit. Emma stabbed the last piece of the cheesecake crust with her fork as her father-in-law left. She appreciated Josef, liked him a lot, in fact, and yet at moments like this he always made her feel that she was a complete failure when it came to raising a child.

The warm air was full of the buzzing of bees

eagerly gathering nectar in the rosebushes and flower beds surrounding the terrace. Farther away in the park, a lawn mower was droning, and there was a smell of freshly mown grass.

"Do you happen to have the guest list with you?" Renate asked, tearing Emma out of her gloomy thoughts. "Oh, you don't know how much I'm looking forward to seeing all my children again at last."

Emma pulled the folder out of her shoulder bag and slid it across the table to her mother-in-law. She was happy that Corinna had left the guest list and the design and mailing of the invitations to her. It gave her the feeling that she really belonged to the family and wasn't merely a guest. She had drawn up the list from an existing Excel file; she didn't recognize 95 percent of the names. Renate, on the other hand, emitted a little cry of joy at each check mark that indicated a guest had accepted the invitation.

Her genuine enthusiasm touched Emma.

Renate was a woman who went through life with a cheerful smile, simply ignoring anything negative. She was not the least bit interested in what was happening in the world, and didn't read the newspaper or watch the news on TV. With scarcely disguised contempt, Florian described his mother as unworldly, naïve, and tiresomely superficial. It was true that her persistent cheerfulness was sometimes hard to take, but it was certainly preferable to the constant harping and morose pronouncements of Emma's own mother.

"Oh God, how the time flies." Renate sighed, wiping tears from her eyes. "They've been grown men and women for so long, but I can still see them as children when I read their names."

She patted Emma's hand.

"It makes me so happy that you and Florian can be there for the party."

"We're happy, too," replied Emma, although she was not completely sure whether Florian really was glad about the reception and the summer festivities. He wasn't exactly enthralled by his parents' life work, in which they had invested the greater part of their fortune.

"No!" Emma stopped Louisa from spearing another piece of cake. "You've still got half a piece on your plate."

"But I only like the soft part," Louisa protested as she chewed.

"You have to eat the crust, too. Or do you want Grandma to throw it in the garbage?"

Louisa started to pout.

"Want more cake!" she demanded.

"But dear, you've already had two big pieces," said Renate.

"But I want more!" the child insisted with a greedy look.

"No. That's all," said Emma firmly, taking the

plate out of Louisa's hand. "We're going to eat supper soon. Why don't you tell Grandma what you did at day care today?"

Louisa pressed her lips together defiantly, then realized that she really wasn't going to get a third piece of cake. She burst into tears and climbed down from her chair, looking around wildly.

"Don't you dare!" Emma yelled in warning, but it was too late. The little girl kicked at the ceramic birdbath, which fell off its stone support and broke into pieces.

"Oh my, the lovely birdbath!" cried her grandmother.

Emma saw that Louisa had already spotted her next target, a flowerpot full of geraniums. She jumped up and grabbed her daughter by the arm before she could cause any more damage. Louisa squirmed, shrieking at a frequency that could shatter glass, kicking and flailing about. Emma was used to her daughter's temper tantrums, but the intensity of Louisa's rage startled her.

"I want cake! I want cake!" she screeched, totally beside herself, her face red as a lobster. Tears sprayed from her eyes, and she threw herself to the ground.

"Stop making a scene," Emma hissed. "We're going upstairs until you've calmed down."

"Stupid Mama! Stupid Mama! Cake! I want ca-a-a-ke!"

"Just let her have another piece," Renate interjected.

"Absolutely not!" Emma snapped at her mother-in-law. How was she ever going to make any headway with Louisa if her in-laws kept torpedoing her like this?

"Cake! Cake! *Cay-ay-ake!*" Louisa was ratcheting herself up to genuine hysteria; her face was dark red, and Emma was about to lose her patience.

"We'd better go upstairs," she said. "Sorry. Something's been bothering her the past few days."

She dragged her shrieking and howling daughter into the house. The peaceful afternoon was over.

There were days that consisted of nothing but a string of ordinary banalities, too uneventful to remember at all. Most people let days like these simply flow by, measuring the passage of the years by birthdays, holidays, or some other memorable event—that was what their lives were reduced to in hindsight. For years, Pia had kept a diary, in which she jotted down key words for what had happened each day. Sometimes she amused herself by rereading what insignificant crap she'd recorded, but these brief notes gave her a satisfying feeling of living her life more consciously and not letting a single day go by unnoticed.

Pia braked and then moved to the right to allow a tractor to pass. It had turned into the underpass from the other side. She waved to Hans Georg, the farmer, whose land was up in Liederbach, where he pressed hay and straw for her each year, and he waved back.

On days like today, she often left her diary blank. What was she going to write? "Girl's body found. Stubborn youth interviewed. Autopsy from 12:00 to 4:00. Took 126 useless tips on the phone. Media inquiries fended off. Ate nothing all day. Kathrin Fachinger pacified. Mowed the lawn after work." Not likely.

Pia had reached Birkenhof. She touched the garage door opener and the green door slowly swung upward. This luxury was one of many improvements that she and Christoph had made to the house after the city of Frankfurt had finally dropped its threats to demolish it. The case had been dragging on for years. Pia could smell the tangy scent of freshly mown grass through the rolled-down car window, and she knew that Christoph had arrived home before her. The strip of lawn on the left side of the gravel driveway between the birches that gave the property its name had just been mowed.

It had been the right decision not to buy the Rabenhof estate in Ehlhalten. The mere renovation would have taken forever. Since the building commission had finally given the green light last summer for the remodeling of the house at Birkenhof, they preferred to spend their money on fixing up that somewhat outmoded residence.

Pia pulled up in front of the garage and got out of the car. After ten months of living in a construction site amid scaffolding, building rubble, torn-up floors, and cans of paint and mortar, everything had finally been finished a couple of weeks ago. The house had been extended upward by a story and had a new roof, new windows, new insulation, and, above all, a proper furnace, since the old electric heating had cost them a horrendous amount each month. Now a modern heat exchanger and solar cells on the roof provided for heating and hot water. These investments had, of course, strained their credit to the limit, but a real home had now been created from what was a stopgap living arrangement. Christoph's lovely furniture had at last been brought out of storage, where it had been relegated when he sold his house in Bad Soden.

After her stressful day, Pia longed for a shower, something to eat, and a glass of wine on the terrace. The horses were still in the paddock, the front door of the house stood wide open, but there was no sign of the dogs. She could hear the motor of the tractor in the distance. Christoph was probably busy in the back meadow, with the dogs keeping him company. Then the old red tractor appeared, and on the foldaway seat next to the driver, a small blond figure was jumping up and down, waving with both arms.

"Piiiiiiiaaaa! Pia!" a bright voice rang out over the clatter of the motor. Good God! With all the commotion that had kept her on pins and needles all day long, she'd totally forgotten that Lilly was arriving today. Pia felt her spirits sink. Bye-bye peace and quiet and relaxing with a glass of wine.

Christoph stopped underneath the walnut tree, and Lilly clambered down from the tractor as quickly as a monkey and came running over to Pia.

"Pia! Pia! I'm so excited!" she cried, her whole freckled face beaming. "I'm so happy to be back in Germany."

"I'm glad to see you, too." Pia gave her a wry grin and threw open her arms to give the child a big hug. "Welcome to Birkenhof, Lilly."

The little girl threw her arms around Pia's neck and pressed her face to her cheek. Her joy was so genuine that it touched Pia to the heart.

"It's soooooo beautiful here, it really is!" the girl gushed. "The dogs are so sweet and the horses, too, and everything here is so lovely and green, much nicer than at home."

"Well, I'm glad to hear it." Pia smiled. "How do you like your room?"

"It's awesome!" Lilly's eyes lit up and she held Pia's hand tight. "You know what, Pia? You two don't seem like strangers at all, since we're always Skyping. And that's so cool. I probably won't even get homesick."

Christoph had put away the tractor and came across the courtyard, followed by the four dogs, their tongues hanging out, reaching almost to the ground.

"Grandpa and I drove around in the tractor, and the dogs ran alongside the whole time," Lilly recounted excitedly. "I helped him put the horses in the paddock, and you know what? Grandpa made my absolutely favorite meal, just like I dreamed of: roulades!"

She opened her eyes wide and rubbed her tummy. Pia had to laugh.

"Hello, Grandpa," she said to Christoph with a grin. "I hope you left me a bite of Lilly's favorite food. I'm as hungry as a bear."

Louisa had finally fallen asleep. For two hours, she had sat in a corner of her room, staring into space with her thumb in her mouth. When Emma had tried to touch her, she'd moved away. At last the child had dozed off, exhausted, and Emma had put her to bed. This odd behavior had scared Emma more than the earlier uncontrollable outburst. She clamped the baby monitor under her arm and left the apartment. The talk with Corinna wasn't until seven o'clock, but Emma hoped to have a brief chat with her father-in-law alone. Maybe he could give her some advice about how to deal with Louisa.

The door to her in-laws' apartment on the floor below was ajar. Emma knocked and stepped inside. Because of the heat, the shutters were closed, bathing the room in a faint twilight and pleasant coolness. The smell of freshly brewed coffee hung in the air.

"Hello?" she called. "Josef? Renate?"

No answer. Maybe they were still outside on the terrace.

Emma stopped in front of the big mirror in the entry hall and was shocked at her appearance. She made a face. She certainly didn't look very attractive. Damp strands of hair had come loose from her bun and were straggling down the back of her neck; her face was flushed and as shiny as bacon rind. Her buttocks and thighs had always been problem areas, but she'd managed to hide them reasonably well. Now they'd grown to almost elephantine proportions, and her legs had swollen in the heat. Depressed, she ran both hands over her butt. It was actually no wonder that Florian hadn't shown any desire to sleep with her in months, the way she looked!

Suddenly, she heard voices and pricked up her ears. Emma wasn't the sort of woman to listen at closed doors, but the conversation was so loud that she couldn't help hearing several sentences. A door was flung open, and Emma now recognized Corinna's voice, sounding unusually incensed.

". . . have no intention of canceling the whole party!" she hissed.

Emma didn't catch her father-in-law's reply.

"I couldn't care less! I kept warning him that he'd better not push it too far," Corinna snapped back. "I've really had it up to here. As if I didn't have anything else to do."

"Wait a minute! Corinna!" Emma's father-in-law called.

Quick footsteps were approaching, and it was too late to retreat to the kitchen or some other room.

"Oh, hello, Emma." Corinna gave her an oddly appraising look, and Emma responded with a strained smile. She hoped her friend didn't think she'd been eavesdropping.

"Hello, Corinna. I . . . I was a bit early and . . . I . . . I heard voices and . . . then I thought maybe you'd already started."

"I'm glad you're here." Corinna no longer showed even a hint of her annoyance. Her usual cheerful expression had returned. "We can go over a few points regarding the guest list and the seating chart before the others get here. Let's go outside on the terrace."

Emma nodded, relieved. Although she would

have liked to know what had set Corinna off, she couldn't ask without admitting that she'd been listening, however inadvertently. Her gaze shifted to the open door of the study, and she saw her father-in-law sitting at his desk, his head buried in his hands.

Monday, June 14, 2010

The mood in the ready room of the Regional Criminal Unit in Hofheim was tense. All weekend, the phones had been ringing incessantly. Hundreds of tips from the public had come in, and dozens of people said they had seen the girl. Some of the tips had sounded promising at first, but they had not stood up to closer inspection.

There was no missing person's report, no hot trail in the Mermaid case, not even a lukewarm one. They were not a single step closer than they had been on Friday, and with each passing day, the chance of a swift resolution to the investigation grew slimmer.

Pia recapped the results of the autopsy.

"The girl was around fifteen or sixteen years old. Multiple injuries all over the body point to severe abuse over a long period. Most of these injuries had not been treated by a physician. These include broken bones in the upper arm, forearm, and collarbone that had not healed properly." The brutality concealed behind these precise words was unimaginable. "There were numerous scars on her buttocks, arms, and legs, as well as traces of sexual abuse and marks that looked like cigarette burns. In addition, the victim suffered from extreme vitamin D deficiency, significant skin pallor, and ricketslike changes in bone structure, which lead to the conclusion that the girl had not been exposed to sunlight for a very long time."

"How long had she been in the water?" asked a colleague who normally worked in another group, but all officers in the Regional Criminal Unit who were not working on another case had been assigned to assist the Special Commission.

"Time in the water was estimated at twelve to twenty-four hours," Pia went on. "Time of death cannot be precisely determined, but it was probably two days before the body was found."

Kai Ostermann wrote these key details on the whiteboard, which had previously been empty except for the photos of the corpse and the discovery site.

"Cause of death was drowning," Pia continued. "She had been injured so severely by blunt trauma—probably kicks and blows to the abdomen and chest—that she had little chance of surviving. During the autopsy, ruptures to the liver, spleen, and bladder were found, which had caused massive internal bleeding in the abdominal cavity.

If she hadn't drowned, she would have died soon afterward from internal bleeding."

It was deathly quiet except for the muted ringing of a telephone in the next room. The twenty-four men and five women gathered in front of Pia didn't move a muscle. There was no coughing, no throat clearing, no moving of chairs. Pia read in the faces of the team what she herself was feeling: sadness, bewilderment, and repulsion. It wasn't always easy to deal with the terrible results of crimes of passion, but what this girl had suffered, possibly over a period of years, burst all bounds of the imagination. Most of Pia's colleagues were fathers, and for them it was difficult, if not impossible, to maintain any sense of emotional distance in a case like this.

"But the biggest surprise so far is the fact that the girl didn't drown in the river, but in chlorinated water," Pia said, concluding her report. "We're still waiting for a conclusive analysis. Does anyone have any questions?"

No one spoke. No questions. She sat back down and turned over the floor to Kai Ostermann.

"The girl was dressed in cheap clothes from a department store, off-the-rack merchandise, manu-factured in the millions," said Kai. "Impossible to trace where, when, and from whom they were purchased. There are no dental records because she had apparently never been to a dentist. Except for the puzzling scraps of fabric found in her stomach, no conclusions can be drawn from the contents that would give us a lead. We're really left with nothing."

"And the media are putting on the pressure," Pia added. "They're making comparisons to the case from nine years ago. You know what I'm talking about."

Everyone nodded. Nine years before, a girl of presumably Middle Eastern origin had been found dead in the Main River off Wörthspitze Park, wrapped up in a bedspread with a leopard pattern, her feet weighted down with a cement umbrella stand. The Leopard Special Commission had made immense efforts to discover the identity of the girl; team members were sent to Afghanistan, Pakistan, and northern India, and flyers about the girl had been posted all over. But in spite of the high reward offered, only two hundred tips came in, none of which provided a viable lead.

"How do you intend to proceed?" Dr. Nicola Engel asked.

"I would like to have an isotope analysis done so that we can find out where the girl was from, and where she has lived in the past few years. That could bring us a good bit further," said Bodenstein, clearing his throat. "In addition, we need an analysis of the river currents in the Main so we can determine where the body was deposited in the water."

"I've already arranged for that," said Christian Kröger. "I marked it urgent."

"Good." Bodenstein nodded. "That's the first step, and in the meantime we'll keep in close contact with the press and the public. I'm still hoping that somebody will remember something and report it to us."

"Okay," the commissioner agreed. "What about the boy who was found near the body?"

"I was able to speak with him yesterday," said Pia. "Unfortunately, he can't remember a thing. A classic blackout. Not surprising, with blood alcohol of point thirty-three."

"And the other young people?"

"They say they didn't even see the dead girl." Pia snorted. "Two of them weren't particularly drunk, and I'm sure they're lying. Still, I don't think they saw anything that would be of any help to us. It was really just a chance encounter."

Her cell buzzed.

"Excuse me," she told the group, taking the call as she left the room. "Hello, Henning. What's up?"

"Remember the scraps of fabric from the girl's stomach?" replied her ex, as usual without bothering to say hello or to offer any other introductory remarks. "The material consists of cotton and an elastic fiber. Possibly she ate it out of hunger— that might explain why it was in her stomach. We were able to reconstruct some of the scraps. It

154

might be interesting for your team. I'll send you three photos as an e-mail attachment."

Since the team meeting in the conference room was already breaking up, Pia went up to her office and sat down at her desk. She opened the e-mail program and waited for the server to download the mail from Henning. She drummed her fingers impatiently on the edge of her keyboard. Naturally, Henning hadn't taken the trouble to compress the attachment, so it took her computer a couple of minutes to download three 5.3-megabyte photos. Finally she was able to open the first picture, and she stared in bafflement at the screen.

Kathrin Fachinger and Kai Ostermann came into her office.

"What have you got there?" Ostermann asked curiously, looking over her shoulder.

"Henning sent me photos of the fabric scraps from the girl's stomach," Pia said. "But I can't make out anything."

"Let me take a look."

She rolled her chair back a bit and turned over the keyboard and mouse to Kai. He shrank the photos. Then the three colleagues examined the pictures of the scraps.

"The biggest piece is seven by four centimeters," said Kai. "They're letters! The fabric is pink, with white print on it."

Kathrin and Pia bent over to look.

"That could be an *S*," Kathrin guessed. "An *I* and then *N* or *M*, and *D* or *P*."

"And on this picture I can decipher an *O*," said Kai.

"S-I-N(M)-D(P) and O," Pia jotted down on her blotter.

Kai read the e-mail that Henning had sent with the photos.

"The stomach acid had already begun to attack the fabric. There was no foreign DNA detectable. No teeth marks were found on the fabric; it had been cut or torn into small pieces."

"But how did it get into her stomach?" Kathrin wondered aloud.

"Henning thinks she could have eaten it because she was hungry," replied Pia.

"Good God." Kathrin grimaced. "Just imagine. How desperate would you have to be to eat cloth?"

"Maybe somebody forced her to do it," Kai suggested. "Considering everything this girl was subjected to, it seems plausible."

They heard raised voices in the corridor.

". . . haven't got time for such nonsense," they heard their boss say. A moment later, Bodenstein appeared in the doorway.

"We just got a tip that sounds promising," he announced. "Pia, we're leaving at once."

Frank Behnke appeared behind him.

"You're calling this nonsense? An official

investigation of the Office of Internal Affairs?" he asked smugly. "Get down off your high horse, Mr. *von* Bodenstein, or there might be unpleasant consequences."

Bodenstein turned to look down at Behnke, who was a head shorter.

"I refuse to be threatened." His voice was icy. "Once my current case is solved, I will put myself at the disposal of the Grand Inquisitor. Until then, however, I have no time for you."

Behnke's face first turned red, then pale. His gaze shifted and he looked past Bodenstein. Only now did he notice his former colleagues.

"So, Frank," said Kathrin with a derisive grin. "You're looking good in your new role."

Behnke had always had a problem with women, especially with female colleagues who were of equal or superior rank. But Kathrin Fachinger was his special object of hatred because she had reported him for assault, and that had brought about his suspension.

His lack of self-control remained his weak point.

"I'm going to get you, too!" In his fury, he allowed himself to utter a potentially incriminating remark, and before witnesses, too. "All of you! You're in for a real surprise."

"I've often wondered what sort of person you'd have to be to spy on your own colleagues," Kathrin retorted in disgust. "Now I know. You have to be a relentless conspirator who's eaten up by inferiority complexes. A pathetic loser, frankly speaking."

"You're going to eat your words," Behnke hissed as it dawned on him that he'd shown his weakness. He turned on his heel and marched off.

"You really could have kept that remark to yourself, Kathrin," Bodenstein chided his younger colleague. "I don't want any unnecessary trouble."

"Sorry, boss," said Kathrin without the slightest regret. "But that toxic midget isn't going to be making any trouble for me. I know too much about him . . . and about Erik Lessing."

This cryptic remark gave Bodenstein pause. He raised his eyebrows.

"We'll talk about this later," he said in an admonishing tone.

"Gladly." Kathrin stuck her hands in the pockets of her jeans and stuck her chin out belligerently. "I'd like nothing better."

"She was angry because she didn't get her way. That's completely normal at that age; all children act up every now and then." Florian got up and put his coffee cup in the sink. "Really, Emmi, I don't think you should make such a big deal of it. Today she was completely back to normal, wasn't she?"

Emma gave her husband a dubious look.

"Yeah. Sort of."

"It's just a phase." Florian took her in his arms. "This isn't easy for any of us."

Emma hugged him around the waist, leaning against him. Moments of closeness like this were rare, and she was afraid that they'd become even rarer once the baby arrived.

"We ought to go away for a few days. Just you and me and Louisa," he said, to her surprise.

"Do you have time?"

"I can probably take off four or five days." He let her go and put his hands on her shoulders. "I haven't taken any vacation time in ten months, and for the past few weeks I haven't been very nice to you."

"True." Emma smiled.

"It's because . . ." He fell silent, searching for the right words. "I know that you like it here, but for me it feels somehow . . . claustrophobic to be back living in my parents' house all of a sudden."

"But it's only temporary," said Emma, even though that wasn't what she thought.

"Is that how you see it?"

She saw the skepticism in his eyes.

"Okay, you're right. I do feel pretty good here," she admitted, "but I can see that it's strange for you. If you get another job abroad, the children and I could stay here at first, but if you stay in Germany, we should look for a place of our own."

Finally, the smile reached his eyes. He seemed relieved.

"Thanks for understanding," he said, turning serious again. "The next few weeks will determine what the future holds for me, and then we can make plans."

He disappeared into the bedroom to pack his suitcase, because he had to leave soon. He was going on a lecture tour in the new federal states of Germany. Even though he'd be away again for a few days, Emma's heart felt lighter than it had in weeks. She placed both hands on her belly.

Just five more weeks and the baby would be here.

Florian had finally admitted that he didn't feel comfortable staying here, after hardly talking to her in weeks except to discuss day-to-day matters.

Everything was going to be all right.

Half an hour later, they said good-bye, and she successfully resisted the urge to hold on to him and never let him go.

"I'll call you when I get there, okay?"

"Okay. Have a great trip."

"Thanks. Take care of yourself."

A little later, he clattered downstairs; the door opened with a faint squeak of the hinges, then closed with a gentle thud.

Emma heaved a sigh, then headed for the laundry room. Maybe she was just too sensitive at the moment. Corinna was probably right: For Florian, the whole situation was far from easy. And once the baby arrived . . .

Emma opened the door to the laundry room and turned the old-fashioned light switch until it clacked and the fluorescent lights on the ceiling came on. Through a high window, a little daylight fell into the room, which contained a washing machine and a dryer. Clotheslines were hung across the room, and it smelled of detergent and fabric softener. As she sorted the piles of laundry into dark, light, hot wash, and delicate fabrics, Emma's thoughts wandered to the beginnings of their relationship.

When she and Florian realized that they both came from the Taunus, they suddenly had a feeling of home out there so far away from Germany. In the middle of nowhere, they had eagerly spoken of mutual acquaintances, and that had given them a closeness that had actually never existed. They hadn't had much time to get to know each other, because only a short time later she found that she was pregnant, and they had married rather precipitously in the camp, because Florian had to go to India. For months, they had communicated only by e-mail, and she had fallen in love with the man she glimpsed behind the insightful comments, the incisive introspection, the words full of affection and flattering desire. He wrote about openness and trust and how happy he was he had found her. But when he was standing right in front of her in flesh and blood, everything changed. Their conversations seemed superficial, never reaching the quality, depth, and intimacy of all those e-mails. She was always conscious of the stale aftertaste of disappointment and inhibition, the subliminal fear of pressuring him and asking too much of him due to her need for closeness and tenderness. Embraces never lasted as long as she wanted them to, so she was unable to enjoy them because she was expecting at any moment that he would let her go and reinstate the distance between them. He never seemed capable of giving her the feeling of security that she yearned for with every fiber of her body.

Emma had believed and hoped that this would come with time, that he would open up to her and realize what she wanted from him, but that hadn't happened. And ever since they'd moved into his parents' house, she'd felt more than ever that she didn't really know her husband.

"Oh, damn it, you're thinking way too much," Emma chided herself. "That's just the way he is."

She grabbed his jeans, turned them inside out, and searched the pockets so as not to wash coins, tissues, or keys along with the clothes. Her fingers touched something smooth; she pulled it out to see what it was. In disbelief, Emma stared at the object from the pants pocket, her mind refusing to believe what it might mean. She went hot, then ice-cold; she felt a stab in her heart, and tears of pain welled up in her eyes.

In a split second, her whole world had collapsed

with a clap of thunder. In her palm lay a torn-open condom packet. It was empty.

Hello, Mrs. Herzmann. Unfortunately, your cell phone is turned off, so I'm trying to reach you on the landline. Please call me no matter how late it is. It's extremely important. Thank you.

Leonie Verges had never called Hanna before, but her voice had such an urgent undertone on the answering machine that Hanna grabbed the phone and dialed her therapist's number, although she was exhausted and wanted only to have a cold beer and go to bed. The woman must have had her hand on the receiver, because she picked up on the very first ring.

"Mrs. Herzmann, I'm sorry to bother you so late. . . ." Leonie Verges paused because she probably realized that she wasn't the one who had called. "Oh . . . I mean thanks for calling me back."

"Is everything all right?" Hanna asked. She'd gone to see the therapist to regain some sense of calm and composure. Her fourth divorce in twenty years had given Hanna more to deal with than she ever would have imagined, so after separating from Vinzenz, she'd decided on psychotherapy. No one could know about this, because if anyone got wind of it, the story would be all over the front page of the *Bild* tabloid in big headlines. Hanna had happened to find Leonie Verges on the

163

Web. Her practice was far enough away, but not too far, from where Hanna lived. In her photo, the psychotherapist looked quite pleasant, and her specialty seemed to fit Hanna's problems.

But after twelve therapy sessions, Hanna was no longer so sure that it was the right thing for her. Rummaging around in the depths of her past didn't really suit her attitude toward life. She was a person who lived in the here and now and was always looking forward. After the last session, she'd actually felt like telling the therapist that she didn't want to make another appointment, but at the last second she'd changed her mind.

"Yes . . . I mean, no," Leonie Verges blurted out. "I don't know quite how to tell you this. . . . It's a rather . . . well . . . delicate matter. Could you possibly come over to my office?"

"Now?" Hanna's gaze shifted to the clock on the display of the phone charger. "It's already ten o'clock. What's this about anyway?"

She had no desire to get back in her car and drive to Liederbach.

"It's . . . it . . . it's a very explosive story, which might be extremely interesting for you as a journalist." Leonie Verges lowered her voice. "I can't tell you any more on the phone."

Precisely as Ms. Verges had slyly intended, Hanna's journalistic instincts reacted to this wording like Pavlov's dog to the sound of a bell. She realized she was being manipulated, but her professional curiosity was stronger than her fatigue.

"Give me half an hour," she said, and hung up.

Meike didn't intend to go out again, so she magnanimously lent Hanna her Mini. Five minutes later, Hanna backed out of the driveway. She put the top down and stuck her iPhone in the console, then selected the music she wanted to hear. Hanna listened to music only when she was driving or jogging. The tiny car had a gigantic Harman/Kardon stereo system in it, and even with the top down, the sound was sensational.

At this time of night, the air was warm and pleasant, and the nearby forest exuded a beguiling fragrance. All her weariness was gone.

Freddie Mercury, the most gifted singer of all time, began to sing. His voice sent a pleasant shiver down Hanna's back, and she turned up the volume until the bass notes of "Love Kills" vibrated in her diaphragm.

The Mini jolted along the road, which in recent years had acquired a lot more potholes and patches, until it now looked like a patchwork quilt. At the main highway, Hanna turned left.

"Now I'm really curious to hear what this is all about," she said to herself, and stepped on the gas.

Kathrin Fachinger's remark kept whirling through Pia's mind all afternoon. How did she know secrets from Behnke's past? To her dismay, Bodenstein hadn't said another word on the topic, but Pia suspected that it had something to do with the case that her boss had mentioned when they drove over to the forensics lab. But how could Kathrin know anything about that?

When Pia returned home at half past nine, Lilly was already in bed. She took off her shoes and got a cold beer from the fridge. Christoph was sitting on the new deck, which they'd added to the rear of the house as part of the renovation. She'd called him earlier to tell him not to wait for her with dinner.

"Hi," she said, giving him a kiss.

"Hi." He took off his reading glasses and put down his book next to a stack of newspapers and computer printouts.

"What are you doing?" Pia sat down on the bench, removed the elastic from her hair, and stretched out her legs. The steady roar of the nearby autobahn was almost inaudible here, and the view of the neighboring yards and the apple orchards of the Elisabethenhof stretching all the way to the Taunus hills in the distance offered a much more attractive backdrop than the view from their old deck. Crickets chirped and there was a smell of damp earth and lavender.

"Actually, I was trying to write an article for a journal, which I've been putting off for days," said Christoph, yawning heartily. "I promised to have it done by tomorrow, but somehow I just can't seem to concentrate."

Pia assumed that Lilly had been keeping him on the go all day, but contrary to her fears, the visit seemed to be off to a good start. The little girl had spent the whole day at the zoo and had behaved well. Christoph had left her in the care of the zoo's two teachers.

"So? Are they still alive?" Pia asked with a teasing undertone.

"Yes, they seemed quite fond of her."

"They probably wouldn't dare say anything negative about the granddaughter of the zoo director," said Pia, who was still of the opinion that Lilly was a spoiled brat.

"Then you don't know those two very well," replied Christoph. "The zoo is not a dictatorship."

The candle in the lantern on the table flickered as three suicidal moths danced dangerously close to the flame. The four dogs dozed on the basalt plates, which radiated the heat of the day like a floor heater. They were now joined by the fat black tomcat and his gray tabby partner, both of whom had showed up in the spring and claimed Birkenhof as their home. The female cat was rather aloof, but the tom strutted with dignity through the tangle of stretched-out dog legs until he found a spot he liked. He curled up between the forepaws and belly of Simba, the husky half-breed. A rumble issued from the dog's throat, but it was an expression of contentment, not a threat.

Pia smiled at the sight of this unusual animal camaraderie and felt the stress and tension of the day melt away.

"Speaking of dictatorship . . ." She took a swig of beer. "Today we heard a real bombshell. A classic case of neighbor denouncing neighbor in the best Stasi style—and in Glashütten, of all places."

"Sounds exciting."

"Mostly shocking." Pia, who'd thought nothing could really surprise her anymore, was again stunned by the profound malice of human beings.

"An old married couple from Glashütten called us," she told Christoph. "They claimed their neighbors had kept the girl that we found in the river hidden in their house for the past six months and exploited her as a maid. The poor thing had to do the most degrading tasks, and she was never allowed outdoors in the daytime. She turned as pale as an albino. And she'd been missing for several days."

She shook her head at the thought of the girl's situation.

"The old couple told us genuine horror stories—mistreatment, nighttime sex parties, screams, orgies of beatings. On Tuesday night, they said, they saw the neighbor loading a body into the trunk of his car. Oliver asked why they hadn't reported it to the police earlier, and they said they were afraid because the man was so violent. So we went to the house and rang the bell, with four colleagues as backup. A woman opened the door, holding a child in her arms. God, was that embarrassing!" Pia rolled her eyes. "There stood my old classmate Moni, whom I'd just seen at the reunion. She was smiling innocently, happy to see me. I tell you, I wanted to sink into the ground, I was so ashamed."

Christoph listened with a mixture of amusement and disbelief.

"It turned out that the Swedish au pair, whom we met, is in perfect health, but she has a sun allergy, which is why she doesn't like to go outside. And there had been several parties in recent weeks, because first Moni's husband celebrated his birthday, and then she did."

"What about the body in the trunk?"

"A golf bag."

"You're kidding."

"Nope. At first, Moni was mad as hell, but then she had to laugh. They built their house there three years ago, and the house belonging to the neighbors' best friends was torn down when they moved to an old folks home. And since then, the old couple has had nothing better to do than make up stupid stories. They said that Moni's eldest son was a drug dealer, and that he got in trouble at school because of it, and at church they said that the daughter was a hooker."

"Sounds like grounds for filing a suit for defamation of character."

"That's also what my boss advised Moni." Pia still couldn't believe it. "Otherwise, that crazy old couple will never realize what sort of trouble they're stirring up with all their lies."

" 'The very meekest cannot be at peace if his ill neighbor will not let him rest,' " Christoph said, quoting Schiller's *William Tell*. He got up, stretched, and yawned again. "It's been a long day, and Lilly will probably be in top form at six in the morning. Grandpa has got to see about getting to bed."

Pia looked at him and giggled.

"Please don't make a habit of doing that," she admonished him.

"What do you mean?" asked Christoph, confused.

"Talking about yourself as 'Grandpa' in the third person. It's so unsexy. . . ."

Christoph grinned. His teeth gleamed white in the dark. He gathered up the magazines and papers, grabbed his empty glass and the bottle of red wine.

"How about if Mommy jumps into a quick shower and then comes to bed with Grandpa?" he teased.

"Only if I can get in under your rheumatism blanket," Pia countered.

"I'd like nothing better," he replied, blowing out

the candle. The dogs jumped up, yawned, shook themselves, and trotted inside, while the cats preferred to remain outside.

"Let's just check on Lilly," said Christoph.

They went to their former bedroom, which now served as a guest room. He put his arm around Pia's shoulder, and for a moment they watched the child sleeping peacefully.

"She isn't really that bad," said Christoph softly. "And she painted you a picture today."

He pointed to the desk.

"Oh, that's sweet." Pia was touched, but then she took a closer look. Her good feelings vanished. "Did you actually look at this picture?"

"No," said Christoph. "She did it in secret."

Pia held up the paper for him to see, and Christoph had to leave the room because he was laughing so hard.

"What a little monster," she muttered.

The picture showed a fat figure with a blond ponytail standing next to a horse and four dogs, and on the top it said *For Pia, my deer step gramma.*

The big gate to the estate was closed, and it took Hanna a moment to find the doorbell in the dim glow of a streetlight. Usually, the gate of the courtyard stood wide open, allowing any passerby to see the lovingly arranged garden inside. Leonie Verges undoubtedly had a green thumb. If she

171

weren't a psychotherapist, she could have easily gotten a job as a gardener. The courtyard was blooming in sumptuous abundance; statues stood among pots, tubs, and beds in which flowers and shrubs had been planted. In a protected spot right next to the wall, there was even an apricot tree.

Hanna heard footsteps behind the gate; then a bolt was shoved back and the little door on the left opened.

"Ah, it's you," said Leonie in a hushed voice.

Was she expecting some other visitor at this hour? She stuck her head out and looked past Hanna to peer up and down the empty street.

"Has something happened?" Hanna was slightly irritated by the odd behavior of her therapist, whom she knew only as a calm and levelheaded woman.

"Come in," Leonie replied, bolting the door behind her. Hanna's gaze fell on a huge automobile that stood in the middle of the cobblestone courtyard like a tank on guard, its monstrous presence desecrating the magic of this peaceful Garden of Eden. The light of the courtyard lamps glinted off the car's black lacquer, tinted windows, and chrome.

The clock in the nearby church tower struck eleven times, and all of a sudden Hanna had an uneasy feeling. She hesitated.

"What—" she began, but the therapist pushed her gently but firmly toward the front door.

Inside, the heat of the day still lingered; it was stifling, and Hanna began to sweat. Why was Leonie Verges sitting around inside with her company instead of outside in the courtyard?

She stopped in the hall and grabbed Hanna's wrist.

"I'm not sure whether it's a good idea to drag you into this matter." She was almost whispering. Her dark eyes seemed unnaturally large. "But the others are . . . well . . . of another opinion."

The *others?* Given the closed gate, the huge black car, and Ms. Verges's peculiar behavior, it almost sounded as if members of some sort of secret society might be waiting to admit her into their midst with some repulsive initiation rite.

"Leonie, wait." Hanna did not whisper. She didn't like secretiveness, and after this horrendous day she was in no mood for unpleasant surprises. "What's all this about?"

"We'll explain everything," the woman said evasively. "Then you can decide for yourself what you think of it."

She let go of Hanna's wrist and led the way down the hall to the kitchen. A low murmuring broke off when Hanna stepped through the doorway. At the kitchen table sat a man, who now turned to face her. The room seemed too low and too small for the mountain of muscles and suntanned, tattooed skin that now stood up from a kitchen chair. The man must have been at least six

six, and the sight of him instantly set off alarm bells in Hanna's brain. A dark, sharply trimmed beard, his long hair in a braid, and alert dark eyes that scanned her from head to toe in a second. The man was wearing a white T-shirt, jeans, and cowboy boots, but the dark blue tattoo on his neck was clearly visible. Hanna swallowed hard. That kind of tattoo was worn only by members of the Frankfurt Road Kings, a notorious motorcycle gang. What the hell was one of them doing in her therapist's kitchen?

"Good evening," said the giant in an oddly hoarse voice, holding out his hand. On the ring finger of his right hand he wore a heavy silver ring adorned with a skull. "I'm Bernd."

"Hanna," she replied, shaking his hand.

Only then did she notice the second man. A glance from disturbingly glacier blue eyes shot through her whole body without warning like an electric shock, making her knees tremble for a moment. She hardly noticed the rest of his face. He was a little taller than she was, but next to the giant, he looked like a dwarf. At that instant, Hanna was only too aware of how she looked— no makeup, her sweaty hair tied in a sloppy knot, T-shirt, jeans, running shoes. She hardly ever left the house looking like this, not even to go jogging.

"What would you like to drink?" Leonie Verges asked. "Water, diet Coke, nonalcoholic beer?"

"Water, thanks," she said, feeling her initial

174

annoyance changing to curiosity that went beyond purely professional interest in a good story. What was the purpose of this strange team? Why were these two men sitting in Leonie Verges's kitchen at eleven o'clock at night? Why were they—without knowing her—convinced that she should be included in whatever they were planning? She accepted the glass of water and sat down on the corner bench at the small square table with the checked oilcloth. Mr. Blue Eyes took a seat to her left, and Leonie and the giant sat on the kitchen chairs.

"Do you mind if I smoke?" asked the giant, unexpectedly polite.

"Go ahead."

He pulled out a pack and snicked his Zippo. A brief smile played across his stony face, as if noticing the craving in Hanna's eyes.

"Please help yourself." He shoved the pack over to her. She took a cigarette, thanked him with a nod, and saw that her fingers were trembling. She hadn't had a smoke in four weeks, and the first drag had the effect of marijuana on her central nervous system. A second and third drag, and the vibration inside her vanished. She felt the gaze of Mr. Blue Eyes like a physical jolt; her skin grew hot and her pulse quickened. She realized that he hadn't introduced himself. Or had she missed it? Asking him now seemed embarrassing.

For a moment, there was a tense silence as they

assessed each other. Finally, Leonie spoke. She was sitting calmly on her chair, almost like in a therapy session, but beneath her laid-back exterior Hanna noticed a nervousness, and lines had appeared around her eyes and mouth—lines that were usually barely noticeable.

"I've called you here tonight for reasons that are not entirely altruistic," she said. "We will tell you what it's about, and then you can decide for yourself whether you think it might be an interesting story for your show or not. If you aren't interested, simply forget this conversation. But before we tell you the details"—she paused briefly—"you ought to know that it's a highly explosive matter, which could be extremely unpleasant and dangerous for a lot of people."

This sounded like trouble, and right now Hanna needed more of that like a zit on her nose.

"Why did you decide to approach me?" she asked. She reached for the carafe of ice water on the table at the same time as Mr. Blue Eyes. Their hands touched, and she snatched hers back as if she'd been burned.

"Pardon me," she muttered in embarrassment.

He just smiled briefly, then poured water for her and then himself.

"Because you have no qualms about taking on hot-button topics," replied the giant instead of Leonie. "We're familiar with your show."

"I don't normally talk about my patients,"

Leonie put in. "My oath of confidentiality forbids it, of course, but in this special case I was released from that constraint, and I hope you will understand why."

Hanna's curiosity was definitely piqued, but she was still hesitant. This was not the way she usually worked. She and her team found topics that interested her, in the newspapers—on the Web, on the street. But to be honest, lately this type of research had lost its appeal. She'd interviewed Hartz IV families, single-trick cheats, teenage mothers, criminal migrant children, victims of quacks, and the like on her show dozens of times, and nobody was bowled over by them anymore. It was high time for a story that would draw really big ratings.

"What's this about?" she asked, taking her voice recorder out of her pocket. "If you're familiar with my broadcast, then you also know what we focus on. Human-interest stories with a fateful twist are what we do."

She placed the recorder on the table.

"Is it all right if I record this conversation?"

"No," said the man with the blue eyes, whose name she didn't know. "No recording. Just listen carefully. If you don't want to do it, this meeting never happened."

Hanna looked at him. Her heart began to pound. She couldn't stare him down for long. In his eyes she saw a mixture of strength and vulnerability that fascinated and disturbed her at the same time. And this time, she saw more than just his eyes. A sharply chiseled, lean face with a high forehead. Straight nose, prominent chin, a wide, sensitive mouth, his hair slightly graying—a remarkably attractive man. How old could he be? Forty-five or forty-six? What did he have to do with the giant biker guy? Why was he sitting here in Leonie Verges's kitchen? What secret was weighing on his soul?

She lowered her eyes. In that very second, she'd made up her mind. She was interested by whatever the story might be, but something else was the deciding factor. This good-looking stranger with the piercing blue eyes had completely and unexpectedly touched something deep inside her, something she hadn't thought even existed.

"Tell me what it's about," Hanna said. "I'm not afraid of hot-button topics. And I never say no to a good story."

Thursday, June 24, 2010

The team meetings at K-11 took place in the usual room on the second floor; the ready room behind the watch room had been cleared out a few days before and returned to its original purpose.

Two weeks after the discovery of the girl's body in the river, they were no closer to solving the case, despite a great deal of effort. The officers in the Mermaid Special Commission had followed up on countless tips and interviewed dozens of people, but nothing had panned out. No one knew the dead girl; no one missed her. An isotopic analysis had shown that the girl had grown up in the vicinity of Orsha, in Belarus, but had spent the last years of her short life in the Rhine-Main area. Even the male DNA that had been secured from under her fingernails and had given them a brief glimmer of hope had brought them no further, because it could not be found in any database.

All ships that had passed along the Main River within the relevant period had been located and inspected, although the police had been forced to restrict themselves to the vessels that had radar or had been registered at the locks. They had even checked the restaurant ships that were anchored in Frankfurt, as well as the tour boats. But there was nothing they could do about all the private sport boats that zipped about on the Main. The options for putting a body directly into the river from a bridge or even from the riverbank were so numerous that it would have required a colossal expenditure of personnel and technical efforts, with little hope of measurable results.

The media, craving results and some progress in the case, accused the police of acting blindly and wasting the taxpayers' money.

"Unfortunately, even the cooperation with our

colleagues in Minsk has not brought us any further," Oliver von Bodenstein said as he took stock, feeling frustrated. "There is no missing person's report in Belarus that matches the description of the deceased. A flyer campaign in the region of Orsha has also produced no results so far."

Neither the girl's clothes nor the fabric remnants from her stomach had produced any concrete leads in the investigation.

Bodenstein gazed at the silent team. The tension of being constantly in the public eye, along with two weeks of constant work with no weekends off, had taken their toll. He saw exhaustion and resignation in the faces of his colleagues, and he had the greatest sympathy for their state of mind, because he felt exactly the same way. He had seldom experienced a case in which there was so little to go on.

"I propose that you all go home and get some rest," he said. "Stay in touch, though, in case something does come up."

There was a knock on the door, and Dr. Nicola Engel came in. At the same moment, Ostermann's laptop emitted a discreet trill.

"We received permission," announced the commissioner. "Bodenstein, next week you'll be going to Munich. Our Mermaid case will be featured on *Germany's Most Wanted*. In any event, it's worth a try."

Bodenstein nodded. He had already discussed it with Pia. Unfortunately, summer vacation started tomorrow in the state of Hessen, and many people would be gone, but the TV show was one last chance for the police to get some helpful information from the public.

"Hey, people," said Kai Ostermann. "I just got an e-mail from the lab in Wiesbaden. They've finally analyzed the water from the girl's lungs."

The fact that the girl had drowned in chlorinated water was one of the biggest riddles in this case. Bodenstein wasn't the sort to rely heavily on lab results, but he'd insisted on an analysis of the water. He harbored the almost despairing hope for some kind of helpful lead.

"And?" he asked impatiently. "What did they find?"

Ostermann scanned the report.

"Sodium hypochlorite, sodium hydroxide," he read aloud. "Those are the chemical components of chlorine tablets for swimming pools and Jacuzzis. Traces of aluminum sulfate were also found. Unfortunately, nothing that would give us a genuine lead. So I'm afraid we're still looking for the needle in the haystack."

"She didn't drown in a public swimming pool. Somebody would have noticed," said Kathrin Fachinger. "How about if we start an appeal in the press and ask people to call in if they have a pool on their property?"

"That's crazy," Pia countered. "In this region, there must be thousands of houses with swimming pools, and even more with Jacuzzis."

"We're not going to get a call from whoever owns the pool where the girl drowned," said Kai.

"If we try to check out all the private swimming pools, we'll have enough work to keep us busy for years," added Cem Altunay, who had postponed his trip home to Turkey to see his wife and kids. "Do you want to make every pool owner submit to a water analysis?"

"Very funny," Kathrin snapped in a huff. "I just wanted to point out that—"

"All right," Bodenstein said, interrupting his young colleague. "This may not be a hot lead at the moment, but it could be a valuable piece of the puzzle once we have a specific suspect."

"Are we just about done, then?" Pia glanced at her watch. "I've got a half day of vacation today."

"Yes, that's it for now," said Bodenstein with a nod. "But please remain available just in case."

Everyone nodded and the meeting broke up. Kai grabbed the investigation folder, tucked the laptop under his arm, and followed Cem and Kathrin down the hall.

"We have to get going, too," said Dr. Engel.

Bodenstein turned around.

"Where to?" he asked, surprised.

"In my calendar, it says that today at two P.M. you've got the interview at State Criminal Police headquarters," she replied. "Have you forgotten?"

"Damn it, yes." Bodenstein shook his head. At six, he and Cosima had a meeting with the notary and the buyers of the house. They'd already moved the appointment to early evening because of the investigation. He hoped the stupid interview wouldn't take any longer than an hour.

After the confrontation with Bodenstein ten days ago, Frank Behnke had shut down his provisional inquisition court in one of the neighboring offices and retreated empty-handed to the State Criminal Police. But two days later, an official summons had fluttered onto Bodenstein's desk: *Hearing to obtain testimony regarding the closing of the police investigation involving bodily injury to Mr. Friedhelm Döring on 7 September 2005, due to the suspicion that certain criminal offenses were not properly investigated and obstruction of justice on official duties occurred.*

"Why do you want to go with me?" Bodenstein asked his boss as she followed him down the hall. "It has to be a total waste of your time."

"I refuse to permit such an accusation to be made against one of my unit leaders," she said. "Behnke is on a personal vendetta, and I intend to remind him of something, if necessary."

• • •

"Hello there, Hanna." Wolfgang got up from his desk and came over to her with a smile. "How lovely to see you."

"Hello, Wolfgang." She allowed him to kiss her on both cheeks. "Thank you for agreeing to see me on such short notice."

"Well, you've got me really curious," he said, offering her a seat at the conference table. "Would you like something to drink?"

"No thanks." Hanna hung her bag over the back of her chair and rubbed her palms on her bare upper arms. "Well, maybe a mulled wine."

In the big office, a dim twilight prevailed, and the air conditioning produced a chill that made her shiver.

"It must be a shock for you to go outside. It's ninety-five degrees out there."

"By the time I leave the office, it's eleven at night. Then it's no longer so hot." Wolfgang smiled and sat down across from her. "I haven't heard from you in a long time."

There was a gentle reproach in his voice, and Hanna felt instantly guilty.

"I know I haven't been much of a friend lately, but there's a reason for it." She lowered her voice. "By chance, I've run into a crazy story. A real doozy. But it's so incredible that first I had to check out some of the details with a couple of people. I swear to you, it could be really big. And

I'd prefer to lead off with this topic in the first show after the summer hiatus; then we could hype it big-time in the weeks leading up to it. Half of Germany will be sitting in front of the tube at nine-thirty sharp."

"You're all aglow with enthusiasm," Wolfgang said. He cocked his head and smiled. "Is there more behind this than what you're telling me?"

"Nonsense!" Hanna uttered a brief laugh, which even to her sounded a bit too phony. Wolfgang knew her well; she kept forgetting that. "But I've never had my hooks into such a gigantic story. And I've got an absolute exclusive."

She had masterfully resolved the crisis that Norman had instigated with his thoughtless blabbing. Her public display of remorse had turned around what had threatened to destroy her image. The TV station and the shareholders had been satisfied; they'd found a capable new producer and decided to move on, putting aside what had happened. After three days, her car had emerged like new from the paint shop, and she wasn't surprised when Meike informed her that for the rest of her vacation she'd be moving to Sachsenhausen to stay at the apartment of a girlfriend who was spending the summer in Chile or China. Everything that had seemed so incredibly important to her earlier was now of no consequence. Since that evening in her therapist's kitchen, something had changed, and she could hardly grasp what it was.

"The topic is absolutely sensational. The person involved wants to remain anonymous, of course, but that shouldn't be a problem." She pulled a couple of sheets of paper out of her bag and held them out to Wolfgang. As he reached to take them, she pulled her hand back. "It's top secret, Wolfgang. I trust that you won't mention this to a soul."

"Of course not," he assured her, acting a bit offended. "I've never betrayed anything you've told me in confidence."

She handed him the four single-spaced pages, and he began to read.

She had a hard time curbing her impatience.

Read faster, she thought. Say something, will you?

But he remained silent, his face expressionless. The only visible sign of emotion was a furrow at the bridge of his nose that got deeper the longer he read.

Hanna had to stop herself from slamming the palm of her hand on the table.

Finally, he looked up.

"Well?" she asked expectantly. "Didn't I tell you? This story is pure dynamite! The human tragedy behind it is of apocalyptic proportions! And there are no suspicious circumstances involved; I've spoken personally with most of those affected. They gave me names, places, dates, facts. As you can imagine, at first I could hardly believe it. With a big PR campaign, this story is going to produce ratings like we haven't seen in years."

Wolfgang still said nothing. Eloquence wasn't his strong point. Sometimes it took him minutes to formulate a request into awkward wording, and she often felt stupid because she talked so fast and said so much. She would interrupt him and race ten thoughts ahead before he'd answered the original question.

"Hanna, I don't want to rain on your parade, but if you ask me, the topic is actually rather . . . banal. It's been covered in the press ad nauseam," he finally said after an enervating pause. "Do you really believe that anyone would still be interested?"

Her sense of eager anticipation collapsed like a house of cards when she saw the skepticism in his eyes. She was hugely disappointed, but she was also angry—at him, but, above all, at herself. Once more she'd been overhasty, too enthusiastic.

"Yes, I do. I also think that this particular topic can't be discussed often enough in the public arena." She reached out her hand and tried to make her voice sound calm. "I'm sorry that I've wasted your valuable time."

He hesitated, made no move to hand her the

pages; instead, he placed them on the desktop and arranged them into a neat stack.

"Ultimately, it's your decision what topics you want to deal with on your show." Wolfgang smiled. "But you wanted my advice, so I'm giving it to you." He turned serious. "Don't do it."

"Excuse me?" She thought she hadn't heard him correctly. What did he have in mind?

He lowered his eyes, but she had noticed the emphatic way he had voiced his objection. Furrows of tension appeared between his eyebrows. What was prompting such a strong reaction?

"As your friend, I advise you not to run this story," he said in a lowered voice. "It's an explosive issue. You have no idea what you're getting into. I have a bad feeling about it. If what it says here is true, then people are involved who will not welcome publicity of this kind."

"Are you worried about the station's reputation?" Hanna asked. "Are you afraid of lawsuits? Or what is it?"

"No," he replied. "I'm worried about you. You're not judging the situation correctly."

"We've been dealing with hot potatoes for years," Hanna countered. "It's the hallmark of my show."

They gazed at each other for a long time in silence, until he gave up with a sigh.

"You're going to do what you want to do; I know that." He reached out his hand and put it on top of hers. "I'm only asking you to think it through one more time."

She really liked Wolfgang. He was her oldest and dearest friend. She knew his strengths, but she also knew his weaknesses. Wolfgang was a number guy; he was rational, dependable, and cautious. But it was precisely these good qualities that kept getting in his way, because on the flip side he was also an indecisive vacillator, a cowardly bean counter who simply lacked the courage to take a risk.

"Okay." Hanna nodded and gave him a forced smile. "I'll do that. Thanks for your advice."

The Main-Taunus shopping center was swarming with shoppers. It took Pia a long time to find a spot in the parking garage.

"So what are we shopping for?" Lilly asked, gamboling along beside her.

"I have to pick up my shoes at the shoe repair," said Pia. "But first you and I have to find something to wear tonight."

"What's happening tonight?"

"I told you already." Pia took Lilly's hand so she wouldn't lose her in the crowd. "Miriam's grandmother is having a party, and we're going to it."

"Is Grandpa coming, too?"

"No, he's in Düsseldorf today."

"Oh, that's a shame."

"You mean you don't like my company?" said Pia with a grin.

"Oh, of course I do," Lilly declared. "But I like it best when we're all together."

Pia stroked the girl's hair. Sometimes Lilly could drive her nuts with her constant chatter, but her disarming honesty was always so touching. She was actually going to miss the girl when she flew back to Australia in two weeks.

"Could we buy a DVD, too?" Lilly begged as they walked by the Media Mart. Pia cast a quick glance in the shop window at the crush of people and shook her head.

"First we have to get the important stuff done."

All week long, she'd told herself to drive to the mall and look for a summer dress, but when she got home late in the evening, she never felt like dealing with the crowds. She'd found a nice dress on the Web, but of course it wouldn't be available in her size until the first days of fall. By then, she'd no longer need a summer dress.

"Oh, look, ice cream!" Lilly pointed excitedly at the ice-cream stand and tugged on Pia's hand. "I'd really like to have an ice-cream cone. It's so hot."

"They won't let us into the department stores with ice cream." Pia ushered her past. "Later."

Before they reached the shop where Pia hoped

to find a dress, Lilly had spied five things that she absolutely had to have.

Pia was getting fed up.

"I'm not going to take you shopping ever again if you keep trying to make detours," she said firmly. "First we're going to buy the clothes, and then we'll look at other things."

"You're no fun," said Lilly with a pout.

"Neither are you," said Pia, unmoved.

Whether that was pedagogically correct or not, she had no idea, but it worked. The little girl shut up.

In the first store, Pia found nothing she liked. In the second, she narrowed it down to two dresses, but neither of them fit right, and they looked as baggy as overalls on her. This didn't help Pia's mood. She hated trying on clothes in the cramped changing rooms in this heat, and it didn't help to see her sweaty reflection in the mercilessly harsh fluorescent light. Maybe somebody should give the department store owners a tip: Dim lights in the changing rooms would surely increase sales. In the third store, she finally found something suitable. She told Lilly to wait outside, but as soon as she was down to slip and bra and putting on the dress, Lilly stuck her head in.

"Is it going to take long? I have to go to the bathroom," she said.

"I'm almost done. You're going to have to hold it awhile."

"How long?"

"Five minutes."

"But I can't hold it that long," the girl whined.

Pia didn't answer. Sweat was running down her face and back, and she couldn't zip up the back of the dress.

"You're too fat," said Lilly.

That did it.

"Get out!" Pia yelled. "Wait outside like I told you. I'll be right there."

The little witch stuck out her tongue and then pulled open the curtain all the way to make her even madder. Two narrow-hipped young gazelles in size zero tops stared at Pia and giggled idiotically.

In her mind, Pia cursed Miriam's grandmother for having a stupid charity party, and she cursed herself for agreeing to drive to Frankfurt. The sight of the dress calmed her down a bit. It fit well and she looked good. It wasn't even that expensive.

When she came out of the dressing room, Lilly was gone. Pia figured she was probably hiding somewhere among the clothes racks, just to annoy her. Pia went to the checkout counter and got in the line that looked the shortest. A big mistake, as it turned out, because the woman in front of her was buying fourteen items and her credit card didn't work. Pia nervously kept a lookout for Lilly. Finally, she was able to pay. She put the shopping bag under her arm and headed off to find the girl.

The little rascal wasn't in the women's department or the men's. She asked a salesclerk where the rest rooms were, which turned out to be in the basement, and took the escalator down. But Lilly wasn't there, either. Gradually, Pia's anger turned to concern. She wasn't used to being responsible for a child. After she'd searched the whole store in vain and asked every salesclerk if they'd seen a little girl with blond pigtails, she went out into the mall. Throngs of people were wandering through the place. How could she possibly find Lilly in this crowd? She started to feel upset. She thought about cases in which children had disappeared without a trace in shopping centers, because they walked off with some stranger who promised them an ice cream or a toy.

Now frantic, she hurried into the costume jewelry store where Lilly had seen a pink pearl necklace that she just had to have. No trace of her. Nobody seemed to have seen her. Not even at the ice-cream stand, or the DVD section of the Media Mart on the second floor. In a panic, Pia ran back to the fountain. She rudely bumped into strangers, who hurled curses after her. At first, she'd imagined that she would tell Lilly off, but after half an hour she was only praying silently to find the girl unharmed.

There was a line waiting at the information booth.

"Please, could I cut in?" she gasped. "I'm looking for a lost child."

Most people were understanding and let her go ahead of them, until she got to two grandmothers who stubbornly insisted that their business was more important than a lost child. As cool as ice, one of them bought three gift certificates, and the other asked where some store was and didn't understand what the woman in the booth was trying to explain. Finally, it was Pia's turn.

"Could you please help me find my—" She stopped. How exactly should she describe her relationship to Lilly? Could you please make an announcement? I'm trying to find the granddaughter of my live-in boyfriend? How crazy did that sound?

"Yes?" The chubby, bored slowpoke at the information desk gave her a blank look. Without embarrassment, she was scratching at her cleavage with multicolored lacquered nails that looked like claws.

"I've . . ." Pia began a second time, then decided on the uncomplicated version.

"My daughter is lost," she blurted out. "Could you please page her for me?"

"What's her name?" asked the fat lady lethargically. "Where should she meet you?"

"Her name is Lilly. Lilly Sander."

"What?"

Man, she was stupid!

Pia spelled it out impatiently. "L-I-L-L-Y. Tell her to meet me at the fountain. Or no, wait—the ice-cream shop is better. She doesn't know her way around here."

Finally, the cow got it and made a halfway intelligible announcement, but Pia doubted that Lilly would realize that it was for her.

"Thank you," she said, and headed for the ice-cream stand to keep an eye out for Lilly. What else could she do? Her knees were shaky, her stomach was cramping, and she realized that what she was feeling was fear. Pia forced herself not to think about all the things that could happen to a pretty, blond seven-year-old girl.

For the first time in her life, she understood what really went on in the minds of parents with missing kids. This kind of helplessness and uncertainty was pure hell. So how horrible must it be to endure these feelings for weeks, months, or even years? She also grasped how little consolation it must be for parents when the police assured them they would do everything humanly possible to find the child.

Pia thought she saw Lilly in every blond girl who passed by. Her heart leapt each time, followed by disappointment that brought tears of despair to her eyes. People strolled past her, and at last Pia could no longer stand the waiting and inaction. She took off at a brisk pace. She had to search on her own; otherwise, she would go crazy. She forgot all the hollow advice she had given to parents of missing kids about the need to stay calm. Loaded down with her shoulder bag and department store bag, she hurried into the store where she'd last been with Lilly. She went back to the ice-cream stand, to the costume jewelry shop, to the crafts store where Lilly had seen some stuffed animal she wanted. Finally, she went back to the Media Mart. She asked a zillion people if they'd seen Lilly, but nobody had.

Finally, she decided to take her shopping bag to the car so that she could look for Lilly without feeling encumbered. On the way to the parking garage, she considered calling her colleagues on the beat. Officers in uniform who asked people questions were usually taken more seriously than a sweaty, panicky woman.

But what was she going to tell Christoph? She couldn't return home without finding his granddaughter! Pia fumbled to get the car keys out of her bag. Then she looked up and couldn't believe her eyes. Arms around her knees, Lilly was huddled on the ground next to the rear tire of the car.

"Pia!" she yelled, jumping to her feet. "Where have you been?"

With a deafening crash, the whole north face of the Eiger slid from Pia's heart. Her knees

196

suddenly turned soft as butter, and she began to sob with relief. She dropped her bags and car keys and pulled the girl into her arms.

"Good Lord, Lilly! You really gave me a scare," she whispered. "I've been looking all over the mall for you."

"I had to go to the bathroom so bad." Lilly flung her little arms around Pia's neck and rubbed her cheek against Pia's. "And then I couldn't find you. I . . . I thought you . . . you were mad at me and drove off without me. . . ."

The little girl was sobbing, too.

"Oh, Lilly dear, I'd never do that." Pia stroked her hair and rocked her in her arms. She never wanted to let her go. "What do you say we go have an ice-cream cone and then buy you another dress, hmm?"

"Oh yeah." Beneath her tears, there was a glimmer of a smile. "Ice cream sounds great."

"Well, let's go, then." Pia stood up. Lilly clutched her hand tightly.

"I'll never let you go again," Pia promised.

After a quarter of an hour, the matter under discussion, which was Behnke's attempt to discredit his former boss, had been roundly dismissed. Based on the available records and reports, Bodenstein was able to prove indisputably that he had investigated the suspicious circumstances in the case of the aggravated assault against

Friedhelm Döring in 2005, before he'd had to terminate the investigation due to lack of evidence.

The three-person commission from Internal Affairs was satisfied, and Bodenstein and Dr. Nicola Engel were found blameless of any wrongdoing. Behnke had sat in silence, red in the face and seething like a pressure cooker. Bodenstein wouldn't have been surprised to hear a shrill whistle come out of his ears.

While Nicola Engel was still speaking with the director of the presiding office to which the Department of Internal Affairs belonged, Bodenstein waited outside in the hall and spent the time checking his iPhone. No important developments. He was glad that the whole matter had been dispatched so swiftly, because he didn't want to arrive late at the appointment with the notary and the buyer. Last week, he'd reached an agreement with the bankrupt owner of half of the duplex in Ruppertshain, and the day before yesterday he'd gotten the green light from the savings bank for the financing. Inka had contacted the contractor firms at once, and they could resume work in mid-July. The prospect of being able to live within his own four walls in less than six months from now, and to stop renting lodgings at his parents' estate, had given Bodenstein a real burst of energy. After two long, dismal years with no sense of purpose, he now felt that he was finally standing at the rudder and able to determine the direction his life would take. Some men suffered a midlife crisis after fifty, but it had struck him a year earlier. While he waited for the commissioner, he thought about furniture that he wanted to buy, and about the design of the garden. He wondered whether it was going to be painful to clear out the house that he and Cosima had built and lived in for twenty-five years.

"Bodenstein!"

He turned around. Frank Behnke was coming toward him. Barely suppressed anger flashed in his eyes, and for a moment Bodenstein had the crazy idea that Behnke was going to pull out his service weapon and gun him down in the corridor of State Criminal Police headquarters just to be rid of his own pent-up frustration.

"I don't know what kind of strings you pulled," he snarled. "But I'm going to find out. You're covering up something big-time."

Bodenstein scrutinized the man who had once been a close colleague. He felt neither malicious glee nor animosity toward Behnke, who had failed in his efforts to prove Bodenstein guilty of dereliction of duty. He felt sorry for Behnke. Something had gone fundamentally wrong in his life. His bitterness was eating him up, and now his inferiority complex and vengefulness had taken him over completely. For a long time, Bodenstein had protected his younger colleague, showing him more leniency than was fair to the rest of his team. Too long. Behnke hadn't listened to any of his admonitions and in the end had pushed things so far that Bodenstein had been forced to distance himself from the man in order not to be pulled into the maelstrom of events.

"Frank, let's put this behind us for good," Bodenstein said in a conciliatory tone of voice. "For my part, I'll forget the whole thing here and now, and I won't hold it against you."

"Oh, how gracious of you!" Behnke gave a spiteful laugh. "I don't give a shit whether you're going to hold anything against me or not. You dropped me like a hot potato when Kirchhoff joined the team. I'm not going to forget that. Ever. From that day on, I was relegated to second best. And I know for a fact that Kirchhoff and Fachinger have always complained about me. Those two bitches made me look ridiculous. And you let them do it."

Bodenstein frowned in disbelief.

"Okay, let's back up here for a moment," he replied. "I won't permit you to speak of our female colleagues in that tone. It's all completely untrue—"

"The hell it is!" Behnke shouted, cutting him off, and Bodenstein realized what enormous and pathological proportions Behnke's jealousy had assumed. "You've always been henpecked. Your wife made you a cuckold. And . . ." He paused for effect, crossing his arms and smirking with spite. "And I happen to know for a fact that you fucked Engel!"

"That's right," said a voice behind him. Nicola Engel gave him an icy smile, looking very self-composed. "And not only once, dear colleague. We were engaged at one point. About thirty years ago."

Bodenstein watched Behnke wrestling desperately with his self-control as what he viewed as a triumph again dissipated like smoke before his eyes.

Nicola Engel stepped closer, and he retreated, a reflexive gesture of subordination that infuriated him even more.

"I hope you're aware that you were given your last chance in this job, and you remain on the force solely thanks to my intervention," she said in a low voice that was nevertheless razor-sharp. "In the future, you should not allow personal motives to guide your work, or else you'll wind up at the Police Academy cleaning blackboards. I've already spoken with your superior and assured him that Bodenstein and I will not waste another word on this whole unpleasant matter. I've saved your ass for the third or fourth time now, Behnke. And now we're finally quits. I hope we understand each other."

Frank Behnke gulped with clenched teeth and nodded reluctantly. The hostility in his blue eyes was murderous. Without a word, he turned and left.

"There's going to be more trouble with him," Nicola Engel prophesied glumly. "He's a ticking time bomb."

"I shouldn't have protected him for so long," said Bodenstein. "That was a mistake. He should have been sent for therapy."

Nicola Engel raised her eyebrows and shook her head.

"No. It was too bad he survived that suicide attempt."

The coldness with which she made this statement shocked Bodenstein. And yet he again realized why she'd climbed the career ladder so fast, while he hadn't. She knew no scruples. Doubtless, Dr. Nicola Engel had the stuff to reach the very top.

Ever since Florian had moved out, Emma had felt vulnerable and unsure. The proof of his unfaithfulness and his persistent silence in the face of her reproaches and questions had made her aware that deep inside she'd never been really sure about him. She couldn't rely on him, and that depressed her the most, more even than the fact that he had betrayed her.

The center of Königstein was packed, and Emma had to drive all the way up to the Luxemburg Castle to find a parking place. She might not have taken the whole situation so seriously if she hadn't been so hugely pregnant. But things might not have gone so far if she hadn't looked like a walrus. She fought back the tears as she crossed the playground and headed for the pedestrian street through the spa park. She hoped she wouldn't run into anyone she knew. She was in no mood to chat or indulge in superficial small talk. People expected pregnant women to be blissfully anticipating the baby and not walking around weeping.

At the bookshop, Emma picked up three books she had ordered, then went over to Café Kreiner next door and sat down at the last free table under the awning. She was bathed in sweat, and her legs felt like they were going to burst at any moment. Even so, she ordered a dish of chocolate ice cream with extra whipped cream. A few extra pounds no longer mattered.

But what was going to happen? In a little more than two weeks, the baby was due, and then she'd be living with two young children with her in-laws, without a real home, without a husband, without money. The uncertainty had been robbing her of sleep lately, hanging over her like an ominous shadow. And what was worse, Florian was going to pick up Louisa for the weekend. She'd thought he'd be glad to be rid of his family for a while, but to her surprise, he had insisted on his right to have his daughter over every other weekend. Emma was absolutely not happy about the idea, and she had agreed only reluctantly. Should she retract her consent? She didn't even know where he would be taking Louisa. Apparently, he was living in a boardinghouse. That was hardly the proper surroundings for a five-year-old girl who also happened to be going through a difficult phase.

Emma slurped up her chocolate ice cream. The people around her were talking and laughing, carefree and happy. Was she the only one who had problems?

No one knew yet what had happened between her and Florian. For everyone else, his absence was perfectly normal, since he was often gone for weeks or months at a time in some foreign country. Emma had told her in-laws something about a lecture tour, and they'd accepted the lie without question. But today, when Florian picked up Louisa, she was going to have to tell them the truth.

"Hello, Emma."

She gave a start and looked up. Standing in front of her was Sarah, loaded down with shopping bags.

"I didn't mean to startle you." Her friend set down her handbag and purchases next to the table. "Could I join you for a moment?"

"Hello, Sarah. Yes, of course."

"It's sure hot today. Whew."

Sarah didn't mind the heat; she never sweated, even when it was one hundred degrees in the shade. Florian's adopted sister was a petite doll with big dark eyes and delicate facial features. Her glossy black hair was plaited as usual into a thick braid. She was wearing a lime green sleeveless summer dress with matching suede open-toe shoes, a perfect contrast to her velvety, golden-brown skin, which she'd inherited from her East Indian ancestors. Emma desperately envied her figure, which she was able to maintain without starving herself or taking up sports.

"You look a little down." Sarah put her hand on Emma's arm. "Is something wrong?"

Emma heaved a sigh and shrugged.

"What's bothering you?" Sarah asked.

Emma tried to think of a noncommittal reply. Nothing, she wanted to say. I'm fine.

"Is it something with Florian?"

It was spooky how Sarah could be downright clairvoyant. Emma bit her lip. She was a disciplined, pragmatic person, not one of those women who wailed and cried on their friends' shoulders. Even as a child, she had been used to solving her own problems; it was always hard for her to talk about them. She would rather bury her worries under restless activity, and so far that method had worked for her.

Suddenly, she realized she was thinking way too much. That wasn't good.

"You can talk to me about it," Sarah said gently. "You know that. Sometimes it helps just to talk about what's wrong."

Talk, talk, talk! That's exactly what Emma didn't want to do.

"Florian is cheating on me," she whispered at last. And then the tears came.

"He hasn't slept with me since last November," she sobbed. "Before we used to have sex at least three times a week, and now . . . if I try to touch him, he pulls away. It's so humiliating."

She wiped away her tears, but new ones kept streaming down her face, as if a dam had burst inside her.

"I mean, he did contribute to me looking like this, after all. It seems to me that . . . that he wants to punish me. Damn it, I hate being pregnant. And I'm not looking forward to the baby at all."

"Emma!" Sarah leaned over and took her hands. "You can't say that. A baby, a new human being, it's the most wonderful thing in the world. It's the greatest privilege that we women have. Of course it's difficult and painful, and we have to make great sacrifices, but that's all forgotten once the baby arrives. A lot of men are unconsciously jealous. Some even feel suddenly scared of their partner and the baby growing in her belly. They might act irrationally, but that will pass. Believe me. You have to make some allowances for your husband. He's not hurting you on purpose."

Emma stared at her friend in disbelief.

"You . . . you're saying it's acceptable, the way Florian is behaving?" she whispered. "Ten days ago, I found an empty condom wrapper in his jeans, and he owes me an explanation! He didn't say a word when I asked him whether he was seeing someone else. Instead, he packed up his things and moved out, to some . . . some boardinghouse in Frankfurt. I got the impression he was really happy to get away from here. Away from me and his parents! And then he suggested that I stay here until the baby is born."

Sarah listened mutely.

"Who knows what he did or how often he betrayed me when he was alone for weeks in some camp," Emma blurted out. "Damn it, I can't take it anymore."

She shook off Sarah's hands. Black spots were dancing before her eyes, and she felt dizzy. The heat was making her circulation go crazy. The baby had woken up, and she felt it kicking her. All at once, she felt like she was carrying an alien being in her belly.

"I feel so alone," she sobbed in despair. "What am I going to do with Louisa when I have to go to the hospital? How is this all going to work out? Where am I going to go with two kids and no money?"

Sarah stroked Emma's arm.

"But you'll be in good hands with us," she said

sympathetically. "You can have your baby at our place in the birthing center. Louisa can stay with Renate, Corinna, or me, and she can visit you anytime. And if everything goes well, you'll be home the next day."

Emma hadn't even thought of this option. Her situation, God knows, was no different from that of many other women. The Sonnenkinder Association specialized in helping unhappy women like herself—women who had been left in the lurch by their men. Sure, that wasn't really any consolation; on the contrary, it made her realize the true extent of her plight. At the same time, an ominous suspicion crept into her mind. Because Florian hadn't wanted a second child, was he deliberately unloading her on his parents, so that he wouldn't have to assume any responsibility or have a guilty conscience when he went off with another woman? Was all this a carefully calculated ploy, an elegant solution to get rid of her?

She cast a suspicious glance at this woman who had so easily adopted her as a friend. Maybe Sarah knew about the whole thing. Maybe Corinna and her in-laws did, too.

"What is it?" Sarah sounded genuinely concerned, but that could be feigned, too. Suddenly, Emma felt that she could no longer trust anyone. She opened her wallet, placed five euros on the table, and got up.

"I . . . I have to go pick up Louisa," she stammered, and made her escape.

Instead of the announced intercity express, a regular intercity train rolled into the Hamburg Main Station on track 13 fifteen minutes late. This meant that his seat reservation, which he'd been glad to get, considering the crowds waiting on the platform, was now useless. The train was so full that he couldn't find a seat and had to stand in the corridor, his backpack wedged between his feet.

The most dependable thing about the German railroad was its lack of dependability. Sure, you could download the tickets to your smartphone and make reservations online, but in reality daily train travel didn't look much better than it had thirty years ago.

He had never liked being confined in a small space with so many strangers, and he'd always preferred to fly or drive. The woman next to him smelled like she'd taken a bath in a cloying cheap perfume and then washed her clothes in it, too. From the left, a sharp body odor assaulted his nose, and he could tell that one of his fellow travelers had recently eaten garlic.

His hypersensitive sense of smell, which he'd once been so proud of, turned out to be a torment in situations like this.

At least the short trip to the north had been worth it. He had gotten what he wanted. Of course, he'd taken only a couple of quick looks at the photos that were stored on the inconspicuous USB stick, but they showed precisely what he had secretly hoped: thousands of photos and a few video files of superb quality that would be worth a small fortune on the black market. If the cops found the stick on him, his probation would be rescinded, but that was the chance he had to take.

He checked his cell. No calls, no texts. He'd really hoped she'd get in touch.

He took a look around the railway car. In his gray Brioni suit, a relic from his former life, and wearing a shirt and tie, he looked no different from the other business types. No one took any notice of him except for a pretty brunette sitting in the window seat across the aisle; she kept staring at him whenever she thought he wasn't looking. She smiled coquettishly and a bit invitingly, but he didn't smile back. The last thing he wanted was to carry on a conversation. Actually, he'd wanted to read or sleep on the way back, but neither was easy to do standing up. Instead, he gave in to daydreams, indulging in pleasant memories that were being clouded by increasing doubts.

Why wasn't she calling him? This morning, he'd texted her to say that all day he'd be reachable only by phone or text message. Since then, he'd waited nervously for her reply—in vain. The longer his cell remained silent, the greater his doubts. In his mind, he went over every conversation and every sentence, trying to call up in his memory whether he could have somehow offended her, hurt her feelings, or made her mad. The euphoria with which he'd set off this morning on the trip to Hamburg had now disappeared.

Not until half an hour before the train reached Frankfurt did he feel his cell vibrating in his pants pocket. Finally! Only a text, but still. As he read it, he had to smile, and when he looked up, the dark-haired woman's gaze met his. She briefly raised her eyebrows, turned her head, and demonstratively looked out the window. He was rid of her.

The stage lights went off; the camera people rolled back their cameras and removed their headsets. The studio audience applauded.

"That's it, people!" the director called. "Thank you all."

Hanna took a deep breath and tried to relax her cramped facial muscles after two straight hours of smiling. The ninety-minute summer special on the topic "Fate or Accident," the season finale, had demanded all her concentration. The guests had been difficult to control. It had been hard work to make sure they all got time to speak, and the director had kept squawking at her in her earbud, until she finally barked at him during the warmup, asking him to please keep his trap shut—she knew what she was doing.

At least her team had worked well together. Meike and Sven, the new producer, had done a perfect job in rehearsal. Hanna escaped to her dressing room before the audience could storm her with requests for autographs. She didn't feel much like going to the wrap party on the roof terrace, but her team and the guests deserved to see her for at least half an hour. Her makeup was itching, and thanks to the heat of the spotlights, she was drenched in sweat. She'd gotten almost no sleep the night before, yet her body was buzzing with energy and a zest for life. For days, she'd felt as if she were standing underneath high-voltage lines, and the whole hassle with Norman was long forgotten.

Hanna reached for her cell phone, fell into an easy chair, and took a couple of swigs of lukewarm mineral water. Shit, no reception again in this fallout shelter! The studios of Antenne Pro and the other stations that belonged to the holding company were located in an ugly industrial section of Oberursel. The editors, finance people, and other office workers had their offices on the second floor, but management had outsourced themselves to a property more suitable to their status—for the past two years, the big shots had been housed in an Art

Nouveau villa in Palmengarten, in the Westend of Frankfurt.

"Hanna?" Meike came in, as usual without knocking. "Are you coming up? The guests are already asking for you."

"Ten minutes," replied Hanna.

"Five minutes would be better," said Meike, slamming the door behind her.

There was no point in changing clothes. Up on the roof terrace, it was probably still over eighty-five degrees. And if she wanted to go home soon, it would be better to go up there right now, before everybody got tipsy and wouldn't let her leave. Hanna exchanged her high heels for flat ballerina slippers, grabbed her purse, and left the dressing room.

On the roof, there was a party going on, and it was a bigger celebration than usual. The summer and Christmas specials were always a huge challenge for all the staff; unlike on the normal show, the guests were prominent individuals and a lot more demanding than the no-names, who were so intimidated by the whole television scene that they made no demands at all.

On the stairs, the cellular reception improved, and Hanna's smartphone woke up. She stopped on the landing below the roof terrace and scanned her messages. Congratulations from Wolfgang for the successful show, a callback request from Vinzenz, and various other texts and e-mails, but not the one she was waiting for. Hanna felt a pang of disappointment. Patience was not one of her character traits.

"Hanna! Wait up!" Jan Niemöller always took two steps at a time. "That was really a super show. Congrats!"

"Thanks."

Breathless, he stood next to her and made an attempt to hug her, but Hanna retreated.

"Please don't," she said. "I'm a sweaty mess."

The smile vanished from Niemöller's face. She walked the rest of the way up the stairs, and he followed.

"Have you already talked to Matern?" he asked.

"No. Why?"

"He called me this afternoon and sounded a little weird. Did you guys have a fight?"

"What makes you say that?"

"Well, he was sort of hemming and hawing. Something about the first show after the summer hiatus."

"Oh, really?" Hanna stopped and turned around. Hadn't she told Wolfgang expressly not to mention a word about that matter?

"What's going on? What's it all about?" Niemöller looked at her with a mixture of envy and mistrust. "For days, you've been almost unreachable."

"I'm working on a big deal," said Hanna, relieved that Wolfgang had apparently kept his

214

mouth shut. But she was really going to take him to task. "It could be huge."

"So what's it about?"

"You'll find out when I know more."

"Why all the secrecy?" her comanager complained, looking suspicious. "Usually, we make decisions together about what to do on the show. Or is something going on behind my back?"

"There's nothing going on," Hanna snapped. "And things haven't proceeded far enough to talk about it yet."

"But you've already told Matern—" Niemöller began, offended like a prima ballerina who has lost the role of the black swan to a rival.

Hanna interrupted him. "Jan, don't be childish. You'll find out everything soon enough. And Wolfgang happens to be not only the program director but also a good friend."

"I hope you're not making a mistake," Niemöller grumbled enviously.

Hanna glanced one last time at her smartphone before she stuck it back in her bag, then switched on her professional smile.

"Come on," she said, trying to be conciliatory as she linked arms with him. "Let's go celebrate. We all deserve it."

"I don't feel like partying," said Niemöller, pulling away. "I'm going home."

"All right." Hanna shrugged. "Good night, then."

If he thought she was going to beg him to go along, he was wrong. He was really getting on her nerves with his possessiveness. Maybe she ought to look for another man to take over the job, or better yet, a woman.

The guest list of people assembled in the park of the magnificent city palace of Miriam's grandmother in the posh Holzhausen district read like a who's who of Frankfurt and Lower Taunus society. Old names, new names, old money and new money amused themselves side by side; they were in a generous mood. When Charlotte Horowitz sent out invitations to a performance by talented new musicians, everybody came. Today, a seventeen-year-old pianist was the center of attention. Because of the episode at the Main-Taunus Center, Pia arrived late and caught only the last few bars of a truly virtuoso presentation.

She wasn't really disappointed, because she was mainly concerned with the exquisite food. You could always count on the quality of Grandmother Horowitz's spread.

At the buffet, she ran into Henning.

"So, fashionably late once again?" he remarked archly. "That's eventually going to attract attention."

"Only from you," Pia replied. "Nobody else is keeping tabs on me. Besides, I'm not that crazy about piano noodling."

"Pia is a Philistine," said Lilly in her know-it-all voice. "Grandpa told me that yesterday."

"How right your Grandpa is," said Henning with a grin.

"I admit it." Pia's eyes roved over the tempting delicacies, and she tried to decide where to start. She was starving.

Miriam came up to her with arms outstretched and kissed her on both cheeks.

"Chic dress," she remarked. "New?"

"Yeah, picked it up today at Chanel," Pia joked. "A steal at two thousand euros."

"That's not right," Lilly put in excitedly.

"It was a joke," Pia said. "Why don't you tell Miriam about our adventure today, which is why we arrived late and missed this *wonderful* pianist."

She winked at her friend. Miriam knew she couldn't care less about her grandmother's musical protégés. Lilly recounted the adventurous shopping center story in detail, not forgetting to mention the price of Pia's dress—9.95 euros. That was approximately the cost of two square inches of Miriam's dress.

"This child is going to send me to an early grave." Pia rolled her eyes.

"Pia, look at that boy—I know him from the Opel Zoo." Lilly pointed to a couple standing with a group of people; their son seemed to be about eight.

"Don't point your finger at people," Pia scolded.

"What should I point with, then?" Lilly asked.

Pia took a deep breath and shrugged.

"Forget it. Go and play. But please stay close by and check in with me every fifteen minutes."

The girl took off obediently, heading straight for the boy. She certainly wasn't shy.

"Tell me, Henning, the man standing next to the boy, isn't that State Attorney Frey?" Pia asked, squinting her eyes. "What's he doing here?"

"Markus Frey is on the board of the Finkbeiner Foundation," Miriam explained before Henning could reply. She was spooning an iced cucumber soup with a caramelized shellfish crust from a little shot glass. "Do you know him?"

"Do I ever. I know all the state attorneys in Frankfurt," replied Pia. "He showed up recently at the scene where a dead body was found, and then he attended the autopsy."

"Have you made any progress in the case?" Henning asked, then lowered his voice. "By the way, here comes Charlotte. Better act fast. Don't try to hide it—I can tell that you're lusting after all that food."

Pia gave him a withering look. But it was too late. Miriam's grandmother had spied her. For unknown reasons, the old lady had taken a liking to Pia many years before, and after she'd cleared up the murder of a close acquaintance a few years ago, she invited Pia on every conceivable occasion. It was half an hour before Pia got anywhere near the buffet.

The air had turned oppressive, and the mosquitoes were exasperating. The weather report had predicted a powerful storm for that evening, and Pia wanted to get home before it broke. She hurried to load up a plate with delicacies and went in search of Miriam, finally finding her with Henning and a few other acquaintances in one of the pavilions beneath the magnificent old chestnut trees in the garden. The mood was cheerful; they all knew one another, and teasing repartee flew back and forth. Once more, Pia's dress was the preferred target of Henning's snide comments, and finally she'd had enough.

"Anyone who runs around wearing glasses like that should keep his mouth shut when it comes to fashion," she said, and the group laughed.

"That just shows how clueless you are." Henning grimaced. "The frames alone cost eight hundred euros; I won't even tell you what the lenses cost."

"Where'd you get them?" Pia said with a grin. "Bought Nana Mouskouri's old pair, perhaps?"

The group exploded in laughter, and Henning, who didn't appreciate jokes made at his expense, was insulted.

Suddenly, Pia remembered Lilly, whom she hadn't seen in quite a while.

Many of the guests were heading inside, and some had already left, since tomorrow was a workday. At any rate, people didn't tend to stay until midnight. It wouldn't be polite. There was no trace of Lilly in the park, and Pia instantly got nervous again. One episode of excitement per day was quite enough.

"Maybe I should have a GPS implanted under the girl's skin," she told Miriam and Henning, who were helping her search. "I must have aged ten years today."

Finally, they found Lilly in the conservatory. She and her playmate from the Opel Zoo were asleep on one of the sofas, and Lilly had chosen Chief State Attorney Frey's thigh as a pillow. His hand was resting lightly on her head as he chatted with two other gentlemen sitting across from him in easy chairs.

"Beauty and the Beast," Henning muttered mockingly. "How idyllic."

"Ah, Ms. Kirchhoff, Dr. Kirchhoff." The state attorney smiled. "I take it this little girl belongs to you. I didn't want to wake her up, but I'm afraid I have to get going."

"I'll free you at once." It was a bit embarrassing for Pia to be thought a bad mother. "I'm sorry. I hope Lilly wasn't too much trouble."

"No, not at all, no worries; we had a nice chat." Frey moved over a bit and got up, then carefully picked up the sleeping child and handed her to

Pia. "An enchanting little girl, so self-confident and happy."

Lilly hung like a sack in Pia's arms, her head resting on Pia's shoulder.

"Can you manage, or should I carry her to the car?" asked Frey with concern.

"No, thank you. I'm fine," said Pia with a smile.

"I have three children myself," explained the SA. "The young man here, Maxi, is my youngest, and he and Lilly know each other from the zoo school."

"I see," said Pia.

People continued to surprise Pia. The state attorney, hard as nails, apparently had a butter-soft, human side to him.

She politely took her leave. On the way to the car, Lilly woke up.

"Are we going home soon?" she murmured.

"We certainly are," said Pia. "It's already eleven. Your grandpa is probably wondering where we are."

"I had a nice time with you today." Lilly yawned and threw her arms around Pia's neck. "I like you sooooo much, Pia. You're my German mama."

She said it so simply, with such childlike honesty, that Pia had to swallow hard. Her initial lack of enthusiasm and annoyance had evaporated.

"I like you, too," she whispered.

• • •

Hanna turned off the autobahn at the Krifteler Triangle and took the L3011 toward Hofheim. Sweaty and exhausted, she longed for a shower or, even better, a dip in the pool. Most of all, she needed to get a few hours' sleep, because tomorrow night she had to host a gala at the Wiesbaden Spa, and she had to be in top form.

Naturally, she hadn't managed to escape the wrap party after only half an hour. Jan had simply taken off, angry and hurt like a little boy, leaving her alone with the guests. Until shortly after midnight, she'd been able to grin and bear it, but then she'd used the approaching storm as an excuse to leave the party. She'd had a hard time concentrating on the conversations, so many things were spinning around in her head. Meike. The scratches on her car. These strange matters that her therapist was mixed up in. Norman, who had threatened her on the phone but never called back. But mostly she was thinking about Mr. Blue Eyes. Even during the broadcast, she had caught herself thinking of him a couple of times.

They had become very close, and not merely physically, but Hanna still didn't know much about him; she couldn't really figure him out. Even a couple of years ago, she might have thrown herself blindly into an affair, but after making so many bad decisions with regard to men, she had grown cautious. A song she liked began on the radio. She pressed the button on the steering wheel to turn up the volume and then sang along. The wind had picked up and lightning was flashing across the sky. In Oberursel, the storm had already swept through, turning the streets into raging rivers. In a few minutes, it would hit here, too. In the light of her headlights, something zipped across the road in front of her, and she instinctively turned the wheel to the left. A bolt of adrenaline shot through her body and she took her foot off the gas. Fortunately, no oncoming car was approaching, or it would have been a close call. A couple of hundred yards past the off-ramp to Kreishaus, she put on her blinker and turned in the direction of Langenhain. Shortly before the forest, a dark-colored car pulled out to pass her.

"Idiot!" Hanna muttered, hitting the brake in shock. What suicidal maniac would choose to pass at such a blind spot? Then she saw it. In the rear window of the car ahead of her a red signal had lit up: POLICE—PLEASE FOLLOW.

This was too much! They were probably driving behind her, saw her evasive maneuver, and assumed she was drunk. At the wrap party, she'd indulged in only two shandies. That probably didn't add up to more than .005 blood alcohol.

The dark-colored car eased to the right, heading for the big forest parking lot. With a sigh, Hanna put on her blinker, turned down the music, and stopped behind the police car. She rolled the window down.

Two men got out; an officer in plainclothes shone a flashlight into her car.

"Good evening," he said. "Vehicle check. Driver's license and registration, please."

Hanna reached for her handbag on the passenger seat and took out her wallet. She was glad that she had all the necessary papers with her. That meant she could be on her way sooner. She drummed her fingers impatiently on the steering wheel as the plainclothes cop went back to his cruiser. The second officer remained standing off to the side, a short distance from the front of her car.

Should she write Mr. Blue Eyes a text? Or was it better to wait until he sent one? In any case, she didn't want to create the impression that she was chasing him.

The first heavy raindrops splashed on the windshield, and the wind came up quickly in the surrounding big trees. Why was this taking so long? It was already almost 1:00 A.M.

Finally, the officer came back.

"Please step out of the vehicle and open the trunk."

If she refused to comply, she might have to take an alcohol test, so it was better to do exactly what they asked. They were probably bored on the night shift, and a car like hers always attracted attention and aroused envy. Since she'd been driving the Porsche Panamera, she'd been stopped by the cops more often than ever before. Hanna pressed the button that opened the trunk, then got out.

Cool raindrops struck her sticky skin. She could smell the forest, wild leeks, wet asphalt, and that metallic smell that the earth exuded in the summertime when it got wet after a long dry spell.

"Where do you have the warning triangle, the safety vest, and the first-aid kit?"

God, they really were sticklers. The rain got stronger, and Hanna shivered.

"There are the warning triangle and vest." She pointed to the underside of the trunk lid. "And here's the first-aid kit. Satisfied?"

Lightning flashed.

Out of the corner of her eye, Hanna saw a movement. The second officer was suddenly standing behind her; she could feel his breath on the back of her neck, and her brain instinctively registered danger.

These aren't cops! The thought shot through her head as powerful hands grabbed her upper arms. She ducked forward and took a step back at the same time. The attacker loosened his grip, so she was able to spin around and ram her knee into his genitals. Hanna's reaction was pure reflex. In the self-defense course she'd taken after that crazy guy had stalked her for almost two years, the instructor had emphasized "freeing yourself from various holds" and taught her how to defend herself if she was attacked. The man staggered, doubled up, and cursed. Hanna used the moment to flee, but she hadn't reckoned with the other guy. A blow struck her on the back of the head. Dazzling points of light exploded before her eyes like fireworks, her knees gave way, and she collapsed. She could hazily make out the legs and shoes of the men, but her perspective had changed. She saw the muddy soil on which puddles were forming in the downpour, but she didn't understand what was happening. For a moment, she felt weightless and lost her orientation. Then all of a sudden, it was dry, dark, and warm. Everything happened so fast that she didn't even have time to feel afraid.

She loved being in the horse stable. For her it was the most beautiful place in the whole world. None of her siblings liked horses as much as she did, and they often held their noses when she came out of the stall smelling like horses. She loved acrobatic riding and was good at it, and because she was so petite and light, she was allowed to take part not only in the compulsory exercises but also in the free sections. She enjoyed the feeling of security and lightness that flowed through her each time she performed acrobatics on horseback. Other people could barely do the same tricks on solid ground.

After her lesson, she had helped Gaby, the equestrian acrobatics teacher, to take care of Asterix. She was allowed to scrape out the horse's hooves and lead him into his box. Asterix was the dearest horse in the whole world, white, with warm brown eyes and a mane like silver. The other girls from the equestrian acrobatics class had already left, but she didn't feel like going home. She sat down under the feed box in Asterix's stall and gazed at the way the white horse contentedly chewed his hay.

Gaby's voice sounded right behind her head. "Hey, you're still here. Better get moving, or you'll have to spend the whole night in the stall."

She wouldn't have minded one bit. This was where she felt safe. Here the nightmares were far away. Gaby opened the stall door and came in.

"What's the matter? Should I give you a ride home?" The equestrian acrobatics teacher squatted down and looked at her. "It's already almost dark outside. Your parents are going to be worried."

She shook her head. At the thought of going home, she felt sick with fear, but she couldn't say anything. It was a secret that she couldn't tell anyone else; she'd promised Papa. But last night, she'd had such bad dreams and was so terrified of the wolves. Because they were going to come and eat her up if she ever told anyone about the secret. That's what Uncle Richard had told her. She was so scared that she hadn't dared go to the toilet and had peed in her bed. That's why Mama was really mad this morning, and her siblings had laughed at her.

"I don't want to go home," she said softly.

"Why not?" Gaby gave her a searching look.

"Because . . . because . . . my papa always hurts me."

She didn't dare look at the young woman. She waited tensely for something terrible to happen now that she'd broken her promise. But nothing happened, and so she raised her head. Gaby was looking more serious than she'd ever seen her.

"How do you mean?" she asked. "What does he do?"

Her courage melted away, and she didn't dare say any more, but suddenly she had an idea.

"Could I maybe go home with you?" she asked. Gaby liked her; she was proud of her best pupil, as she always said. Along with a couple of other girls, she'd already been to the equestrian acrobatics teacher's house; they'd looked at photos of horses and drank cocoa. Gaby was grown-up and was never afraid of anything. She would protect her from the wolves.

"I'm afraid not," said Gaby, to her disappointment. "But I can drive you home and have a talk with your mother."

She looked at Gaby and fought back tears.

"But what about the bad wolf?" she whispered.

"What bad wolf?" Gaby straightened up. "Did you have a bad dream?"

Disappointed, she lowered her eyes and got up. Gaby tried to give her a hug, but she wriggled loose.

"Bye, Asterix," she said to the horse, then stepped out of the stall and left the stable without saying a word. Only now did the fear come, the tears burning behind her eyelids like fire. What if the wolves did something to Gaby now because she hadn't kept her mouth shut, because she had told her about the secret?

Friday, June 25, 2010

"Her cell phone is still off. And she's not answering her landline, either."

Meike looked at the group and saw clueless and worried faces. For half an hour, the new members of Herzmann Productions had been sitting around the oval table in the conference room, downing quarts of coffee and becoming more and more fuzzy-headed. Like a herd of sheep without an alpha sheep, she thought derisively.

"Have you tried texting her?" asked Irina Zydek, who had been Hanna's assistant forever and was almost part of the furniture in the office. For some inexplicable reason she was crazy about Hanna even though she was never treated very nicely. Over the years, she had looked on with stoic composure as a long series of husbands, admirers, lovers, CEOs, producers, production assistants, editors, female volunteers, and controllers came and went. Anyone who didn't stay on good terms with Irina didn't have a ghost of a chance to get near the great Hanna Herzmann. Irina was loyal to the point of surrendering her own identity, and even though she might appear to be a gray mouse, inside she was a Cerberus, hard as iron and incorruptible.

"How's she supposed to read texts if her cell is turned off?" Meike countered. "She just over-slept. Or her battery's dead."

Irina got up, went over to the window, and gazed down into the courtyard.

"Hanna has never been late without notifying me in all the years I've known her," she said. "I'm starting to worry."

"Whatever." Meike shrugged. "She'll turn up. It was a late one last night."

Most probably she was in bed with some guy. Hanna had something going on with a man; she knew that for a fact. Meike was only too familiar with the typical symptoms of infatuation. Once her mother's hormones took over, everything else faded away. In recent weeks, she'd seemed changed somehow; she would turn off her cell phone and was sometimes unreachable for hours. Besides, she hadn't offered a word of protest when Meike announced that she was going to live in the city all summer, in the middle of Sachsenhausen, instead of in her mother's house behind the seven hills, in the middle of nowhere. Actually, Meike had expected begging, tears, and pleading—yes, she'd even secretly looked forward to that sort of response. But Hanna had scarcely reacted to her news. "If you think that's better" was all she had said. Once again, some guy was more important than her daughter, and now Meike's assumption seemed to be confirmed. Naturally, Hanna had told her nothing, and Meike would rather have bitten off her tongue than to ask. She didn't give a damn about her mother's personal life, and if she hadn't needed the money so badly, she never would have agreed to take this job.

"One of us ought to drive over to her place and see if she's okay." Jan Niemöller looked wiped out. His eyes were bloodshot and he was unshaven and nervous. "Hanna was acting so strange yesterday."

Sure, she wanted to hook up with her boyfriend, Meike thought scornfully, but she stopped herself from making a bitchy remark. Negative comments about her mother didn't go over well here. Irina and Jan were now discussing the best way to proceed, and Meike asked herself what their motivation might be.

It was absurd the way Jan was making a fool of himself. A heated rivalry existed between him and Irina. It went so far that neither of them would stay home even with a fever of 104, out of sheer terror that the other might be scoring points to win Hanna's favor. They waged regular battles of jealousy, competing to see who could do something with or for Hanna, who, in turn, exploited this silly kindergarten war to her advantage.

Irina and Jan were always discussing things. Meike shoved her chair back, threw her bag over her shoulder, and stood up.

"I see no reason to drive out to Langenhain at the moment, but I'll do it if that will finally give the two of you some peace of mind."

"Oh, that's so nice of you," they both said in a rare display of unity.

"If she calls in the meantime, I'll let you know." Irina beamed with relief.

Meike was happy to get out of the office. Today she definitely wouldn't be going back there. Not in this awesome weather.

The officers at K-11 had returned to the daily routine, temporarily at least, after two hectic weeks. There were no new leads or tips, and the hot-line phone hardly ever rang. In the papers, the story of the dead girl in the river had long since been pushed off the front page by current events and disasters.

But Bodenstein was still working intently on the case. Late that afternoon, he'd spoken on the phone in detail with an editor from *Germany's Most Wanted* and had great hopes for the scheduled broadcast. The only drawback was the planned date of the broadcast, in the middle of the first week of summer vacation in Hessen. He had spread out the "Mermaid" case files on the visitor's table and had organized the documents that he wanted to take with him to Munich next week. It wasn't the first time that Bodenstein would be speaking to the public from a television studio. Twice before, the program had produced helpful tips that in the end led to the arrest of the perpetrator, although on a third occasion, his appearance had brought no result. He was just making notes of the facts that the editor needed in advance, along with photos and exhibits, when there was a knock on his door.

"We have an emergency call, boss," said Kai Ostermann. "I've already told Pia, and she'll be here in ten minutes."

His eyes fell on the meticulously organized documents.

"But I could also try to send Cem and Kathrin. They're still at that suicide site in Eppstein."

"No, no, it's all right. I'll take it." Bodenstein looked up. A little fresh air wouldn't hurt. "Maybe you could make sure these photos and the scraps of clothing go out today. I've written down the address."

"No problem." Ostermann nodded. "By the way, you'll have to go to Weilbach. A woman in the trunk of a car. That's all I know."

"Whereabouts exactly?" Bodenstein got up. He was wondering whether to take his jacket. Last night, the temperature had turned deceptively cool. But today, it was more unbearable than ever, because an almost tropical humidity of 70 percent had settled in.

"Somewhere in the field behind the Weilbach rest stop on the autobahn heading for Frankfurt. I sent Kröger over there, too."

"Good." Bodenstein took his jacket from the back of the chair and left the office.

The case of the dead girl in the river weighed on him. In his career with the Criminal Police, he'd been on two cases that, despite intense efforts, had never been cleared up. He had still been with K-11 in Frankfurt when a thirteen-year-old boy was found dead in a pedestrian underpass in the city's Höchst district, and in 2001 the body of a young girl was found at the Wörthspitze in the Main River at Nied. Both times, it was young people, hardly more than kids, who were the victims of gruesome crimes. Their murders remained unsolved, and the perps were still on the loose. Was it about to happen a third time? The success rate in solving homicides was relatively high in Germany, but it was a very bad sign that after more than two weeks there were still no hot leads.

"Hanna?"

Meike stood in the hall and listened. Although she had a key to the front door, she had rung the bell twice. She had no desire to surprise her mother in flagrante with a man in her bed.

"Hanna!"

Nothing. The bird had flown the coop. Meike went into the kitchen, then through the dining and living rooms to her mother's home office. She glanced into the room, which looked as chaotic as always. Upstairs in the bedroom, the bed hadn't been slept in and the wardrobe doors were standing open. A few articles of clothing had been removed from their hangers in the wardrobe, and several pairs of shoes lay scattered on the floor.

Her mother probably hadn't been able to decide what to wear to the broadcast. The clothes her stylist picked out for her seldom found approval in her eyes; she liked her own clothes better. The bedroom didn't look like it had been the setting for a passionate night of love; it looked instead as though Hanna hadn't been home at all.

Meike went back downstairs.

She didn't like this house; it gave her the creeps. When she was a kid, it was nice to live on a street with no cars driving past. With the neighbor kids, she roller-skated and rode go-carts; they had played Chinese jump rope and hopscotch and wandered through the woods. But then the house had turned into an enemy. After months of fighting, her parents had finally separated. Her father suddenly vanished, and Meike's mother had left her alone with constantly changing au pairs. As she grew older, it had been sheer hell to live in such a stagnant place by the woods in Langenhain, removed from any sort of excitement.

Meike opened the mailbox, took out a stack of letters, and quickly looked through them. Once in a while, some mail came for her. A note that was stuck between the letters dropped to the floor. Meike bent down and picked it up. It was a page torn out of a calendar.

Waited until 1:30, she read. *Would have liked to see you. My cell battery is dead! Here's the address. BP knows about it. Call me. K.*

What could this mean? And what was this address in Langensebold?

Meike's curiosity was aroused. She would never admit it, but the change that had come over her mother during the past weeks made her mad. Hanna was acting very secretive and refused to tell anyone where she was going or where she'd been. Not even Irina. Was "K" her new boy-friend? And who was BP?

Meike glanced at her cell phone. It was just a little past eleven. More than enough time to drive over to Langensebold and check out that address.

Bodenstein pressed the button to open the door and stepped into the security screening area. He nodded to the officer on duty, who was sitting in the guard room behind bulletproof glass, to let him out. Pia was already waiting in the car and had the motor running. He got in and sighed with relief. She had gotten hold of an official car with air conditioning, and it was pleasantly cool inside.

"Do we know anything more?" Bodenstein asked, fumbling with the seat belt.

"Female body in a car trunk, they said," Pia replied. She turned left in the direction of the autobahn. "Did everything go all right at your appointment with the notary yesterday?"

"Yep. The house is sold."

"Was it bad?"

"Amazingly, no. Maybe it will be when we move our stuff out. But if all goes well with the house in Ruppertshain, leaving will be easier." Bodenstein thought about his meeting with Cosima last night at the notary's office in Kelkheim. For the first time since their ugly separation almost two years ago, he'd been able to look at her and talk to her rationally, without getting upset. He had no feelings left, either good or bad, for the mother of his three children, and the woman with whom he had spent over half his life. And that was both frightening and a big relief. Maybe this was how they would continue to deal with each other in the future.

On the drive to Weilbach, he told Pia about the hearing at State Criminal Police headquarters and Behnke's defeat. The shrill ring of Pia's cell interrupted him, postponing any decision about whether or not to tell his colleague about the showdown in the corridor between Behnke and Nicola Engel.

"Can you take this?" Pia asked. "It's Christoph."

Bodenstein answered the phone and then held it up to Pia's ear.

"I don't know how late we'll be today. We just got called out again, and we're on our way over there now," she told Christoph. "Hmm . . . yes . . . grilling is perfect. There's still some pasta salad in the fridge, but if you're stopping at the store anyway, could you get some detergent? I forgot to write it down."

A typical everyday conversation between two people in a relationship, like Bodenstein used to have with Cosima. In the past two years, as he'd gone through a private state of emergency, he'd often missed this feeling of closeness. No matter how much he tried to tell himself that the freedom he now had was an exciting new opportunity, he longed for a real home and another person with whom he could share his life. He wasn't cut out for living alone for any length of time.

Pia listened to Christoph for a while, occasionally muttering in agreement, but all of a sudden she smiled in a manner Bodenstein had seldom seen.

"Okay," she said, ending the call. "I'll call you later."

Bodenstein turned off the phone and placed it on the center console.

"Why are you grinning like that?" he asked.

"Oh, that little girl," Pia replied lightly without looking at him. "She's so cute. You wouldn't believe the things she comes up with." She turned serious again. "It's almost a shame that she has to leave so soon."

"A couple of days ago, you were singing a different tune," Bodenstein said, amused. "You were totally worn-out and you were crossing off the days to her departure on your calendar."

"You're right. But in the meantime, we have come to an agreement, Lilly and I," Pia admitted. "Having a kid like that in the house really does change everything. Most of all, I underestimated the burden of responsibility. Sometimes she's so independent that I forget how much she still needs to be protected."

"You're right about that," Bodenstein said with a nod. His youngest daughter had turned four in

December, and now that she spent every other weekend with him, or sometimes a couple of days midweek, he noticed how much attention such a small child required, but also how much joy she gave him.

They left the A66 at the autobahn exit in Hattersheim and turned onto the L3265, heading for Kiesgrube. They could already see the scene of the crime in the distance, because there was a helicopter standing in a meadow, its rotor blades lazily turning in neutral.

At the edge of a neighboring wheat field, they saw police vehicles, a medical examiner's car, and an ambulance. Pia slowed down and put on the blinker, but before she could turn onto the dirt road, a uniformed colleague motioned for them to park by the side of the highway. They got out to walk the last fifty yards on foot. A wall of humid heat seemed to slam into Bodenstein as he followed Pia along the narrow grass shoulder; the dirt track had been turned to mud by the thunderstorm and was roped off. The wheat had not survived the previous night unharmed, and the downpour had broken many of the stalks or bent them to the ground.

"Please go around the outside!" shouted Christian Kröger, pointing toward the field, in which a narrow path was marked with tape fluttering in the wind. The leader of the evidence team and his three colleagues had already put on their white overalls with hoods—not a job to be envied in this searing heat. There was no shade tree anywhere in sight.

"What have we got?" Bodenstein asked when they reached Kröger.

"A woman in the trunk of a car, naked and unconscious," Kröger told them. "Not a pretty sight."

"She's not dead?"

"You think they send a chopper to take corpses to forensics?" Kröger snapped. "No, she's still alive. Two people from autobahn maintenance spotted the car from the rest stop and thought it was odd. They drove over here—unfortunately, they didn't think to take care about destroying evidence."

One of the seven deadly sins in Kröger's eyes. But who apart from a policeman would immediately think of a crime when an empty car was found abandoned in a field?

"The car wasn't locked, and the key was in the ignition. And then they found her."

In passing, Bodenstein looked into the open trunk of the black Porsche Panamera and saw big dark spots, presumably blood. Two EMTs were busy in the ambulance.

"The woman was seriously injured," one of them replied to Bodenstein's question. "And completely dehydrated. One or two more hours in the closed trunk in this heat and she wouldn't have survived. We're just trying to get her ready for transport. Her circulation is totally fucked."

Bodenstein wasn't bothered by this rather unprofessional expression. EMTs were front-line fighters, and the crew of a rescue helicopter was bound to see things that were much more gruesome than a normal person could stand. He glanced at the face of the woman, which was disfigured by bruises and lacerations.

"She was beaten up and raped," the EMT said soberly. "And very brutally."

"My colleague said she was naked," said Bodenstein.

"Naked, hands and feet bound with cable, and gagged with a rag," said the EMT. "What a bunch of bastards."

"Boss?"

Bodenstein turned around.

"I spoke to the two guys who found the woman," Pia said in a low voice, stepping into the shade of the ambulance. "They told me that the parking lot behind the rest stop is known in certain circles as a meeting place for people who want to have anonymous sex."

"You mean she could have met somebody there and wound up with the wrong guy?" Bodenstein's eyes swept across the field to the rest stop. There were so many sick and perverted people running around in this world that sometimes he could hardly bear to think about it.

"It's possible," Pia said with a nod. "Our colleagues have checked the license plate. The vehicle is registered to a firm in Frankfurt. Herzmann Productions on Hedderichstrasse. There were no papers or purse in the vehicle. But the name Herzmann sounds familiar."

She frowned as she tried to remember.

Suddenly, the name popped into Bodenstein's head. He wasn't a big TV watcher, but maybe he'd read something recently, or maybe it was simply because the alliteration made the name easy to recall.

"Hanna Herzmann," he said. "The TV host."

A bed, a table, a chair, a cabinet of light-colored veneered wood. A small window, barred of course. In the corner, a toilet without a lid, a washbasin, above it a metal mirror. The smell of disinfectant. Eighty-five square feet that would be his whole world for the next three and a half years.

The heavy door closed with a thud behind him. He was alone. It was so quiet that he could hear his pulse beating in his ears, and the desperate need overcame him to grab his cell phone and call somebody, anybody, just to hear a human voice. But he no longer had a cell phone. Or a computer. Or his own clothes. As of today, he was a man who took orders, a prisoner, completely and utterly at the mercy of the moods and regulations of indifferent guards. He could no longer do what he wanted. The law had taken away his privilege to decide how to spend his time.

I'll never be able to stand it, he thought.

Ever since the day the Criminal Police showed up with a search warrant, tossed his house and office, and confiscated his computer, he'd been in a state of shock. He remembered Britta's disbelief, the disgust in her eyes when she set his luggage at the door and said she never wanted to see him again. The next day, the temporary injunction was issued that forbade him from seeing his children. Friends, his colleagues, his partner—they had all abandoned him. And finally the police had arrested him. Flight risk and suppression of evidence. Bail denied.

The weeks that lay behind him, the pretrial custody, the trial itself—it had all seemed utterly unreal to him, a labyrinthine nightmare from which he would eventually awake. When the female judge read the verdict, he realized they were really going to send him to prison for three years. His children, who were more precious to him than anything, would be twelve and ten years old the next time he saw them, but he had still believed he was strong enough to endure all of it. He had kept his composure when they led him in handcuffs from the courtroom through the storm of flashing cameras belonging to the sensation-greedy mob of reporters. He had spent so many years of his life among them, the right side of the law.

Even the medical exam and the humiliating procedures that stripped away the rights of every new arrival in the joint had failed to provoke any visible agitation from him. When he put on the worn institutional clothing that many other men had worn before him and the guard indifferently stuffed his clothes in a sack and took his wristwatch and briefcase, his mind had still refused to accept the irrevocable nature of his situation.

He turned around and stared at the scratched cell door. A door with no handle or lock, one that he would never open himself. At that instant, it became bitterly clear that this was now his reality, and he would never awake from this nightmare. His knees went weak; his stomach rebelled. He was suddenly overcome by a naked, panicky fear. Of being alone and helpless. Of the other prisoners. As a convicted child molester, he ranked at the very bottom of the prison hierarchy, and for his own safety they had put him in solitary.

He had lost all control of his life and couldn't do a thing about it. His independent life belonged to the past, his marriage was in ruins, and his reputation had been irrevocably destroyed. Everything that had formed his personality and his life, his whole identity, had vanished along with his suit, shirt, and shoes, now consigned to a green clothes sack.

Starting today, he was nothing but a number. For 1,080 endless days.

The shrill ring of a bell tore him out of a deep sleep. His heart was pounding, he was soaked with sweat, and it took him a few seconds to understand that he'd been dreaming. This dream, which had not haunted him in ages, was so oppressively real that he could hear the squeaking of the rubber soles on the gray linoleum and smell the unmistakable prison stench of piss, male sweat, food, and disinfectant.

With a groan, he got up and went to the table to look for his cell phone, whose ringtone had woken him. It was hot and sticky in the trailer. He'd wanted to take only a short nap, but then he'd fallen sound asleep. His eyes burned and his back ached. He'd stayed up until dawn reading through stacks of notebooks and newspaper articles, listening to cassette tapes, poring over reports of conversations, minutes of meetings, and diary entries, taking notes the whole time. It was anything but easy to filter out the most important facts and put them into context.

He found the cell phone under a pile of paper. Only a couple of calls, but to his surprise not the one he was waiting for so anxiously. With the click of a mouse, he awakened the laptop from standby mode, entered his password, and scanned his in-box. Disappointment flowed through his body like an insidious poison. What was going on? Had he done something wrong?

He stood up and went to the dresser, where he hesitated a moment before pulling out the drawer. Among the T-shirts he found the photo and took it out. The dark eyes. The blond hair. The sweet smile. He really ought to get rid of the photo, but he just didn't have the heart to do it. His longing for her hurt like a knife wound. And there was absolutely nothing that could ease the pain.

You have reached your destination, announced the voice of the GPS navigation program. *Your destination is on the left.*

Meike stopped the car and looked around helplessly.

"Where?" she murmured, taking off her sunglasses. She was in the middle of a forest. After the glaring sunshine, she could see nothing but trees and underbrush, a thick, dark green, here and there dappled with golden patches of sun. Then she noticed a gravel road and a tin mailbox like the ones in American movies. Refusing to be deterred, Meike put on the blinker, turned, and jolted along the winding forest road. The tense feeling grew. Who was BP? And who was K? What awaited her at the end of the forest road? She passed the last rows of trees. Bright light nearly blinded her. Around a curve, a veritable fortress unexpectedly appeared. A metal gate with surveillance cameras, an opaque fence crowned with a razor-wire barrier. Signs warned the uninvited visitor of the danger of guard dogs, high voltage, and land mines.

What the hell was all this? A paramilitary off-limits area in the middle of Main-Kinzig county? What kind of story was her mother chasing? Meike shifted into reverse and backed down the gravel road the way she had come until she reached a fork in the road. The other track looked like it was seldom used, but it led in the direction she wanted to go. When she was far enough off the main highway that nobody could see her conspicuous red car, she got out the binoculars from the glove box, closed the sunroof, and continued on foot. After about fifty yards, the track ended. Meike kept to the right and soon reached the edge of the woods. The metal gate was quite a ways off, but here she was out of sight of the cameras that were located above the gate. A short distance farther on, Meike spied a raised blind on the edge of a Christmas-tree farm. Luckily, she was wearing jeans and running shoes, because the stinging nettles and thistles were over three feet tall. The blind looked like it hadn't been used in a long time; the wooden rungs of the ladder were covered with moss. Meike felt her way cautiously up the ladder, trying out the stability of the wooden seat at the top before she sat down on it. She had a perfect view from up here.

She adjusted the focus of her binoculars and

found herself looking at a building. In front of the open gates, there were at least twenty motorcycles, heavy machines with flashing chrome, mostly Harley-Davidsons, but also two or three Royal Enfields. Next to them, separated by a chain-link fence, was a junkyard in which piles of motorcycle and auto parts, tires, and oil drums were stored. In the shade of a huge chestnut tree next to the building stood tables and benches. A swing barbecue grill was smoking, but not a soul was in sight. On the other side of the big courtyard, the guard dogs advertised on the warning signs were dozing in the sun inside caged dog runs.

Except for the distant drone of a prop plane, it was completely quiet. Honeybees and bumblebees buzzed in the surrounding thickets, and deep in the forest a cuckoo called.

From her elevated vantage point, Meike inspected the rest of the gigantic fenced area. Between tall trees stood a residence, surrounded by a well-tended garden with carefully trimmed bushes, blooming flower beds, and emerald green lawns. A little way from the terrace, the blue water of a swimming pool glittered, and farther back in the yard was a children's playground with swings, sandboxes, jungle gyms, and a slide. A peaceful paradise among razor-wire fences, big motorcycles, and aggressive attack dogs. Very strange. What was this place?

Meike took a few photos with her iPhone; then she activated the GPS locator in Google Maps. She zoomed in on the satellite image, but, to her dismay, it seemed to be a few years old, because neither the fence nor the junkyard was visible. Previously, the property must have been a simple farm, before some obscure organization had entrenched itself here. The whole thing reeked of criminal energy. Drugs? Stolen cars and motorcycles? Human trafficking? Maybe something political?

Meike grabbed the binoculars again and looked at the house.

Suddenly, she jumped in shock. Behind one of the windows on the ground floor stood a man. In one hand he held binoculars and in the other a cell phone that he had pressed to his ear. And the man was looking right at her! Shit, they'd discovered her.

She climbed hastily down the ladder. A rung cracked and broke, and Meike lost her balance and fell backward into the stinging nettles. Cursing, she got to her feet, and not a second too soon, because from the woods a big black car with tinted windows was heading toward her, followed by four motorcycles. But the procession didn't drive into the courtyard. Instead, it kept coming straight on the overgrown dirt road, directly toward the blind. Meike didn't hesitate for even a second. She fought her way through the nettles, thorny bushes, and undergrowth into the forest. Fear had always been a foreign concept to her. In Berlin, she had lived in one of the worst neighborhoods in the city, and she knew how to defend herself if she was attacked. But this was different. She was in the middle of nowhere and hadn't told anyone where she was going.

The car and the motorcycles stopped, and car doors opened. Voices. Meike ventured a look back, saw bandannas, gold chains, black leather, beards, tattoos. Was the fortress the headquarters of a motorcycle gang? A dog barked but then fell silent. She heard crackling sounds in the under-brush. They were sending one of those attack dogs after her! Meike ran as fast as she could, hoping she could make it to her car before the animal caught up with her. She didn't doubt for a second that on this gigantic property there were a thousand ways to make uninvited guests disappear without a trace. Images of cesspools, vats of acid, and concrete blocks flashed through her mind. The gang would probably break up her Mini in no time and hide it in their junkyard or run it through the compactor with her body in the trunk. Then she caught sight of something red among the trees. Meike felt as if her heart might jump out of her chest at any moment. She had a stitch in her side and could hardly get any air, and yet she managed to pull out the car keys and press the remote door lock. At that instant, the dog appeared in her path. The black muscle-bound creature came rushing toward her with its teeth bared. She saw snow-white teeth in a wide-open dark red maw and heard loud panting.

"Down!" yelled a man's voice, and Meike obeyed without thinking. In the next second, a deafening gunshot thundered. The dog, which had already launched itself forward, seemed to pause in midair. Then its body crashed with a thud against the fender of the red Mini.

"I saw Hanna last night at the after-show party." The director of Herzmann Productions was a tall, lanky man in his late forties. He had a shaved head and sported a goatee, even though he was getting a bit old for that. He peered at Pia with bloodshot little rabbit eyes through the thick lenses of black horn-rimmed glasses. No doubt he hadn't gotten much sleep the night before.

"When was that?"

"Around eleven." Jan Niemöller, dressed in black from head to foot, shrugged. "Maybe ten past. After that, I left the party. I can't say how long she stayed."

"Until shortly before midnight," said Irina Zydek, Hanna Herzmann's assistant. "Before the thunderstorm."

"Did she say whether she planned to go any-where else?" Pia asked.

"No." Niemöller shook his head. "She never

did. She always kept her private life confidential."

"You talk about her as if she were dead," Irina Zydek said indignantly, snorting. "Hanna isn't secretive—she just doesn't tell you everything."

Niemöller was insulted and didn't reply. Obviously, there was no love lost between the two.

"Ms. Herzmann had no papers on her, no cell phone, and no handbag when she was found," Pia said. "We traced the license plate to her company. Where does she live?"

"In Langenhain, which is part of Hofheim," replied the assistant. "Rotkehlchenweg Fourteen."

"What can you tell us about her personal life?"

"A few months ago, Hanna . . . I mean, she and her husband separated," said Jan Niemöller.

Pia noticed his hesitation.

"*She* separated from her husband—or *they* separated from each other?" she asked.

"Hanna separated from Vinzenz," Irina said firmly.

"You seem to know a lot about your boss," said Pia.

"Yes, I do. I've been Hanna's assistant for more than fifteen years, and she has few secrets from me." Irina Zydek smiled bravely, but her eyes had filled with tears.

"Do you have the address and telephone number of Mr. Herzmann?"

"Kornbichler," Irina corrected her. "Vinzenz

Kornbichler. Hanna didn't take his name when they married; she kept her own. I'm sorry, but I only have his cell number. Just a moment. I'll look it up."

As Irina searched on her tablet for the number, Pia looked around the big conference room. Hanna Herzmann was omnipresent. Radiantly beautiful and self-confident, she smiled from at least a dozen photos hanging on the snow-white walls. What would it feel like to have your own face always looking at you? Famous, successful individuals often had some kind of character flaw. Was Hanna Herzmann's vanity?

Pia looked at all the framed posters and photos and thought of the cruelly beaten face of this woman she had seen so often on TV. Who could have done that to her?

Half an hour ago, the police had received word from the hospital that Hanna Herzmann had suffered critical internal injuries, which made an emergency operation necessary. Details would follow later after an extensive forensic examination was made.

The wanton brutality of the perp gave rise to the suspicion that powerful emotions must have been involved: hate, rage, disappointment. And only someone who either knew the victim personally or had perhaps had some sort of relationship with her would have harbored such feelings.

"Have there been any problems or changes

recently? Trouble with someone? Threats?" asked Bodenstein, who had remained in the background until now.

By now, Hanna's assistant and the manager of the firm had recovered from their initial shock and horror upon hearing the bad news. For a while, it was silent in the big room. Through the half-open window came muted street noise, and a commuter train rushed past.

"When anyone is as successful as Hanna, there are always people who envy her," Niemöller said evasively. "It happens all the time."

"But to beat up someone, to rape her and then lock her naked in the trunk of her car, that doesn't happen all the time," replied Bodenstein mercilessly.

Jan Niemöller and Irina Zydek exchanged a quick glance.

"About three weeks ago, Hanna fired our longtime producer," Irina conceded at last. "But Norman would never do anything that terrible. He wouldn't hurt a fly. Besides . . . he's not into women."

It always astounded Pia to hear what incredibly erroneous assessments people could make with regard to their fellow human beings. Even the most placid individual could turn to violence or even to murder if he got into a situation that seemed to have no way out, putting him into an emotional state of emergency that he could not control. Often alcohol played a role, and a man who wouldn't hurt a fly could then emerge as a brutal killer who lost all inhibitions in an excess of violence.

"According to statistics, ice-cold professionals commit the fewest crimes of violence," Pia told them. "In most cases, the perpetrators come from the victim's immediate circle of friends and acquaintances. What's the full name of the man Ms. Herzmann fired? And where can we find him?"

Irina Zydek reluctantly recited a name and address in Bockenheim.

"I recall seeing Ms. Herzmann's name recently in the headlines," Bodenstein said. "Wasn't there something about guests on her show who felt poorly treated?"

"Things like that happen occasionally," said the manager, trying to play down the controversy. "People talk on camera about all sorts of things and don't notice till later what they blabbed about. Then they complain. That's how it goes."

He seemed very annoyed by the fact that Bodenstein wasn't sitting at the table but instead was prowling about the room.

"In this case, I believe it was something more than just a complaint," Bodenstein insisted, now standing by the window. "Ms. Herzmann apparently rectified the whole matter on one of her shows."

"Yes, that's right." Jan Niemöller squirmed uncomfortably on his chair, his prominent Adam's apple twitching up and down.

"We'd like to have the names and addresses of every person who has ever lodged a complaint." Bodenstein pulled out a business card and placed it in front of Niemöller. "It would be good if that could be done ASAP."

"Unfortunately, it's a rather long list," the manager admitted. "We have—"

Irina Zydek interrupted him. "Oh God! I have to call Meike. She has no idea what's happened."

"Who's Meike?" Bodenstein asked.

"Hanna's daughter." The assistant grabbed her cell and pressed a button. "She's working with us during her summer vacation as a production assistant. When Hanna didn't show up this morning at the editorial meeting and couldn't be reached on her cell, Meike drove over to her mother's place. She should have checked back in by now."

"When will Papa finally get here?" asked Louisa for at least the tenth time. Each question struck Emma like a knife in her heart.

"At two o'clock. In five minutes."

The little girl had been kneeling on the wide windowsill in the kitchen ever since Emma had picked her up an hour earlier than normal from day care. She was holding her favorite stuffed animal as she kept her gaze on the street below. She was fidgeting with impatience and seemed anxious to get away. This hurt Emma more than the knowledge of Florian's infidelity.

Louisa had always been a daddy's girl, although Florian wasn't home much and had only seldom looked after his daughter. When he *was* home, the two were inseparable, and Emma felt shut out. Now and then she even got jealous of this almost symbiotic connection between father and daughter, which made her feel superfluous.

"There! I see Papa's car!" Louisa shouted, climbing down from the windowsill. She grabbed her little bag, ran to the front door of the apartment, and hopped excitedly from one foot to the other. Her cheeks were glowing, and when Florian came up the stairs a couple of minutes later, she tore open the front door and flew into his arms, shouting with joy.

"Papa, Papa! Are we going to the zoo? Are we going right now?"

"If you like, sweetie." Smiling, he rubbed his cheek on hers, and she threw her little arms around his neck.

"Hello," Emma said to her husband.

"Hello," he replied, avoiding her glance.

"Here's Louisa's bag," she said. "I packed a few clothes, a pair of pajamas, and a spare pair of shoes. And two diapers. Sometimes she needs them at night. . . ."

The lump in her throat threatened to stifle her voice. What an awful situation. Was this whole process going to repeat itself every two weeks— this cool, businesslike handover? Should she ask Florian to move back in, and simply ignore his unfaithfulness? But what if he didn't agree? Maybe he was glad to have escaped from her.

"Are you serious about the separation?" she asked in a hoarse voice.

"You threw me out of the house," he reminded her, still without meeting her gaze. He was a stranger, someone she no longer trusted. And that made it even worse to surrender her child to him.

"You still owe me an explanation."

Not a word from Florian, no justification, no apology.

"Let's talk about it next week," he said evasively, as usual.

Louisa was wriggling impatiently in Florian's arms. "Come on, Papa," she urged him, oblivious to the cruel effect her words had on her mother. "I want to go now."

Emma crossed her arms, fighting so hard against the rising tears that she almost forgot to breathe.

"Please take good care of her." Only a whisper issued from her lips.

"I've always taken good care of her."

"When you were around." She couldn't help the bitter tone in her voice. This reproach had been smoldering inside her for too long.

Both Florian and his parents spoiled Louisa, which meant that she was the only one who set rules and boundaries for the child. And for that reason, she was not particularly popular with Louisa. "You were never more than a weekend father. You've always left me to deal with the everyday problems. Now you shower her with everything she doesn't get from me for peda-gogical reasons. It's really unfair."

Finally, he looked at her, but he said nothing.

"Where are you taking her?"

She had a right to know; she'd learned that from the woman at the child-protection agency and a family law attorney with whom she'd spoken at length on the phone over the past week. In order to deny a child's parent the right to see her, there had to be serious grounds, such as alcohol or drug abuse. The woman from the agency had explained to Emma that for young children, spending the night away from home was often not permitted, but that was left to her discretion.

For a long time, she'd pondered whether to insist that Florian bring Louisa back in the evening, but she'd finally decided not to. For days, Louisa had been looking forward to the weekend with her papa, and the last thing Emma wanted was to make her daughter a victim of selfish parental power plays.

"I have an apartment in Sossenheim," Florian

said coolly. "A basement in-law apartment. Only two rooms, plus kitchen and bath, but it's probably sufficient."

"And where will Louisa sleep? Do you want to take her travel cot?"

"She'll sleep with me." He put the child down and grabbed the bag that Emma had packed. "That's what she did almost every night when I lived here."

That was true. Night after night, Louisa had appeared in their bedroom, and Florian had always let her sleep next to him, although Emma had protested and said that the child had to get used to her own bed. In the morning, when she got up, the two would stay in bed, snuggling, tickling, and romping with each other. They would no doubt do the same thing tomorrow morning. With one difference: Emma wouldn't be there. And suddenly, a word flashed through her head, an ugly, nasty word, which the woman at the agency had mentioned when she listed the reasons why a parent might have visitation rights revoked.

"Have you ever considered what an impression that might give?" Emma heard herself saying. "A grown man and a little girl alone in an apartment? In the same bed?"

She noticed Florian's jaw muscles tighten and his eyes widen. For a moment, they stared at each other in silence.

"You're sick," he said then, full of contempt.

The front door opened downstairs.

"Florian?" The voice of Emma's mother-in-law came from the entry hall.

Louisa reached for her father's hand.

"I have to go say hi to Grandma and Grandpa." She pulled Florian toward the door.

Emma squatted down and stroked her daughter's cheek, but Louisa no longer had eyes for her mother.

"Have fun," Emma whispered.

She couldn't hold back the tears a second longer. She left her husband and daughter standing there and fled to the kitchen. But she couldn't resist the desire to watch them go. She stood at the kitchen window and saw Florian buckle Louisa into her child seat in the backseat of the car. His father stood on the steps to the front door; his mother had gone with him to the car and, with a smile, handed him Louisa's bag. What had he told them? Certainly not the truth.

Then Florian got in the car and drove off. Through a veil of tears, Emma saw her in-laws waving good-bye. Then she pressed her fist to her mouth and began to sob.

I've lost my husband, she thought. And now I'm also losing my child.

Christian Kröger and his team were already waiting in front of the house when Pia and Bodenstein arrived at Rotkehlchenweg.

"What are you doing here?" Kröger asked in surprise. "Is she dead?"

"Whom were you expecting?" Bodenstein asked.

"Well, somebody from the Thirteenth," he replied.

Their colleagues from K-13 were in charge of sex crimes, but two of them were on vacation and the third wasn't particularly upset to hear that K-11 had taken over the case.

"I'm afraid you're just going to have to put up with us," Bodenstein said.

Irina Zydek had given them a house key after they had tried in vain to reach Meike Herzmann. The house, which a real estate agent had extolled as an "entrepreneur's villa," stood at the end of a cul-de-sac on property adjoining the woods, and it had certainly seen better days. The roof was covered with mossy lichen, the white trim had greenish spots, and the flagstones up to the house and the travertine steps fairly screamed for a thorough steam cleaning.

"The first thing I would do is cut down the fir trees," Pia said. "They're blocking all the light."

"I could never understand why people would plant fir trees in the front yard," Bodenstein agreed. "Especially not when they live right next to the forest."

He stuck the key in the front door lock.

"Stop! Get away from the door!" Kröger roared behind him in a voice filled with panic.

Bodenstein let go of the key as if he'd burned himself, while Pia backed up in shock and instinctively grabbed for her weapon. Had Kröger seen some wires that were part of an ignition mechanism or a bomb? Or was a sniper lurking in the bushes?

"What's going on?" Adrenaline was pumping through Pia's limbs.

"You need to put on overalls and booties over your shoes." Kröger brought them two sealed plastic bags with crime-scene uniforms. "We can't have you leaving your hair and skin flakes all over."

"Are you going nuts?" Bodenstein barked at his colleague from the evidence team. "You almost scared me to death, yelling like that!"

"I'm sorry," Christian Kröger said with a shrug. "I haven't been getting much sleep the past few days."

Pia holstered her weapon, took one of the packets from him, and tore it open. On the front porch, she and Bodenstein pulled on the overalls and slipped the plastic booties over their shoes.

"May we go in now?" Bodenstein asked with exaggerated courtesy.

"Knock yourself out," Kröger grumbled. "You're not the ones who'll have to deal with the bean counters in the finance department when we have to do a DNA analysis on you in the lab, just because your genetic microtraces are strewn around some crime scene."

"All right, then," said Pia, trying to mollify her colleague.

Inside, the house was much larger than it looked from the outside. Travertine, wrought iron, and dark wood dominated a large, somber entrance hall with a stairway leading up to the second floor. Pia looked around and then went over to the console table that stood to the left of the front door.

"Someone picked up the mail today and put it here," she said. "The mailman must have shoved it through the mail slot."

"Probably the daughter picked it up." Bodenstein went into the kitchen. Looking at the kitchen table, he saw dirty glasses and four empty beer bottles, and plates and silverware with remnants of food sat in the sink. In the living room, there was a rumpled blanket on the black leather couch, as if someone had taken a nap there. On the coffee table were more glasses and an ashtray with a couple of cigarette butts. A veritable DNA paradise for Kröger's people.

The floor-to-ceiling windows offered a view of the terrace and an extensive garden. The home office was across the entry hall. Compared to the rest of the house, it looked messy. They saw balled-up paper and file folders; the drawers of a wheeled file cabinet stood open, and the contents of a wastebasket lay strewn across the floor. Pia let her gaze wander over the room. It was only an instinct, indefinable and disquieting, but after seeing so many crime scenes, she always noticed if something was off-kilter; any disturbance had an almost physical effect on her. In this instance, there were no obvious signs of a struggle or blood traces.

"Somebody was here," she said to Bodenstein. "A stranger. He rifled through the desk and papers."

Her boss didn't ask how she knew. They had worked together a long time, and often enough Pia had been correct with her intuitive hunches.

They entered the room. Here, too, the walls were plastered with framed photos of the owner, but there were also family photos in between. Various men, but always the same girl, from childhood to young woman.

"That must be Meike." Pia looked at the photos. A happy, laughing child who had metamorphosed into a fat, pimply teenager with a sullen expression. She didn't look happy in the shadow of her radiantly beautiful mother. "And there seem to have been a few men in her life."

"Mr. Kornbichler, in any case," said Bodenstein, leaning down to take a look under the desk. "I don't see any laptop or PC."

"Maybe she keeps it in the bedroom. Or it was stolen."

Pia stepped up next to her boss and inspected the papers strewn about. Notes, research materials, contracts, drafts for a presentation—all hand-written.

"I wonder why Hanna Herzmann would feel the need to meet men for anonymous sex at a rest stop on the autobahn," Pia said, thinking out loud. "She doesn't seem to have any trouble finding a man."

"That's not the point," Bodenstein countered. "People who do that aren't doing it to find a partner. They do it for kicks. The thrill. The danger. Who knows, maybe that's exactly what she was looking for."

Pia's cell rang. It was the doctor who had examined Hanna Herzmann before the operation. Pia put the phone on speaker, and she and Bodenstein listened to the report with growing revulsion. Hanna had not only been raped, which would have been bad enough. No, the perp had abused her vaginally and rectally with some object, which had caused serious internal injuries. In addition, she had been beaten and kicked with extreme brutality, resulting in fractures of her facial bones, ribs, breastbone, and upper right arm. The woman had been put through hell and it was sheer luck that she'd survived.

"Sounds like pure hatred," said Pia when she ended the call. "I'm positive that something personal was involved."

"I don't know." Bodenstein wanted to stick his hands in his pockets but found that the overalls had no slits to allow him to do it. "Abuse with an object is not personal."

"Maybe the perp wasn't physically able to rape her," Pia surmised. "Or else he was gay."

"Like Norman, her former employee."

"Precisely."

"We're going to have to talk to him right away."

They continued their tour of the house but found nothing upstairs that would indicate that a stranger had gone up there, too. In the bedroom, the bed was untouched and clothes were scattered around the room; in the bathroom, there was also nothing unusual. The other rooms seemed unused. In the basement, there was a sauna, a furnace room, a housekeeping room, and an indoor swimming pool. Another room held a deep freeze and a shelving unit full of cartons. Bodenstein and Pia returned to the main floor.

"What's going on here?" In the open doorway stood a young dark-haired woman, who was giving them a scandalized look. "What is this? What are you doing here?"

Bodenstein and Pia pushed back their hoods.

"Who are you?" asked Pia, although she'd recognized the woman's face at once. Hanna Herzmann's daughter had developed from a defiant adolescent in the photos in her mother's office into a young woman. She looked as though

268

she'd been crying. The smeared eyeliner had left black flecks on her cheeks. Had she already heard the news?

"No, who are *you?*" countered Meike Herzmann in an imperious manner. "Can you explain what's going on here?"

She didn't look like her mother. With those gray eyes and ash-blond hair, she seemed colorless, and her facial features didn't really go together: her chin was too pointed, her nose too long, her eyebrows too heavy. Only her mouth was remarkable, with the very full lips and perfect snow-white teeth, undoubtedly the result of years of martyrdom to braces.

"I'm Pia Kirchhoff from Kripo in Hofheim. This is my boss, Chief Detective Inspector Bodenstein. And you are Meike Herzmann, right?"

The young woman nodded, grimaced, and scratched her upper arm. Her arms, hardly more substantial than those of a twelve-year-old, were extremely flushed and full of pustules; she probably suffered from neurodermatitis.

"Do you live here?"

"No. I'm only here for the summer." As she spoke, her eyes followed the officers of the evidence team, who were walking around inside the house. "So, what's going on here?"

"Something has happened to your mother," Pia began.

"Oh yeah?" Meike Herzmann looked at her. "Is she dead?"

For a moment, Pia was shocked at the unsympathetic, indifferent coldness with which she had uttered this brief query so spontaneously.

"No, she's not dead," Bodenstein said, taking over. "She was attacked and raped."

"It was bound to happen." The young woman's expression was as hard as granite, and she snorted contemptuously. "The way my mother has been running around with men her whole life, it doesn't surprise me at all."

Leonie Verges looked at her watch, annoyed. She'd been waiting half an hour now for Hanna Herzmann. Couldn't she at least have sent a text saying that she'd be late? They'd been working together toward this day for almost two weeks now; Leonie had been for months, if not years.

When Leonie had first met her patient Michaela, eleven years ago in the psychiatric clinic in Eltville, she'd had no idea what a huge challenge this woman would turn out to be. Soon after Leonie finished her studies, she began working with traumatized individuals, but she had never encountered anyone with such unusual symptoms before. Michaela had spent a large part of her life in psychiatric clinics, but the vague diagnoses ranged from schizophrenia to paranoid personality disorder, autoaggressive character

270

neurosis, schizoaffective disorders, and even autism. For decades, the woman was treated with the strongest psychopharmaceuticals without anyone ever being able to determine the actual cause of her abnormal behavior or what would trigger an episode.

In countless conversations, Leonie had finally learned in fragments what had happened to Michaela. It had been a tough test of her patience, because the woman seemed to have no complete or coherent memory of her past. On some days, a totally different person seemed to be sitting across from her, someone who behaved differently and spoke differently, no longer knowing what she had talked about in the last therapy session. More than once, Leonie was about to discontinue the therapy and give up, but then she had finally understood what was really going on with her complicated patient: Michaela's ego consisted of many different personalities that existed independently of one another. When one personality took control of her consciousness, the others were consigned to the background and had no knowledge of any of the others.

Michaela herself had been completely shocked at Leonie's diagnosis and had reacted defensively. But there was no doubt. According to the classification system of the American Psychiatric Association, the DSM-IV, she had symptoms of the most severe form of dissociation. Michaela suffered from a multiple personality disorder, which was also called dissociative identity disorder.

It had taken two years for Leonie to discover what was wrong with Michaela, and by then things had become very difficult, because her patient initially didn't want to accept that the lengthy blackout periods she couldn't remember had been experienced by other parts of her ego. Leonie soon realized that the woman must have had horrible experiences that led to this extreme dissociation of her personality. As a matter of fact, the picture that eventually emerged from dozens of memory fragments was so cruel and terrifying that Leonie had often been tempted to doubt the truth of the story. How could any human being experience something like that and survive? But Michaela had survived, and she did it by splitting off from these events in early childhood, or by dissociating from them. In this manner, children in particular were able to deal with traumatic occurrences such as war, murder, serious accidents, and disasters.

After more than ten years, Michaela was still not cured, but she knew what was wrong with her, what a "switch" (from one identity to another) could trigger, and she was able to cope with it. She had learned to accept the other personalities. For years, she had lived a completely normal life. Until the day when the dead girl was found in the Main River.

Leonie grabbed her phone. She had to get hold of Hanna Herzmann, because Michaela couldn't sit here forever waiting for her. The decision she'd made ten days ago was courageous—but also dangerous. The decision to make the whole story public could have serious repercussions for everyone involved, but Michaela and all the others were aware of the danger.

Hanna's cell phone was still turned off, so Leonie tried her again on her landline. The phone rang five times before someone picked up.

"Herzmann."

A woman's voice, but not Hanna's.

"Er . . . is . . . er . . . could I speak with Hanna Herzmann?" Leonie stammered in surprise.

"With whom am I speaking?"

"Leonie Verges. I . . . er . . . Ms. Herzmann is one of my patients. She had an appointment at four P.M."

"My mother isn't here. Sorry."

Before Leonie could say a word, she got a busy signal. The woman, apparently Hanna's daughter, had simply hung up. Odd, and worrisome. Leonie didn't particularly like Hanna Herzmann, but now she was seriously concerned. Something must have happened. Something that was so serious that it had kept Hanna from coming to this important appointment. Because today she was supposed to meet Michaela in person for the first time.

"Ms. Herzmann?" The female cop knocked on the door of the guest bathroom. "Is everything all right?"

"Yes," replied Meike, flushing the toilet.

"We're leaving now," the officer said. "Please come down to the police station in Hofheim so that we can take your statement."

"Yes, I will."

Meike looked at her face in the mirror above the washbasin and grimaced. Blotchy skin, swollen eyelids, smeared mascara—she looked like shit. Her hands were shaking, and she still had ringing in her ears. Maybe the shot that had been fired barely fifty feet away from her had shattered her eardrum. The forest ranger had saved her life, although he'd really just wanted to give her a scare because she'd driven her car into the middle of the forest. But even worse than people driving around in the woods were people who let their dogs run around during the closed season. There was no excuse for that.

While searching for the eyeliner in her purse, Meike fished out the fateful message that had come in the mail today. Should she give it to the police? No, better not. Hanna had absolutely no sense of perspective when it came to research for her show, and she would tear Meike's head off if she told the cops anything about a project that was still secret. Plus, if it had anything to do with that motorcycle gang, the police would be the worst place to take it.

Meike gave up trying to redo her makeup. She was shaking even harder, so she ran cold water over her wrists.

She had escaped the bikers by simply driving away. The forest ranger might have noticed her license plate number, but he would hardly give it to those biker types. On the way back, she'd howled in fury as she drove straight to Langenhain to confront her mother. But here she'd found the cops in the house, claiming that Hanna had been attacked and raped, and asking stupid questions.

Meike was aware that her indifferent reaction must have seemed odd to the two police officers. She was all too familiar with the look she had seen in their eyes: a look of disgust. People often reacted to her that way, and it was her own fault because she provoked the response with her gruff attitude.

She used to try to be polite and nice to everyone. Even when she was feeling totally different inside, she had smiled and lied. In her fat phase, the shrinks had explained to her that her excessive weight was simply because she gobbled up everything in sight. That's when she started saying exactly what she thought. At first, she was convinced that it would help her to be honest and upright, but over time she had begun to feel a malicious glee at antagonizing people, even though it made her highly unpopular. And she wasn't shocked by what the cops had just told her. On the contrary, it merely exacerbated her anger toward Hanna. Why did her mother have to get involved with those sorts of people? All those antisocial individuals, those damaged psychos and criminals? Anyone who ventures into danger will die from it. That was one of the stupid proverbs that her father kept tossing around, but unfortunately, it had a core of truth.

When the police asked her whether Hanna had any enemies or had run into trouble with anyone lately, Meike had mentioned Norman Seiler and Jan Niemöller. Last night, Jan had been waiting in his car in the parking lot and had waylaid Hanna when she came out of the TV station. Meike also gave the police the name of her current stepfather and told them that someone had recently vandalized Hanna's car.

She thought again about the message. Had Hanna found out something about a biker or done something to provoke the anger of the gang? Had she been attacked by them? Should she have mentioned this to the police?

Meike's knees were shaking so hard that she had to sit down on the toilet seat lid. The fear that she'd almost managed to suppress now flooded over her in a black wave. She felt sick to her stomach. She wrapped her arms around her upper body and bent over.

Hanna had been beaten and raped. She was found unconscious, naked, and tied up in the trunk of her car. Oh God! That couldn't be true! It simply *mustn't* be true! She wouldn't go to the hospital, ever. She didn't want to see her mother like this, so weak and sick.

But what was she going to do? She *had* to talk to someone about all this—but who? Suddenly, the tears came, streaming down her cheeks, and couldn't be stopped.

"Mama," Meike sobbed. "Oh, Mama, what am I going to do?"

Her cell buzzed incessantly in her pocket. She pulled it out. Irina. Thirteen calls, four messages. No, she definitely didn't want to talk to her. Or to her father, and she had no girlfriends she could talk to about something like this. She wiped away the tears with a piece of toilet paper, then opened her contact list, scrolling from *A* down. She stopped at one name. Of course. There was somebody she could call. Why hadn't she thought of that earlier?

The social descent of Vinzenz Kornbichler had been colossal. From the spacious villa at the edge of the forest, he had been catapulted by fate to the sofa bed in a two-room apartment on the fourteenth floor of an apartment silo in the Limes district of Schwalbach. When he opened the door, Pia understood what Hanna Herzmann must have

277

liked about the man, at least from a purely visual perspective. Vinzenz Kornbichler was in his early forties and unquestionably attractive, in a robust, boyish way: brown cocker-spaniel eyes, thick dark blond hair, an appealing, even pretty face.

"Come in." His handshake was firm, his gaze direct. "I can't invite you into the living room, I'm afraid. It's a mess, because I'm only staying here temporarily."

Bodenstein and Pia followed him into a sparsely furnished little room: a sofa bed, dresser, and small desk, a narrow mirror on the wall, behind the door a folded ironing board and a laundry rack.

"How long have you lived here?" Pia asked.

"A couple of weeks."

"Why? You and your wife have a lovely house."

Kornbichler frowned. His muscular upper arms told of countless hours in the fitness gym, while his neat clothing and carefully manicured hands revealed that he placed great value on his appearance.

"My wife has grown tired of me," he said lightly, but with a bitter undertone in his voice. "She tends to switch out her husbands every so often. She threw me out over a trifle and closed all my accounts. After six years of doing *everything* for her."

"What sort of trifle was it?" Pia wanted to know.

"Oh, it was insignificant. I just had a little something on the side, and she made a federal case out of it," he replied evasively, looking past her into the mirror. He seemed to like what he saw, because he smiled with satisfaction.

He didn't offer any further explanation for his expulsion from paradise. He didn't blame himself for the unfair treatment he'd received and seemed not to notice how suspicious he was making himself appear with each word he spoke.

"It sounds like you're rather angry," Pia said.

"Of course I'm annoyed," Vinzenz Kornbichler admitted. "I gave up my business for my wife's sake, and now here I am with no home, no money, nothing! And she doesn't even answer the phone when I call."

"Where were you last night?" Bodenstein asked him.

"Last night?" Kornbichler looked at him in surprise. "What time?"

"Between eleven o'clock and three in the morning."

Hanna Herzmann's husband frowned in thought.

"I was at a bistro in Bad Soden," he said after a moment. "From about ten-thirty on."

"Until when?"

"I'm not sure exactly. Twelve-thirty or one, I guess. Why do you want to know?"

"Are there any witnesses who could corroborate your presence there?"

"Yes, of course. I was with a couple of friends. And the staff will no doubt remember me. Has something happened?"

Pia gave him a sharp look. His innocence seemed genuine, but maybe he was just a good actor. Was it possible that he had no idea what had happened, or why they wanted to speak with him?

"What type of car do you drive?" asked Pia.

"A Porsche. A 911, 4S, convertible." Kornbichler grimaced. "Until she takes that away, too."

"And where were you before you went to Bad Soden?" Bodenstein asked the exact question that Pia had been going to ask next. Sometimes, Pia thought with a hint of amusement, she and Bodenstein were like an old married couple. It was no wonder, after conducting hundreds of interviews and interrogations together.

The question obviously made Kornbichler uncomfortable.

"I drove around the area a bit," he said, waffling. "Why is that important?"

"Your wife was attacked and raped yesterday," Pia said. "She was found this morning, seriously injured and unconscious in the trunk of her car. And her neighbor told us that you were at her house yesterday."

Markus Maria Frey had changed from his slick suit into jeans and a T-shirt. Right now, he was standing with two other fathers at the outdoor gas grill. All week, he'd been looking forward to the school celebration. Despite his tight calendar of appointments, he always made time for his children; he was the chairman of the parents' association and had played a substantial role in organizing the party. All proceeds from the sale of food and drink and any donations would go toward construction of the new school library. The line waiting at the grill seemed endless. As fast as they took meat and sausages off the grill, the food was whisked out of their hands. The citizens of Königstein were generous when it came to charitable causes, and the school parents' association had agreed to round upward the amount that was taken in.

The weather was being cooperative, and the mood was relaxed and festive.

Frey stayed at the grill until his relief arrived; then he was assigned to be a referee and assistant at the games on the athletic field—sack races, wheelbarrow races, bobbing for apples, tug-of-war. The children and their parents were having a great time, and Frey had at least as much fun just watching. How eager and focused the children were, with their red cheeks, shining eyes, and happy laughter. What could be better? They swarmed around him when the awards were handed out to the winners, but he also had consolation prizes and encouraging words for the kids who had lost. Children gave meaning to life.

The afternoon flew by. There were tears of disappointment to wipe away, adhesive bandages to apply to a skinned knee, and squabbles to settle.

"So, if you ever get bored at the state attorney's office, you're always welcome here with us at the day care," someone said behind him. Frey turned around and looked into the smiling face of Mrs. Schirrmacher, the director of the city day-care centers.

"Hello, Mrs. Schirrmacher," he said, returning her smile.

"Thank you," chirped the little girl whose braid had just been newly plaited. She ran off to play.

"The children are hanging on you like leeches."

"Yes, I know." He watched the girl go as she jumped into the tumult at the bounce house. "It makes me happy, and I find it really relaxing."

"I wanted to talk to you about our theater project," Mrs. Schirrmacher said. "I wrote you an e-mail about it. Perhaps you recall it."

Frey had a great fondness for the educator who was so involved in her job. With imagination and enthusiasm, she worked very hard on behalf of the children in her care, some of whom came from troubled families. She continually had to contend with the shrinking budget in the strained communal coffers.

"Of course I remember. I've already spoken with Mr. Wiesner from the Finkbeiner Foundation about it."

They strolled across the grounds to the tents, where there was still a line at the grill and drink stands.

"Normally, we don't support outside projects, but in this case we decided to make an exception," Frey went on. "It's a very ambitious program, and it will also benefit children from disadvantaged families. So you can count me in. Including a donation of five thousand euros."

"Oh, that's wonderful! Thank you so much." Mrs. Schirrmacher's eyes glittered with tears, and in her excitement she pressed a kiss to his cheek. "We were afraid that we'd have to give up the whole project because of lack of funding."

Markus Maria Frey smiled, a bit embarrassed. He always found it awkward to receive gratitude for such a trifle.

"Papa?" Jerome, his eldest son, came running up, out of breath, a cell phone in his hand. "It rang a couple of times already. You left it at the grill stand."

"Thanks, big guy." He took the cell and tousled his son's disheveled hair. The phone promptly rang again.

"Please excuse me for a moment," Frey said, reading the name on the display. "I have to take this."

"Yes, of course," Mrs. Schirrmacher said, and Frey moved a few paces away.

"It's just not convenient," he said into the phone. "Could I—"

He stopped speaking when he heard the tension in the caller's voice. In silence, he listened, and within seconds his anger turned to bewilderment. Despite the heat, he found himself shivering.

"Are you a hundred percent certain?" he asked in a low voice, glancing at his watch. He was standing in the shade of a huge cherry laurel, and the lovely sunny day seemed suddenly clouded by a gray veil. "I'll meet you in an hour. Find a place we can meet and let me know, okay?"

His thoughts were churning like crazy. Could a person in Germany simply vanish from the surface of the earth—for fourteen years? A burial without a body? A gravestone, flowers, and candles on an empty grave? After everything that had happened, the news of the death made him sad, but mostly relieved. The danger that had threatened everyone had seemed averted once and for all.

Frey ended the call and stared into space for a moment.

He realized what it meant, if what he'd just heard was true. It was undoubtedly the worst thing that could have happened. The nightmare was going to begin all over again.

"Good God!" Kornbichler straightened up and his eyes opened wide. "I . . . I didn't know that. How is . . . I mean . . . oh shit. I'm really sorry."

"Why were you in Langenhain? Why did you go there?" Pia asked.

"I . . . I . . ." He ran his hand through his hair, fidgeting nervously as he sat on the sofa bed. "You . . . You don't think that I raped and injured my wife, do you?"

He didn't sound outraged; he sounded shocked.

"We haven't come to any conclusions," replied Bodenstein. "Right now, you just need to answer our questions."

"Why didn't anyone call to tell me about this?" Kornbichler shook his head and looked at his smartphone. "Irina or Jan should have informed me."

"What were you looking for in your wife's house in Langenhain?" Bodenstein asked, repeating Pia's question. "And why didn't you tell us at once that you'd been there?"

"You asked about the period from eleven to three in the morning," Kornbichler countered quickly. "I had no idea what this was all about."

"So why did you think that Kripo wanted to talk to you?" Pia asked.

"Honestly, I had no clue," he said with a shrug.

Pia watched the play of emotions on his face. Vinzenz Kornbichler was clearly insulted and angry, but was he capable of the kind of brutality that Hanna Herzmann had been subjected to?

"Does your wife have any enemies?" Bodenstein asked. "Was she ever threatened in the past?"

"Yes, there was a guy who stalked her once,

quite seriously," Kornbichler said. "It was shortly before Hanna and I met. By then, he'd been convicted and sent to prison."

That sounded interesting. Kornbichler didn't know the man's name, but he promised to ask Irina Zydek about it.

"And there's a former employee, Norman Seiler. He has a gigantic grudge against Hanna," the man went on. "She fired him two weeks ago, without notice. And then there's Niemöller—he has always seemed suspicious to me. He's got a huge crush on Hanna, but she doesn't pay him any attention. And there are lots of people whose lives were exposed when they were talk-show guests—some of them are pretty mad at Hanna because of that."

Pia had been taking notes. Norman Seiler certainly had a motive that would be any police officer's dream, but unfortunately, he also had an airtight alibi. The day before yesterday, he'd flown to Berlin and had just returned this morning. All appointments he'd mentioned had been checked and confirmed. But Jan Niemöller's alibi was considerably weaker. He claimed he'd driven home after the wrap party and gone straight to bed. But Meike Herzmann had observed him sitting in his car, waiting for Hanna. His bleary-eyed appearance also contradicted his claim that he'd been sound asleep.

"One evening, I happened to drive through

Langenhain," Vinzenz Kornbichler now said. He hesitated before he went on. "It was late, shortly before midnight, and there was a vehicle I didn't recognize parked in front of the house. A black Hummer. I thought, Oh great, my successor has already moved in. Actually, I wanted to leave right away, but I . . . I couldn't resist. So I got out of my car and went into the yard. I saw not only one guy there, but two."

Pia cast a glance at Bodenstein.

"When was this?" she asked.

"Hmm . . . night before last. Wednesday night," replied Kornbichler. "I had a funny feeling. Even though Hanna threw me out, I still love her."

Pia dug deeper. "Why did you have a funny feeling?"

"One of the guys was huge, with a beard and bandanna . . . the kind of guy you wouldn't want to run into even in broad daylight. He had so many tattoos that he looked like a Smurf. Completely blue, except for his face."

"And what did you observe?" Bodenstein asked. "Were the men threatening your wife?"

"No. They just sat there talking; I think they'd had something to drink. Around twelve-thirty, the giant Smurf left, and a few minutes later Hanna got in the car with the other guy. I followed them." Kornbichler gave an embarrassed smile. "Don't think I'm a stalker, but I've been worried about Hanna. She never told me much about her research, but she often has full-blown psychopaths on her show."

"Where did they go?"

"In Diedenbergen, I saw that my tank was almost empty. I had to stop for gas on the autobahn, so I lost track of her."

"Where did you stop for gas? At the Weilbach rest stop?" Pia had the geography of the Main-Taunus region pretty well memorized.

"Yes, exactly. Around that time of night, it's the only gas station open."

She glanced at her colleague. Hanna Herzmann had been found thirty-six hours later in the trunk of her car, not five hundred yards from that very rest stop where the husband she'd thrown out had stopped for gas. Only a coincidence?

"Did you notice the license number of the black Hummer?" Bodenstein asked.

"I'm afraid not. It was such a small plate, like on a moped, and it was dark."

What Vinzenz Kornbichler was telling them could definitely be true. The glasses on the coffee table in the living room of Hanna Herzmann's house could indicate that she'd had visitors.

But the fact that Kornbichler kept driving past his ex-wife's house showed that he still had strong feelings for her. The man was feeling insulted, injured, broke, and jealous—all of it making for a highly explosive mixture. A single spark could set him off. Had the sight of Hanna getting into a car at night with a strange man been that spark?

"That was on Wednesday," she said. "What happened on Thursday?"

"I already told you." Kornbichler frowned.

"No, you didn't." Pia gave him a friendly smile. "So? What did you do at her house on Thursday?"

"Nothing. Nothing special. I just sat in the car for a while." His body language betrayed his nervousness: his hands fiddled with his smartphone, his gaze kept shifting, and he was jiggling one foot. At the beginning of the conversation he'd made a commanding, even relaxed impression, but his self-confidence was leaving him with each second that passed.

Pia took from her shoulder bag the clear plastic sleeve with the photos of Hanna Herzmann's face beaten until it was unrecognizable and held it without comment in front of Kornbichler's nose. He glanced at the picture and recoiled.

"What's this supposed to be?" He tried to sound indignant, but he couldn't pull it off.

"I propose that you accompany us, Mr. Kornbichler." Bodenstein got up.

"But why? I told you that I—" Kornbichler said, agitated.

"You are under provisional arrest," Pia said, interrupting him. Then she read Kornbichler his rights and obligations according to paragraphs 127 and 127b of the criminal code. "Since you have no permanent place of residence, you will be housed at state expense until we have checked out your alibi for Thursday night."

It was cold. She was freezing, and her body felt as heavy as lead. Somewhere in her mind, she felt a throbbing that was a distant foreboding of pain and torment. Her mouth was dry as dust, her tongue swollen so thick that she couldn't swallow. As if through cotton she heard a faint, steady beeping and buzzing.

Where was she? What had happened?

She tried to open her eyes, but she couldn't no matter how hard she tried.

Come on, she thought. Open your eyes, Hanna.

It took all her willpower to open her left eye just a sliver, but what she saw was blurry and out of focus. A gloomy twilight, blinds pulled down in front of the windows, bare white walls.

What kind of room was this?

Footsteps approached. Rubber soles squeaked.

"Ms. Herzmann?" A woman's voice. "Can you hear me?"

Hanna heard an unarticulated sound that changed to a dull groan, and it took a few seconds to realize that she had made this sound herself.

Where am I? she wanted to ask, but her lips and tongue were numb and refused to obey her.

A hint of concern crept through the thick fog

surrounding her. Something was wrong. This was no dream; this was reality.

"I'm Dr. Fuhrmann," said the woman's voice. "You're in the intensive care unit of Höchst Hospital."

Intensive care. Hospital. At least that explained the irritating beeping and buzzing. But *why* was she in the hospital?

No matter how much Hanna racked her brains, she had no memory of why she was in this condition. Just emptiness. A black hole. Total blackout. The last thing she could remember was the argument with Jan after the party. He'd suddenly appeared in front of her in the parking lot, as if he'd sprouted right out of the ground. He'd given her a real fright. He'd been extremely angry, grabbing her arm so hard that it hurt. She probably had a bruise on her upper arm today. But what was that all about?

Scraps of memory flitted through her head like bats, gathering into fleeting, fragmentary images, and then tearing apart. Meike. Vinzenz. Blue eyes. Heat. Thunder and lightning. Sweat. Why had Jan been so mad? And again those bright blue eyes with the laugh lines. But no face, no name, no memory. Rain. Puddles. Blackness. Nothing. Damn.

"Are you in pain?"

Pain? No. A dull ache and pounding that she couldn't locate—unpleasant but not unbearable.

And her head was throbbing. Maybe she'd had an accident, crashed her car. What kind of car did she drive anyway? Strangely enough, the fact that she couldn't remember her car scared her more than anything else about her condition.

"You're getting a strong sedative that will make you sleepy. . . ."

The voice of the doctor sounded like a distant echo, which blurred and dissolved into a meaningless series of syllables.

Tired. Sleep. Hanna closed her left eye and faded away.

When she woke up the next time, it was almost dark outside. She had a hard time keeping one eye open. Somewhere a lamp was on, but it cast only a pale glow over the empty room. Hanna noticed a movement next to the bed. She saw a man sitting on a chair. He wore a green smock with a green cap; his head was bowed and his hand rested on her arm, which had tubes running out of it. Her heart skipped a beat when she recognized him. Hanna closed her eye again. She hoped he hadn't noticed that she was awake. She couldn't bear for him to see her like this.

"I'm sorry," she heard him say in a voice that sounded so strange. Had he cried? On account of her? Something really bad must have happened to her.

"I'm so sorry," he said again in a whisper. "This isn't what I wanted."

• • •

Bodenstein sat at the desk in his office, thinking about Meike Herzmann. He had seldom seen such bitterness in such a young face, so much anxiety and barely suppressed rage. Obviously, she had been under enormous pressure, but that made it all the more peculiar to see the indifference with which she had reacted to the news of the attack on her mother. That wasn't normal. Vinzenz Kornbichler had displayed a similar lack of emotion. At first, the man had made an open and forthright impression, but over the course of the conversation, this impression had radically changed. He didn't have to tell them that he had already been to his wife's house on Wednesday. Admitting that had made him look suspicious. Was it unintentional? Or had he felt an urge to confess, as many perps did when their guilty conscience got the better of them?

Where had Hanna Herzmann driven with the unknown man after her husband had been forced to abandon the pursuit?

Vinzenz Kornbichler's story checked out insofar as he actually had filled up with gas on Thursday morning at 1:13 A.M. at the autobahn rest stop at Weilbach. This was corroborated by the surveillance camera at the gas station. His alibi for Thursday evening—the bistro in Bad Soden—was going to be verified today by police colleagues. The rest of what he'd told them might or might not be true.

Bodenstein read once again the preliminary report from the forensic medical examination of Hanna Herzmann. He wondered how she was doing. Had she awakened from the anesthesia and realized what had happened to her? Physically, she might recover eventually, but Bodenstein doubted that mentally she'd ever be able to forget the abuse she'd endured.

Her injuries were similar to those of the dead girl in the river. What kind of monster must this guy be? Who could be capable of such bestial brutality? For over twenty years, Bodenstein had dealt with murderers, but he'd never been able to comprehend what could bring a person to the point of killing another human being. Only when he personally ended up in a situation in which despair, humiliation, and helplessness had caused him to lose self-control and he'd attacked his own wife did he realize how rapidly a person could turn into a murderer. He had been terribly ashamed and bitterly regretted resorting to violence, but since then he understood what must be going on inside a person who committed a crime of passion. Not that he could ever excuse such behavior or accept frustration or rage as justification for extinguishing a human life. Yet it was somehow more comprehensible than the excess of violence that had been exerted on

Hanna Herzmann and the young girl whom they now called "the Mermaid."

Bodenstein heaved a sigh. He took off his reading glasses, yawned, and rubbed his sore neck. It was dark outside. Already after eleven. It had been a long day. Time to go home.

Just as he'd switched off the desk lamp and put on his jacket, the phone on his desk rang. A number with a Hofheim prefix. Before the call forwarding could send it to his cell, Bodenstein picked up the receiver and said hello.

"Good evening, this is Katharina Maisel," said a woman. "You spoke with my husband today; we're neighbors of Ms. Herzmann. I'm sorry for calling so late."

"No problem," Bodenstein replied, trying to suppress a yawn. "What can I do for you?"

"I just got home, and my husband told me about the terrible thing that happened." In Katharina Maisel's voice he heard the nervousness that gripped most people when they called the Criminal Police. "I noticed something. At first I didn't think it was anything unusual, but now . . . considering what happened . . ."

"I see." Bodenstein went back around his desk, turned on the lamp, and sat down. "Tell me. What did you see?"

Mrs. Maisel had been in her garden at around 10:00 P.M., watering her flowers. Glancing over at Hanna Herzmann's house, she saw a man she'd never seen before. He arrived on a motor scooter and had waited at the edge of the woods for a while. After about ten minutes, he noticed that she was looking at him suspiciously. Then he stuck something in the letter slot in the front door of Hanna Herzmann's house and drove off.

"That's interesting." Bodenstein had jotted down a couple of notes. "Can you describe the man? Or his motor scooter?"

"Yes, I can. He passed by me not ten yards away and even nodded politely. Hmm, he was around mid-forties, I guess. Well groomed, very thin, about five ten or so. Short hair, dark blond, already a bit gray. His eyes were the most noticeable. I've never seen such incredibly blue eyes."

"You're a very good observer," Bodenstein said. "Would you recognize the man if you saw him again?"

"Definitely," Mrs. Maisel said. "But that wasn't all. I couldn't sleep that night. It was so hot, and our son had gone out in his car alone for the first time. I was worried because of the thunderstorm. So I kept looking out the window. From our bedroom, you can look down at Ms. Herzmann's driveway. Around ten after one, she came home and drove into her garage, as usual."

In a flash, Bodenstein's fatigue was gone. He sat up straight.

"Are you positive?"

"Yes. I know Ms. Herzmann's car. She always

opens her garage with the remote and closes the door behind her right away. She didn't have to go out again. From the garage, there is direct access to the house."

"Did you actually see Ms. Herzmann?" Bodenstein asked.

"Well . . . I recognized her car. It's nothing unusual; I didn't look that closely. Fifteen minutes later, our son came home, and then I went to bed, too."

Bodenstein thanked the neighbor and said good-bye. He had no reason to question what she had seen, but her observation was a riddle for him. Previously, he and Pia had assumed that something had happened to Hanna on her way home, but now it looked as though she'd been attacked and raped in her house. Vinzenz Kornbichler was aware of his wife's routines, and he also knew that there was direct access from the house to the garage. Later, the perp must have shoved Hanna Herzmann into the trunk of her car and driven her to Weilbach. But how had he gotten away from there afterward? Were there two perps involved? Did Kornbichler have an accomplice? Or were they on the wrong track altogether? Maybe the tattooed giant Kornbichler said he'd seen had something to do with it.

Bodenstein reached for the phone and dialed Christian Kröger's cell phone. He picked up at once.

"Did you examine the garage of the Herzmann house?" Bodenstein asked after quickly summing up the statement he'd just received from the neighbor.

"No," Kröger replied after a brief pause. "Damn, why didn't I think of the garage?"

"Because we had no idea that the house might be a crime scene." Bodenstein was well aware of his colleague's perfectionism and knew how much it rankled when he happened to overlook something.

"I'm driving over there right now," Kröger said firmly. "Before that crazy woman destroys any evidence."

"Who do you mean?" Bodenstein asked, slightly annoyed.

"The daughter, of course. She's off her rocker. But at least she left me a front door key."

Bodenstein glanced at the clock. Midnight, but now he was wide awake and wouldn't be able to sleep anyway. "You know what, I'll go over there, too," he said. "Can you be there in half an hour?"

"If you bring the evidence van. Otherwise, I'll have to stop by Hofheim."

His fingers flew over the keyboard of his laptop. The thunderstorm last night had brought only a brief cooling; today it was hotter and more humid than ever. All day long, the sun had mercilessly baked the trailer, heating up the tin box. The computer, fridge, and TV kept radiating more heat, so it no longer made any difference whether it was 104 degrees or 106. Even though he was hardly moving, the sweat ran down his face, dripping from his chin to the tabletop.

Originally, he had tackled the job with the intention of filtering out only the most important facts from the confused jumble of notes, diary entries, and reports. Her suggestion to make a whole book out of it haunted him. Concentrating on work distracted him from asking himself whether he had said or done anything to anger her. She used to be dependability personified. It was so unlike her to miss an appointment without notifying him in advance. It was a mystery to him why he hadn't heard a word in more than twenty-four hours. At first, her cell was still on, but now it was off, and she wasn't answering any texts or e-mails. Everything had been fine when they parted early Thursday morning. Or had it? What had happened?

He stopped and reached for the water bottle, which almost slipped out of his hand. Condensation had loosened the label, and the contents were almost at room temperature.

He stood up and stretched. His T-shirt and shorts were soaked with sweat and he longed to cool off. For a moment he allowed himself to think about his air-conditioned office in the old days. Back then, he'd taken this luxury for granted, along with the coolness of a well-insulated house with triple-pane windows. In the past, he could never have worked in such sweltering heat. But a person could get used to anything if he had to—even extremes. To survive you didn't need twenty tailored suits or fifteen pairs of handmade shoes or thirty-seven Ralph Lauren shirts. You could cook on a single hot plate with two pots and a pan, and you didn't need a fifty-thousand-euro kitchen with granite countertops and a cooking island. All superfluous. Happiness was to be found in the scarcity of material things, because if you didn't have any possessions, you didn't have to worry about losing them.

He closed the laptop and turned off the light so as not to attract more moths and mosquitoes. Then he took an ice-cold bottle of beer from the fridge and sat outside in front of the awning on the empty beer case. The trailer park was unusually quiet. The combination of heat and alcohol seemed to have paralyzed even the most ardent partyers among his neighbors. He took a swig and gazed into the hazy night sky, in which the stars and crescent moon were only vaguely visible. A beer at the end of the day was one of the few rituals he still held on to. He used to have a beer every evening with colleagues or clients in a bar somewhere downtown, a way of relaxing before he went home. That was a long time ago.

In the past few years, there had hardly been anything that had weighed on his heart, so he had survived fairly well. But now things were different. Why hadn't he been able to maintain a professional distance? Her silence made him feel more unsure than he wanted to admit. Too much closeness was just as damaging and dangerous as false hope. Especially for an ex-con like him.

He heard engine noise approaching. A full, throaty rumble, the typical Harley sound at low rpm. He was about to receive a visitor, and he raised his head in alarm. None of the boys had ever shown up at the trailer park before. The beam of a headlight grazed his face. The machine stopped in front of the garden fence, the motor rumbling in neutral. He got up from the beer case and hesitantly walked over.

"Hey, *avvocato*," the rider greeted him without dismounting. "I've got a message from Bernd. Didn't want to tell you on the phone."

He recognized the man in the faint illumination from the streetlight that stood fifty yards away, and acknowledged his greeting with a nod.

The man handed him a folded-up envelope.

"It's urgent," he said in a low voice, and then rode off into the night.

He stood there until the sound of the motorcycle faded in the distance; then he went inside his trailer and tore open the envelope.

Monday, 7:00 P.M., it said on the note. *Prinsengracht 85. Inner city. Amsterdam.*

"Finally," he thought, taking a deep breath. He'd been waiting a long time for this contact.

Friday used to be her favorite day of the week. Michaela had always looked forward to Friday afternoon, when she could do trick riding at the stables. But she hadn't been there in two weeks. Last week, she said she had a stomachache, and it wasn't even a lie. Today she told Mama she didn't feel good. And that wasn't a lie, either. She'd started feeling bad at school, and at lunch she'd only been able to get down a bite before she threw up. Her siblings had disappeared right after lunch. Today was the start of fall vacation, which meant the start of the Indian tepee camp they'd all been looking forward to so long. In a clearing in the woods, they would put up Indian tepees and sit around the campfire in the evening, grilling hot dogs and singing songs.

Michaela got into bed, leaving the door ajar, and listened to the sounds in the house.

The telephone rang. She jumped out of bed as if she'd had an electric shock and dashed out of the room, but—too late. Mama had already picked it up downstairs.

"She's in bed . . . threw up . . . don't know what's wrong with her. . . . Aha . . . hmm . . . I see. Thanks for telling me. Yes, of course. It's

302

nonsense. Her vivid imagination sometimes baffles us. . . .Yes. Yes, thank you. Next week, I'm sure she'll be glad to come. The riding stable is all she lives for."

Michaela stood at the top of the stairs, her heart pounding like crazy. She felt dizzy with fear. That must have been Gaby, calling to ask about her. What had her mother told her? She hurried back to her room, got into bed, and pulled the covers over her head. Nothing happened. The minutes passed and turned to hours. Dusk was falling outside her window.

Now the others would be doing tricks, riding Asterix. How she wished she were there. Michaela pressed her face into her pillow and sobbed. Papa came home. She could hear him talking to Mama downstairs. Suddenly, her door opened. The light flared on and the bedcovers were torn away.

"What's this crap Gaby's been telling us?" Papa's voice sounded irate. Her mouth was dry and her heart was in her throat from fear. "Tell me! What kind of bullshit story did you make up this time?"

She swallowed hard. Why hadn't she just kept her mouth shut? Gaby had betrayed her. Maybe she was afraid of the wolves, too.

"Come with me," said Papa. She knew what was going to happen now—she'd been through it enough times before. Still she got up and followed him. Up the stairs. To the attic. He closed the door behind him, took the riding crop from one of the roof beams. She was shivering as she pulled off her clothes. Papa grabbed her by the hair, flung her down on the old sofa under the sloping roof, and began hitting her.

"You lying piece of shit!" he hissed with rage. "Go on, turn over on your back! I'll teach you to tell lies about me!"

He beat on her like crazy, the whip whistling through the air, hitting her between the legs. Tears streamed down her face, but only a faint whimper escaped her lips.

"I'll beat you to death if you ever tell anybody something like that again." Papa's face was contorted with fury.

Michaela, who only knew her father as a cheerful and loving man, had disappeared. A little bit earlier, downstairs in her bedroom, Sandra had already surfaced from the depths of her subconscious. Sandra always appeared whenever Papa got so furious and beat her. Sandra was able to stand the blows, the pain, and the hatred. Michaela wouldn't remember anything about it the next day, surprised to see the bruises and welts on her skin. But she would never again mention a word about it to anyone else. Michaela was eight years old.

Saturday, June 26, 2010

The scare the day before had evolved into a terrifying nightmare: the dark biker types, the slavering hounds, the trigger-happy ranger, the cops. Vinzenz and Jan had played some kind of role. Meike could no longer remember who or what she'd been running from, but she was panting like a racehorse after the Grand Prize at Baden-Baden when she woke up just after midnight bathed in sweat. She took a shower, then wrapped herself in a bath towel, and sat out on the small balcony. The heat in the early-morning hours was tropical, and going back to sleep was out of the question.

Since yesterday, Meike had been speculating incessantly about what her mother could have been working on and whether it had anything to do with the assault. Even Wolfgang didn't have the faintest idea. He was totally shocked when she told him what had happened to Hanna, and after she told him about her encounter with the bikers and the attack dog, he'd offered to let her stay at his house for the time being. Meike had been pleased, but she'd politely declined. She was too old to go into hiding somewhere.

She braced her feet against the balcony railing. After the cops had left yesterday, she'd searched through her mother's home office. Nothing. Her laptop had vanished without a trace, and her smartphone, too. Her eyes scanned the façade of the building across the street. Most of the apartment windows were wide open to let in some fresh air during the heat wave. No lights were visible except for in a window on the fourth floor, which displayed a bluish shimmer. A man was sitting at his desk with his PC, dressed only in underpants.

"Of course!" Meike jumped up. The PC at Hanna's office. Why hadn't she thought of it sooner? She threw on some clothes, grabbed her backpack and keys, and left the apartment. The Mini was parked a couple of blocks away because she hadn't been able to find anyplace closer last night. She could make it to Hedderichstrasse faster on foot than by going to get the car.

The hour between two and three in the morning was the quietest time of the night. She saw only a few cars. Two winos were sitting at the tram stop at the corner of Brückenstrasse and Textorstrasse and shouted to her drunkenly. Meike ignored them and kept walking fast. A city at night was always creepy, even when the streets were well lit and even potential rapists should be sound asleep. Besides, in her shoulder bag she had both pepper spray and a 500,000-volt Taser, which she had brought with her yesterday from the house in Langenhain, making sure to put in a new battery.

Vinzenz's predecessor, Marius, Hanna's husband number three, had bought it for Hanna in an excess of concern when that stalker was lying in wait everywhere, but she'd never carried it with her. Would the Taser have protected her on Thursday night before the attack if she'd had it with her? Meike's fingers closed tighter on the grip of the device when a man came walking toward her. She wouldn't hesitate one second to use it.

Fifteen minutes later, she opened the door of the office building with the passkey. The elevator was shut down at night, so she had to climb the stairs to the sixth floor.

She knew the password to Hanna's PC. Her mother never changed it; she'd used the same combination of letters and numbers for all her log-ins, even for online banking, foolishly enough. Meike sat down behind the desk, turned on the lamp, and booted up the computer. It took all the self-control she could muster not to think about her mother. Trying to assuage her guilty conscience, she told herself that she could help Hanna more here than sitting by her bed at the hospital.

Outside the windows, it was getting light. Hanna had tons of e-mails; Meike scanned the senders and scrolled down. The last e-mail her mother had read was at 4:52 P.M. Since then, 132 new messages had come in. Jeez, there was no way she could read all of them. Meike resorted to reading the subject lines. The names of the senders didn't mean anything to her.

A message from June 16 caught her attention. *Re: Our conversation,* it was titled. The sender was Leonie Verges. This name triggered a vague memory in Meike's mind. It wasn't very long ago that she'd heard it—but in what connection?

Hello, Ms. Herzmann, she read. *My patient is ready to speak with you in person, under certain conditions. Though in no way does she want to appear in public. You are familiar with the reasons for this. She requests that her husband and Dr. Kilian Rothemund be present during the conversation that will take place at my office. As we discussed, I will send Dr. Rothemund the documents. Please get in touch with him so you can examine them at his office. Yours truly, Leonie Verges.*

Meike frowned. Patient? Was her mother on the trail of some medical scandal? Dr. Kilian Rothemund . . . Kilian. K!

Was the handwritten note with the address of the biker gang from him?

Meike switched from the e-mail account to the Web and entered "Leonie Verges" in Google. On sites for Pointoo, Yasni, 123people, and jameda, she instantly found an explanation: Leonie Verges was a psychotherapist and had her practice in Liederbach. She didn't have her own Web site,

308

but Meike found her photo on the site for the Center for Psychotraumatology, along with her address and a short CV. Now Meike also remembered where she'd heard that name: Yesterday, when the cops were in the house, they had phoned the therapist and asked about Hanna.

So at least that mystery was solved. Meike searched for "Dr. Kilian Rothemund." In a few seconds, the search engine listed 5,812 hits. She eagerly clicked the first link and began to read.

"Oh shit," she muttered as she realized who—or rather, what—Dr. Kilian Rothemund was. "That's disgusting."

"The rape undoubtedly took place in the garage of her house," Bodenstein began as he opened K-11's morning meeting. "The object that Hanna Herzmann was abused with was an extension of a wooden parasol stand, and we have just received news from the lab that the blood on the wood is the same blood type as Hanna Herzmann's. In addition, there were traces of vomit, which correspond to the forensic findings."

He had hardly slept last night. He and Kröger had stayed at the house until after three, photographing and securing blood traces, shoe prints, and fingerprints in the garage. Then he drove home, hoping to get at least a couple of hours' sleep, but in vain. The chronology of the sequence of events was confusing and contradicted the first theory that they had proposed yesterday.

"The perp may have waited in the garage for Hanna," Pia said. "That points to Vinzenz Kornbichler. He must certainly know how to gain access to the house, even if he no longer has a key."

"I thought the same thing at first," Bodenstein said with a nod. "But he was at a bistro called the S-Bar in Bad Soden until about ten to one, which our colleagues checked out yesterday. Then he spent another half hour outside on the street talking with two acquaintances. No, he's definitely ruled out. But I'm wondering why Hanna Herzmann took so long to drive home."

She had left the party in Oberursel around midnight, and her car was seen at ten after one by her neighbor when she drove into the garage. Using Google Maps, Kai Ostermann had calculated the route from the industrial area An den Drei Hasen in Oberursel, where the TV studios were located, to Rotkehlchenweg in Hofheim-Langenhain: 31.4 kilometers, driving time twenty-six minutes. Even if she drove slowly because of the thunderstorm, it wouldn't have taken a whole hour to cover that distance.

"There can be a zillion reasons for that," Pia remarked. "She could have stopped at another gas station. Maybe she even took a whole different route."

"I sent colleagues to all the gas stations between

the two points." Kai looked up from his laptop. "If she took the A661, the A5, and the A66 to the Krifteler Triangle, there are only two gas stations on the autobahn: the Taunusblick rest stop and the Aral station before the turnoff to Bad Soden. If she drove through the Taunus, there were no gas stations at all that would have been open."

"Meike Herzmann said that Jan Niemöller was waiting in the parking lot for her mother and spoke with her," Bodenstein said. He'd been sitting up half the night racking his brains to figure out a possible sequence of events. "Yet he claimed that he last saw her around eleven. He was lying about that. I sent someone to pick him up at his house and bring him here."

"So the perp could have been lurking in the garage for Hanna, or else he got into her car somewhere on the way to her house," Pia said, thinking out loud. "Then he stuffed her into the trunk and drove to Weilbach. Why there? And how did he get away?"

"Maybe he had an accomplice," Cem Altunay suggested. "Or he ordered a taxi at the rest stop."

"No way," Ostermann countered. "There are surveillance cameras at the rest stop."

"What about that stalker Kornbichler mentioned? Anything new on that?" Pia asked.

"Yeah, our colleagues also checked that out yesterday." Bodenstein permitted himself a sarcastic smile. "It would have been so simple, but the man was killed in an accident last year, so it couldn't have been him."

The door of the conference room flew open. Christian Kröger stormed in and slapped a photo on the table.

"We got a hit in the AFIS database," he announced. "Fingerprints that we found both on the inside and outside of the car, as well as in the kitchen and on a glass in the house, belong to one Kilian Rothemund."

"Why is he in our system?" asked Dr. Nicola Engel, who hadn't spoken until now. She leaned over and reached for the photo to examine it more closely.

"Child molestation and possession of pornographic photos and videos," replied Christian Kröger, dropping into the empty chair between Cem and Pia. "He did three years for that."

Bodenstein frowned. Kilian Rothemund—he'd heard that name before.

"Up until his conviction in October 2001, he was a lawyer in Frankfurt," said Kai Ostermann, whose memory was computerlike. "First business law, then criminal law. The firm of Bergner Hessler Czerwenka. In those days, they represented the Frankfurt Road Kings."

"Yeah, I remember," said Bodenstein. "That was a pretty messy trial."

"And it would explain why he would abuse Hanna Herzmann with a piece of wood," said

Kathrin Fachinger. "But what would a pedophile want with a grown woman?"

For a moment, there was silence around the table. Could this suspect be their perp?

"Could I take a look at the photo?" Bodenstein asked. Nicola Engel shoved it over to him. A rather good-looking man in his mid-forties with blue eyes and a serious expression. A man who at first sight did not look like he had sick sexual tendencies. A memory stirred in Bodenstein's subconscious, urgently demanding attention. What had the photo triggered in his mind?

The telephone on the table rang, and Ostermann picked it up.

Bodenstein passed the photo on to his colleagues as he tried to marshal his thoughts.

"He's got eyes like Paul Newman," Pia remarked in passing, and she was right. All of a sudden, the puzzle pieces fell into place, and Bodenstein remembered.

His eyes were the most noticeable. I've never seen such incredibly blue eyes. That's what the neighbor, Katharina Maisel, had told him yesterday on the phone. Excitement seized him— it was the feeling he got whenever a confusion of hunches and disjointed facts suddenly revealed a red thread, a logical structure, a viable clue.

"I think we're on the right track," Bodenstein said, without noticing that he'd interrupted Ostermann in mid-sentence. "On Thursday evening around ten o'clock, Hanna Herzmann's neighbor observed a man who arrived on a motor scooter and put something in Ms. Herzmann's mail slot."

He shoved back his chair and looked around the room.

"The way she described the man, it could very well have been Kilian Rothemund."

The night had been pure hell. For the first time since Louisa was born, Emma was separated from her daughter for longer than twelve hours. She paced restlessly, did the ironing, and even cleaned out the kitchen cabinets. At last, she lay down on Louisa's bed in total exhaustion. Her brain had conjured up a steady stream of images. Florian with another woman, the way he kissed her and made love to her. That was bad enough, but even worse was the thought that Louisa might like this woman. In her mind, Emma could see Florian, the other woman, and Louisa doing puzzles and playing Memory, watching the Disney Channel and *Ice Age*, having a boisterous pillow fight, going for walks and eating ice cream, the three of them laughing and having fun while she sat alone and abandoned in her in-laws' house, torn by worry and jealousy. Emma had picked up the phone a dozen times to call Florian, but she didn't do it. What would she say? How's Louisa? Is she sleeping well? What has she been eating? Are you with another woman? Ridiculous. Impossible.

Emma had begun to count the hours until Sunday afternoon. How was she going to endure this pain, this tormenting loneliness, every other weekend?

Sobbing, she buried her face in Louisa's pillow, beating on the stuffed animals in helpless rage. Florian could simply start a new life, while she would soon be completely occupied by a newborn. And doubtless he would seize the opportunity to bind Louisa even closer to him. Eventually, her exhaustion was stronger than her worry, and she dozed off on the child's bed.

At seven o'clock, Emma woke up, muscles stiff from lying in such an uncomfortable position because the bed was much too short and something had dug into the back of her neck. She shook out the pillow and underneath found the kitchen shears that she'd been looking for recently. Why were there shears in Louisa's bed?

Emma took them into the kitchen and resolved to ask Louisa about it when she returned on Sunday. Taking a shower gave her little relief, but at least she no longer felt sticky and sweaty.

Corinna had set up a meeting for nine o'clock at her office to discuss the birthday festivities on July 2. By this time, everybody must know that Florian has moved out, she thought. Emma feared their sympathy even more than prying questions, but she decided to go anyway. Maybe it would distract her from her worry for a while. She powdered her shiny face and put on mascara, which smudged instantly. With a cotton swab, she removed the black flecks above her eyes. The pedal-operated trash can in the bathroom was overflowing. She bent down with a sigh, pulled the container out of the holder, and carried it to the kitchen to empty it into the big garbage receptacle. Suddenly, she gave a start. What was that? Under crumpled Kleenex and cotton swabs lay a lump of light brown fabric. When she pulled it out, a green glass eye rolled across the floor.

Emma recognized the fabric scraps at once as the hand puppet that was one of Louisa's favorite toys: a light brown wolf with a red fabric tongue and white canine teeth made of felt. She smoothed out the scraps on the kitchen table and shuddered, imagining her five-year-old daughter wielding the big kitchen shears. When had she done that? And more important, why? Louisa loved Wolfi more than all her other stuffed animals and hand puppets, and she had a huge number of them. Wolfi had the place of honor next to her pillow, and she often carried him around in the daytime, too. For a long time, she'd refused to go to sleep at night until Emma had put on a little show with Wolfi. Emma tried to remember when she'd last seen the puppet, but she had no luck. She sat down on a kitchen chair, rested her chin on her hand, and gazed at the scraps from the hand puppet. Something didn't mesh with Louisa's personality. Was her changed behavior in recent weeks really only a difficult phase? Did the child feel somehow neglected because her parents were too involved with themselves? Was this act of destruction a childish attempt to draw attention? If so, wouldn't she have left the scraps lying on the floor of her room, instead of hiding them somewhere nobody would find them? It was strange. And worrisome. Continuing to gloss over what was going on was no longer any use. She had to get to the bottom of what was wrong with Louisa—as soon as possible.

Leonie Verges filled one watering can after another with fresh tap water. Normally, she did this in the evening so that the water would be room temperature and somewhat stagnant by morning, because that was what the roses and hydrangeas liked best. But yesterday, she'd forgotten. When she had purchased the property on Niederhofheimer Strasse twelve years ago, it had been rather run-down, with the courtyard and barn full of old junk and trash. It had taken months to dispose of everything, build trellises, and lay out flower beds, but now the old estate had been turned into the paradise she'd imagined. Climbing roses grew along the wall in luxuriant profusion, and the pavilion in the rear of the grounds had almost disappeared under the light pink blossoms of her favorite rose, New Dawn, which had a fragrance similar to apples.

On the round garden table with the mosaic top, which she'd rescued from the junk pile and refurbished, a radio played cheerful music. Leonie hummed along with the melody as she watered the hydrangeas flourishing in the semishade in tubs and wicker baskets. Despite all her professionalism, it was often difficult to blot out the human pain with which she was confronted daily. The courtyard garden provided an excellent retreat from her work. When she was trimming rosebushes, fertilizing, repotting, and watering, she could let her thoughts roam as she relaxed and gathered new strength. After she'd watered the plants, she began snipping off the withered blooms of the geraniums.

"Ms. Verges?"

Leonie spun around in shock.

"Excuse me," said a man she'd never seen before, "we didn't mean to startle you. But you were so engrossed in your work that you must not have heard the doorbell."

"I can't hear the doorbell out here," replied Leonie, staring at her visitor suspiciously. The man was in his mid-forties, wearing a green polo shirt and jeans, and his lack of muscle tone indicated that he spent most of his time sitting at a desk. He was neither particularly attractive nor strikingly ugly, but he had a friendly, average face with an alert gaze. The woman was considerably younger. She was very thin, and her angular face seemed to consist mainly of heavily made-up eyes and bright red lips. They didn't look like Jehovah's Witnesses, who usually sent out a man and a woman together. Leonie was in no mood for visitors, and she was annoyed that she'd forgotten to close the big main gate.

"What can I do for you?" she asked, tossing the withered geranium leaves and petals into a bucket. Often customers of the bakery across the street wandered into her garden because they thought her property was a plant nursery.

"I'm Meike Herzmann," replied the young woman, "Hanna Herzmann's daughter. This is Dr. Wolfgang Matern, the program director of the TV station where my mother works, and a good friend."

"I see." Leonie's suspicion grew. How had these two gotten her name and address? Mrs. Herzmann had sworn never to mention their relationship to anyone.

"On Thursday night, my mother was attacked and raped," said Meike. "She's in the hospital."

Briefly, she described what had happened to her mother, omitting none of the ugly details. She spoke in a matter-of-face tone, with no sign of empathy. Leonie felt shivers run down her back. Her premonition that something bad must have happened to Mrs. Herzmann proved to be well founded. She listened in silence.

"That's just horrible. But what do you want from me?" she asked when Meike finished.

"We thought you might know what my mother's been working on. You wrote her an e-mail ten days ago saying that one of your patients was ready to meet my mother. And you mentioned the name Kilian Rothemund."

Leonie now turned ice-cold. At the same time, fury began boiling insider of her. Hadn't she explained strongly enough how dangerous this whole thing could be? Despite all her warnings, Mrs. Herzmann must have spoken to somebody about it and stored her e-mails in an easily accessible computer. Damn it! By doing that, she'd jeopardized everyone and might have ruined the plan they'd carefully worked out. Leonie had had a bad feeling about this from the very beginning. Hanna Herzmann was a selfish woman who craved attention, and in her arrogance she firmly believed that she was invincible. Leonie felt absolutely no sympathy for her.

"By chance, I found an address in Langensebold," Meike went on. "It's an isolated farm, presumably the headquarters of a motorcycle gang. I was there, but they let a dog loose on me."

Fear surged like an insidious poison, and Leonie started to sweat. She had to try to keep her expression under control, so she crossed her arms and pressed them to her chest.

"Have you gone to the police about this?" she asked.

The man, who hadn't spoken until now, cleared his throat.

"No, not yet," he said. "I've known Hanna for a long time; she's worked for our station for fourteen years. And I know how sensitive she is when it comes to her research. So the first thing we wanted to do was find out if the attack might have something to do with her work."

Obviously, there was some connection, but he seemed to think it was better to play dumb.

"Ms. Herzmann has been in therapy with me for a few weeks," Leonie replied with a regretful undertone in her voice. "She didn't tell me what she was working on. The e-mail referred to a former patient of mine whom Ms. Herzmann happened to know. That's all I can tell you."

Leonie felt Meike scrutinizing her with an almost hostile expression. You're lying, her eyes said, and I know it. But Leonie had no choice; she had to protect Michaela at all costs.

The man thanked her and handed her his card. She stuck it in the pocket of her gardening apron.

"Just in case you happen to think of something else that might be helpful," he said. Briefly, he put his arm around the young woman's shoulders. "Come on, Meike, let's go."

They left the courtyard, and Leonie watched them get into a car with Frankfurt plates parked in one of the five spots in front of the bakery. Then she closed the main gate, barred it, and went into the house. She had to make an urgent call—very urgent. No, it would be better not to use the phone. For a moment, she stood undecided in the hall, then she grabbed the car keys hanging on the hook next to the front door. She would drive over there. Maybe it wasn't too late for damage control.

Kai Ostermann had spent three hours ascertaining that Kilian Rothemund had absolutely no subsequent police record. After he was released from prison, he no longer seemed to exist officially. He did not receive any money from the government, nor did the government receive any from him. The cell phone number of his probation officer had been changed, and on the landline there was only an answering machine that said there was no possibility of leaving a message.

"Here it is." Pia stopped the car in front of a cubic glass building with a flat roof and a well-tended front yard. "Oranienstrasse One twelve."

They got out and crossed the street. Even before noon, the asphalt was very hot, and Pia could feel the heat through the soles of her running shoes. In front of the two-car garage stood a snow-white SUV, so someone must be home. During his research, Kai had found Rothemund's old address in Bad Soden. Bodenstein was hoping that the new owners might know what had become of the previous occupants.

Pia rang the doorbell next to the mailbox labeled with the discreet initials K.H.

"Hello?" a voice said in the intercom.

"Criminal Police. We would like to speak with you," said Pia.

"One moment."

The moment lasted a long three minutes.

"Why are they taking so long?" said Pia, blowing a strand of hair from her forehead. Some people tore the door open at once out of sheer curiosity when they rang, while others were struck by vague feelings of guilt at a visit from Kripo and tried to delay the encounter.

"Maybe they're running some compromising documents through the shredder," Bodenstein said with a grin. "Or they're hiding Grandma's body in the basement."

Pia gave her boss a surreptitious glance. This type of humor was something altogether new for him, just like his current habit of not shaving regularly and no longer wearing a tie. There was no doubt that Bodenstein had changed in the past few weeks, definitely for the better, in her opinion, because it certainly hadn't been easy to work with an eternally depressed and absentminded boss.

"Very witty." Pia was just about to ring the bell

again, when the door opened. A woman appeared in the doorway. Mid-forties, willowy, very well groomed. She was still attractive, but her looks were starting to fade. After forty, the skin took its revenge for too much sun and too little body fat.

"I was just in the shower," she said apologetically, running her hand through her damp, dark hair, which showed a few white strands.

"No problem. Fortunately, it's not raining yet." Bodenstein presented his ID and introduced himself and Pia. The woman gave him an uncertain smile.

"What can I do for you?"

"Ms. . . ." Bodenstein began.

"Hackspiel. Britta Hackspiel," she replied.

"Thank you. Ms. Hackspiel, we're looking for someone who once lived here. A man named Kilian Rothemund."

The smile on her face vanished. She crossed her arms and took a deep breath. Her whole posture signaled a defensive attitude.

"Why am I not surprised?" she said through clenched teeth. "I don't know—"

She stopped, wanting to say something, then changed her mind.

"Please come in. We don't need to let the whole neighborhood know that the police are here again."

Bodenstein and Pia entered a glassed-in anteroom. The whole house seemed to consist primarily of glass walls.

"Kilian Rothemund is my ex-husband. I divorced him when he had to go to prison. That was in 2001, and I haven't seen him since." Britta Hackspiel tried hard to maintain her composure, but inwardly she was in turmoil. Her hands revealed her distress, as she kept rubbing her upper arms. "I couldn't bear to be married to a pedophile. My children were still young back then, and I've often wondered whether that perverse swine might have molested them, as well."

Revulsion and hatred were evident in her voice. Nine years had not softened her emotions.

"What that man did to me, the children, and my parents is simply unimaginable. The disgusting reports in the media were a nightmare for all of us. I don't know if you can comprehend how humiliating and appalling it is when the husband you thought you knew suddenly turns out to be a child molester." She looked at Pia, who could see how deeply wounded the woman was. "Our friends turned away from me, and I felt like an innocent person condemned to death. I often asked myself whether it could have been my fault. I spent three years in therapy because I felt partly to blame."

The family members of convicted felons often had feelings of guilt, seeing themselves as responsible for what had happened. This was even worse if they lost their friends and neighbors. Pia could only imagine how dreadful it must feel to be suddenly branded the wife of a child molester and have to bear the shame for crimes committed by someone in the family.

"Why didn't you move away from here?" she asked.

"Where to?" Britta Hackspiel uttered an unhappy laugh. "The house wasn't paid off yet, and there was no money left. In the divorce settlement, I was awarded everything, but if my parents hadn't helped me out financially, it all would have gone down the tubes."

"Do you know where your ex-husband is living now?" Bodenstein asked.

"No. And I don't want to know, either. The court revoked all visitation rights; he isn't allowed to come near the children. If he violates these conditions, he'll be sent straight back where he belongs: in prison."

So much bitterness. A damaged woman whose wounds would never heal.

A black BMW pulled into the double garage next to the white SUV, and a large man with a sparse gray hair stepped out, along with a boy and girl.

"My husband and my children," explained Britta Hackspiel nervously. "I don't want them to know the reason for your visit."

The boy was about twelve years old, the girl about fourteen, a little beauty with big dark eyes and skin like milk and honey. Her long blond hair reached to the middle of her back, and Pia understood Britta's fears. She had a fleeting thought of Lilly.

The girl must have been a little younger than Lilly was now when Britta Hackspiel learned of her husband's perverse tendencies. Along with the terrible realization that she didn't really know her own husband, she'd had to worry about the children and endure the ostracism of society. Unfortunately, too many children were sexually abused by their own fathers. The closed microcosm of the family allowed for a cruel exertion of power, and despite all the public service campaigns, this topic was still taboo.

Pia handed Britta Hackspiel her business card.

"Please call me if you happen to think of anything else," she said. "It's very important."

The girl came up the steps. Stuck in one ear was a white iPod earbud, and over her shoulder she carried a sports bag with a hockey stick protruding from it.

"Hi, Mama."

"Hi, Chiara." Ms. Hackspiel smiled at her daughter. "How was practice?"

"Awesome," replied the girl without enthusiasm. She gave first Bodenstein, then Pia a quizzical look.

"Okay," Bodenstein said, turning to go. "Thanks so much for the information. And have a nice weekend."

"You, too. Good-bye." Ms. Hackspiel folded Pia's card into a small rectangle, first across, then lengthwise. She wasn't going to call. The card would probably wind up in the trash. And Pia could understand why.

At 4:00 P.M., the APB was issued for Kilian Rothemund.

The photo wasn't very current, of course. It was nine years old, from the police computer, but better an old photo than none at all. Additional results came in from the crime lab in Wiesbaden, lending the Hanna Herzmann case a whole new perspective. Fingerprints on one of the glasses from the coffee table in Hanna's house had been partially wiped off, but the lab had still been able to find one usable print.

"Bernhard Andreas Prinzler," said Kai Ostermann at the afternoon meeting. The whole K-11 team, including Christian Kröger, had showed up in the conference room. "A real heavy. His rap sheet is as long as a roll of toilet paper. Manslaughter, aggravated assault, illegal weapons possession, promotion of prostitution, coercion, extortion. The man has worked his way through almost the entire penal code. But his last conviction was fourteen years ago. For a long period, he was also one of the leaders of the Frankfurt Road Kings."

"The tattooed giant Kornbichler had reported seeing in the living room," said Pia. "So who was the other man Hanna Herzmann later drove away with?"

"That was Kilian Rothemund," replied Kai. "His prints are all over the house. And he didn't bother to wipe them off his glass."

"Unlike Prinzler," Bodenstein added. "Why would he wipe off the glass if he was just visiting someone?"

"It probably becomes a habit for somebody who has regular run-ins with the law," Christian Kröger suggested.

"Or maybe Prinzler intended to come back," said Cem Altunay.

"Somehow it doesn't add up." Pia shook her head. "Prinzler and Rothemund visit Hanna Herzmann, sit with her in the living room, and chat like old friends. Later, Ms. Herzmann rides away with Rothemund. That evening, he returns to her house and shoves something in the mail slot—"

"So what did he actually put in there?" asked Kathrin Fachinger, interrupting.

"We don't know yet. Meike Herzmann isn't answering her cell phone," said Pia. "She hasn't called back, has she, Kai?"

"Not here, no."

Bodenstein stood up, picked up a marking pen, and added the names Kilian Rothemund and Bernd Prinzler to the list on the whiteboard. Then he crossed out Norman Seiler and Vinzenz Kornbichler.

"What about Niemöller?" He turned around. "Who talked to him?"

"Kathrin and I did," said Cem Altunay. "He has no alibi for Thursday night. He claims he had an argument with Ms. Herzmann about a research matter. He apparently was insulted that she wouldn't tell him what she was working on. Supposedly, he drove straight home from Oberursel and got drunk in his apartment out of sheer frustration. Unfortunately, there are no witnesses to corroborate his story."

"It didn't seem to me that he was lying," Fachinger added. "To be honest, he's such a dry stick-in-the-mud. I really can't imagine him doing something like that."

Bodenstein made no comment. It was impossible to tell by looking at someone what he was capable of. Bodenstein didn't think that Jan Niemöller was the perp, either, but he hoped to get useful information from him about Hanna Herzmann's actions, especially about the research she was involved with at the moment.

"Any news from the hospital?"

"Ms. Herzmann still isn't able to be questioned," Cem put in. He and Kathrin had been to the hospital in Höchst, but Hanna hadn't come out of the anesthesia from the second operation yet, and the doctors still considered her condition to be critical.

"Rothemund must be staying somewhere in the

vicinity," Bodenstein said. "He rode a motor scooter to Langenhain."

"I've got Prinzler's address." Kai looked up from his laptop. "He lives at Peter-Böhler-Strasse One forty-three in Ginnheim. I've got a gut feeling that Rothemund could be hiding out at his former client's place, because he owes him a favor. It might interest you to know that Kilian Rothemund was Prinzler's defense attorney in several court cases. In two cases of aggravated assault, Rothemund got him acquitted due to lack of evidence."

Bodenstein nodded. That actually sounded quite promising. At any rate, they could assume that Prinzler would not let himself be taken without resistance.

"Let's go over there right now," he said, glancing at his watch. "Kai, call our colleagues in Frankfurt. I'll need backup team of at least six men. They have to be there at precisely five-thirty P.M."

Maybe they'd get lucky and the Hanna Herzmann case would be cleared up in a couple of hours so that they could get back to concentrating on the Mermaid, who still lay nameless in a freezer at the Frankfurt Institute for Forensic Medicine.

Hanna had lost all track of time. How long had she been lying here? A day? A week? What date was it? What day of the week?

It drove her crazy that she couldn't remember anything. But no matter how hard she tried, there was nothing in her head but impenetrable fog. She realized that was a specific gap in her memory, because she knew her name, her birthday, and she could recall even the smallest details, up until the argument with Jan after the wrap party.

The doctors had told her this morning, before they took her to the OR for the second time, that she had suffered a skull fracture and a severe concussion; temporary amnesia was not unusual in such cases. They had advised her not to push herself too hard. At some point, her memory would return on its own. Skull fracture. Severe concussion. Why did they have to operate a second time? Why could she hardly move?

The door opened and the dark-haired female doctor whom she'd seen several times came over to her bed.

"How are you feeling?" she asked in a friendly voice.

Dumb question. How would anyone feel lying in Intensive Care with no memory and not even a single visit from her own daughter?

"Pretty good," Hanna murmured. "What happened, actually? Why did I need an operation?"

At least she was able to articulate halfway understandably. The doctor checked the monitors behind Hanna's bed, then pulled up a chair and sat down.

"You were the victim of a crime. Someone attacked and raped you," she said with a serious expression. "This caused serious internal and external injuries. We had to remove your uterus and part of your intestine and perform a colostomy."

Hanna stared at the woman in silence. Comprehension came in shock waves. She hadn't had an accident. She'd been *raped*. That couldn't be true. Things like that happened to other people, not to her. She was the one who reported on that sort of event. Victim of a crime? No, no, no! She didn't want to be a victim, someone people would gape at and pity.

"Does . . . do the media know about this?" Hanna murmured. She could picture the headlines on the front pages of the tabloids: HANNA HERZMANN BRUTALLY RAPED. Maybe even with a photo showing her helpless and half-naked. The image made her shudder in horror.

But to Hanna's relief, the doctor shook her head.

"No, the hospital has imposed a news blackout. But the police would like to speak with you."

Of course. The police. Now she was a *victim*. A rape victim. Sullied, abused, violated. She'd had so many women on her show who'd been raped, and she'd talked to them about trauma, fear, and perpetrators, about psychotherapy and self-help groups that went on for months or even years. She had feigned sympathy and under-standing, but secretly she had despised these women. It's your own fault, she'd thought, if something like that happens. Anyone who runs around dressed like a hooker or cowers like a scared rabbit should expect to be attacked and raped. And now the same thing had supposedly happened to her? The thought was absolutely intolerable.

"Don't be too hard on yourself. If you like, you can speak with a psychologist." The doctor put her hand briefly on Hanna's arm. Looking in her eyes, Hanna saw sympathy, which was the last thing she wanted.

She closed her eyes. Just don't think about it, she told herself. The best thing would be to stop trying to remember. If she didn't remember, then maybe she could repress the fact that it had happened. As soon as possible, she needed to call her agent so that he could think up a suitable story for the press and the public. It would be impossible to hide that something had happened to her. An accident would be good. Yes, she could live with a car crash. *In the glare of the headlights, something dashed across the street in front of her, and she instinctively spun the steering wheel to the left.* Hanna twitched in shock, the situation had suddenly seemed so real. She'd been on her way home when an animal ran in front of her car. She'd managed to avoid hitting it and then . . . Loud music. The animal in the headlights. A badger or a raccoon. POLICE—PLEASE FOLLOW. The warning triangle. Flashes of memory shot like lightning through the fog in her brain, random and unwelcome. She had been raped. Who had found her? Some strangers who had seen her weak, ugly, and abused?

Hanna balled her hands into fists and fought against the rising tears. Good God, what a disgrace! How would she ever be able to live with it?

Instead of the two patrol cars, a complete SWAT unit was waiting when Bodenstein, Kröger, Altunay, and Kirchhoff pulled up to Peter-Böhler-Strasse.

"What's this all about?" Bodenstein asked the team leader in annoyance when he saw the men in their black battle uniforms. A moment later, he realized that when he called for backup Ostermann had mentioned that the target to be arrested was a Road King, so his request was forwarded by the dispatcher to the Department of Organized Crime, and the Special Assignment Unit was then notified.

"Were you guys just planning to ring the bell and march inside?" asked the SWAT team leader in a condescending tone.

"Certainly," Bodenstein replied coldly. "And that's exactly what we're going to do now. I don't want to cause a fuss and provoke the man unnecessarily. Not when he may have a pile of testosterone-boosting weapons."

The team leader gave him a scornful look. "I have no desire to sit around afterward writing up reports for hours because you provincial sheriffs have underestimated the situation," he said. "I will coordinate the action. My boys know what they have to do."

More and more passersby were taking notice, and residents were sticking their heads out of windows in curiosity or leaning over balcony railings. Pia shook her head impatiently. Her boss was once again letting his innate sense of courtesy get in the way.

"If you guys stand around discussing this much longer, the bird will have been warned and flown the coop," she put in. "And I want to go home sometime today."

"What were you expecting to—" began the SWAT team leader, but his arrogant tone of voice and his macho attitude finally got to Bodenstein.

"Just stop," Bodenstein said, interrupting the man. "We're going in now before the TV cameras show up and our target sees his house on the local *Hessenschau* news. You'll stay down here and guard the exits."

"You're not even wearing a bulletproof vest," griped the officer, who felt his honor had been insulted. "My boys and I will accompany you."

"If you insist," Bodenstein said with a shrug, and set off. "But stay back."

Building number 143 was one of many faceless gray apartment blocks from the sixties. On this warm Saturday evening, most of the residents were outdoors. People were sitting on their balconies, children were playing soccer on the lawns between the buildings, and a few youths were tinkering with a car. Just as the police approached the building, the door opened. Two young women with strollers came out, giving them suspicious looks.

"What's going on here?" one of them asked when she saw the SWAT team.

"Nothing. Move on," snapped the SWAT team leader.

Of course this had the opposite result. The two women stayed where they were, and one even pulled out her cell phone. Pia urged the officers to hurry. The whole action was attracting far too much attention.

"Prinzler," Cem read from the list of residents on the wall. "Fourth floor."

The foyer was filled with the smell of food cooking.

"Pia and I will take the elevator, you guys the stairs," Bodenstein said to Altunay and Kröger, pressing the button.

"Wouldn't you rather take the stairs?" Pia asked innocently.

She knew what her boss would say, but she couldn't help teasing him. Last summer, he had loudly declared that he was going to lose a few pounds without any stupid fitness or nutrition plans, because in the future he would simply take the stairs instead of the elevator. Since then, she'd seen him take the stairs only two or three times when there was a functioning elevator.

The elevator arrived.

"Every day I bitterly rue having taken you into my confidence regarding my fitness plans," replied Bodenstein after the elevator doors closed. "You're going to tease me till the end of my days about that thoughtlessly uttered remark. I propose we take the stairs back down."

"As usual, that is." Pia grinned knowingly.

Moments later, they stood in front of a scratched-up door adorned with a dusty wreath of plastic flowers. The mat bade a hearty welcome to visitors. Bodenstein rang the bell. Behind the thin plywood door, a radio was blasting, but there was no other sound. After a second ring, the radio was turned off. Bodenstein knocked.

Suddenly, everything happened at top speed. When the door opened slightly, the two SWAT team members stormed past Bodenstein and threw themselves against the door, which slammed against the wall. A shrill cry came from the apartment, followed by a second cry, a dull thump, and a choking cough. Like lightning, a white cat zipped between Pia's legs and into the stairwell, meowing loudly.

Pia and Bodenstein stepped into the apartment. They were met by a startling sight. A petite old lady with neatly permed white hair stood in the hallway, holding a spray can, while at her feet the SWAT team leader was curled on the light gray carpet, and the other officer was leaning on the wall. He was coughing and his eyes were running. What a mess.

"Hands up!" The old lady pointed the spray can aggressively at Bodenstein. He had never been threatened by an eighty-year-old woman with gold-framed reading glasses on the tip of her nose, but he swiftly obeyed as a precaution in view of her fierce resolve.

"Please calm down," he said. "My name is Bodenstein, from the Criminal Police in Hofheim. Please excuse the rude behavior of my colleagues."

"We're taking Grandma with us," croaked the team leader, struggling to get up. "I'm charging her with assault."

"Then I'll charge you with breaking and entering," countered the old lady quickly. "Get out of my apartment right now!"

More residents were gathering in the stairwell, rubbernecking and whispering.

"Are you all right, Elfriede?" called an old man.

"Yes, yes, everything's fine," replied the fearless senior citizen, setting the spray can of tear gas on the shelf of the wardrobe. "But after this fright, I think I need a sherry."

She gave Bodenstein a stern look.

"Come with me, young man," she said. "At least you have some manners. Not like these two louts, who almost slammed the door in my face."

Bodenstein and Pia followed her into the living room. Rustic oak furniture, floral-patterned wallpaper, a serving cart cluttered with knick-knacks, overstuffed furniture loaded down with embroidered pillows, pewter plates and steins in a cabinet. The gigantic plasma TV was a real anachronism. Hard to believe that a six-foot-seven tattooed giant frequented this apartment wearing motorcycle boots and a denim vest with a gang logo on the back.

"A small glass for you?" the old lady asked Bodenstein.

"No, but thank you very much," he replied.

"Please have a seat." She opened a glass cabinet containing a remarkable collection of various alcoholic drinks, took a glass, and poured herself a healthy shot. "So, what's the meaning of this invasion, then?"

"We're looking for Bernd Prinzler," replied Bodenstein. "Is he your son?"

"Ah, Bernd. Yes, that's my son. One of four. What's he gone and done now?" Without embarrassment, Elfriede Prinzler tossed back the sherry.

Christian Kröger appeared in the doorway.

"The apartment is empty," he said. "Also no sign that anyone else stayed there recently."

"Who were you expecting? My son? I haven't seen him in years." The old lady sat down in the easy chair that faced the television. She started to giggle.

"You must pardon the tear gas," she went on, chortling in amusement, and Pia realized that this was not the first glass of sherry she'd had today. "But there are so many ruffians running around here; that's why I always keep a spray can handy. Also when I go shopping or to visit the cemetery."

"I'm sorry about that," said Pia. "Our colleagues were a bit overzealous. We didn't mean to scare you."

"I've seen worse." Elfriede Prinzler waved it off. "You know, I'm eighty-six, and life is a bit boring now. At least today something happened, and we can talk about it for the next few weeks."

Good that she was taking it with a sense of humor. Other people would have pressed charges in this sort of situation. And justifiably.

"What do you want from Bernd anyway?" Mrs. Prinzler asked.

"We want to ask him a few questions," replied Bodenstein. "Do you know where we could find him? Do you have a phone number for him?"

Pia looked around and went to a sideboard with framed photos from earlier times. On the wall

341

were sepia photos depicting a young Elfriede Prinzler and her husband.

"No, I'm sorry, I don't." The old lady shook her head regretfully. "My other boys come to see me regularly, but Bernd, he lives his own life. That's how he's always been. Once in a while, I get a letter for him, and I forward it to a post office box in Hanau." She shrugged. "As long as I don't hear anything about him, I'm content. No news is good news."

"Is this Bernd?" Pia asked, pointing at one of the silver frames. Hulk Hogan with dark hair, standing in front of a black car; next to him a woman, two children, and a white pit bull terrier.

"Yes," Elfriede Prinzler confirmed. "Too bad the way he's tattooed, isn't it? Like a sailor, my husband always said—God rest his soul."

"How old is that picture?"

"He sent it to me last year."

"Would you mind if I borrow it?" Pia asked. "I'll send it right back next week."

"No, of course, go ahead and take it."

The white cat came back inside and jumped up on Mrs. Prinzler's lap, purring.

"Thank you." Pia took the photo out of the frame and turned it over. It was a photo post-card, the kind you could have made in Internet cafés.

Merry Christmas 2009 from Bernd, Ela, Niklas, and Felix. Take care of yourself, Mom! was written on the back. Even bikers sent Christmas cards to their mothers.

Pia examined the cancellation mark closely, and secretly rejoiced. The postcard had been stamped in Langensebold, and part of the license plate of the car was visible.

Fifteen minutes later, they left the building; a crowd had gathered out in front. Altunay called Kai Ostermann and gave him the post office box address, although the prospect of finding out anything from the postal service over the weekend was negligible.

"A pure waste of time, the whole action," Kröger grumbled on the way to the car. "What a screwup."

"Not completely," said Pia, handing him the photo postcard, which she had stuck in an evidence bag. "Maybe you can get a lead from this."

"You're a genius," Christian Kröger said as he looked at the photo. "Well, if that isn't the black Hummer that was parked in front of Hanna Herzmann's house."

Sunday, June 27, 2010

The street lay in the dim glow between two streetlights as if it were dead. At ten to four in the morning, there wasn't much going on at the Rudolph Tavern, either; all the windows were dark. Bernd had impressed on her to keep an eye out for unfamiliar cars before she went outside and opened the gate. He had offered to drive her home, but she had declined. She rode along the street at walking speed, turned left into Haingraben, and then back onto the Old Niederhofheimer at the Rudolph. Nothing conspicuous. She knew all of her neighbors' cars; the others she'd seen had the local MTK prefix on the plates. If things kept up like this, she was going to develop paranoia. Leonie stopped in front of her property, got out, and opened the small door in the gate. The motion detector reacted, the floodlight above the front door flared, bathing the courtyard in blazing bright light. She shoved the bolt aside and opened the big gate. She wasn't particularly afraid, since she'd been living alone for years, and yet for the past few days she'd had an odd, queasy feeling when it got dark. Her gut feelings seldom deceived her. If only she'd trusted her own instincts and kept Hanna Herzmann out of the whole thing, she wouldn't be having these problems now. Her resentment toward this arrogant, attention-starved woman had soared to immeasurable proportions. Because of her, they'd just had a real fight!

Leonie drove the car into the courtyard, closed the gate, and conscientiously shoved the bolt home. Inside, she went into the kitchen and got a bottle of diet Coke out of the fridge. She was so thirsty that her tongue was sticking to the roof of her mouth. She finished the half-liter bottle in no time. With one hand, she typed in a text message. *All OK—made it home.*

She slipped off her shoes and used the toilet that was actually reserved for her patients. She'd been tormented by miserable flatulence all day, but she simply hadn't been able to release it anywhere else. After she'd relieved herself, she cracked open the window and then left the bathroom. In the hall, she switched off the light and nearly jumped out of her skin. Right in front of her stood two masked figures, dark baseball caps pulled down over their faces.

"W—what are you doing here?" Leonie tried to make her voice sound firm, although her heart was pounding with fear. "How did you get in here?"

Damn! Her cell phone was lying on the kitchen table. Slowly, she backed up. Maybe she could run upstairs, lock herself in the bedroom, and shout for help out the window. Was there even a key in that door? Another step backward. Twenty-five feet to the stairs. Don't look in that direction, she thought; just run and hope to have the advantage of surprise. With a sprint, she could do it. She tensed her muscles and took off, but the bigger of the two men reacted like lightning. He grabbed her arm and yanked her roughly back. Another hand grabbed her by the neck and knocked her head so hard against the wall that she fell to her knees in a daze. First she saw stars, then everything double. A warm fluid ran down her cheek and dripped from her chin onto the floor. She thought about Hanna Herzmann, about what had happened to her. Were these men going to beat her up, too, and rape her? Leonie was shaking all over as the fear turned to naked panic, when she heard a ripping sound. The next moment, she was grabbed by the feet and dragged across the floor to the therapy room. She saw the door frame and clutched at it desperately, kicking her feet. A painful kick in the ribs took her breath away, and she let go.

"Please," she whimpered in despair. "Please don't hurt me."

Meike opened her eyes and took a couple of seconds to figure out where she was. Then she luxuriantly stretched her arms above her head. Outside the window, the birds were singing, and sunlight seeped through the shutters, sketching bright stripes on the shiny parquet floor. Last night had been a late one. She and Wolfgang had gone out to eat in Frankfurt and had drunk quite a lot. Again he had invited her to stay at his house, because he didn't like the idea of her alone in the house in Langenhain. This time, she'd accepted his invitation. She didn't mention that for a few weeks now she'd been staying at a friend's apartment in Sachsenhausen, not with Hanna. She'd loved her godfather's magnificent white villa ever since she was a kid. She used to stay here overnight quite often when her mother was away on a trip. Wolfgang's mother had been like a third grandmother to her. Meike truly loved her. Her suicide nine years ago had deeply shocked Meike. She couldn't understand why someone who lived in such a lovely house, had plenty of money, and was popular and welcomed everywhere would hang herself in the attic. Christine had suffered from severe depression, Hanna once explained. Meike could still vividly remember the funeral. It was on a beautiful sunny day in September; hundreds of people had paid their respects beside the open grave. She was fifteen at the time, and she'd been most impressed that Wolfgang cried like a child. His father had always been kind to her, too, but ever since she heard him yell at Wolfgang and insult him, she'd been afraid of him. Shortly after Christine Matern's funeral, Hanna had remarried. Georg, her new husband, was terribly jealous of Hanna's friendship with Wolfgang, so after that they'd seldom visited the villa in Oberursel.

Yesterday, Meike had spent the whole day with Wolfgang, and she had enjoyed their time together. He never treated her like a child, even back when she was a kid. All those years he'd been her friend and confidant, the only person with whom she could talk about things that she could never discuss with her father and definitely not with her mother. Wolfgang had visited her in the various psychiatric clinics, he never forgot her birthday, and he always tried to mediate between her and Hanna. Every now and then, Meike would ask herself why he didn't have a wife. When she learned about homosexuality, she wondered whether he might be gay, but there was no sign of that, either. One time, she asked her mother about him, but Hanna had merely shrugged. "Wolfgang is a loner," she'd replied, "and always has been."

Hanna. Meike's guilty conscience was triggered by the thought of her mother. She still hadn't gone to see her at the hospital. Yesterday, she'd phoned Irina, who had been there, of course. But what Irina told her only reinforced Meike's decision to postpone the visit. She shuddered and pulled the covers up to her chin. Irina had chided her for not getting in touch. She would go there eventually, but not today, because Wolfgang wanted to drive out to the Rheingau in his cool Aston Martin convertible and take her to lunch. So you'll have something else to think about, he'd said last night.

The smartphone on the nightstand buzzed. Meike reached out her hand, pulled out the charging cable, and unlocked the phone. In the past twenty-four hours, she'd received 220 anonymous calls. She never answered when anyone called with an unlisted number, and definitely not if it might be the cops. This time, she had a text waiting for her.

Hello, Ms. Herzmann. Please get in touch with me. It is very important! Yours truly, P. Kirchhoff.

Important? For whom? Not for her.

Meike deleted the text and hugged her knees to her chest. Why couldn't they leave her in peace?

The call came into the switchboard of the Regional Criminal Unit at ten after nine in the morning. The dispatcher informed Bodenstein fifty seconds later, and he, in turn, called Pia, but she was on her way to the hospital in Höchst to see Hanna Herzmann.

As Bodenstein was driving toward Hofheim, he summoned Kai, Cem, and Christian to the station and also called the state attorney's office to petition for a search warrant immediately for the home of Kilian Rothemund. Forty-five minutes after he made the calls, the whole team except for Pia had gathered in the watch room. Even after listening to the recording three times, nobody could say whether it was a female or male voice that in two brief sentences revealed what no one had known previously.

The man you're looking for lives at the trailer park on Höchster Weg in Schwanheim. And he's there now.

This was the first concrete tip since the regional

newspapers all over southern Hessen had printed the photo of Kilian Rothemund.

"Send two patrol cars to the trailer park," Bodenstein told the dispatcher. "We're leaving right away. Ostermann, if the search warrant arrives, then—"

He broke off. Yes, then what?

"I'll send it as an e-mail attachment to your iPhone, boss," Kai Ostermann said with a nod.

"Will that work?" Bodenstein asked in astonishment.

"Sure. I'll scan it in," Ostermann said with a grin. Bodenstein had no trouble using his iPhone, but modern communications technology sometimes baffled him.

"And how—"

"I know how it works," said Kröger, interrupting Bodenstein impatiently. "Come on, let's get going before this guy slips through our fingers again."

Half an hour later, they reached the trailer park on the banks of the Main River. Two patrol cars were parked in the lot in front of a low building painted yellow, which housed a restaurant with the pompous name of the Main Riviera, as well as the bathrooms for the trailer park residents. Bodenstein left his jacket in the car and rolled up his sleeves; his shirt was already sticking to his back this early in the morning. Next to the overflowing garbage cans, which gave off an unpleasant odor, empty beer cases were stacked to the roof. An open window with torn wire mesh in front of it allowed a view into a filthy, cramped kitchen. Dirty utensils and glasses covered every free surface, and Bodenstein shuddered at the thought of having to eat anything that was prepared here.

One of his uniformed colleagues had tracked down the proprietor of the Main Riviera. Bodenstein and Kröger stepped onto the terrace, which was made of concrete flagstones. A big sign announced THE GARDEN CAFÉ. In the evening, the increasing blood-alcohol level of the guests probably convinced them that the strings of lights and plastic palm trees suggested a sort of vacation ambience. But in the bright sunshine, the dilapidated, ugly state of the premises was mercilessly revealed. Places like this made Bodenstein feel deeply depressed.

At a table with a plastic tablecloth under a faded umbrella, the couple who ran the place sat peacefully having their breakfast, which seemed to consist mainly of coffee and cigarettes. The emaciated bald man was leafing through the *Bild am Sonntag* tabloid with nicotine-yellowed fingers and was not particularly pleased about a police visit early on a Sunday morning. He was wearing a pair of cook's checked trousers and a dingy yellow T-shirt. Bodenstein suspected that it had been a very long time since either article of clothing had seen the inside of a washing machine. The penetrating odor of old sweat emanating from the man merely confirmed his suspicion.

"Don't know him," the man muttered after casting an uninterested glance at the photo that Kröger held under his nose. His wife coughed and stubbed out her cigarette in an overflowing ashtray.

"Let's see it." She held out her hand. She wore gold rings on her sausage fingers, whose nails looked like red-polished talons. Too much black mascara and teased hair pulled back into a ponytail revealed a style popular in the sixties, when she was young. The Schwanheim version of Irma la Douce. She was big, voluptuous, and energetic. Obviously, she would have no problem handling drunken guests. A sickly sweet aroma of garbage wafted over the terrace. Bodenstein grimaced and held his breath for a moment.

"Do you know this man?" he asked, almost choking.

"Yeah. That's Doc," she said after studying the photo. "He lives in number forty-nine. Down that way. Green awning in front of the trailer."

The thin man gave his wife a dirty look, which she ignored.

"I don't want any trouble here." She gave Kröger back the picture. "If our tenants are in trouble with the cops, it's not my problem."

A very healthy attitude, Bodenstein thought. He thanked her and hurried to leave the Main Riviera and its proprietors, who began arguing loudly. They had to find the trailer before the bald guy could warn Kilian Rothemund by phone. He sent his colleagues to search in every direction, because there was no rhyme or reason to the space numbers in the huge area. Cem Altunay finally found the trailer with the number 49 near the far end of the grounds. The awning may have been green forty years ago, but the number was right. A couple of young people were sitting on garden chairs in front of the trailer next door and looked on curiously.

"Nobody home," yelled a young man wearing a jersey with *Deutschland* emblazoned on it.

Oh, great.

The teenagers came here only on summer weekends to party, as they said. Their trailer belonged to the uncle of the patriotic soccer fan. They didn't know their neighbor very well, but they identified him easily from the photo. Yesterday, Kilian Rothemund had had a visit from a guy on a Harley, and this morning he took off on his motor scooter. They never talked much to him, mostly just saying hello or good-bye.

"The guy doesn't have much to do with anyone here," said the young man. "He mostly just sits at his laptop inside his trailer. Once in a while, he has a visitor, usually some weird people. Over at the café, they said he used to be a lawyer, but now he works in a french fry stand. That's life, I guess."

Bodenstein ignored the last wise remark.

"What about his visitors?" he asked. "What sort of people are they? Men, women?"

"All kinds. I heard he helps people who have trouble with the authorities and stuff. Your lawyer at the trailer park, sort of."

The other teens laughed.

The nephew of the trailer owner said he would be willing to serve as a witness during the search of the trailer. Kröger had already opened it with no trouble.

"What do I have to do?" the teen asked, squeezing through the sparse hedge.

"Not a thing. Just stand at the door and watch," replied Bodenstein as they walked under the awning.

"Can I go in?"

"All right, but don't touch anything," Kröger warned him. He'd already put on his latex gloves and booties. Inside the trailer, it was stuffy, but everything was neat and clean. Kröger began opening the cupboards.

"Clothes, pots and pans, books—the usual stuff," he commented. "The bed is made. But I don't see any laptop."

He checked the few drawers and found a creased photo under a stack of underwear.

"Once a child molester, always a child molester." He handed Bodenstein the photo with a disgusted expression. It showed a pretty blond girl about five or six years old.

"That's his daughter," said Bodenstein. "She's fourteen now. But he's not allowed to see her or his son."

"Understandable." Kröger continued the search but found nothing at first glance that was either suspicious or compromising.

"I'll call my boys," he said. "We're going to have to toss this place thoroughly. Did Kai send you the search warrant?"

"Er, I don't know." Bodenstein took out his smartphone. "Where do I look?"

Kröger took the phone from him and pressed the HOME button.

"You haven't even entered a password," he reproached him. "If you lose the thing, anyone can use it to make calls."

"I always forget my passwords," Bodenstein admitted. "It gets so frustrating when I enter the wrong numbers three times in a row."

"A real tech guy, huh?" Kröger shook his head and grinned. He pressed the letter symbol next to the number 1, which showed he had a new message. "Here's the e-mail from Kai. Look, you just have to scroll down in the text and you'll find the link to the pdf."

"You do it," Bodenstein told his colleague,

reaching out his hand for his phone. "I have to call Pia."

Christian Kröger sighed.

"Wait, I'll forward the mail to me; then you can make your call. Really, Oliver, I think you need a basic course in dealing with modern communication methods."

Bodenstein secretly agreed with him. Somehow he'd missed the boat since Lorenz was out of the house. But maybe he could get some private coaching from his eight-year-old nephew without anyone finding out about it.

Kröger handed him the phone, and he tapped in Pia's number. But at the same moment, he got an incoming call. Inka! What could she want from him on a Sunday morning?

"Hello, Oliver," she said. "Tell me, are you still thinking about Rosalie?"

"Rosalie?" Bodenstein frowned. Had he missed or forgotten something? "What about her?"

"Today at noon, she has the cooking contest at the Radisson Blu," Inka reminded him. "Cosima isn't here, and we promised her we'd go."

Shit! The cooking contest had completely slipped his mind, even though he had sworn to his daughter that he'd be there. Being chosen to participate was a high honor. She would refuse to accept any excuse about professional obligations preventing him from coming, and his sister-in-law Marie-Louise would hold it against him forever.

"What time is it now?" he asked.

"Twenty to eleven."

"I actually did forget about it," Bodenstein admitted. "But of course I'll be there. Thanks for reminding me."

"No problem. Let's meet at quarter to twelve in front of the hotel, okay?"

"All right. See you soon." He ended the call and uttered a rather vulgar curse, which was rare for him. It caused Kröger to glance at him, aghast.

"I have to go. Family matter. Tell Pia to call me if something comes up."

Sheer exhaustion had made her fall asleep, and in an uncomfortable position at that. It was completely dark in the room except for a few narrow beams of light coming through the closed shutters, telling her that it was bright daylight outside. How long had she been asleep? The hope that she had only dreamed the night's events evaporated when she felt the cord restraints that cut painfully into her wrists. The duct tape that they had stuck over her mouth and wound around her body several times was tightly fastened and pulled at her hair every time she moved. But that was the least of her worries. They had bound her to a chair that stood in the middle of the therapy room, her ankles strapped to the chair legs, her hands pulled behind her back and fastened to the back of the chair. A tight plastic strap around her waist fixed her to the damned chair. The only thing she could move was her head. Although her situation was more than shitty, at least she was still alive, and she hadn't been beaten or raped. If only she weren't so thirsty and didn't have this awful pressure on her bladder.

On her desk, the phone rang. After the third ring, it broke off, and she heard her own voice. *Hello, you have reached the psychotherapeutic practice of Leonie Verges. I will be out of the office until July 12. Please leave me a message and I will call you back.*

The answering machine beeped, but nobody said anything on the tape. All she heard was hoarse breathing, almost like wheezing.

"Leonie . . ."

She twitched in shock at the sound of the voice before she realized it was coming from the machine.

"Are you thirsty, Leonie?" The voice had obviously been disguised. "You will get even thirstier. Did you know that dying of thirst is probably the most painful death there is? No? Hmm . . . The rule of thumb is: Three to four days without water and you're dead. The first symptoms begin after one to one and a half days. The urine turns quite dark, almost orange, from the lack of water, and then you stop sweating. The body sucks all the water out of the organs, which don't need it as urgently. The stomach, intestines, liver, and kidneys shrink. It's unhealthy, to be sure, but not immediately fatal. The good thing is that you no longer have to pee."

The caller laughed maliciously, and Leonie closed her eyes.

"The water is directed to the most vital organs, the heart and the brain. But at some point they begin to shrink, too. The brain no longer functions properly. You develop delusions, panic attacks, and can no longer think clearly. And then you fall into a coma. After that it's only a matter of hours until you die. Not a pretty thought, is it?"

Again the revolting laugh.

"You know, Leonie, you should have chosen the people you associate with more carefully. You have definitely picked the scum of the earth. And that's why you now have to die of thirst. Nice of you to hang a sign on your door so no one will disturb you before you fall into a coma. And if someone finds you in a few days, with any luck you'll be a very appetizing corpse. Unless a fly wanders into your house and lays its eggs in your nostrils or in your eyes. But that would be no concern of yours anymore. So long! And don't take it too hard. We all have to die sometime."

The scornful laughter echoed in Leonie's ears. There was a click and then silence. Until then, Leonie had consoled herself with the fact that she hadn't really been harmed and that somebody was bound to find her soon. But now the hopelessness of her situation dawned on her, and fear hit her like a piledriver. Her heart began to race and the sweat broke out from every pore. She desperately tried to free herself from her bonds, but they were so tight that they refused to budge even a millimeter. By sheer force of will, she quelled the rising tears. Every tear she cried would be a dangerous waste of her bodily fluids, and she was also afraid that her nose would get stopped up and she would suffocate because she couldn't breathe through her mouth.

Stay calm! she implored herself, but it was easier thought than done. She was sitting in her house, and on the door hung the sign that she had idiotically put up yesterday: ON VACATION UNTIL JULY 12. The sign and the drawn shades were a clear indication that no one was home. Her cell phone was on the kitchen table. The landline phone stood on her desk, twenty feet from her chair and thus unreachable. How long had she already been sitting here? Leonie balled her hands into fists and opened them again. They hurt like hell, as if her circulation had been blocked. She tried to look back over her shoulder at the clock hanging on the wall, but it was too dark for her to make out anything. She couldn't expect any help from outside, so she would have to help herself. Or die.

Emma was so out of it that she didn't notice the red light at the intersection with the road to

Kronberg and barely avoided crashing into the back of the car braking in front of her. She braced herself with both hands on the steering wheel and spat out a furious curse.

Ten minutes ago, Florian had called her from the emergency room at the hospital in Bad Homburg, where he had taken Louisa. They had gone to Wehrheim to the Lochmühle pony ride, and she had fallen off. They had discussed this a zillion times before. Louisa was still too little; she would have to wait a year or two for things like pony riding. But Louisa must have begged her father, and since he wanted to score points with her, he'd allowed himself to be persuaded. The light changed to green and Emma turned left toward Oberursel. She was going much faster than the speed limit, but she didn't care. Florian hadn't told her the details of what had happened to Louisa, but if he'd taken her to the ER, it couldn't be good. Emma pictured her little daughter with crushed bones and gaping wounds. The only positive thing about this fiasco was that now she could notify the child-protection agency and insist that Louisa go back home with her tonight. No more staying in some strange boardinghouse or apartment.

Twenty minutes later, she stormed into the lobby of the hospital. There was no one in the waiting room of the ER, and she rang the bell next to the milky pane in the door. Several minutes passed before somebody finally deigned to open it.

"My daughter is here," she blurted out. "I want to see her. Now. She fell off a pony and—"

"What's your name?" The pimply young pup in hospital blues was used to excitable relatives and was not easily ruffled.

"Finkbeiner. Where is my daughter?" Emma tried looking over his shoulder but saw only an empty corridor.

"Come with me," he said, and she followed him with a pounding heart into one of the examination rooms.

Louisa lay on the examination table, small and pale, with a big white bandage on her forehead, her left arm in a splint. Emma almost broke down in tears when she saw her child alive in front of her.

"Mama," the girl whispered, feebly raising one hand. Emma's heart bled at the sight.

"Oh, my darling!" She paid no attention to Florian, who stood there sheepishly, or to the doctor. Emma hugged Louisa and stroked her cheek. She was so fragile, her skin so translucent that the blood vessels were almost visible. How could Florian have allowed this delicate creature to be subjected to such danger?

"You mustn't be mad at Papa," Louisa said softly. "I wanted to go riding."

In a corner of Emma's heart, jealous rage flared

up. Unbelievable how Florian had manipulated the girl.

"Mrs. Finkbeiner?"

"What's wrong with my daughter?" Emma looked the doctor in the eye. "Did she break anything?"

"Yes, her left arm. Unfortunately, the fracture is a bit displaced, so we'll have to operate. The concussion will heal in a few days," replied the doctor, a wiry woman with a reddish blond pageboy and bright, alert eyes. "In addition . . ."

She paused.

"Yes, what?" Emma asked nervously. Wasn't this bad enough?

"I would like to speak with both of you. Nurse Jasmina will stay with Louisa. Please follow me."

Emma could hardly bear to leave her daughter alone in the big, sterile examination room, but she followed the doctor and Florian into a nearby office. The doctor sat down behind her desk and motioned toward the two chairs. Emma sat down uncomfortably next to her husband, careful not to touch him.

"It's a bit awkward for me to say this, but . . ." The doctor looked from Florian to Emma. "Your daughter has injuries that lead me suspect that she may have been . . . abused."

"Excuse me?" said Emma and Florian in unison.

"She has bruises and contusions on the inside of one thigh and injuries to her vagina."

For a moment, there was dead silence. Emma felt paralyzed with horror. Louisa abused?

"You must be out of your mind!" Florian exclaimed, jumping up. His face turned first red, then very pale. "My daughter fell off a pony and landed badly. I'm a doctor myself and I know that such injuries could be caused by a fall."

"Please calm down," said the doctor.

"I have no intention of calming down!" Florian yelled in rage. "That's an incredible accusation you're making. I don't have to stand for this!"

The doctor raised her eyebrows and leaned back.

"It's only a suspicion," she replied calmly. "We have become much more attuned to these signs. Of course these injuries could have been caused by something altogether different, but they're rather typical for sexual abuse, and they're not fresh. Maybe you ought to take some time to think this over in peace and quiet. Has your daughter seemed different lately? Has she exhibited behavioral problems that you may not have noticed before? Or has she been acting more aggressive?"

Emma instantly thought about the cut-up plush wolf and about Louisa's recent violent outburst in her in-laws' garden. She was suddenly freezing and began to tremble inside. When she'd told Florian about Louisa's odd behavior, he'd dismissed her concern by claiming that it was a normal phase of development. But was it? Her instincts had told her that something wasn't right with the child. Good God! Her hands were gripping the armrests of the chair. She didn't dare dwell on the monstrous thoughts that began flashing through her mind. What if Florian had abused his own daughter, who idolized him and trusted him? What if she herself had triggered this abuse by throwing her husband out of the house? She kept reading and hearing about such atrocities that took place behind closed doors, about fathers who raped their daughters and got them pregnant and threatened them into never telling anyone. Emma never would have believed that wives and mothers hadn't suspected a thing, but perhaps that really was possible.

She couldn't even look at the man whose child she was now carrying. Louisa's father. Her husband. He was suddenly as foreign to her as if she'd never seen him before.

Pia put down the toilet seat and sat down. With a piece of toilet paper, she wiped the cold sweat from her brow and forced herself to breathe calmly and steadily. With great difficulty, she'd managed to make it out of Hanna Herzmann's room in the intensive care unit and over to the women's rest room, where she had vomited her guts out. This past year, it had happened to her for the first time while observing the autopsy of a murder victim. Only Henning had noticed, but he hadn't mentioned it. Since then, it had kept happening; her blood pressure would drop at the sight of a victim of violence and she would feel so sick that she had to throw up.

Pia hauled herself to her feet and stood in front of the sink, peering into the mirror. A pale ghost with dark circles under her eyes stared back at her. She didn't know why after twenty years on the force she suddenly couldn't take it anymore. She'd never talked about this with anyone before, not with Christoph or with her colleagues, because she certainly didn't want Nicola Engel to send her to the psychologist. That might get her condemned to a desk job. Of course she could have avoided situations like this, invented excuses, and sent colleagues in her stead, but she very deliberately had declined to do that. If she gave in to this weakness, she might as well call it quits as a police officer.

Fifteen minutes later, she left the rest room, took the elevator to the ground floor, and walked to her car. Bodenstein had called her a couple of times on her cell. She called him back, but he didn't pick up.

When she arrived at the station, she was still feeling the effects of her visit to Hanna Herzmann. It was not the same thing to read the results of the most brutal violence in a sober forensic medical report as it was to see the consequences with her own eyes. The woman no longer looked anything like herself. Her face was swollen with bruises, her body covered with lesions, bruises, and welts. Pia shuddered when she thought about Hanna Herzmann's dull, extinguished gaze, which had met hers for a few seconds before the woman closed her eyes again.

From her own experience, Pia knew the feeling of being violated. The summer after graduation, she'd met a man on vacation who would not accept that their affair had been only a summer flirtation. He followed her to Frankfurt, stalked her, and finally attacked her in her apartment and raped her. Pia had never mentioned this episode to her ex-husband, and she kept trying to repress and forget it, but without success. No woman who had ever encountered the raging determination of a man to harm her physically would ever forget the humiliating feeling of helplessness, the endless minutes spent fearing death, and the complete loss of physical integrity and self-determination. Pia found that she could no longer stand to be in her apartment, where the rape had happened, so she had given up her law studies after two semesters and joined the police force. She had often thought about why she had made this decision at the time. She was sure that the rape had played a significant role, no matter how unconsciously. As a policewoman, she felt in a position to defend herself, and not only because of the pistol she was allowed to carry. Her self-awareness had changed, and in her training she had learned how to win a two-person fight despite physical inferiority.

She entered the office she shared with Kai and was not surprised to see him sitting at his desk, even though it was the weekend.

"The others are still in Schwanheim," he told her. "Rothemund wasn't there when they got to his trailer."

"Oh, great." Pia tossed her backpack onto one of the visitor's chairs and sat down behind her desk. Her stomach still felt queasy. "Where's the boss?"

"On his way to some secret family function. Now you're the boss."

The last thing she needed.

"By the way, there are new results back from the lab," he said. "The semen detected in Hanna Herzmann's vagina undoubtedly came from Kilian Rothemund—a positive DNA match. I sent a patrol car to Vinzenz Kornbichler's house, and he picked the photo of Rothemund out of the four mug shots I showed him. He's the man Herzmann rode away with that night."

Pia nodded. Rothemund was quickly becoming the prime suspect. Even though she wasn't surprised, it still didn't make sense to her. She pulled up the photo of Rothemund from the POLAS database and studied it carefully.

What had Hanna Herzmann done to warrant such hatred? At first glance, Rothemund looked cultivated and rather charming. What sinister motives lurked behind that handsome face and those blue eyes of his?

"You know what I've been thinking about?" Kai said, tearing her out of her reverie.

"No."

"According to the river-current calculation, our Mermaid should have reached somewhere near where the Nidda empties into the Main. The trailer park where Rothemund lives is only a mile or so upriver."

"You mean he might have something to do with the Mermaid?" Pia asked.

"It may be far-fetched," Kai admitted, "but the injuries suffered by the Mermaid and Ms. Herzmann are similar. Both were vaginally and anally penetrated; both show injuries caused by blunt trauma."

Pia's gaze shifted back to Rothemund's photo on her monitor.

"And he looks so normal. Almost charming," she said.

"Yeah. You can only see the surface—you can't see inside him."

"What's the deal with the DNA that related to the Mermaid case?" Pia asked. "Anything new?"

"No." Kai shook his head and grimaced. "And that shakes up my theory of Rothemund as the

Mermaid killer, unfortunately. The DNA was not registered in any public files, not even by Interpol."

Pia's cell rang. It was Christian Kröger. He and his team were finished with Rothemund's trailer.

"Did you find anything interesting?" Pia asked. Her stomach had recovered in the meantime and was growling audibly.

"The trailer was clinically clean. The bed freshly made, everything carefully cleaned with a chlorine cleanser. He even got rid of all the stuff in the drains. We found only a couple of smeared fingerprints on the door. The only thing that might be of interest was a strand of hair."

"A hair?"

"A long dark brown strand. It was stuck between the cushions of the corner bench. Just a moment. Don't hang up, Pia. . . ."

Pia heard Kröger talking to someone.

Hanna Herzmann had long dark hair. Had Kilian Rothemund driven her home Wednesday night? Had she been inside his trailer? But what connected the two? Did Hanna's research have something to do with the Road Kings?

"What did the owner inquiry on Bernd Prinzler's car turn up?" Pia asked Kai, as Kröger's conversation seemed to be turning into a lengthy discussion.

"Another dead end." Kai took a swig of coffee. He was a caffeine junkie, drinking jet black coffee from morning to night; it didn't even bother him if the coffee got cold. "The car may be registered to Prinzler, but at Mama's address. All we can do is hassle him for not registering the proper address on time."

Pia sighed. This case was getting complicated. Meike Herzmann hadn't checked in. The main suspect was a fugitive; the second suspect was a prime example of how easy it was in Germany to hide behind post office boxes and fake addresses. Nobody seemed to know what Hanna Herzmann had been working on, and the telecom company was taking its time supplying them with the records for Hanna's cell phone.

"I'm back." Kröger sounded irritated. "I *hate* it when state attorneys mess around in my work."

"A state attorney showed up for the search of a trailer?"

"Chief State Attorney Frey in person." Kröger snorted.

They talked briefly; then Pia got another call. She was hoping that it might be Meike Herzmann, so she took it, although she didn't recognize the number.

"Pia? It's me, Emma. Is this a good time?"

It took Pia a couple of seconds to realize who was speaking. Her old schoolmate's voice sounded shaky, almost as if she were about to cry.

"Hello, Emma," Pia said. "No, you're not interrupting anything. What's up?"

"I . . . I . . . have to talk to somebody," Emma replied. "I thought you might know what to do or know someone who could give me advice. Louisa, my daughter, had to go to the hospital. And there . . . the doctor . . . oh, I just don't know how to say this."

She sobbed.

"Louisa . . . she . . . she has injuries that might indicate that she . . . was sexually abused."

"Oh my God."

"Pia, do you think we could meet somewhere soon?"

"Yes, of course. How about right now?" Pia looked at her watch. A little before one. "Do you know the Gimbacher Hof between Kelkheim and Fischbach?"

"Yes, I do."

"I could be there in twenty minutes. Then we can have coffee and you can tell me everything. Okay?"

"Sure, that'll be fine. Thanks. See you soon."

"See you." Pia put away her phone, stood up, and slung her backpack over her shoulder. "So get this, Kai. Chief State Attorney Frey showed up during our search of Rothemund's trailer."

"I'm not surprised," replied Kai without looking up from his monitor. "Frey's the one who put Rothemund in prison back then."

"Oh, really? How come you know that?"

"I read documents." Kai raised his head and

grinned. "Besides, back then I was still in Frankfurt. That was right after I went back to work, with my peg leg. It was a high-profile case. The spectacular fall of the handsome Dr. Rothemund. The press really had a field day: Frey and Rothemund had been fellow students, and after passing the second state bar exam, they both began working at the state attorney's office, before Rothemund switched sides and became a defense attorney. Frey could have handled the whole case more discreetly, but at a press conference he really hung his old pal out to dry. I'm surprised that you never heard about it."

"At that time, I was on the housewife track, spending my free time mainly in the basement of the forensics institute," Pia recalled. "Oh well. I'm going to grab a bite to eat. Call me if anything comes up."

The heat and thirst were unbearable. Was it a hallucination, a trick that her parched brain was playing on her? Leonie had lived for years in this house; it was almost two hundred years old and had thick walls, which were better insulated than the ones of flimsy Sheetrock that people put up these days. The best part was that the house stayed warm in winter and cool in summer. Why was it so hot in here now? Sweat was running into her eyes, which burned like fire. Twice she had counted to 3,600 so that she wouldn't lose her sense of time in the dark and go crazy. She had come home at a quarter to four in the morning. Since then, she'd dozed off occasionally, but because she hadn't peed herself yet, no more than a few hours could have passed in the meantime. Although the shutters were closed, she could see that the sun was shining on the right-hand window of the therapy room, which faced the west. So it was afternoon now. Four or five o'clock. She would know exactly when the sun went down.

Her tongue felt furry and swollen in her mouth. She couldn't remember ever experiencing such awful thirst. She asked herself who could have done this to her, but the even bigger question was: Why? What had she done to deserve such a punishment? The caller had said she'd picked the wrong friends. Whom did he mean? Did it actually have something to do with Hanna Herzmann or with the case that Hanna had gotten involved in? But they weren't *friends;* they were *patients.* A huge difference.

The telephone on the desk rang, and Leonie gave a start.

"Leoniiiiie . . . Oh, you're still sitting there so nicely on your little chair."

The sound of this nasty, mocking voice banished Leonie's fear for a moment and transformed it to rage. If she could have, she would have screamed at him and told him what a sadistic, sick piece of shit he was. Even though it wouldn't have helped, she would have liked to say that to him.

"Are you nice and cozy warm, hmm? You have to be warm when you die, so I turned up the heat."

So that was the explanation for this blistering heat.

"Can you remember what I told you about the stages of dying from thirst? I have to correct myself. The higher the heat, the faster it goes. Let me set your mind at ease. You won't have to suffer more than three or four days."

A low, filthy laugh.

"And you haven't even cried. You are really being brave. You're still hoping that somebody will find you, right?"

How could he know that she hadn't cried? Could the guy see her? In this darkness? Leonie turned her head back and forth, trying to make out something like a camera, but there wasn't enough light to see much other than shadowy contours.

"Now you're looking for the camera, aren't you? I gave myself away. You know, Leonie, you really ought to die fast. But there are so damned many people in the world who pay a hell of a lot of money to watch an actual struggle against death on DVD. Yours, of course, we'll have to edit a bit. Who wants to watch an ugly cow like you sitting on a chair for twenty-four hours?" The voice was dark, soft as velvet. No discernible regional dialect. "But the end will certainly be grandiose. The cramps, the spasms . . . oh, no, I haven't seen it before. I'm really looking forward to this. And it'll be truly exciting if nobody finds you. You probably won't decay, simply dry out and turn into a mummy."

At that moment, Leonie realized that the man on the telephone was a sick psychopath, someone who got off on inflicting pain on other people. She'd dealt with such individuals a few times, back when she was still working at the locked psychiatric ward in Kiedrich. These experiences had convinced her to specialize in working with traumatized women who had been the victims of such perverse beasts.

Suddenly, there was a beep, and the voice stopped. The tape on her old-fashioned answering machine was full.

It was completely quiet except for the sound of her own breathing. Her nose was dried out, and each breath was an effort. It felt like she was in a sauna, the tiny nose hairs burning in the hot air. But she was no longer sweating. The knowledge that there was no chance she would ever get out of this room, that she would die here, in her own home, where she had always felt happy and safe, struck her with elemental force. She didn't care that this deviant bastard was watching her. With all her strength, Leonie strained against her bonds; she screamed as hard as she could under the duct tape, until her vocal cords ached and her head felt like it was going to burst. She refused to allow the fear of death to conquer her. She did not want to die!

The expansive garden café of the Gimbacher Hof was busy. At the tables and benches in the shade of enormous old trees, there was hardly a free seat to be found. The historic country inn located in the valley between Kelkheim and Fischbach was a popular daytime excursion destination, especially for families and hikers. Pia had first noticed this when she saw all the children romping boisterously in the playground. But she'd been so focused on State Attorney Frey and Kilian Rothemund that she hadn't thought much about it. Meanwhile, Emma seemed oblivious to all the commotion swirling around her. She was still in shock. And it was no wonder. For her, the situation was a disaster. Her worry about Louisa was combined with concern for her unborn child and the horrible suspicion that her husband might be a pedophile.

Pia had given Emma the phone number of an experienced therapist at the Frankfurt Girls Home, since she clearly needed professional help. Child abuse was a topic that Pia had never had to deal with professionally. Of course she had followed the scandalous cases that were always coming up in the media, but she had never felt more than a superficial sadness. To see Emma so desperate, helpless, and full of worry about the physical and mental well-being of her little daughter had moved Pia deeply. Maybe she had grown more sensitive because of Lilly. Parents had an enormous responsibility for such small creatures. Children could be protected to some degree from external dangers. But what happened when your own partner, the person you trusted most, revealed such dark and hidden depths?

After an hour, Emma had to leave to go see Louisa at the hospital. Pia watched her old school friend drive off and then walked over to her own car parked farther down the hill. It was the expression in Emma's eyes, the mixture of fear, rage, and deep hurt, that made her think of Britta Hackspiel. Kilian Rothemund was a convicted child molester. At the trial, of course, he had vehemently denied it, but the proof of his guilt had been overwhelming and decisive. The prosecution had presented photos that showed Rothemund in unambiguous poses, naked in bed with little children, as well as thousands of photos and dozens of videos of the most heinous kind on his laptop.

Now that the lab had identified the semen in Hanna Herzmann's vagina as Rothemund's, Bodenstein was firmly convinced that he was the one who had beaten and raped Hanna and stuffed her in the trunk of her car, perhaps together with Bernd Prinzler. Still, they could only speculate about the motive of the two men. Although the circumstantial evidence clearly pointed to the guilt of Rothemund, Pia harbored a slight doubt. Hanna Herzmann was a grown woman: forty-six years old, self-confident, successful, beautiful, with a very feminine figure. She embodied everything that would turn off a man disposed to pedophilia. Anger and hatred might be an explanation for the incomprehensible brutality. Rape had nothing to do with lust, but with power and domination. Still, something was bothering Pia about the case. This solution seemed too simple and obvious.

She drove straight through Kelkheim, crossed the train tracks, turned left toward the center of town, and followed the Gagernring to the main highway. There she signaled to turn right, then changed her mind and turned left to drive through Altenhain to Bad Soden. A few minutes later, she stopped in front of the house where Kilian Rothemund had once lived. The street was fairly crowded with parked cars, so Pia drove the unmarked police car up to the edge of the field and then had to walk back. When she rang the bell, Britta Hackspiel's new husband opened the door; Pia had seen him only briefly yesterday. His friendly, welcoming smile vanished at the sight of her.

"It's Sunday afternoon," he reminded Pia needlessly when she asked for his wife. "Does it have to be now? We have company."

People frequently tried to get rid of Pia at the door, but it was part of her job as a detective to pay unwelcome visits, and it no longer bothered her.

"I just have a couple of questions for your wife," Pia countered, unperturbed. "It'll only take a minute."

"Why can't you leave my wife alone?" he snapped. "God knows she's been through enough already because of that pig, yet she keeps on being reminded of him. Go away. Come back tomorrow."

Pia scrutinized the man, and he returned her gaze with undisguised aversion. In appearance, Richard Hackspiel was the complete opposite of Kilian Rothemund: heavy and bloated, with the big nose, red face, and watery eyes of an alcoholic. There was something arrogant about him, and Pia wished she could have asked him whether it bothered him to live in the same house where "that pig" used to live.

"I'm not a vacuum cleaner salesperson," said Pia with a charming smile, because she knew that would provoke this man to a white heat. "Either you go get your wife or I'll have her picked up by a patrol and we can have a chat at the station. It's your choice."

It wasn't really her style to flaunt her authority, but that was the only language some people understood. Pressing his lips tight, Hackspiel went inside and came back a moment later with his wife.

"What's it about this time?" she asked coolly, her arms crossed. She made no move to invite Pia inside.

"Your ex-husband." Pia didn't want to waste any time. "Do you think he's capable of beating a woman so badly that she's beyond recognition? Torturing her, and locking her naked in the trunk of a car?"

Britta Hackspiel swallowed and her eyes widened. Pia could see the struggle going on deep inside her.

"No. I don't think he's capable of that. Kilian never hit anyone as long as I was with him. Although . . ." Her face went hard. "Although I never would have believed that he would get aroused by little children. I'd known him for twenty years. Even when he was working hard, he was still first and foremost a family man, and always very conscientious. He never neglected the children and me."

Her shoulders slumped forward. The cool demeanor, which was her defense mechanism, dissolved. Pia waited for her to resume speaking. At moments like this, it was better simply to let someone talk, especially when the situation was as emotionally charged as it was for Britta Hackspiel.

"He was a loving father and husband. We always talked to each other and made plans, and we had no secrets from each other. Maybe . . . maybe that's why I was so . . . stunned when everything came out." She had tears in her eyes. "I never would have thought that of him. But suddenly our whole life was just one big lie."

"The press wrote at the time that your ex-husband had once been friends with the state attorney who instituted proceedings against him," Pia said. "Is that correct?"

"Yes, that's true. Markus and Kilian studied together and were very good friends. The summer when Kilian and I met, he and Markus were touring on their mopeds. At some point, the friendship fell apart." She heaved a resigned sigh. "Kilian became a defense attorney and made a lot of money. I don't know exactly what happened between them, but the devastating press campaign was instigated by Markus."

"Did you ever question the accusations that were made against your husband?" Pia asked.

Britta Hackspiel drew in a shaky breath, fighting for self-control.

"Yes, at first I did. I believed his claims of innocence because I thought I knew him. Until I saw those . . . those disgusting videos." Her voice was now only a whisper. "Then there was no doubt. He lied to me; he abused my trust. I can never forgive him for that. Of course we're still connected through the children, but as a human being he is dead to me."

A cracking sound on her left ankle made her stiffen. Her heart skipped a beat. One of the cables that the bastard had used to bind her foot to the chair leg seemed to have split. Now she could move her foot, even touch the floor with the tip of her toe. New hope flooded through every vein in her body. She mobilized all her strength and braced her toes against the floor. It was actually possible to move the chair backward a bit. An inch, and then another. Leonie was barely getting enough air, as the slightest movement strained her weakened body. Bright spots were dancing before her eyes, but outside it was pitch-dark. No light fell through the gaps in the shutters, so it must be nighttime, she realized. It was more than twenty-four hours ago that she had drunk the diet Coke in the kitchen. Her hands clenched around the wooden armrests and she pressed her toes against the floor, but no matter how hard she tried, the chair wouldn't move any farther. The pine floorboards in the therapy room were worn and uneven, and the chair legs were caught on some obstacle. Full of despair, she tensed every muscle in her body. Suddenly, she felt the chair tipping back. She couldn't bend forward because her upper body was bound tightly to the back of the chair. The chair toppled backward and her head struck the wooden floor. For a couple of seconds, Leonie remained motionless and stunned. Had her position improved or worsened? She lay helpless on her back like a beetle, with one foot, the only somewhat movable part of her body, sticking up in the air. Her chest rose and sank violently, but she noticed that it was no longer as hot. Hot air rises, and on the floor it was a little cooler. Leonie tried to imagine the layout of the room. How far was she from the desk? But how would that help her? She still couldn't move. Full of rage, she strained at her bonds, fighting against the hopeless situation. The telephone on the desk rang. The answering machine turned on, but the automatic voice said only that the tape was full. The pig had surely seen what had happened. Her heart was pounding in her throat. Would he come here and kill her? Where could he be? How long would it take? How much time did she have left?

Monday, June 28, 2010

It was already almost nine o'clock, and Corinna had scheduled a meeting in the administration building for nine. Emma dreaded the upcoming celebration on Friday. It was the last time she would have to see Florian, so she would put on a good front and not ruin her father-in-law's birthday party.

She took the shortcut across the lawn, which was still damp from the rain last night. The doctor at the hospital had assured her that Louisa was doing fine. The caseworker at the child-protection agency had left a message asking for a return call from Emma, who was firmly determined to see that Florian was officially prevented from any contact with Louisa.

The conversation with the therapist had done nothing to allay Emma's concern; instead, it had reinforced her worst fears. She'd told the woman about the hospital doctor's suspicion and about Louisa's altered behavior in the past few weeks, which Florian had called a normal developmental phase for a five-year-old. The therapist had been cautious with her assessment. There might actually be a completely different explanation for why Louisa had cut up her favorite plush animal, alternated between tantrums and exhausted lethargy, and displayed unusual aggression toward Emma. In any event, it was very important to keep a vigilant eye on her behavior. Sexual abuse by fathers, uncles, grandfathers, or close friends of the family was, unfortunately, much more widespread than commonly believed.

"Little children understand instinctively that what is being done to them isn't right. But when the abuse comes from someone they trust, they don't try to defend themselves," the therapist had told Emma. "On the contrary: the perpetrator usually succeeds in making the child complicit. 'This is our secret, and you can't tell Mama or your brothers and sisters that I love you so much, or else they'll be sad or jealous.' Something along those lines."

When Emma asked how she ought to react in the future, and what she could do in the next few weeks, after the new baby was born, the therapist could offer no particularly constructive advice. Her only suggestion was that Emma stay with someone she trusted.

Great. Emma trusted Corinna and also her in-laws, but how could she prevent them from allowing Florian to see Louisa? Her only recourse was to tell them about her suspicions. Emma couldn't imagine what sort of reaction his family would have if she accused Florian of molesting his own daughter. They'd probably think she was hysterical or just plain vindictive.

Deep in thought, she walked past the rhododendron bushes, which over the past decade had turned into a veritable jungle.

"Hello," somebody said, and Emma jumped. On a wrought-iron bench sat an elderly woman in a white smock, smoking a cigarette. She wore a hairnet over her white hair, and her bare feet were stuck into a pair of plastic sandals.

"Hello," Emma replied politely. Only now did

386

she recognize Helga Grasser, whom she knew only by sight. She was the mother of the Finkbeiners' factotum Helmut Grasser.

"So," said the old woman, stepping on her cigarette to grind it out. "Are things that bad?"

"Two weeks to go," said Emma, assuming the woman's question referred to her pregnancy.

"That's not what I meant." Helga Grasser got up with a groan and came closer. She was big and stout, her reddened face a network of wrinkles and burst veins. A penetrating smell of sweat issued from her smock, which seemed a size too small and was straining across her stomach and breasts. Emma could see pinkish skin and shuddered. The old woman was wearing nothing underneath.

"I'm on my way to a meeting." Emma wanted to escape quickly, but with a sudden lunge, Mrs. Grasser grabbed her by the wrist.

"Where there is light, there is also shadow," she whispered significantly. "Do you know the story about the wolf and the kid goats? No? Shall I tell it to you?"

Emma tried to escape, but the old woman was gripping her arm like a vise.

"Once upon a time, there was a goat who had six little kids and loved them like a mother loves her children," Helga began.

"As far as I can recall, there were seven kids," Emma put in.

"In my story, there are six. Now listen. . . ." The old woman's dark eyes glistened, as if she wanted to tell Emma a good joke. Emma's discomfort grew. Corinna had once told her that Helga Grasser was a bit slow, but she was indispensable in the kitchen as a dishwasher. Florian had made many blunt comments about the mental state of Helmut Grasser's mother. Ever since contracting meningitis forty years ago, Helga Grasser had been totally gaga. All the kids used to be scared of her because she particularly liked telling them bloodthirsty horror stories. She had spent many years in the locked psychiatric ward; Florian didn't seem to know why.

"One day," the old woman whispered hoarsely, shoving her face close to Emma's, "the goat had to go away, so she called all six kids together and said, 'Dear children, I have to go away for a few days. Watch out for the wolf and don't go up in the attic! If he finds you there, he will eat you up, skin, hair, and all. The villain may disguise himself, but you can recognize him by his rough voice and his black fur.' The kids said, 'Dear Mother, we'll be very careful. You can leave now. Don't worry.' Then the old goat bleated and confidently went on her way."

"I really have to get going," Emma said, interrupting the woman, who was wiping drops of spittle from her cheek with her free hand.

"You think I'm crazy, too, don't you?" She let

go of Emma's arm. "But I'm not. Years ago, some bad things happened here. Don't you believe me?"

When she saw Emma's bewildered expression, she cackled, baring her two canine teeth, which were all that remained in her lower jaw. On top, two gold teeth protruded from her gums.

"Then ask your husband sometime about his twin sister."

Corinna came walking around the corner. Her eyes fell on Emma's pale face.

"Helga! Are you telling horror stories again?" she asked sternly, her hands on her hips.

"Bah!" said the old woman, and tottered off toward the kitchen.

Corinna waited until she had disappeared behind the rhododendron bushes, then put an arm around Emma's shoulder.

"You look really frightened," she said with concern. "What did she say to you?"

"She told me the story of the wolf and the seven kids." Emma forced a laugh and hoped that she sounded amused. "She's really something else."

"You shouldn't take Helga too seriously. Sometimes she makes up things, but she's harmless." Corinna smiled. "Come on, let's go. We're going to be late."

The reception desk of Herzmann Productions was deserted, as were all the offices. Pia and

Bodenstein went around opening doors and eventually burst in on a staff meeting that was going on in the conference room. The nine people sitting around the table were listening to a man, but he fell silent at the sight of the Criminal Police. Jan Niemöller, the manager of Herzmann Productions, jumped up and brought the meeting to a close. As everyone filed out, he introduced Pia and her boss to the speaker, Dr. Wolfgang Matern, CEO of Antenne Pro. Judging by the crestfallen look of the staff as they left the room, he had not been presenting good news.

"We would like to speak with you, as well." Pia blocked Meike Herzmann's way as she tried to slip out unnoticed. "Why didn't you call me back?"

"Because I didn't feel like it."

"Was that the same reason why you didn't visit your mother?" Pia asked.

"That's none of your damned business," Meike hissed.

"You're right," said Pia with a shrug. "I was at the hospital. Your mother is not doing well. And I want to find out who did this to her."

"That's what we taxpayers expect of you," Meike snapped. Pia would have liked to tell this little bitch what she thought of her, but she controlled herself.

"On Friday morning, you went over to your mother's house. You picked up the mail and put it on the sideboard," she said. "Did you notice any particular letter or note at the time?"

"No," Meike said. Pia did not miss the quick glance over to the CEO of Antenne Pro, who was talking to Bodenstein.

"You're lying," she said, determined to knock the stuffing out of her. "Why? Are you in cahoots with the people who attacked your mother? Did you have something to do with it? Maybe you were even hoping that your mother would die so you could inherit her money."

Meike Herzmann first turned red, then pale, indignantly gasping for breath.

"It's illegal to withhold evidence and obstruct an investigation. If it turns out that's what you're doing, then you're in big trouble." Pia saw the uncertainty in the young woman's eyes. "Please write down the address where we can reach you. And in the future, answer your cell phone when we call, or else I'll have to arrest you for refusing to cooperate."

That was nonsense, of course, but Meike Herzmann seemed to have no experience with the law. She also seemed quite intimidated. Pia left her standing there and went over to join Bodenstein and Dr. Matern, who, according to his own testimony, had no idea what Hanna Herzmann had been working on.

"I'm the president and CEO," he said. "We work with a lot of production companies. There's no way for me to keep track of who is doing what for each program, even for weekly shows. Bottom line, I'm interested only in the viewer ratings. I have nothing to do with the content."

He stated that he'd known Hanna for many years and that their relationship was friendly but professional. Pia listened in silence. Matern was a businessman through and through, polite, noncommittal, and slippery as an eel. Given the fact that Hanna Herzmann was the ratings queen of the station, and the station did own 30 percent of Herzmann Productions, it would not be in Matern's interest to lose his cash cow on a long-term basis. Just as Pia was about to ask him about Kilian Rothemund and Bernd Prinzler, her cell rang. Christoph! Her thoughts flew to Lilly. She hoped nothing had happened. Whenever Christoph knew she was in the midst of a sensitive investigation, he almost never called her, but sent a text instead.

"Hi, Pia." She heard Lilly's voice and was relieved. "I haven't seen you in so long."

"Hi, Lilly." Pia lowered her voice and moved to the other side of the conference table. "We saw each other last night. Where are you now?"

"In Grandpa's office. You know what, Pia? I got a tick! In my hair. But Grandpa operated and got rid of it."

"Yikes. Did it hurt?" Pia had to smile as she turned to face the wall. She listened to Lilly for a while, then promised her she'd get home earlier.

"Grandpa wants me to tell you that we're making a reeeeeally delicious potato salad."

"Well, that's one more reason to get home early."

Pia saw Bodenstein signaling to her that he was leaving. She said good-bye to Lilly and stuck the phone in the back pocket of her jeans. She was truly sorry that the little girl would have to leave soon.

"I find it odd that no one on Hanna's staff knows anything about her research nor do any of her other colleagues," Pia said to her boss as they left the office and headed for their car. "And the daughter seems really suspect. How could anyone have so little sympathy for her own mother?"

She was not satisfied at all with the results of her conversations. Seldom had an investigation moved so sluggishly as with the two current cases. At their morning meeting, Commissioner Engel had put the pressure on for the first time, and rightly so, because there'd been no progress in either the Mermaid case or Hanna Herzmann's. Bodenstein had asked his colleagues in Hanau for their cooperation. A round-the-clock stakeout of the box at the Hanau post office seemed to be their last chance to learn the whereabouts of Bernd Prinzler. An examination of the records of all Residential Registry offices in all of Germany had produced no satisfactory results.

"After *Germany's Most Wanted* is broadcast on Wednesday night, something will happen," Bodenstein prophesied. "I know it."

"All right, your word in God's ear," replied Pia drily, unlocking the car. She looked up because she sensed someone was watching them. Meike Herzmann was standing at a window on the sixth floor, staring down at them.

"I'm going to get you, too," Pia murmured. "I'm not going to let you get away with lying to me."

Emma's in-laws had already left for the airport by the time Emma got home after her meeting. All morning, the strange encounter with Helga Grasser had been on her mind. Of course she could have called Florian and asked him directly why he'd never told her about having a twin sister. But after everything that had happened lately, she simply couldn't bring herself to do that.

Emma hesitated when she reached her in-laws' front door. The door was never locked, and she could come and go as she pleased. Still she felt like an intruder as she stepped into the house and looked around. Renate kept her photo albums in the living room cabinet. They were arranged by year, and Emma started with the album from 1964, the year Florian was born. An hour later, she had leafed through dozens of albums. She had seen pictures of Florian, his foster and adopted siblings, and a zillion other children at all ages, but no girls that looked like they might be Florian's twin sister.

With a mixture of disappointment and relief, Emma broke off her search and left her in-laws' house. Had Corinna been right? Was Helga Grasser really just a crazy old woman who liked to tell stories? But why had she changed the details in the fairy tale about the wolf and the seven kids? Emma stuck the key in the lock of the door to the apartment. Why had she spoken of only *six* kids? Had she meant Florian and his siblings? Florian, Corinna, Sarah, Nicky, Ralf—if so, then one was missing. But who? Emma's gaze shifted to the wooden stairs that led to the attic. She'd been up there only once, when Renate had shown her the house. Hadn't Helga Grasser mentioned an attic in her fairy-tale version?

Emma pulled the key back out of the lock and climbed up the narrow steps. The plywood door was stuck and she had to press her shoulder against it until it swung open with an awful creak. Stuffy, hot air gusted toward her. The heat of the past few days had accumulated beneath the poorly insulated roof. Scant light came through the tiny attic window, but it was bright enough for her to see carefully stacked moving cartons, discarded furniture, and all sorts of other junk that had piled up over forty years. A thick layer of dust covered the creaky wooden floor, and spiderwebs hung from the rafters. The whole attic smelled of wood, dust, and mothballs.

At a loss, Emma looked around and then pushed aside a moth-eaten velvet curtain that was fastened to a crossbeam. She gave a start when she saw a woman facing her in the dim half-light, and it took a few seconds before she realized that she was looking at her own reflection. A large mirror was leaning against the wall. Its glass had turned cloudy over time. Behind the curtain, there were also crates and cartons, all meticulously labeled. Winter jackets, a Carrera racecourse, Playmobil, wooden toys, receipts, Florian's books, Corinna's schoolwork, baby clothes, Halloween costumes, Christmas tree ornaments, and Christmas cards from 1973 to 1983.

Josef and Renate wouldn't be back from Berlin until tomorrow, so she had plenty of time to look through all the boxes and chests of drawers. But where to start?

Finally, Emma pulled out a box labeled *Florian: kindergarten, grammar school, high school.* She had to sneeze when she opened the lid. Her mother-in-law had certainly saved everything: notebooks, schoolbooks, Florian's artwork, receipts for school milk, swimming awards, programs from school plays, even a gym bag with the initials FF cross-stitched on it. Emma leafed through one notebook after another, looking at the clumsy writing, the fading ink. Did Florian know that these relics of his childhood still existed?

Emma closed the box and put it back in place, then moved on, looking at scratched furniture, rickety children's chairs, an old-fashioned baby scale, a wonderful antique typewriter that would probably bring a tidy sum on eBay. She kept sneezing; her T-shirt was sticking to her back and her eyes were itching. She was just about to give up, when she spied a carton hidden beneath the sloping ceiling behind the bricked-up fireplace. She didn't recognize the name that was printed on the side in big block letters, and it aroused her curiosity. She squatted down, which was not easy in her condition, pulled out the carton, and opened it. Unlike Florian's carefully packed childhood memories, this box looked as though someone had simply tossed everything inside. Books, notebooks, drawings, a doll, stuffed animals, photos, documents, articles of clothing, a flowered poetry album with a lock, a red hood. Emma lifted out a shoe box, opened it, and pulled out a black-and-white photo with a white border like people had in the sixties. Her heart skipped a beat and then started racing in a wild staccato. The photo showed a smiling Renate with two little blond children on her lap, and in the foreground two cakes, each with two candles. Emma turned the photo over, fingers trembling. *Florian and Michaela, 2nd birthday, December 16, 1966* was written on the back.

• • •

Back at her desk, Pia typed in "Wolfgang Matern+Antenne Pro" into Google. She instantly got hundreds of hits. Wolfgang Matern, born 1965, was the son of Dr. Hartmut Matern, the noted media mogul. He was one of the first to see the lucrative possibilities of commercial television in Germany, and he exploited the opportunity to amass a fortune. Even today, Matern senior, at seventy-eight, held the office of chairman of a diversified holding company, which owned various commercial television and cable networks as well as numerous other firms. The company also held part interests in other enterprises. Wolfgang had studied business administration and political science, earning a doctorate in the latter. On the Web site of the Matern Group, which was headquartered in Frankfurt am Main, he was listed as a member of the board, in addition to being the program director and chief operating officer of several commercial broadcast stations that belonged to the company conglomerate. Pia found innumerable photos of him, most of which showed him with his father at various public events, lectures, awards dinners, or television galas. The Web had absolutely nothing to say about the private lives of the Materns. As genuine media professionals, they no doubt knew how to protect themselves from intrusive scrutiny. Not much changed when she entered

Wolfgang Matern's name by itself. A sheer waste of time.

There was no news from the hospital; Hanna Herzmann was still not able to be questioned. Kilian Rothemund remained at large, and at the Hanau post office, no one had yet come to pick up the mail from Prinzler's box.

Since she had nothing better to do, Pia searched all the available social networks, but Wolfgang Matern was not on XING, Facebook, or Classmates.com.

"Do you have any other ideas where I might find information about this man?" Pia asked her colleague.

Kai rattled off a few sites without looking up from his monitor: LinkedIn, 123people, Yasni, CYLEX, firma-24.de.

"Tried them already." Pia leaned back in resignation, clasping her hands behind her head. "Damn it, this guy was my last hope. Why does it all seem so mysterious? Somebody must know what Hanna Herzmann was working on. Why can't I find what it was?"

"Did you already check out the daughter?"

"Yeah, of course. But she seems to have almost no presence online."

"Try Stayfriends," Kai suggested, looking up. "Oh man, I'm as hungry as a bear. Got any snacks?"

"Nope. You scarfed down my last bag of chips.

Go and find some food before you start getting grouchy." Pia put her fingers on the keyboard again and entered the Web address of Stayfriends: www.stayfriends.de.

"Kebab or burger?" Kai asked, getting up from his chair.

"Kebab. Extra spicy, with double meat and feta," Pia replied. "I knew it!"

"What?"

"I knew something was fishy about this Wolfgang Matern." Pia grinned in triumph and pointed at her screen. "He's actually registered at Stayfriends, just like Hanna Herzmann. And get this: Those two went to the same school, yet he swore that their relationship was only professional. Why would he do that?"

"Maybe he's afraid of getting involved in something," Kai guessed. "Be right back."

Pia focused all her attention on the site. She clicked on the profiles of Hanna Herzmann and Wolfgang Matern as well as the 1982 class photo of the eleventh grade of the Königshofen private high school in Niedernhausen. Since she wasn't a "gold member," she couldn't see any more details on the site, but it didn't matter. The connection was there, and Wolfgang Matern had lied to Bodenstein. He had known Hanna Herzmann better and longer than he'd claimed. Even more important, he and Hanna had studied at the Ludwig-Maximilian University in Munich and were both members of the same alumni club from their secondary school. Pia spent the next hour and a half going through photos of Hanna Herzmann on the Web; unfortunately, there were thousands of them. She was finishing off the rest of her cold kebab when she found what she was looking for. It was a photo from 1998 that had appeared in an illustrated magazine, and it showed a radiant Hanna in her wedding dress with her second or third husband. On the other side of her stood Wolfgang Matern, and in front of him was Meike as a sullen, chubby preteen. *Wolfgang Matern (34), son of media mogul Hartmut Matern, close friend of the bride and godfather of her daughter Meike (12), acted as witness* read the caption.

"Ha!" Pia exclaimed as she clicked on the photo and sent it to the printer. She was already extremely curious about what the program director of Antenne Pro would say. With the still-warm printout, she went to Bodenstein's office and almost ran into him in the doorway.

"Look what I—" she began, but Bodenstein interrupted her.

"Kilian Rothemund's motor scooter was found at the main train station and impounded," he said brusquely. "And a witness recognized Rothemund. He got on an intercity express to Amsterdam at ten-forty-four this morning. I spoke with our Dutch colleagues, and they'll be waiting for him when he arrives at five-twenty-two this afternoon. If we're lucky, we'll have him in custody in a few hours."

Meike had opened all the windows in the apartment to get some air flowing through. She was sweating even though she was wearing only a bra and slip. At the office, nobody had noticed when she took Hanna's computer home with her. Even the supersmart blond cop chick hadn't thought of that computer. Since this morning, Meike had found herself with plenty of time on her hands because she no longer had a job. Irina and Jan had promised to keep her on the payroll at the company; everyone else had been forced to take their annual vacation until it was clear whether Hanna would be able to appear before a camera again. Antenne Pro was fair: no replacement show was aired in her time slot; instead, there were reruns of *In Depth*.

Yesterday had been one of the best in Meike's life: breakfast at the magnificent villa in Oberursel, lunch at the Schwarzenstein fortress in the Rheingau, riding in the Aston Martin convertible, and champagne in the evening on the terrace of the Hotel Frankfurter Hof with a view of the illuminated bank skyscrapers. Meike had never experienced anything like it. She had noticed people casting curious glances in her direction, obviously wondering whether she and

Wolfgang were a couple. An age difference of more than twenty years was nothing unusual; lots of women dated much older men. Wolfgang was her godfather; she'd known him ever since she could remember, and had never viewed him in any other way. Until today. Suddenly, she'd noticed what nice hands he had and how good he smelled. She'd had to force herself not to keep staring at his lips and his hands. Once she started thinking about what it must be like to kiss him and sleep with him, she couldn't get the idea out of her mind. She'd never been truly in love. She hadn't even had a serious boyfriend, and she didn't have much to be proud of when it came to her few adventures with the opposite sex. Yesterday, she'd gotten a glimpse of how wonderful it could be to belong to someone. Wolfgang was so solicitous and charming: he'd opened the car door for her, pulled out the chair for her, focused all his attention on her, his arm around her shoulder.

She'd lain awake half the night analyzing every word that Wolfgang had said. He had held out the prospect of an internship at Antenne Pro, although she had not yet completed her studies. But he thought she would be perfect for the position, since she'd already gained a great deal of experience by working at a TV station. Why had he done that? Because she was Hanna's daughter? If Meike thought carefully about it, he hadn't really said or done anything that could be interpreted as an expression of love. He had simply been nice to her. The euphoric feeling of happiness in which she had indulged herself all day had then turned to disappointment. Her hormones went crazy as soon as a man was nice to her. Clear proof of her own shortcomings.

"Ouch!" Meike hit her head as she was untangling the cables underneath the desk and fumbling the right plugs into the right slots on the back of Hanna's computer. Fortunately, the friend whose apartment she was looking after had left her own computer along with the monitor, mouse, and keyboard on her desk. Meike rubbed the sore spot on her head and booted up Hanna's computer. It worked. She clicked on the menu and configured the WLAN in the system settings. In a few moments, she was online. First, she checked her mother's Facebook fan site, which Irina managed and supplied with content. No word of the attack or the hospital. Irina would certainly delete any posting that might mention such details. On Google, she found no new entry, either; the latest update referred to the broadcast with the ridiculed candidates and the summer special. Next in line were the e-mails. Over a hundred new messages were waiting in the in-box of the business account, and fourteen had come into the private address. One name instantly caught Meike's eye, and she stopped short. Kilian

Rothemund! What did her mother have to do with that child molester?

She clicked on the e-mail and read the brief text, which had been sent on Saturday at 11:43 A.M.

Hanna, why don't you answer? Did something happen? Did I say or do something that made you mad? Please call me. Unfortunately, I can't talk to Leonie anymore. She's not answering, either, but on Monday I'm still going to go to A and meet with the people with whom B got in contact. They are finally ready to talk to me. I'm thinking of you. Don't forget me. K.

What the hell did all that mean? Meike stared helplessly at the screen, reading the mail over and over. *I'm thinking of you. Don't forget me.* What was going on between Rothemund and her mother? She had no doubt that "K" stood for Kilian Rothemund, who had put the note with the address of that rabid biker gang in Langensebold in Hanna's mail slot, but none of it made any sense. What did Leonie Verges have to do with Kilian Rothemund and Hanna? Had Hanna been working on a story about the Frankfurt Road Kings? Rothemund used to be a lawyer, and he knew the bikers because he'd represented them. But this lying therapist didn't fit in the picture.

Meike rested her chin on her hand to think. Should she call up Wolfgang and tell him about the e-mail? No. This morning, *he* had promised to call *her.* She wasn't going to play the fool and keep calling him like some infatuated teenager.

Maybe there were more e-mails. Normally, Hanna downloaded her mail to her laptop, but with luck, she hadn't done so since Thursday. Meike carefully went through all the folders on the computer. Her mother was the type of user who was a horror for computer nerds. She almost never deleted anything, and she backed up data according to a system that was purely intuitive and illogical. After an hour, Meike gave up in disappointment. For a few minutes, she sat there thinking. If she wanted to find out more, then she would have to go talk to that therapist again.

The digital clock on the toolbar of the monitor showed 8:23 P.M. Not too late to drive to Liederbach.

As darkness descended, the ugly terrace of the Main Riviera was transformed under the glow of hundreds of multicolored lights into a grotesque stage set. Schmaltzy Italian pop hits were coming out of the loudspeakers, and the few guests who had wandered in began to think they were on an Italian vacation. Sitting in the bar, the regulars from the trailer park were wearing flip-flops and tracksuits, staring at a gigantic TV screen showing a soccer match. Bodenstein felt like having a cold beer, and his stomach was rumbling. A warm wind had come up that smelled of rain. In the distance, he saw lightning and could hear the roll of thunder, yet he decided to sit at one of the empty tables on the terrace. He ordered a mug of wheat beer. When the waiter set the beer on the table, he made a tick mark on the beer coaster, then handed Bodenstein a menu encased in sticky brown plastic.

"No thanks. I don't want anything to eat." Although Bodenstein's stomach was growling pitifully, he couldn't force himself to order any food. A glance at the plate on the next table had taken away his appetite: a giant schnitzel, hanging over the edge of the plate, covered with hollandaise, with a pile of fries dumped on top. The salad looked like something mowed off the shoulder of the autobahn, with bottled dressing poured over it. The meal was worlds apart from the artful delicacies that Rosalie had conjured up yesterday, which had earned her third place in the cooking contest of the Chaîne des Rôtisseurs.

"Suit yourself." The waiter shrugged and vanished.

Bodenstein took a sip of his beer.

His Dutch colleagues had missed Kilian Rothemund in Amsterdam, if he had even been on that train. The itemized list of calls from Hanna Herzmann's phone had given them only a few helpful tips, because the most frequent numbers on the bill were to or from prepaid cell phones that couldn't be traced. Bernd Prinzler was still missing. Nobody had emptied his post office box, and none of his contacts in Frankfurt had supplied any concrete information, but that didn't surprise Bodenstein. The only thing he'd learned was that Prinzler hadn't had anything to do with the Frankfurt chapter of the Road Kings in years.

The first heavy raindrops splashed on the umbrella.

The people at the table next to him fled inside, and Bodenstein grabbed his glass and beer coaster to follow. He stood in the open doorway, looking out at the rain, which came rushing across the Main like a gray wall, driving a squall of wet wind toward him.

"Hey, there's a draft! Close the damn door!" called one of the customers. None of the waiters reacted, so Bodenstein closed the sliding glass door. He could feel the regulars giving him suspicious and curious looks, but he pretended not to notice. A goal was scored in the soccer game, and the men at the bar cheered and yelled to one another. The loudest of them was a beefy, red-faced guy in a black undershirt, who paid for his know-it-all bellowing with a violent coughing fit. He slid off his bar stool, stumbled through the bar, and tore open the door that Bodenstein had just closed. Coughing, he staggered outside and leaned against the wall under the eaves, gasping for breath.

"Should I call an ambulance?" asked Bodenstein, who had followed him out. His pals at the bar seemed unconcerned.

"Naw . . . it's going away now," the fat man snorted, waving him off. "It's this shitty asthma. I shouldn't get so worked up. Soccer is like poison to me. . . ."

He snorted and coughed and spat a disgusting yellow loogie into the overflowing standing ashtray next to the door.

"Scuse me," he said. He wasn't totally without manners.

"As long as it helps," replied Bodenstein laconically.

"I worked forty years at the Ticona Mine. That's where I got it. Ruined my health. The lungs."

"Ah." Bodenstein guessed that smoking hundreds of thousands of cigarettes was responsible for the condition of his lungs, not working in the mine. But people tend to blame everything but themselves.

"Tell me . . ." the fat man said, recovering his breath. He scrutinized Bodenstein. "Aren't you a cop?"

"Yes, I am. Why?"

"I heard you're looking for Doc. Anything in it for me if I tell you something about him?" He rubbed his thumb and forefinger together, and his eyes flashed with sly greed.

"A reward has been offered for information leading to an arrest," Bodenstein confirmed.

One of the waiters stuck his head out the open sliding door.

"Everything okay with you, Karl-Heinz?" he

asked. "The boss says don't croak before you pay your tab."

"He can shove that tab where the sun don't shine. Bring me another pilsner." With a groan, Karl-Heinz shoved off from the wall and lowered his voice to a conspiratorial whisper. "I don't know if it'll lead to an arrest or not. We live right across the street from Doc. And we're home more or less all day, my wife and me."

He paused to let his information sink in, increasing the suspense. Bodenstein waited patiently. From long experience, he knew that people like Karl-Heinz had an uncontrollable urge to tell all, so he wouldn't hesitate for long. And that turned out to be true.

"Recently, say two, three weeks ago," he went on, "Doc had another visitor. And I don't mean somebody who needed advice. No, she was a real young thing. Blond. Pretty. Half-naked. My wife thought she couldn't be more than fifteen. And you know what?"

Brief pause.

"She just walked right into the trailer. We never saw her come out. And a couple days later, they fished the girl out of the Main. I swear to you, it was the same kid. A hundred percent . . ."

The wipers flicked frantically across the windshield, trying to stanch the flood pouring from the skies. Meike drove along at walking speed as she looked for a parking place on the street where Leonie Verges lived. On impulse, she'd jumped in the car and driven off, so it was only on the way from Frankfurt to Liederbach that she had a chance to think about what she wanted to ask the therapist. Her anger at the woman grew with each passing minute. Why had Verges lied to her and Wolfgang, claiming that she knew nothing? She was clearly in cahoots with this child molester and had gotten Hanna mixed up in something.

The parking places in front of the bakery were taken. Meike cursed and turned left at the end of the street to drive around the block again. She didn't want to run through the rain and show up looking like a wet cat. She noticed a big black car parked in front of the barn wall on what was probably Leonie's property. A Frankfurt plate. It was the monster vehicle that belonged to the tattooed biker from Langenscbold. What was it doing here? A few yards farther on, Meike found a spot that her Mini fit into perfectly. By then, the rain had let up a bit. She walked along the street and stopped between two parked cars, scoping out the situation from a safe distance. Leonie Verges's property stretched the whole length of the block, and there was a door in the wall of the barn through which she could probably enter the courtyard.

Meike shivered and pulled her hood up over her head. After the heat of the day, the rain felt cold.

411

What should she do now? Look and see if the door was unlocked? No, she wasn't suicidal. Maybe it'd be best to take a couple of photos of the black Hummer for evidence, because she was pretty sure that this biker gang had something to do with the attack on Hanna. As she was thinking it over, the green wooden door was shoved open. Two men came out and ran with their heads down to the vehicle as if the devil were after them. Meike ducked. An engine roared to life, head-lights flared, and the giant black vehicle rolled past her. She waited a moment, then hurried to the door, which was still standing ajar. It might be impolite to enter through the back door so late at night, but Verges would probably refuse to let her in if she tried the front entrance. Meike went through the barn, which seemed to serve as a storehouse for bags of mulch and pots of all types. The front door of the house stood wide open; the floodlight on the outside wall was on, illuminating the courtyard, which was full of plants and flowers.

"Hello?" Meike called. She stood in the open doorway. "Hello?"

She cautiously took a step inside. Whew, it was hot. There was a light on in a room at the end of the narrow hall; it was shining through a crack under the door, sending a bright line across the reddish tiles.

"Hello? Ms. Verges?"

Meike broke out in a sweat and shoved back the hood from her head. Where was that stupid cow? Maybe she was on the toilet. Meike walked down the hall and knocked on the door of the room with a sign that said COUNSELING. This was where her mother had come. Of course she'd never told Meike that she was in therapy. Typical. Hanna always did her utmost to preserve her perfect façade; it was an obsession for her.

Curious, Meike pushed the door open. A wave of hot, dry air hit her, along with the smell of urine. Her brain took a couple of seconds to register what her eyes were seeing. On the floor in the middle of the room lay Leonie Verges. Someone had bound her to a chair that had tipped over.

"Oh shit," Meike murmured, and went closer. The woman was gagged with duct tape, her eyes were wide open, but she didn't blink. A thick bluebottle fly crawled across her face and disappeared into one nostril. Meike fought an urge to vomit and put her hand to her mouth. Only then did she realize that Leonie Verges was dead.

Karl-Heinz Rösner's wife confirmed what her husband had told him. It wasn't the first time that Kilian Rothemund had had visits from young girls. That was a clear violation of his probation, because the court had prohibited him from going anywhere near underage girls. It was perfectly clear to Bodenstein why the Rösners hadn't said anything to the police at once, so he didn't bother to reproach them. Here nobody cared about anyone else, because everyone was too preoccupied with their own misery. The people in the trailer park had all given up on life, and they weren't the least bit interested in what happened in the world or in their own neighborhood. After Bodenstein had taken another look inside Rothemund's trailer, he paid for his beer at the café and walked slowly back to his car. The thought of what Kilian Rothemund might have done to the girl in his trailer was almost unbearable for Bodenstein. Practically in full view of the public, he had brazenly indulged in his disgusting desires, undeterred because of his utterly indifferent neighbors. What promises had he offered to lure the girl inside? Involuntarily, Bodenstein thought of Sophia and how trusting she was. You could tell a child a thousand times not to take anything from strangers. But what if it wasn't a stranger? What if it was a relative or a good friend of the family who made advances with perverse intentions? Then there was no possibility of protecting the child. There was also no use in trying to shield a child too much from the realities of life, because inevitably the day would arrive when she would have to deal with things on her own. The longer Bodenstein thought about this, the less absurd it seemed that the story about the blond girl might actually be about the dead Mermaid pulled out of the Main. At the trailer park, there was a swimming pool, basically a hole in the ground painted blue, but it did have a functioning chlorine treatment unit.

The thunderstorm was over, the asphalt was steaming, and there was a smell of damp soil. Bodenstein had just reached his car when his phone rang. He had a bad feeling when he saw Pia's name on the display at this time of day.

"We've got a body in Liederbach," she told him. "I'm already on my way over there, and I'll try to reach Henning."

She gave him the address and he promised to drive straight there. With a sigh, he got in behind the wheel. Tomorrow morning, he was going to send Kröger over to the trailer park to take a water sample from the swimming pool for comparison with the chemical analysis of water from the Mermaid's lungs.

Twenty minutes later, he turned onto the street and saw the flashing blue light. Right in front of him was the silver Mercedes station wagon belonging to Dr. Henning Kirchhoff. The evidence team's blue VW van stood next to the wide-open gate to the property. Pia had already mobilized the whole team required whenever a dead body was found. Bodenstein got out and ducked under the crime-scene tape. A few onlookers stood on the sidewalk. Pia was talking to a couple and taking notes. When she spied him, she stopped and walked over to him.

"The dead woman is Leonie Verges, a psychotherapist," she reported. "She's lived here for over ten years but had very little contact with her neighbors. That's the owner of the bakery over there. In the past few days, he's made several interesting observations."

Henning Kirchhoff came across the street with overalls draped over his arm and a metal case in his left hand.

"Hi there," Pia greeted her ex-husband. "I see you've got new glasses again."

Henning Kirchhoff gave her a surly smile.

"Nana Mouskouri wanted hers back," he countered. "Where do I have to go?"

"Over there through the courtyard."

"Is that mental amoeba from your Boy Scout department there, too?"

"If you mean Christian, yes. He's already inside the house."

"Why doesn't that guy ever take a vacation?" Henning muttered as he left. "I could really use a break today."

"The baker wrote down the license plate numbers of two cars because he saw them several times." Pia consulted her notebook. She was talking faster than usual, a sign that she'd discovered something. "F-X 562. A black Hummer. That car belongs to Bernd Prinzler! The other car was a dark station wagon with local plates. I'll get the owner search started."

As usual, Pia was already a few steps ahead of Bodenstein, whose thoughts were still circling around the visit Kilian Rothemund had had from the underage girl. He had to make a real effort to follow the connections Pia had discovered.

"What happened here anyway?" he asked, interrupting Pia's report on their way over to the house.

"The woman was bound to a chair and gagged," Pia replied. "The neighbors thought she was away because there was a sign hanging on her door. That's why nobody missed her."

The small house was full of people in white overalls, and it was unbearably hot.

"The heat was turned up all the way," somebody said. "She must have been lying here for some time."

Bodenstein and Pia stepped into the room. There was a flash as Kröger photographed the corpse and the crime scene.

"Good God, it's like an oven in here," Pia groaned.

"Exactly one hundred degrees," said Kröger. "It was probably even hotter, but the door was open when we arrived. You could open the windows, by the way."

"No, you can't," said Henning, kneeling next to the corpse. "Not until I've measured the body temperature. But Chief Detective Inspector Kröger probably wouldn't know about body temperature."

Kröger ignored Henning's jabs and kept on stoically taking photos.

"How did she die?" Bodenstein asked.

"Most likely very painfully," replied Henning without looking up. "I assume she died of dehydration, as evidenced by her dry, scaly skin and the sunken temples. Hmm. Her eyeballs have turned yellow. That could indicate kidney failure. In individuals who die of thirst, or to be more accurate, of dehydration, the blood thickens due to lack of fluid, and the vital organs then become undersupplied. Finally, death occurs because of multiple organ failure. Usually the kidneys give out first."

Pia and Bodenstein watched as Henning first used pincers to cut through the cables binding the wrists and ankles of the body and then the plastic clothesline with which she was tied to the chair.

"She must have struggled for a long time." He pointed to the skin abrasions and subcutaneous bleeding on her wrists and ankles. Carefully, he removed the duct tape that had been wrapped around her head. Clumps of hair stuck to the tape.

"Also an indication of dehydration, when the hair pulls out so easily," Kröger commented.

"Smart-ass," Henning grumbled.

"Arrogant know-it-all," countered Kröger.

"I know who killed her," said a voice from the doorway. Bodenstein and Pia turned. In front of them stood a pale specter in a completely soaked black hoodie.

"What are you doing here?" Pia blurted out.

"I wanted to talk to Ms. Verges." Meike Herzmann looked like one of those figures from *manga* comics with the pointy face and the huge, heavily made-up eyes. "I . . . I was here before, but that time . . . that time she claimed she didn't know what my mother was working on. That was a lie. I found out that she also knew Kilian Rothemund."

"Oh, really? And when did you intend to tell us that?" Pia would have liked to smack her.

"So who killed Ms. Verges?" Bodenstein interjected before Pia could fly off the handle.

"A biker with lots of tattoos," whispered Meike, staring as if hypnotized at the corpse of Leonie Verges. "He and another man came running out of the yard and jumped in their car just as I got here."

"Bernd Prinzler?" Bodenstein moved to block her view.

Meike Herzmann nodded mutely. Her prickly personality had vanished. Now she was just a little pile of misery filled with guilt.

"By the way, did you notice the minicamera on the heater near the door?" Kröger said suddenly. Bodenstein and Pia turned their heads. Sure enough. Perched on the heating unit that hung on the wall next to the door was a tiny camera, barely as large as a child's fist.

"What's that doing there?"

"Somebody filmed her while she was dying," Kröger said. "What absolute evil!"

Bodenstein ushered Meike into the kitchen. Pia went over to the desk and pressed the PLAY button on the answering machine. Seven new messages. Three times, the caller had hung up right after the announcement, but then a voice issued from the tape.

Are you thirsty, Leonie? asked the caller. *You will get even thirstier. Did you know that dying of thirst is probably the most painful death there is? No? Hmm . . . The rule of thumb is: Three to four days without water and you're dead.*

Pia and Christian Kröger exchanged a look.

"That's disgusting," said Pia. "Whenever I think I've seen everything, something comes along that tops all the previous horrors. Somebody actually watched as she died."

"Or filmed her death," Kröger added. "It's called a snuff movie when someone is actually killed. I'm sure there are plenty of sick idiots who would shell out big money to see this."

Tuesday, June 29, 2010

Emma couldn't come to rest. She missed her little daughter, but at the same time she was afraid of what would happen when Louisa came back home. She'd never felt the responsibility for her child as a burden before, but now she did. It was a burden that she would have to bear all alone. It was her task to protect Louisa and the still-unborn baby.

Emma couldn't understand why Florian had never told her about his twin sister. What else had he kept from her? What would her life be like from now on? She had saved some money, and her father had bequeathed a condo in Frankfurt to her; the rental income from the condo would keep her afloat for a while. In the middle of the night, Emma had even written an e-mail to her previous boss and cautiously asked whether there might be a job for her in the office. She surfed the Net till dawn, visiting forums in which women reported how their children had been abused. She read horror stories about loving husbands and fathers who had turned out to be child molesters. In all these accounts she tried to find parallels to her own life and to Florian. Men who abused children had often had traumatic childhoods themselves or been the objects of abuse; the disposition to pedophilia was also often genetically determined, she read somewhere.

At six-thirty Emma closed her laptop. Only in the last few hours had she become fully aware of the consequences tied to any suspicions that Florian might have abused Louisa. The fact that she considered it a real possibility was tantamount to declaring her marriage a failure. She would never trust him again, never have a peaceful moment when he was alone with a child. It was all so repulsive, so sick! And there was nobody she could talk to about it. Not really. The therapist and the woman from the child-protection agency had listened and given her advice about how she should react, but Emma wanted to talk to somebody who knew Florian, who could reassure her and tell her that this was all utter nonsense. She couldn't go to her in-laws. It would be wrong to confront the old folks with such a topic, especially only a few days before Josef's big birthday party.

Then she thought of Corinna. Florian's adopted sister was always honest with her and had become a friend. Emma appreciated her advice and opinion. Maybe she could tell her something about the mysterious twin sister. Having made up her mind, Emma typed a text message and asked Corinna for fifteen minutes of her time.

Less than a minute later, she had a reply.

You're up early! Come to our house at one

o'clock. Lunch and conversation. Okay? Love, C,
she had written.

Okay, thanks, Emma texted back. She heaved a
sigh of relief. She wasn't happy about having to
question other people about her own husband, but
because of his dishonesty, he'd given her no
choice.

"Please close the window. I'm cold," said Kathrin
Fachinger in annoyance as Christian Kröger
opened the window wide in the conference room.
The thunderstorm last night had brought lower
temperatures, and pleasantly cool air streamed in,
driving out the stuffy heat.

"It's seventy degrees," said Kröger. "And it's
stifling in here."

"Maybe, but I'm sitting right in the draft. I'll
have a stiff neck tonight."

"Then sit someplace else."

"I always sit here."

"Ten minutes of fresh air isn't going to kill you.
I was on my feet all night and need some oxygen,"
said Kröger.

"Stop acting like you're the only one who works
here," Kathrin snapped, jumping up to close the
window, but Christian wouldn't budge.

"Stop squabbling, you two. The window stays
open. Now pull yourselves together," Bodenstein
warned. "Move somewhere else for ten minutes,
Kathrin."

She snorted, packed her bag, and moved. Pia was just drinking her third coffee of the morning and still fighting off one yawn attack after another. She gazed around the table, seeing nothing but exhausted faces and red-rimmed eyes. The new case had brought a whole pile of additional work. They'd already been working almost three weeks, with no weekends off, and they seldom got home on time, so it was beginning to take a toll on all of them—especially since they'd had no tangible results to advance the cases any further. They were fumbling around in the fog, and Pia wasn't the only one who was slowly but surely losing patience. Once again, it had been a very short night. She'd gotten home at ten to three and then needed an hour to calm down before she could get to sleep.

After Kai had reported on the key details regarding the body, it was Kröger's turn. The fingerprints they had found on the door frame and the chair belonged to Bernd Prinzler. The specialists from the State Criminal Police headquarters had tried in vain to find out where the camera in the therapy room had been transmitting and for how long. They also hadn't yet succeeded in cracking Leonie Verges's laptop; without a password, it was as good as useless. The horrific messages on the answering machine had come from a phone with an unlisted number, so that hadn't produced any leads, either.

Kröger and his team had discovered cabinets full of patient files in the house, but it would take a very long time to check all of them. Anyway, it was doubtful that the perp would be included in the therapist's files. According to the Web site of the Center for Psychotraumatology, Leonie Verges had no male patients; she had treated women exclusively.

"It could be that a husband or ex-partner hated her so much that he wanted to kill her," Kathrin suggested.

"We found Prinzler's prints on the door frame and chair," said Pia. "But how did he get into the house?"

"Maybe she let him in, and then he took a key with him after he tied her to the chair and installed the camera," Cem suggested.

"So why did he go back?" Pia was thinking out loud as she looked at the whiteboard where she'd written the name Leonie Verges. Arrows pointed to Hanna and Meike Herzmann, to Prinzler and Rothemund. She had a strong feeling that there was a connection between the attack on Hanna Herzmann and the murder of Leonie Verges; possibly they were even the work of the same perp. Last night, it hadn't occurred to her, but this morning when she woke up, she'd asked herself who had actually called the police and ambulance. It had not been Meike Herzmann. So she'd asked to see the police log about the call to the emergency dispatch number. A man had called at 10:12 P.M. without giving his name. "In Liederbach, Alt Niederhofheim Twenty-two, there's a dead body in the house. The gate and front door are open," he'd told the dispatcher.

"Prinzler's car was seen several times by the neighbors," Pia said. "Was he casing the house, or did he actually know Leonie Verges?"

"If I wanted to case a place, I sure wouldn't drive around in such a conspicuous vehicle," said Kai. "By the way, the infrared radio camera is a mass-produced item. There isn't much hope of tracking down where it was purchased."

Bodenstein, who'd been listening without comment, cleared his throat.

"What I'd really like to know is what Kilian Rothemund had to do with Leonie Verges," he said. "He was with Prinzler at Hanna Herzmann's house. I think we have to concentrate our attention on him. He raped Hanna Herzmann, he's been convicted of child abuse before, he lives in a trailer at a run-down trailer park with no social ties, and he'd had multiple visits from underage girls. I wouldn't be surprised if he had something to do with our Mermaid, too."

"What's his motive?" Pia asked. "He gets off on little kids but rapes a grown woman. And then he makes her therapist die in agony. Why?"

"Because he's sick," said Kathrin. "Maybe Hanna or Leonie found out that he'd violated his parole. Or they found out that he killed a girl, so he wanted to stop them from going to the police."

For a moment, nobody said a word; they were all thinking about this theory.

"And Prinzler could be covering for him or even helping him," Kai added. "He owes Rothemund from the old days."

"But why would they both know Leonie?" Bodenstein asked, puzzled.

Good question. No answer.

"If it's the way Kathrin suspects," Pia put in, "then Hanna Herzmann is in great danger. After all, she isn't dead and might remember something."

"You're right," Bodenstein said with a nod. "We have to protect her, starting now."

The phone on the table rang. Meike Herzmann was waiting downstairs. Last night, she'd been in shock and could hardly manage to say anything coherent, but she'd promised to come to the station today. Kathrin went down to get her from the watch room.

"We'll take up this matter later," Bodenstein decided. "Pia and I will talk to the young woman. Kai, you take care of setting up protection for Hanna Herzmann. Cem, at eleven o'clock you and Kathrin will go to the autopsy of Leonie Verges."

They all nodded, and Cem and Kai got up and left the room.

"Now I'm anxious to see if she's finally going to tell us what she knows." Pia got up, closed the window, and let down the blinds so that the room wouldn't heat up again.

A few minutes later, Meike Herzmann was sitting at the conference table, pale and visibly exhausted.

"I visited my mother last night," she began in a low voice. "She's still in pretty bad shape, and she can't remember anything. But . . . I . . . I know it was stupid of me not to come to you earlier. I . . . I didn't realize how bad the situation was. . . ."

Her voice trembled and she stopped talking. She opened her backpack and took out two pieces of paper.

"This is the printout of an e-mail from Kilian Rothemund that I found on my mother's computer," she said, shoving the first paper across the table. "And this . . . is the note that he put in my mother's mail slot."

Pia looked at the page, which had obviously been torn out of a notebook, and read the few sentences.

Waited until 1:30, she read. *Wanted to see you again. My cell battery is dead! Here's the address. BP knows about it. Call me. K.*

She turned the note over and read the address. Then she scanned the printout of the e-mail.

Hanna, why don't you answer? Did something happen? Did I say or do something that made you mad? Please call me. Unfortunately, I couldn't talk to Leonie anymore. She won't call me back, either, but on Monday I'm going to A anyway and meet with the people with whom B got in contact. They're finally ready to talk to me. I'm thinking of you! Don't forget me. K.

Her anger turned to fury as she looked at the young woman who now sat there meek and subdued, as if someone had caught her with a cheat sheet during an exam at school. What a stupid little bitch.

"Do you know what you've done by withholding this information from us?" she said, controlling herself with difficulty as she shoved the note over to her boss. "We've been looking for Prinzler and Rothemund for days. Leonie Verges might still be alive if you hadn't been so uncooperative."

Meike bit her lip and lowered her head in shame.

"Is there anything else that you've kept from us?" Bodenstein asked. Pia could hear from the sharp undertone in his voice how incensed he was, too. But unlike her, he still had an iron grip on his emotions.

"No," Meike whispered. Her eyes were pleading, her expression despairing. "I . . . I . . . You don't understand. . . ."

"No, I certainly do not," Bodenstein replied frostily.

"You don't know my mother." Suddenly, the tears came. "She gets really mad if anyone messes with her research. That's why I went to this address. I . . . I thought I'd find out something and be able to tell you. . . ."

"You did *what?*" Pia couldn't believe her ears.

"It's an old sort of farm with a junkyard and a tall fence around it." Meike sobbed. "I climbed up on a lookout tower just to see what was inside. But these bikers saw me and sent an attack dog after me. I . . . I was lucky that a ranger or something . . . shot the dog, and I got away."

Pia was seldom speechless, but she was now.

"You have withheld important information," said Bodenstein. "And it may have caused a death. What about your mother's computer that you got the e-mail from? Where is it?"

"At home," Meike said after a pause.

"Good. Then we'll go there now and get it." Bodenstein slapped his palm on the table and stood up. "Your actions will have consequences for you, Ms. Herzmann, I can promise you that."

Next to Corinna, Emma always felt inadequate and somehow pathetic. Right now, she was sitting at the big table in the dining room, soaked with sweat and shapeless, like a whale on dry land. Corinna was cooking in the open-plan high-tech stainless-steel kitchen for her four sons, who came home at all different times from school.

Corinna had been on her feet since six in the morning; she had spent several hours at the office, while also taking care of her family and the housekeeping. Emma already felt overtaxed with only one child. In the past, she had been in charge of the most demanding aspects of her job, including planning, organizing, and improvising, all handled under the most difficult and primitive conditions. At nineteen, she moved out of her parents' house and had always managed her own life by herself without problem. What had changed? When had she stopped trusting herself? She used to be responsible for making sure that tons of food supplies and medical equipment safely reached the most remote corners of the world, while today even a trip to the supermarket presented a challenge.

The kitchen smelled like tomatoes and basil, garlic and sautéed meat, and Emma's stomach growled with hunger. As Corinna emptied the dishwasher, she talked about the final preparations for the big party on Friday.

"I'll be done in a sec," Corinna said with a smile. "You can spare a few minutes, can't you?"

I have all day, Emma thought, but she didn't say it out loud, merely nodding. In silence, she listened to the little everyday anecdotes that Corinna recounted about her husband and sons, and suddenly she felt so envious. How she would have liked to have a home and a husband who spontaneously brought home sushi for dinner, who watered the garden and did all sorts of things with his sons, and who every evening shared a glass of wine with his wife as they discussed the events of that day. How did her life look in comparison? Her only home was a furnished apartment that belonged to her in-laws, and she had a husband who hardly ever told her anything and who had simply abandoned her shortly before the birth of their second child. She didn't even want to think about her terrible suspicions about what he might have done to Louisa. The feeling had begun to grow that she'd lost Florian forever, and in the past few days this feeling had changed to certainty. What had happened could no longer be undone.

"All right, then." Corinna sat down across from Emma at the table. "What did you want to talk to me about?"

Emma mustered her courage.

"Florian never told me that he had a twin sister. Nobody talks about her."

The smile vanished from Corinna's face. She propped her elbows on the table and buried her face in her hands. Emma was afraid she wouldn't get an answer, because Corinna was quiet for so long. Finally, she took her hands away and gave a big sigh.

"The story of Michaela is very sad and painful for the whole Finkbeiner family," she said quietly.

"Even as a little girl, she suffered from mental illness. Today she could probably be helped, but back in the seventies, child psychology hadn't advanced very far, and they didn't know what multiple personality disorder was. They probably just thought she was a stubborn, lying child. That view did her a great injustice, but nobody knew any better."

"That's just horrible," Emma whispered.

"Josef and Renate worried more about Michaela than about the rest of us children," Corinna went on. "But all the love and care eventually did no good. She ran away from home the first time when she was twelve, and was caught shoplifting. After that she was always getting in trouble with the police. Josef was able to smooth over a lot of it through his connections, but Michaela didn't appreciate his efforts. She started drinking and using drugs early on, and she refused to listen to any of us. For Florian, it was especially bad."

All happiness had drained from her eyes, and Emma was sorry she'd brought up a topic that evoked such painful memories for Corinna.

"Why didn't Florian ever tell me about her?" Emma asked. "I would have understood. There's a black sheep in every family."

"You have to understand how terrible it was for him and how much it made him suffer. In the end, it was probably the reason why he left here as soon as he could," replied Corinna. "He was always living in the shadow of his sister, who got much more attention than he did. No matter how loving, diligent, and talented he was, it was always about Michaela."

"What happened to her?"

"She dropped out of school when she was fifteen and started turning tricks to finance her drug habit. At some point, she ended up in the underworld. Josef tried everything to get her out, but she wouldn't accept any help. After a suicide attempt, she spent a few years in a locked psychiatric ward. She never wanted to speak to her parents or to any of us siblings again."

Emma noticed that Corinna spoke about her stepsister only in the past tense.

"Where is she now? Does anyone know?"

On the stove, the pasta water boiled over with a hiss, and at the same time a car pulled up outside the kitchen window. The engine noise stopped, two car doors slammed, and a lively child's voice called, "Mama, I'm hungry!"

Corinna didn't seem to pay any attention. All energy seemed to have drained from her body. She pressed her lips together and looked infinitely sad.

"Michaela died a few years ago," she said. "Only Ralf, Nicky, Sarah, and I attended her funeral. Since then, no one has ever mentioned her name."

Emma stared at her friend in shock.

"Believe me, Emma, it's better that way." Corinna put her hand on Emma's briefly, then got up and went to the stove to put the pasta in the pot. "Don't tear open old wounds. Michaela really brought a lot of trouble down on Josef and Renate."

Torben, Corinna's youngest, stormed through the open French door into the dining room, flung his backpack into a corner, and ran into the kitchen without noticing Emma.

"I'm really really hungry," he announced.

"Wash your hands and take your backpack upstairs. We're eating in ten minutes." Corinna stroked his hair absentmindedly, then looked out at the terrace. "Thanks for picking him up, Helmut. Would you like to stay for dinner?"

Only now did Emma notice the caretaker, Helmut Grasser, standing in the doorway. She stood up.

"Hello, Mr. Grasser," she said.

"Hello, Mrs. Finkbeiner." He smiled. "How are you doing in this heat?"

"So far so good." Emma also managed a smile. She'd hoped to be able to talk to Corinna some more about her suspicions regarding Florian and Louisa, but that wouldn't be possible if Torben and the caretaker were going to join them at the table.

"I guess I'll be going," she said, and Corinna made no attempt to stop her. Her expression was somber, her usual exuberance extinguished. She took the lid off the pan with the simmering meat sauce and stirred it. Was Corinna upset with her because she'd asked about Florian's twin sister?

"Thanks for your candor." Emma didn't dare give her friend the usual hug. "See you tomorrow."

"See you, Emma." Her smile seemed forced. "Don't hold it against Florian."

Bodenstein had squeezed into the passenger seat of Meike Herzmann's Mini, because he didn't trust her not to try and ditch them. Pia got in the unmarked car and followed them into the city. Meanwhile, Kai had applied for an arrest warrant for Bernd Prinzler and a search warrant for his property. Pia still could hardly believe what Meike Herzmann had done. Her cell rang just as she was passing the tower at the fairgrounds, and she answered it.

"Frey here. Hello, Ms. Kirchhoff. I was just informed that you're making progress in the investigation," said the head state attorney. Pia was astounded by how good the communication within the Frankfurt state attorney's office seemed to be.

"Yes, we have the address of a suspect in both the Hanna Herzmann case and the new homicide," she replied.

"The new homicide?"

Aha. So their grapevine wasn't that good after all.

Pia explained to him briefly about the torturous death that Leonie Verges had suffered, and she also reported that Prinzler had been seen in the vicinity of her house.

"Bernd Prinzler is a member of the Frankfurt Road Kings," she said. "We know that he was in contact with Ms. Herzmann, and we found his prints in the house of the deceased Ms. Verges. His vehicle was seen several times by the neighbors in Liederbach. We also found out that Prinzler knows Kilian Rothemund—he's the man we're searching for, to charge him with rape and aggravated assault in the Herzmann case."

"The two do know each other, at any rate," said the state attorney. "The law office in which Rothemund was a partner represented Prinzler and his gang for years."

"We received information that Rothemund has fled to Amsterdam. He was recognized on the train, but unfortunately our Dutch colleagues failed to apprehend him at the train station. We also learned that he violated his probation."

"How?"

"Neighbors at the trailer park have often seen underage girls entering his trailer. For that, he could go back to prison."

"That's absolutely unbelievable."

"I know. For now, we consider it likely that Rothemund may have something to do with the case of the girl found in the river. There is definitely a connection between the attack on Ms. Herzmann and the murder of Leonie Verges, at any rate. So that's it. My boss will be on *Germany's Most Wanted* tomorrow night, and we hope that afterward somebody will call in who saw something or even knows where Rothemund might be."

"That's a real possibility," the state attorney agreed.

Pia had to step on the gas because Meike ran a yellow light at the intersection of Friedrich-Ebert-Park and Mainzer Landstrasse. A red light flashed.

"Shit!" Pia exclaimed.

"Excuse me?" Frey said.

"Sorry. But I was just caught in a speed trap. Red light and phone at my ear."

"That could be expensive." The state attorney sounded amused. "Thanks for the information, Ms. Kirchhoff. How's it going with Lilly, by the way?"

"Everything's fine, thanks." Pia smiled. "Except for the fact that she got a tick that had to be removed in a dramatic operation."

Frey laughed.

"I'm sorry that I've had so little time for her," said Pia. "But with luck, we'll probably clear up these cases soon."

"I hope so, too. If I can do anything for you, don't hesitate to ask."

Pia assured him she would, and ended the call. Only then did she recall what Rothemund's ex-wife and Kai Ostermann had told her. Chief State Attorney Frey and Rothemund had once been the best of friends; then Frey had not only leveled accusations at his old pal but had mercilessly set the media hounds after him. Pia pondered whether to call him back and ask him about that, but she rejected the idea at once. It was none of her business what had happened between the old friends in the past.

A few minutes later, she pulled up in front of the house on Schulstrasse in Sachsenhausen and waited for Bodenstein, who was impounding Hanna's computer from her daughter's apartment. Pia was annoyed with Meike Herzmann, but she was even more annoyed with herself. Yesterday, when she and Bodenstein were at Herzmann Productions, she'd thought about the computer, but then she'd been distracted by Lilly's call about the tick and forgotten to ask about it. That was no mere oversight; it was a serious mistake that she should not have made.

Pia was actually supposed to drive with Cem and Kathrin straight from forensics to Langensebold to arrest Bernd Prinzler, but Dr. Nicola Engel had called them back. Even though, after more than fourteen years, Prinzler had a clean record, he still belonged to the inner circle of the Frankfurt Road

Kings and was known to be dangerous and capable of violence. The commissioner had arranged for a "tactical action" in cooperation with a squad from the Special Assignment Unit. Bodenstein thought that was excessive, but Engel remained firm. She was afraid that Prinzler would not respond to a polite ring of the doorbell. The action had to be decisive and carried out with the element of surprise. Engel was organizing the operation herself, so Pia got to go home early for a change. She'd stopped by the supermarket in Liederbach on her way home and bought things for dinner. Over the past month, Christoph had been responsible for making dinner more and more often. He had a passionate love of food and was a much better cook than Pia, who usually didn't feel like standing in front of the stove after work. But today she did. She turned on the electric grill on the terrace, cut zucchini and eggplant into thin slices, and placed them on the grill. While the veggies sizzled, she mixed up a marinade of olive oil, salt, pepper, and crushed garlic.

The results of the autopsy of Leonie Verges had confirmed Henning's initial theory. The woman had died of multiple organ failure due to complete dehydration: a torturous death. If they'd dis-covered her two hours earlier, they might have been able to save her. It was a gruesome way to die, and Pia didn't want to imagine what the woman must have gone through in the last hours of her life. Had she still hoped for help, or was she aware that she was going to die? But why did she have to die? And why like that? The camera, which had been aimed directly at the chair, and those appalling messages on the answering machine, which Leonie must have heard, displayed an extraordinary level of sadism. Not characteristic of someone like Bernd Prinzler, who'd previously been known for assault and the use of firearms. But Pia had been with Kripo too long to believe that criminals followed any logical patterns.

Hanna Herzmann had been a patient of Leonie Verges; this connection was clear. Had Leonie introduced Hanna to Kilian Rothemund, or vice versa? Rothemund and Prinzler, she knew from before; that was also clear. Pia hoped that Hanna would soon be able to remember something. She was the only one who might be able to shed some light on this complicated case.

Deep in thought, Pia placed the grilled zucchini strips in the marinade and put a layer of eggplant slices on the grill. She plucked a handful of sage leaves from the plant that stood on the kitchen window shelf along with the fresh basil, lemon balm, and rosemary. Lilly loved Pia's special recipe—spaghetti with sage, Parma ham, capers, and garlic—and Christoph always bravely ate it, too.

In front of the house, the dogs began barking in a tone that signaled pure joy—Christoph and Lilly had arrived. Only seconds later, the girl dashed into the kitchen, her pigtails flying and her eyes shining. She hugged Pia, and the words bubbled out of her like a waterfall: *trampoline, Grandpa, pony, leopards, baby giraffe.* . . . Pia had to laugh.

"Take it easy," she said to calm the girl down. "At that speed, I can't understand a word."

"But I have to hurry," Lilly said breathlessly, as honest and serious as only a seven-year-old can be. "Since you're finally here, I want to tell you about everything—absolutely everything."

"But we've got all evening."

"That's what you always say," Lilly replied. "And then your phone rings and you leave Grandpa and me alone."

Christoph came into the kitchen, followed by the dogs. He was holding a paper packet, which he put down on the counter before he gave Pia a kiss.

"She's got a point there." He grinned, inspecting with a critical eye the ingredients that Pia had laid out, and raised his eyebrows. "Sage pasta?"

"Oh, my favorite!" cried Lilly. "I could die for sage pasta! Grandpa bought lamb cutlets. Gross!"

"We'll try to find a compromise," said Pia with a smile. "Pasta and lamb cutlets actually go together nicely. And before that, we're having marinated zucchini and eggplant."

"And before that, we have the bathtub," Christoph added.

Lilly cocked her head critically.

"Okay," she said after a moment. "But only if Pia comes with me."

"It's a deal." Pia abandoned all thoughts of the case. Work would catch up with her again soon enough.

"Hi, Mama."

Meike stood at the foot of the bed. She had to force herself to look at her mother's disfigured face under the faint light cast by the reading lamp located in the strip above the head of the bed. The swelling had gone down a bit, but the bruises looked worse than they had in the morning.

At least now they'd moved Hanna from the ICU to a regular ward. In front of the door stood the uniformed cop that Inspector Bodenstein had ordered.

"Hi, Meike," Hanna murmured. "Get a chair and come sit by me."

Meike did as she was told. She felt miserable. All day, the policewoman's words had been tormenting her. What if Leonie Verges's death was her fault because she hadn't told the police about that stupid note?

There was no excuse or justification for what she'd done, even though she'd talked herself into keeping the note secret in order not to ruin

Hanna's research. In reality, she didn't give a damn.

Hanna stretched out her hand and heaved a sigh when Meike hesitantly took it.

"What's happened?" Hanna asked softly.

Meike was struggling with what to say. This morning, she hadn't said a word about Leonie Verges's death, and she didn't want to mention it now, either. Everything around her seemed to be breaking apart and dissolving. A person she had known and spoken to was now dead. She had been tortured to death while Meike thought only of herself, refusing to acknowledge any possible consequences for others. All her life, she'd felt like a victim, unfairly treated, unloved. She'd tried to gain the affection of others by sheer obstinacy; she had eaten until she was obese and then starved herself until she was anorexic; she had been nasty, unfair, and hurtful, all in a desperate attempt to win love and attention. She had often accused her mother of being egotistical, while she was actually the selfish one. She had only ever demanded but given nothing in return. She had not been a very lovable girl, and it was no surprise that she'd never had a best friend or any friend at all. Someone who didn't like herself couldn't expect to be liked by others. The only person in the world who had accepted Meike as she was, was her mother, of all people. Yet she had pictured Hanna as an enemy because she was jealous of her. Hanna represented everything she so urgently wanted to be but would never achieve: self-confident, beautiful, surrounded by men.

"I know it's not easy for you, either," Hanna murmured, squeezing Meike's hand lightly. "I'm glad you're here."

Tears came to Meike's eyes. More than anything, she would have liked to put her head in Hanna's lap and sob, because she was so ashamed of her mean and spiteful behavior. She thought about all the atrocious things she'd said and done to her mother and wished she had the guts to feel remorse and respond honestly.

I scratched your car and slashed your tires, Mama, she thought. I snooped around in your computer and didn't give the note that Kilian Rothemund wrote to you to the police, simply because I wanted to make myself seem interesting to Wolfgang. Maybe that's why Leonie Verges had to die. I'm jealous and evil and disgusting, and I don't deserve your patience and indulgence.

She thought all of these things but didn't say a word.

"Could you get me a new iPhone? I still have a twin card in my desk at the office," Hanna whispered. "Maybe you can sync it. My access code for MobileMe is written on a note under my desk blotter."

"Sure, no problem. I'll do it tomorrow morning," Meike managed to reply.

"Thanks." Hanna closed her eyes.

Meike sat there for a long time, staring at her sleeping mother. Not until she'd left the hospital and was sitting in her car did it occur to Meike that she hadn't even asked Hanna how she was feeling.

Wednesday, June 30, 2010

At exactly five o'clock in the morning, a helicopter appeared over the treetops. Simultaneously, there was movement at the edge of the forest around Bernd Prinzler's property. Black-clad figures wearing masks broke through the underbrush and surrounded the fenced area. The rising sun was still hidden behind misty swaths of rain-damp air. Bodenstein, Pia, Cem Altunay, and Kathrin Fachinger followed the action from the woods, watching as ten armed commandos from the Special Assignment Unit rappelled from the helicopter hovering a few yards above the meadow near the residence. Bolt cutters sliced through the metal struts of the big gate like butter. Five of the high-powered vehicles with mirrored windows sped across the gravel forest road and turned at high speed into the enclosure. Barely three minutes after the helo's arrival, the fortress had been stormed.

"Not bad," Cem remarked after checking his watch.

"That's what I call shooting cannons at sparrows," Bodenstein grumbled. His stony expression did not reveal much, but Pia knew that he was angry about Nicola Engel's criticism. On the way here from Hofheim, no one had said a word after Bodenstein and Commissioner Engel had gotten into a brief but intense verbal exchange as they passed the Offenbacher Kreuz. Last night, they had used satellite imagery to analyze the situation at the site behind the section of woods between Langensebold and Hüttengesäss and planned the action with an SAU squad and a hundred riot police. Bodenstein had called the action altogether excessive and a total waste of taxpayer funds. Nicola Engel had reproached him sharply, chiding him for not making any progress in the past three weeks. She'd had to justify this failure to the Interior Ministry.

Pia and Cem had merely exchanged glances and very wisely said nothing, because one false word in a situation of such high-explosive tension could have the effect of a fire accelerant.

Startled by the sudden unrest and the noise, a herd of deer fled with graceful bounds through the woods. In the surrounding trees, the first birds were beginning their morning concert, utterly unimpressed by what was going on beneath them.

"Why are so you pissed off about what Engel said?" Pia asked her boss. "If they screw up this raid, it's not our problem."

"That's not what I'm mad about," replied Bodenstein. "Frankfurt and the State Criminal Police know very well where Prinzler lives. They've had him in their sights for a long time, but until yesterday they had no verifiable reason to search his house."

"What? They knew about this place?" Pia asked incredulously. "Why weren't we told about that? When we visited Prinzler's mother, our colleagues in Frankfurt must have known that we were looking for him."

"Because in their eyes, we're just a couple of dumb provincial cops," said Bodenstein, rubbing his unshaven chin. "But this time, I'm not going to let it drop. If it turns out that Prinzler killed Leonie Verges and we could have prevented it if communication with the Frankfurters hadn't been so bad, heads will roll."

The police radio Pia was holding hissed and crackled.

"We're in," she heard a distorted voice say. "One man, one woman, two kids. No resistance."

"Let's go," said Bodenstein.

They headed down the hill, trudging through dry leaves, and then climbed over a ditch to enter the property through the gate the SAU had cut open in their assault. On the left side was a big barn with a barbecue area in front of it. Glancing behind a chain-link fence, they could see a vast number of car and motorcycle parts, sorted and piled up in orderly fashion. The house was farther back, surrounded by an idyllic, expansive yard with ancient trees and blooming bushes. There was a pool and a playground for the children. A regular paradise.

A man was lying on his stomach on the wet lawn not far from the house. He was barefoot, wearing only a T-shirt and shorts, and his hands were bound behind his back with plastic cuffs. Two officers helped him to his feet. In the front door, which had been smashed in, stood a dark-haired woman, her arms around a boy of about twelve, who was sobbing hysterically. A second boy, somewhat older and almost as tall as his mother, refused to cry, but his fright at the dawn attack was clearly etched on his face.

Dr. Nicola Engel, wearing a gray pantsuit, over which she had put on a bulletproof vest, stood in front of the bearded giant like David facing Goliath. She looked composed and self-confident, as usual.

"Mr. Prinzler, you are under provisional arrest," she said. "I assume that you know your rights."

"You are such a bunch of idiots," said Bernd Prinzler, outraged. His voice was deep and rough, definitely not the one on Leonie Verges's answering machine. "Why did you have to terrify my family? There's a doorbell at the gate."

"Precisely," Bodenstein muttered.

"Take him away," said Commissioner Engel.

"May I put on some clothes first?" Prinzler asked.

"No," said Nicola Engel, her voice icy.

Pia could see that the man would have liked to make a rude reply, but he knew all about being arrested. Any insult would not improve his situation. So he contented himself with spitting in the grass right next to Nicola Engel's Louboutins. Then with head held high, he walked between the two SAU men, who looked like dwarfs next to him, and got into one of the black vans.

"Mr. Bodenstein, Ms. Kirchhoff, you may now speak to his wife," said Nicola Engel.

"I want to talk to Mr. Prinzler, not to his wife," countered Bodenstein, which earned him a dirty look, which he chose to ignore. A commotion and babble of voices in the house drowned out her reply. In a room in the basement of the house, the police had found two young women.

"Well, well," said Dr. Nicola Engel with a triumphant note in her voice. "I knew it."

Last night after leaving the hospital, Meike had sent him a text message. She'd been waiting in vain for a reply ever since. She hadn't heard from Wolfgang since Sunday, except for the conversation on Monday morning in his office, but at that time there had been no chance to exchange a personal word with him. She felt that she'd been left in the lurch. Hadn't he promised to take care of her? To stand by her? Why wasn't he getting in touch with her? Had she done something wrong, something to offend him? Several times that night, Meike had awakened and checked her smartphone, but he'd sent neither a text nor an e-mail. Her disappointment grew from one minute to the next. If there was one person in her life she could always depend on, it was Wolfgang. Her disappointment changed to anger, then to worry. What if something had happened to him, too?

By nine o'clock, she could no longer stand it, so she called him on his cell. He picked up on the second ring. Meike, who hadn't expected him to answer, didn't know what to say.

So she said, "Hi, Wolfgang."

"Hello, Meike. I didn't see your text until this morning, and I'd turned off the ringer on my phone," he said. She had the feeling he wasn't telling her the truth.

"No big deal," she lied. "I just wanted to tell you that Mama is doing a little better. I visited her twice yesterday."

"That's good. She needs you right now."

"Unfortunately, she still can't remember anything. The doctors say it may take a while until her memory of the attack returns. Sometimes it never does."

"Maybe that's for the best." Wolfgang cleared his throat. "Meike, I'm afraid I have to go to an important meeting now. I'll call you—"

"Leonie Verges is dead," Meike said, interrupting him.

"Who is dead?"

"Mama's psych lady in Liederbach, where we were on Saturday."

"Good Lord, that's horrible," Wolfgang said, sounding upset. "How do you know this?"

"Because I happened to drop by there. I wanted to ask her about something, on account of Mama. The front door was open and . . . and I saw her. It was . . . awful. I just can't get that sight out of my mind." Meike made her voice sound shaky, like a scared little girl's. This trick had always worked on Wolfgang. Maybe now he'd feel sorry for her and invite her to stay at his house again. "Somebody tied her to a chair and taped her mouth shut. The police said she probably died of thirst. I gave them Mama's computer from her office. Do you think that was the right thing to do?"

It took a moment for him to answer. Wolfgang was a cautious man and always took time to deliberate before he said anything. No doubt he needed a moment to process this information. Meike heard a buzz of voices in the background, footsteps; then a door closed and it was quiet.

"Of course that was the right thing to do," Wolfgang said at last. "Meike, you should keep out of all this and let the police do their job. What you're doing is dangerous. Can't you go stay with your father for a few days?"

Meike couldn't believe her ears. What kind of shitty suggestion was that?

She mustered her courage.

"I . . . I thought maybe I could stay with you for a couple of days. You did offer, after all," she said in her little-girl voice. "I can't go off to Stuttgart and leave Mama all alone."

Again, it seemed to take endless seconds before Wolfgang replied. She had caught him off guard with her request to stay with him; he hadn't actually offered any such invitation. Secretly, she hoped for comforting words and a spontaneous "But of course," yet the longer he made her wait for an answer, the more she knew that he was trying to think of an excuse that wouldn't hurt her feelings.

"I'm afraid that's just not possible," he said at last.

She could hear the discomfort in his voice and knew what a conflict of conscience she had caused him. That gave her a malicious satisfaction.

"We have a house full of guests until the weekend."

"All right, then, I guess not," she replied lightly, although she would have liked to howl in fury at his rejection. "Did you have time to think over the internship idea? I'm out of a job now."

Another man might have told her to stop bugging him, but Wolfgang's innate courtesy prevented him from saying anything like that.

"Let's talk about that on the phone later," he replied, hedging. "Right now, I really have to get to that meeting. They're all waiting for me. Keep your chin up. And take care of yourself."

Meike flung her cell onto the sofa and burst into tears of disappointment. Nothing was going the way she'd hoped. Damn it! Nobody was interested in her. In the past, she would have gone to see her father and demanded his sympathy, but now that he had a new girlfriend, his interest in his daughter had waned. The last time Meike had visited Stuttgart, that bitch had had the nerve to tell her that she should start behaving like an adult instead of like a pubescent fifteen-year-old. Since then, Meike hadn't bothered to visit.

She dropped onto the sofa and thought about what to do, whom she could call. But she didn't have a clue.

The two terrified young women they had found in the basement of Bernd Prinzler's house were anything but enthusiastic about their "liberation." The fact that they were Russians and staying in a less than luxurious room was enough proof to the squad leader that they were prostitutes who were being held against their will. Victims of human trafficking. In the euphoria over this discovery, the police hadn't allowed the women to bring along any personal items. Later at the Frankfurt police headquarters, it turned out that Natasha and

Ludmilla Valenkova were in no way street-walkers. Natasha was working as an au pair for the Prinzlers. She possessed a passport and a valid residence visa. Ludmilla, her older sister, had previously worked for the family as an au pair, but was studying financial IT in Frankfurt. She, too, was living in Germany legally, on a student visa.

All in all the morning's action had proved to be the height of senselessness and had cost a pile of money. Prinzler's attorney, a tough woman in her mid-thirties, had made it clear that she would sue for destruction of property as well as for damages due to pain and suffering. She was planning to ask for a considerable sum for the anxiety the family had suffered.

Pia knew that Bodenstein felt no satisfaction at having been proved right. And it infuriated him that his colleagues in Frankfurt had not yet given him an opportunity to speak with Prinzler. But the morning circus had produced one positive result, because Bodenstein happened to run into an old colleague at police headquarters on Adickesallee who had led the previous arrest of Kilian Rothemund. Lutz Altmüller had also been part of the Leopard Special Commission, which had worked the so-far-unsolved case of the other dead girl, who had been found in the Main River on July 31, 2001. Altmüller was willing to meet with Pia, Christian Kröger, and Cem Altunay, and he had suggested they convene at the Unterschweinstiege Restaurant, not far from the Frankfurt Airport. That sounded good to Pia, because she had promised Bodenstein she would drive him to the airport. His flight to Munich left at two-thirty, and since he had only a carry-on, Kai had already checked him in online and downloaded his boarding pass on his iPhone. Bodenstein would be there in plenty of time if she dropped him off at one-thirty at Departure Hall A.

They drove to the Unterschweinstiege, parked in the parking garage, and walked across the street. Cem and Christian were waiting in front of the former forester's lodge and waved to them as they wandered in search of the restaurant in between the office buildings and the airport hotel.

Chief Detective Inspector Lutz Altmüller was sitting at the first table near the entrance, enjoying an impressive serving of beef brisket with green sauce and salted potatoes. Pia hadn't eaten anything all day, so the sight of his food made her mouth water.

"I thought that as long as we're meeting here at lunchtime, we might as well eat lunch," Altmüller admitted frankly after the greetings and intro-ductions were done. "Have a seat, everyone. Have you eaten yet? I can highly recommend the green sauce."

He brandished his knife and fork, talking with his mouth full.

"Where's Bodenstein?"

"He's flying to Munich," Pia said. "Tonight, he's going to be on *Germany's Most Wanted.*"

"Ah, yes, that's right. He told me about it."

It was hard to imagine that Lutz Altmüller had ever been a successful track and field athlete. In 1996, he had participated in the Olympics in Atlanta, and that had given him a special status on the Frankfurt police force. Since then, his muscles had been transformed into flab, the sad result of eating too much fatty food in combination with lack of exercise.

"So, kids, what do you want to know?" He dabbed his mouth with his napkin, took a swig of hard cider, and leaned back. The chair groaned under the weight of his hefty bulk.

"At present, we're investigating three cases," Pia began. "And we keep running into the names Kilian Rothemund and Bernd Prinzler. Prinzler was arrested this morning, but Rothemund is still a fugitive. We'd really like to learn more about that man."

Lutz Altmüller listened attentively. His body may have turned sluggish in the intervening years, but his memory was sharp. Back then, in July 2001, he'd been one of the Kripo officers who had driven to the site where the girl's body was found, and he'd played a leading role in setting up the special commission. Three days after they found the dead girl, a big commotion arose. An anonymous caller had claimed that he knew where the girl was from. It was their first hot lead—and, unfortunately, also their last. The caller refused to speak with them in person and so had sent his lawyer.

"Kilian Rothemund," Pia guessed.

"Precisely," Lutz Altmüller confirmed. "We met at a pub in Sachsenhausen with Rothemund, who at that time would not reveal the identity of his client. He claimed that the girl may have been the victim of a child-porn ring. His client, also an affected individual, was firmly convinced of this and was able to finger the men who were pulling the strings. All of this was very vague, of course, but it was our first promising lead. Anyway, only a few days later, the state attorney's office initiated an investigation into Rothemund himself, and in raids of his office and home, they found a huge number of incriminating photos, videos, and even a compromising tape that showed Rothemund having sexual intercourse with under-age children."

"But that doesn't make any sense at all," said Christian Kröger. "Why would Rothemund draw attention to himself like that?"

"Good question." Altmüller nodded and frowned. "It was extremely strange. Rothemund was brought to trial and ended up behind bars. His client remained anonymous and was never heard from again. And so the case was never solved."

"Nine years later, we fish another dead girl out of the Main with signs of abuse on her body," said Christian. "And at the same time, this Rothemund again pops into the focus of our investigation."

"So far, we don't know whether he actually has anything to do with our Mermaid," Cem put in. "It's only a hunch."

The waiter appeared at the table and took away Altmüller's plate. Pia ignored her rumbling stomach and ordered only a diet Coke. Cem and Christian also chose not to have anything to eat.

Altmüller waited until the waiter had brought the drinks, then leaned forward.

"My colleagues and I thought at the time that Rothemund was framed," he said in a low voice. "The child-porn Mafia uses all kinds of intimidation methods. They aren't squeamish when there's a danger of exposure, and they have an excellent network. They have connections with public agencies and officials, and at the highest levels of finance and politics. Understandably, nobody is interested in naming names. It often takes years for us to get a conviction or break up a ring, but most of the time we're left empty-handed. They are better equipped, with more money and connections, and more advanced technology— fighting them is simply beyond our means. We're always limping a few steps behind these criminals."

"Why didn't Rothemund defend himself if he was supposed to be innocent?" Pia asked.

"He did. Until the end, he disputed having had anything to do with the material presented in court against him," replied Altmüller. "But the evidence was so overwhelming that the court paid no heed to his objections. Add to that the fact that the public had already prejudged the case in the press. It was very strange. Despite a news black-out, everything leaked out. And then there was that memorable press conference with State Attorney Markus Maria Frey. . . ."

"With whom Rothemund was very good friends at one time," Pia added.

"Yes, that was common knowledge," Altmüller said with a nod. "But the friendship was shattered when Rothemund began to defend big-time criminals and won a few spectacular cases because he was able to prove procedural mistakes and failures on the part of the investigating authorities and the state attorney's office. He was on his way to joining the top league of German criminal defense lawyers; he could afford a big house, tailored suits, and expensive cars. I'm sure that his old pal Frey was simply jealous and searching for an opportunity to knock Rothemund off his high horse."

"By getting him sent to prison like that?" Kröger shook his head. "That's just plain nasty."

"Well, yes . . ." Altmüller grimaced. "Just imagine if you were humiliated in public a few times by your former best friend. Then he makes a really disastrous mistake. What's a state attorney to do? He has to follow up on the matter because of his own position."

"Yes, very true. Especially when it's a matter of child abuse," Cem Altunay agreed. "But Frey could have recused himself from the case because of personal prejudice."

"Maybe. But he might have seen a chance to reinstate and distinguish his own reputation after mistakes had been made by his department. There's a reason why the man became chief state attorney while only in his mid-thirties. He's ambitious, hard as nails, and incorruptible."

"What do you know about Bernd Prinzler?" Pia asked.

"Prinzler was once a very big deal in the Road Kings," Altmüller replied. "People think the Kings are a motorcycle gang that does some dirty business. In reality, they are a tightly organized group with a strict, almost military hierarchy. In the struggle for dominance in the milieu that includes Kosovo Albanians and Russians, there was always collateral damage that sent a few members of the gang to court and to prison. But by and large, we didn't try to stop them, because they imposed order with a heavy hand and saved us a lot of work. In the nineties, Prinzler was vice president of the Frankfurt chapter, and he was both feared and respected. On a couple of occasions, Rothemund successfully saved him from doing time. Then all of a sudden, Prinzler disappeared from the scene. At first, we thought he'd fallen out with his fellow members, and for a while we figured we'd find his body somewhere, but he had simply retired from the daily business and taken over other tasks in the organization."

"What sort of tasks? And why?" Kröger asked.

"I can only speculate about that. We even managed to infiltrate the Kings by using a mole, but he got shot in a raid." Altmüller gave a shrug. "Word was that Prinzler got married and no longer wanted to be on the front line."

"We saw his wife and kids this morning," Cem said. "Two sons between twelve and sixteen years old."

"That would fit," said Altmüller.

Pia had been listening in silence. All the information that Altmüller had given them was whirling around like puzzle pieces in her head as she tried to fit them into the right spots, even though the big picture was still incomplete. Instead of receiving helpful answers to her questions, dozens of new questions had popped up. Had Hanna Herzmann really been doing research on the Road Kings, as they had previously assumed? How had the contact between Rothemund and Prinzler come about? And how did Leonie Verges fit into the whole story?

"When did the raid happen when the infiltrator got shot?" she asked.

Her subconscious was sending her signals that she couldn't interpret or understand, and it was driving her nuts.

"That was a number of years ago," said Altmüller. "I think it was 1998. Or was it '97? I know for a fact that Prinzler was still active then, because Rothemund had successfully gotten him off the hook. And it turned out that it wasn't the Road Kings who shot our mole and two of the gang— it was one of our boys."

"Erik Lessing," said Pia.

Lutz Altmüller, who had just raised his hand to signal the waiter, stiffened, and his usual ruddy complexion—the result of high blood pressure—went pale.

"How do you know that name?" His response was very revealing. Pia's brain was now running in high gear. Erik Lessing. Kathrin. Behnke. Dr. Nicola Engel. Kilian Rothemund. The old case in Frankfurt, which was why Engel and Behnke couldn't stand each other. Why had Behnke always gotten away with everything? Why hadn't they kicked him off the force despite the worst transgressions, and even appointed him to Internal Affairs in the State Criminal Police? Was someone higher up holding a protective hand over him? And if so, why?

"Was that also a screwup by the state attorney's

office?" she asked instead of answering Altmüller. "Could it be that there's some sort of connection with our current cases?"

"Now your imagination is running away with you," said the old chief detective inspector, shaking his head. That was the end of his willingness to share information. He waved for the waiter to pay his bill, saying he had a doctor's appointment. Cem and Christian thanked him for his help. As they all stood up to leave the restaurant, another idea shot through Pia's mind, and she felt a shiver of excitement. Of course, that could be the answer!

"Mr. Altmüller," she said, turning once more to her Frankfurt colleague, "did Rothemund say *anything* back then about his client? Did he mention whether his client was male or female?"

The heavyset man leaned on one of the cocktail tables in the terrace by the entrance and frowned in thought.

"I'd have to take a look at the old files," he said after a moment. "We recorded that conversation with him on tape, and made a transcript of it for the files. I'll have a look and see if I can find it."

"Thank you," Pia said with a nod. "To what extent was this client 'affected'? And by what?"

"Hmm." Lutz Altmüller ran his hand over his bald pate. "I think he meant that his client had also been a victim of the child-porn Mafia.

Unfortunately, we had only that one conversation with him, so we couldn't follow up on it."

The pieces of the puzzle were finally dropping into place as if of their own accord, and Pia grasped what she—sidetracked by Bernd Prinzler—hadn't wanted to see. Suddenly, she was in a big hurry.

"Who is Erik Lessing?" Christian asked her after Altmüller had trudged off. "Why was the old man so shocked when you mentioned that name?"

"That was just a shot in the dark," said Pia. "I'm not so sure I understand it all myself. But we definitely have to take another look at Leonie Verges's house. Somehow, I feel sure that we're going to find the key to everything in her patient files."

During the drive home from the hospital in Bad Homburg, Louisa had just sucked her thumb without saying a word. At home, she had refused to climb the stairs from the car to the apartment. The prospect of chocolate pudding hadn't helped. Asking her to be reasonable or using a stern voice hadn't worked, either. Emma was close to tears. Just as she was trying to schlep Louisa up the stairs, despite her own condition, Helmut Grasser came out of her in-laws' apartment like a rescuing angel. Before Louisa could protest, he'd picked her up, carried her upstairs, and set her down at the door. Corinna and Sarah came by later and brought little presents for Louisa, but they couldn't even coax a smile out of her. Eventually, she went to her room and slammed the door.

Then Emma did burst into tears. It wasn't her fault that her daughter had broken her arm. Still, she felt responsible. What was going to happen now? On the one hand, she wished Florian were there to support her, but on the other, she was afraid that his presence might be exactly the wrong thing. Her girlfriends had tried to console her, assuring her that they'd take care of Louisa. And Emma herself would be close by when she had her baby in the on-site delivery room.

"Maybe Florian will be back by then," said Corinna.

"No, he won't," Emma sobbed. And then the whole story came tumbling out of her. How she had found the empty condom packet in his pants pocket and how when she asked him to explain, he hadn't answered. He had neither admitted nor denied that he'd betrayed her, and after that she'd asked him to move out.

For a moment, Corinna and Sarah were speech-less.

"But the worst thing is that . . . that . . . the doctor at the hospital thinks that Louisa may have been . . . abused." Tears of despair flowed down Emma's face and couldn't be stopped, as if a dam had broken inside her. "She had bruises on the inside of her thighs and in . . . her vagina. And it wasn't caused by falling off a pony. Florian blew his top when the doctor mentioned this, and since then he hasn't contacted me. I can't let him take Louisa every other weekend if I have to worry that he might do something like that to her."

She told Corinna and Sarah about Louisa's changed behavior, about her terrible tantrums, about her aggressive behavior at the kindergarten, about the periods of frightening lethargy, and about the stuffed wolf she had cut up.

"I talked to a therapist from the Frankfurt Girls House and did some research on the Internet," Emma said in a trembling voice. "These types of behavior are typical signs that a young child like Louisa would exhibit in the event of sexual abuse. It's a personality shift, a type of mental defense mechanism, because the child no longer feels safe in her own family."

She blew her nose and looked at the shocked faces of her friends. "Do you understand now why I'm so scared of leaving Louisa alone? And I have no idea how it's going to go once the baby is here and I can't give Louisa my undivided attention."

"What does Florian say to all this?" Corinna asked. "Did you tell him straight out that you suspect him of the abuse?"

"No! When could I have done that? The last time I saw him was when he took Louisa to the hospital."

"You want me to talk to him?" Corinna asked. "He's still my brother, after all."

"Sure. Maybe." Emma shrugged. "I don't know what to do. I don't know anything anymore."

"Just try to calm down," advised Sarah, stroking Emma's arm in sympathy. "Take care of Louisa but don't stress yourself out. A hospital stay is a very traumatic experience for a child her age. And even though you were with her a lot, she was suddenly surrounded by strangers. It'll take her a few days to get settled in again. Everything will be all right."

"I'm going up to see her." Emma sighed and got up. "Thanks for your presents. And thanks for listening." She hugged first Sarah, then Corinna and walked them to the door. After they'd both left, Emma took a deep breath before she went up to Louisa's room.

Louisa was sitting on the floor in a corner and didn't look up when Emma came in. She'd put a fairy-tale CD on her player and was listening to her favorite song about Cinderella. Quiet, almost apathetic, the girl sat there with her thumb in her mouth.

"Would you like a cookie? Or an apple?" Emma asked softly, sitting down facing her on the carpet.

Louisa shook her head mutely without looking at her mother.

"Should we call Grandma and Grandpa so they can say hello to you?"

She shook her head.

"Do you want to cuddle a little?"

She shook her head again.

Emma looked at her daughter, baffled and worried. She wished so much she could help her, reassure her that she was safe and had nothing to fear, but Sarah had probably been right that she shouldn't push her.

"Can I stay here and listen to Cinderella with you?"

Louisa shrugged. Her gaze wandered around the room.

For a while, they sat in silence and listened to the narrator's voice.

Suddenly, Louisa took her thumb out of her mouth.

"I want my Papa to come and get me."

The whole K-11 team sat tensely in front of the TV in Nicola Engel's office. Although it had been a long day for all of them, they were wide awake and excited about Bodenstein's appearance on *Germany's Most Wanted.* An average of seven million viewers watched the program, maybe a few less during vacation time, but it was an opportunity to reach a broad public.

Since there was so little information about the girl from the river, it had made little sense to create a reenactment, but a presentation of the Hanna Herzmann case had been prepared on film. Bodenstein was first up, and they could have heard a pin drop in the commissioner's office when he came on the screen. Pia couldn't really concentrate on her boss's performance, even though his eloquent matter-of-fact style was the equal of the moderator's, and the opposite of that of most of his colleagues from other districts, who seemed wooden and awkward from nervousness. Ever since her conversation with Lutz Altmüller, a wild confusion had reigned inside Pia's head. Sometimes she thought she could clearly see a red thread, a connection, and then fragments of information would dissolve into an unholy mess. At least two people sitting in the room with her could have brought some clarity to her thoughts: Nicola Engel had been the leader of a branch of K-11 in Frankfurt at the time the mole and two of the Road Kings had been shot during a raid in the red-light district. And Kathrin was at least familiar with the name Erik Lessing.

Pia, Christian, and Cem had spent all afternoon going through Leonie Verges's patient records, looking for a tip—but in vain. They had found tragic and depressing case histories of abused, traumatized, and mentally ill women, but nothing that would establish any connection to Rothemund, Prinzler, or Hanna Herzmann.

On the TV, the photo of Kilian Rothemund faded in. He was really a good-looking man, and his bright blue eyes gave him a striking presence. It would really be a stroke of bad luck if no one had spotted him anywhere. What if he were really the innocent victim of some evil conspiracy? Pia tried to imagine how she would react if she learned that a close friend with whom she'd had a minor disagreement was supposedly a pedophile. How would she respond if he assured her that he was innocent? Would she believe him despite the differences they'd had? She stared pensively at the screen, where the number to call to provide a tip had now appeared: 0800/ 22 44 98 98.

"I'm going downstairs to have a smoke," said Kathrin, and got up.

"Wait, I'll come with you." Pia grabbed her backpack and got up, too. Kai had his phone within reach if any calls were forwarded regarding the cases that Bodenstein had presented. She followed Kathrin down the stairs to the basement, past the seldom-used waiting room, and outdoors.

"The boss could have been an actor," Kathrin remarked, lighting a cigarette. "I don't think I'd be able to get a word out if I had to face the camera."

"I hope it gets results." Pia lit a cigarette, too, and leaned against the wall. Although she'd gotten up shortly after three this morning, she didn't feel tired at all. She was electrified by the idea that they might be only millimeters from the breakthrough they'd all been waiting for, something that could give their investigation a decisive turnaround.

For a moment, she smoked in silence. From one

of the neighboring backyards behind the tall chain-link fence, she could hear laughter and voices. The seductive aroma of grilled meat wafted over to her.

"Kathrin," said Pia. "I have to ask you something."

"Shoot." Her younger colleague gave her a curious look.

"Recently, when Frank was here, he mentioned a name. Erik Lessing. Where do you know him from?"

"Why do you want to know?" Her curiosity changed to suspicion.

"Because it may have a connection to our current cases."

Kathrin took a deep breath and blinked as the smoke stung her eye. Then she exhaled.

"When Frank really began to bully me, I'd just begun dating someone," she said. "I was at a seminar in Wiesbaden, and the seminar leader and I . . . well . . . we got closer."

Pia nodded. She remembered the change in Kathrin that had occurred. She had suddenly begun wearing fashionable new glasses, she'd updated her hairstyle, and she'd radically altered what she chose to wear.

"I went out with him for quite a while, but not officially, because he was married. He said he wanted to get a divorce, but somehow it never happened. It took me a while before I realized he just needed a lover to soothe his bruised ego." Kathrin sighed. "Typical. Anyway, it turned out that he knew Frank. They were together in some sort of special unit. The guy had a huge inferiority complex, so he kept telling me about all the heroic things he'd done. And one day he told me about this raid where an undercover agent got shot."

Pia could hardly believe her ears.

"Nobody knew about this raid on a brothel on Elbestrasse; not even the SAU was involved. A few uniforms stormed the place, and it looked like it was just by chance that Erik Lessing and two of the bikers happened to be inside making a collection at just that moment. There was a shoot-out in the back courtyard of the brothel. And now hold on to your hat. . . ."

She paused, but Pia had an idea what was coming.

"It was Frank who shot the three victims—with a weapon that wasn't from the police armory. It was later found in a car belonging to one of the bikers, but he had an airtight alibi for the time of the shootings. His lawyer got the charge dropped before any indictment could be handed down. The whole case was swept under the rug. Frank was sent first to the loony bin, then transferred to Hofheim. The whole story has been kept hushed up until today."

Pia put out her cigarette.

"How did your friend happen to know about it?"

"Frank told him once when he was drunk."

"When was this exactly?"

"1996. Sometime in March, if I remember correctly."

"Do the boss and Engel know that you know the story?"

"The boss wanted to talk to me about it, that day when I mentioned the name Erik Lessing, but so far he hasn't." Kathrin shrugged. "I don't care. I'm only keeping it to use against Frank, in case he tries to mess with me again."

Hanna woke up when the night nurse came into the room. The nurses and orderlies who worked in the daytime respected her wish to be left alone and spoke to her only when necessary. Lena, the night nurse, was an energetic, vivacious blonde who ignored Hanna's silence and babbled away without embarrassment like a Club Med fitness instructor. All that was missing was for Lena to rip off the bedcovers, clap her hands, and force her patient to do sit-ups with all the drainage and infusion tubes still inserted.

"Ooh, that's the new iPhone," she said cheerfully after she'd checked Hanna's temperature and blood pressure. "Wow, that's great. Really cool. I'd love to have one. Bet it's pretty expensive, right? My friend has one, and now he spends all his time downloading apps."

Hanna closed her eyes and let the nurse ramble on. Meike had gotten her a new smartphone and loaded all her data onto it so that Hanna could read her e-mails again. Finally, she knew what day it was. Her sense of time had totally slipped away.

"You were the topic on *Germany's Most Wanted* tonight," Lena told her. "We watched it in the nurses' lounge. It's so gruesome the way they always reenact the crime."

Hanna stiffened and opened her eyes again.

"What did they reenact?" she croaked suspiciously.

Why hadn't anyone told her about this? Irina, Jan, Meike, or at least her agent must have known something about it.

"Well, the way you were discovered in the trunk of your car." Lena propped her left hand on her hip. "And before that, a scene in your garage. Oh yeah, it was just starting when the TV studio cut away to your car."

Good God!

"Did they mention my name?" Hanna asked.

"No. They just kept saying 'The TV host Johanna H.'"

That wasn't very reassuring. What good was a news blackout if her name was bandied about on one of the most watched shows on German TV? Tomorrow, the press would be crawling all over her.

"They think that the attack on you had something to do with the murder of that psychotherapist," Lena went on with the sensitivity of a tank as she stepped into the bathroom.

"What are you talking about? Who was murdered?" Hanna whispered hoarsely.

The night nurse came back, but she hadn't heard Hanna's question.

"Isn't it horrible?" she yammered. "The thought of being bound and gagged and then left to slowly die of thirst . . . No, really. There are some really cruel people in the world. I mean, I see plenty of stuff here, but . . ."

Her words dropped into Hanna's consciousness like stones into water. Shock waves of comprehension drove out the comforting fog in her head. All of a sudden, as if a curtain had been pulled aside, the memory returned without warning. She gasped in horror and felt her body convulse.

The police who weren't police. The thunderstorm. She was locked in the trunk of the car. She remembered her fear, her panicked attempts to get free. She heard the crack as her bones broke, the metallic taste of blood in her mouth. The terrible pain, the fear of death, the sudden certainty that she was going to die. She heard panting and laughing, saw the flashing red light of a camera through a veil of tears, smelled sharp male sweat. *Don't stick your nose into things that are none of your business, you slut! If you do, you'll be dead.*

We'll find you wherever you go, and your daughter, too. Your fans will love it when they see the little video from today.

The terror of that night returned with a force that took her breath away. She tried to remain calm, but the memories that had been slumbering somewhere in the depths of her mind broke over her with the power of a volcanic eruption and hurled her into a pitch-black abyss of horror.

"What's wrong? Do you feel ill?" Only now did the night nurse notice that something wasn't right.

"Try to calm down." She leaned over Hanna, put her hands on her patient's shoulders, and pressed Hanna back onto the bed. "Don't forget to breathe in and breathe out."

Hanna turned her head away, wanting to defend herself, but she had no strength. She heard a shrill, terrified howling, and it took her a few seconds to realize that this horrendous sound was coming out of her own mouth.

Louisa fell asleep at eight-thirty. She'd stopped asking for Florian, and Emma made an effort not to resent what she'd said. Common sense told her that it was normal for a five-year-old to ask for her papa. If she were at Florian's house, she'd probably want to be with Emma. But deep in her heart, she was insulted and hurt at being so blatantly rejected. She's a little kid, Emma tried to convince herself, and she's confused and frightened after being in the hospital. She associates her father with laughter, eating ice cream, playing, and cuddling, and her mother with strict rules and everyday life.

But no matter how reasonably Louisa's behavior might be explained, it was simply unfair the way Florian had bought and won his daughter's love with his sporadic visits. Emma was the one who had always been there for the child, ever since she was born. She had massaged Louisa's little tummy when she had screamed almost nonstop for the first three months of her life; she had rubbed salve on the child's gums when her first teeth were coming in. She had consoled and cared for Louisa, wrapping her in a blanket and carrying her around. Night after night, she had rocked her daughter to sleep, sung songs or read stories to her, given her a bottle, and played with her for hours. And this was the thanks she got!

Emma clasped her hands around the cup of tasteless jasmine tea. She'd been drinking so much tea that it was practically coming out of her ears. Her desire for a strong cup of black coffee, a wonderful bittersweet espresso, or a glass of wine had even started haunting her dreams—when she was able to sleep, that is. She was so exhausted, so unbelievably tired. How she longed to be able to sleep ten hours at a stretch again without the constant worry about her daughter's welfare. But in less than two weeks, a second child would demand her full attention, and then she'd really exhaust all of her physical and mental strength. Nature hadn't arranged things that way by accident, making a woman's body most receptive in her early twenties. The older she got, the more frayed her nerves. She was simply too old to have two little children whom she would now have to raise without the support of a husband.

The day after tomorrow, she would have to face him. Florian would definitely show up for his father's birthday party. Emma pushed away the thought of this confrontation. She had been stuck inside all day because Louisa had refused to leave her room. Now that the girl was sleeping soundly, she would allow herself a short walk in the fresh air to stretch her legs.

Emma turned on the baby monitor and went downstairs. At the front door, she took a deep breath. It was already almost dark. The mild air was filled with the overpowering fragrance of lilacs. She slipped off her Crocs and carried them as she walked barefoot through the damp grass, which felt like a lush carpet. Her nerves were calming down with each step she took; she straightened her shoulders and tried to breathe evenly. She didn't want to go far, only to the fountain that stood in the middle of the grounds, even though Louisa certainly wouldn't wake up before seven in the morning. Emma reached the fountain, sat down on the edge, and dipped her hand in the water, which was still warm from the sun. At the edge of the woods, frogs croaked and crickets chirped.

Emma checked the baby monitor out of habit, but of course she was beyond the range of the wireless connection. She recalled how vehemently Florian had opposed using this device. The radiation that the baby would be exposed to was harmful, he claimed. Just like he believed that modern diapers caused rashes and eczema because they didn't let in any air.

Funny. Why did she only think of negative things when she thought about her husband? Suddenly, a loud bang ripped through the idyllic silence, followed by shrill screams. Emma jumped up and ran back toward the house. But the angry-sounding voice was coming from the direction of the three bungalows. It was Corinna! Emma stopped behind a boxwood hedge and looked over toward the houses. The Wiesners' bungalow was lit up brightly, and Emma saw, to her astonishment, that her in-laws were sitting on the couch in the living room. Sarah, Nicky, and Ralf were also there. Emma had never seen her friend Corinna look so furious. Of course she couldn't hear what she was saying, because the terrace door was closed, but she saw that Corinna was yelling at Josef. Ralf put his hand on her shoulder in a placating gesture. She shook it off indignantly but lowered her voice. Emma stared at the scene, which looked like a stage set. She couldn't make sense of it. Corinna, Josef, and Renate were normally in total agreement. What could be the reason for this obvious ill will? Had something happened? Renate stood up and left the living room. Then Nicky got involved. He said something, then hauled off and slapped Corinna so hard that she staggered. Emma gasped in shock. At that moment, Renate appeared on the terrace and marched straight toward her. Just in time, Emma ducked behind the hedge. When she looked back at the Wiesners' house, everyone had left the living room except for Josef, who sat bent forward on the sofa, his face buried in his hands. Exactly the way Emma had seen him sitting at his desk today, after she accidentally caught Corinna arguing with him. How could she treat her father that way? And why did Ralf sit idly by when Nicky slapped his wife? Emma couldn't make sense of this strange behavior. Maybe everyone's nerves were frazzled before the big party the day after tomorrow. Even Corinna was only human, after all.

During his stay in Holland, Kilian Rothemund had left his cell phone turned off most of the time. Although he had missed the swift development of modern telecommunications while he was in prison, he was well aware that his wireless cell phone could be located by GPS, even when the roaming function was switched off. He wasn't that familiar with Internet cafés, Wi-Fi in hotels, and such things, but under no circumstances was he going to leave a trail to the two men who had met with him only after taking the strictest security precautions. The explosive nature of what they had told him and the material they had handed over to him was enormous. Since Kilian had seen his photo in the top-circulated Dutch daily *De Telegraaf*, he knew that he was the object of an international manhunt. Although he spoke no Dutch, he could read it reasonably well. The search was on for the previously convicted sex offender Kilian Rothemund, but the reason was never mentioned.

One of his trailer park clients had sent him a text and told him that the police had searched his trailer on Sunday and were looking for him. From Bernd, he learned that Leonie Verges was dead. Somebody had tortured her to death in her house in the most gruesome manner. He should have been shocked, but he wasn't. He had seen Leonie last Saturday at Bernd's place. She had claimed that Hanna, despite all the warnings, didn't appreciate the seriousness of the situation and had blabbed about something. Kilian had defended Hanna, but he secretly had some doubts about her loyalty. She hadn't been in touch with him since Thursday, by text or e-mail or phone. He and Leonie had been talking for over an hour when she had said in a spiteful voice that it served Hanna right, what had happened to her. Kilian was flabbergasted when she told him that Hanna had been attacked and raped on Thursday night and since then had been in the hospital. The indifference with which she'd relayed the events had been the last straw for Kilian. They wound up in a terrible argument. Then he jumped on his motor scooter and rode off in the night toward Langenhain, hoping to meet Hanna's daughter there and learn more from her, but the house had been quiet and dark.

Kilian no longer knew if what he'd learned in Holland would still have any significance. They had stuck their hands in a hornet's nest, and the hornets had attacked brutally: Leonie was dead, Hanna lay gravely injured in the hospital, and he was being pursued by the police. Bernd had decided not to tell Michaela about any of this, because no one could tell how she would react to the awful news.

Kilian had spent hours thinking about why his picture had been printed in a Dutch newspaper with a request for information. Did somebody know that he'd gone to Amsterdam, or had it appeared because a press release had been sent to all the major European papers?

Toward noon, he'd made a decision to send the highly volatile material from his conversations in Holland to Germany by mail, in the event that he was apprehended on the way home. He bought a padded envelope and thought long and hard about where to send the package before he addressed it and took it to the post office. Then he sat in a café near the Amsterdam main station waiting for his train, which was due to depart at 7:15 P.M. Five minutes before departure, he paid for the two coffees and piece of cake he'd consumed, took his bag, and headed for the platform.

He was expecting the police to be waiting for him on his arrival in Frankfurt, but not in Amsterdam. As if out of nowhere, men in black riot gear suddenly appeared and blocked his way. One of them held up an ID in front of his face and told him in his best German that he was under arrest. Kilian offered no resistance. Sooner or later, they would extradite him to Germany, and then he'd finally have the proof in his hands that until now had always eluded him: powerful, explicit proof and a whole list of names. The organization had as many heads as a hydra, and they grew back as soon as they were cut off. But with the information he now possessed, he could severely weaken these perverse, unscrupulous bastards and at the same time clear his name and redeem himself. A few days in a Dutch jail didn't scare him.

The first calls with tips came in even before the broadcast was over. Yet probably the most important call wasn't to the studio of *Germany's*

Most Wanted, but to Kai Ostermann, and it got the whole team buzzing with excitement. It was ten after eleven when Pia dialed Bodenstein's number, and he picked up at once.

She sat down on the steps by the watch room, lit a cigarette, and gave him the details, keeping her report short and sweet. A woman had called in to say that she'd seen the dead girl in Höchst in early May on Emmerich-Josef-Strasse. She had just gotten home and was loaded down with shopping bags as she looked for her keys at her front door. A young blond girl with eyes wide in panic came running up to her and in broken German pleaded for help. Only seconds later, a silver car stopped at the curb and a man and woman got out. The girl had cowered in the entryway to the house, holding her arms protectively over her head—a picture of misery. The couple had explained to the witness that their daughter was mentally ill and suffered from delusions. They had apologized politely, and then disappeared with the girl, who had climbed into the car without protest. When asked why she hadn't called the police about this earlier, the woman replied that she'd been on a three-week cruise since early June and had forgotten about the incident until this evening, when she saw the photo of the dead girl from the river. She was 100 percent certain that it was the same girl who had begged her for help, and she promised to come to the station the next day to make a statement.

"Well, that sounds very promising," said Bodenstein. "Now you should see about going home. I'm taking the seven o'clock flight tomorrow morning and will be in the office no later than eight-thirty."

They said good-bye and Pia put away her phone. It took a huge effort of will to get up from the step and drag herself to the car, which was of course parked in the spot farthest away.

"Pia! Wait a minute!" Christian Kröger called behind her. She stopped and turned around. Her colleague came striding toward her, and she asked herself not for the first time whether he was actually human or some sort of vampire who didn't need any sleep. He, too, had been on his feet since dawn, and for the past few nights he'd hardly slept at all, and yet he seemed wide awake.

"Listen, Pia, something's been going around in my head all day," he said as he accompanied her across the scantily lit parking lot between the buildings of the Regional Criminal Unit and the street. "Maybe it's only a coincidence, but maybe not. You remember the car that Leonie Verges's neighbor spotted several times near her house?"

"You mean Prinzler's Hummer?" Pia said.

"No, the other car. The silver station wagon. You wrote down the license number," Christian replied impatiently. "I found out the car is registered to the Sonnenkinder Association in Falkenstein."

"Yeah, so?"

"State Attorney Markus Maria Frey is on the board of the Finkbeiner Foundation, which runs the organization."

"I know," Pia said with a nod, still standing by her car.

"Did you also know that he was a foster child of Dr. Josef Finkbeiner?" Christian gave her an expectant look, but Pia's mental faculties had reached their limit for the day. "He studied law on a scholarship from the Finkbeiner Foundation."

"Yeah, so? What are you getting at?"

Christian Kröger was the type of person who collected tons of odd and abstruse information that he kept stored away in his brain, ready to be called up at any moment. He never forgot anything he'd ever heard. This gift was sometimes a real burden for him, because people he knew often had a hard time following his thought process.

"People like Frey frequently get involved in social issues." Pia almost dislocated her jaw with a yawn, and her eyes filled with tears from fatigue. "So the fact that he's a board member of the foundation set up by his own foster father, to whom he remains closely linked for several reasons, isn't really so strange, is it?"

"Yes, I guess you're right." Christian frowned. "It was just a thought."

"I'm dead tired," Pia said. "Let's talk about this again tomorrow, okay?"

"Okay." He nodded. "Good night, then."

"Yeah, good night." Pia unlocked the car and got in behind the wheel. "By the way, you ought to get some sleep, too."

"Are you worried about me?" Christian cocked his head and grinned.

"Naturally." Pia picked up on his light flirtatious tone. "You know you're my favorite colleague."

"I always thought it was Bodenstein."

"He's my favorite boss." She started the engine, put the car in reverse, and waved to him. "See you tomorrow!"

Thursday, July 1, 2010

Hopeful optimism reigned in K-11. Bodenstein's appearance on *Germany's Most Wanted* had brought in a new wave of tips that now had to be checked out. The witness, Karen Wenning, had arrived at nine o'clock sharp at the station. She had described the incident of May 7 in minute detail, displaying an amazing memory. She was absolutely positive that the girl who had begged so desperately for help was the Mermaid, and she declared herself ready to help the artist from the state police put together ID pictures of the alleged parents.

"She's a mask sculptor at the Frankfurt Playhouse and has a great eye for faces," Pia explained to her boss, who arrived as she and Cem finished questioning the witness. "She's worked in film, TV, and theater."

"Is she credible?" Bodenstein took off his jacket and hung it over the back of his desk chair.

"Yes, absolutely." Pia took a seat in front of the desk and gave him a rundown of what they had learned from the conversation with Lutz Altmüller. Bodenstein listened intently.

"You're doubtful that Rothemund is the perp?" he said with a frown.

"Yes. There's something between him and Hanna Herzmann that goes beyond pure professional interest," replied Pia. "She drove him to the trailer park that Wednesday evening and was with him in the trailer. The strand of hair that was found there came from her. What if those two only had consensual sex that night?"

"Possible," Bodenstein conceded. "What about Prinzler?"

"Our colleagues in Frankfurt have granted me an appointment in Preungesheim for this afternoon," Pia said sarcastically. "By the way, I also found out that the search of the property drew a complete blank, just as you thought. No weapons, no drugs, no stolen cars, no illegal girls."

Bodenstein sipped his coffee and refrained from commenting. Pia continued telling him about how they'd gone through Leonie Verges's patient files, but without result.

"What was the reason for doing that?" Bodenstein asked.

"I had a gut feeling that Hanna Herzmann was not doing research on the Road Kings," replied Pia, crossing her arms. "And I believe that the Herzmann and Verges cases are connected. Maybe it was even the same perp."

"Aha. How do you figure?"

"Kai, Christian, and I have been talking about a possible psychological profile of the perp. We think that he's between forty and fifty, has relationship problems or problems with women in general, and low self-esteem. He has sadistic and voyeuristic tendencies and gets pleasure from other people's suffering, from the pleading and death struggle of his victims. He likes exercising power over people who are superior to him but whom he can degrade and humiliate with bonds and gags. He has no sense of right and wrong, has a hot-tempered personality, but is very intelligent and probably also highly educated."

She smiled when she saw Bodenstein's astounded expression. "Kai's courses have paid off, don't you think?"

"In any event, it sounds impressive," Bodenstein replied. "So which of our suspects fits this profile?"

"Unfortunately, we don't yet know Rothemund or Prinzler well enough to decide," Pia admitted. "That's why I'd like to take Kai or Christian with me this afternoon to Preungesheim."

"Fine with me." Bodenstein finished his coffee. "Is that all?"

"No." Pia had saved the most sensitive topic until last. "I'd like to hear what you can tell me about the death of Erik Lessing."

Bodenstein, who was just about to set down his cup, stopped abruptly. His face shut down, as if a window shade had been pulled down inside him. The cup hovered an inch above the saucer.

"I know nothing about that," he said, finally putting down his coffee cup. Then he stood up. "Let's go over to the conference room."

Pia was disappointed, even though this was the reaction she'd expected.

"Did Frank shoot him and the two Road Kings?"

Bodenstein stopped without turning around.

"What is this?" he asked. "What does this have to do with our cases?"

Pia jumped up and went over to him.

"I think that somebody used Frank to get rid of a dangerous witness—namely, the undercover cop Erik Lessing. Lessing must have learned something from the Road Kings that nobody else was supposed to know. It was neither an accident nor self-defense. It was a triple murder, and somebody gave the order to do it. Frank carried out the order; who knows what they told him. He shot a colleague."

Bodenstein sighed deeply and turned around.

"So now you know everything," he said.

For a moment, it was completely quiet; only the ring of a telephone could be heard faintly through the closed door.

"Why didn't you ever tell me about this?" Pia asked. "I never understood why Frank got that special position, or why you always protected him. Your lack of trust is insulting."

"It has nothing to do with lack of trust," Bodenstein replied. "I had nothing to do with the whole incident, because I was in a different department. The reason why I learned about it at all was—"

He broke off, hesitant.

"Dr. Nicola Engel," Pia said, completing his sentence. "She was in charge of the department that was responsible. Am I right?"

Bodenstein nodded. They stared at each other.

"Pia," he finally said quietly. "This is a very dangerous matter. Even today. I don't know any names, but some of those responsible might still be in high positions. Back then, they never hesitated to kill if necessary, and they will do it today, as well."

"Who?"

"I don't know. Nicola wouldn't tell me the details. Supposedly, in order to protect me. And I didn't really want to know any more about it."

Pia looked at her boss. She asked herself whether he was telling her the truth. How much did he actually know? And all of a sudden, she realized that she no longer trusted him. What would he do, how far would he go, to protect himself and others?

"What are you going to do?" he asked.

"Nothing at all," she lied, shrugging. "It's an old case. God knows, we have plenty of other stuff to keep us busy."

Her eyes met his. Was that something like relief that flashed across his face for an instant?

There was a knock on the door, and Kai stuck his head in.

"I just got a call from somebody who made an interesting observation behind the rest stop at Weilbach on the night Hanna Herzmann was raped." Even Kai, who usually unnerved everyone with his unflappable composure, seemed agitated, which showed what a toll the tension of the past few weeks was taking. "Around two in the morning, the witness was driving along the highway between Hattersheim and Weilbach when a car suddenly came shooting out from a dirt road on the left with its lights off. He almost drove into the ditch from fright, but he got a brief view of the driver's face."

"And?" Bodenstein asked.

"A man with a beard and hair combed straight back."

"Bernd Prinzler?"

"From the description, it's possible. Unfortunately, he can't recall either the make of the car or the license plate number. Big and dark, he said. Might even be the Hummer."

"Okay." Bodenstein thought hard. "We need to bring Prinzler in. I want a lineup to show the witness, first thing tomorrow morning."

Pia got into her car and swore when she almost burned her hands on the steering wheel. The car had been parked in the sun and was as hot as an oven. She needed peace and quiet so she could think over what she'd just learned. Located a couple of hundred yards from the Regional Criminal Unit were the Krifteler Fields, the fruit orchards and strawberry fields that stretched all the way to the A66 autobahn. Pia turned left onto the L3016, locally called "the Strawberry Mile," and drove to the first dirt road. She parked there and continued on foot.

Today the sun reigned supreme, but as usual it was accompanied by muggy air. Thunderstorms were predicted for later in the afternoon. The grassy dirt roads were full of muddy puddles that the last rain had left behind. The skyline of Frankfurt seemed farther away than on clear days, as did the hills of the Taunus in the west.

Pia stuck her hands in the pockets of her jeans and trudged with her head down past rows of plum and apple trees. It had shaken her deeply to learn that Bodenstein was keeping these kinds of secrets. Pia knew and respected him as a man who stood up for his convictions, even if they were unpopular. He was someone with a pronounced sense of justice and high moral values, incorruptible, disciplined, fair, and straightforward. She had regarded his leniency toward Behnke's transgressions as an excusable weakness, a display of loyalty to a long-standing colleague who was in personal and financial difficulties, because that was how Bodenstein had once justified his actions to her. She now realized that his explanation had been a lie.

From the beginning, Pia and Bodenstein had understood each other and worked well together, but there had always been a certain distance between them. That had changed when Bodenstein's marriage broke up. Since then a real relationship of trust, almost a friendship, had developed between them. At least that was what Pia had imagined, but obviously the trust part was an illusion. She recoiled from the thought that her boss might have had more to do with the Erik Lessing case than he was willing to admit. But she didn't intend to pressure him to say more. As soon as Kathrin agreed to tell her the name of her ex-lover, Pia wanted to talk to him. She was also toying with the idea of taking up the matter with Behnke. At first glance, the incident seemed to have nothing to do with the current investigations, but her instincts told her that there was a connection between the triple murders that had been ordered, the attack on Hanna Herzmann, and the murder of Leonie Verges. It couldn't be a coincidence that Rothemund and Prinzler had been key players in the past as well as today.

Her cell phone rang. She didn't pay attention to it at first, but then her sense of duty prevailed. It was Christian Kröger.

"Where are you?" he asked.

"Lunch break," she snapped. "Why?"

"I saw your car parked by the side of the road. Yesterday, I didn't have a chance to tell you something else. When will you be back?"

"At two eleven and forty-three seconds," she replied curtly, which was not usually her style, and she regretted it immediately. Christian, of all people, didn't deserve to suffer the brunt of her bad mood.

"Sorry," she said. "Would you like to join me for a walk through the picturesque strawberry fields? I need some exercise and fresh air."

"Sure, gladly."

Pia told him which way she'd gone and sat down on a boulder that probably served as a property marker. She turned her face to the sun, closed her eyes, and enjoyed feeling the warmth on her skin. With a trill, a lark sprang into the blue sky.

The constant hum of the autobahn in the distance was a familiar sound; her house was no more than two miles away as the crow flies, right next to the A66. Christian apparently didn't have the same need for exercise and fresh air as she did. The blue VW evidence van came bumping along the dirt road. Pia stood up and walked over to her colleague.

"Hey," he said, studying her. "Did something happen?"

His sensitivity again surprised her. He was the only one of her male colleagues who would permit himself such a question. All the others treated her the same as they treated everyone else on the team. And that meant they would probably prefer to bite off their tongues rather than ask about feelings or emotional issues.

"Come on, let's take a walk," said Pia instead of answering. For a while, they walked in silence, and Christian picked a couple of plums and offered her one.

"Plum thief." Pia grinned, rubbed the plum on her jeans, and took a bite. It tasted magnificent, warm from the sun and sweet, awakening childhood memories.

"Theft of comestibles for personal consumption is not a punishable offense." Christian grinned back but then quickly turned serious. "I think there are some blotches in the biography of State Attorney Frey."

Pia stopped in her tracks.

"Why do you say that?" she asked in astonishment.

"I happened to recall reading a newspaper

article," he replied. "It was shortly after Rothemund was arrested. They had interviewed a woman who claimed that the arrest was motivated by personal revenge on Frey's part, because he—Rothemund, that is—had discovered that Frey didn't earn his doctorate; he paid for it."

He spit out the pit of the plum.

"Then last night, I was researching something and stumbled on who Frey's doctoral supervisor was. He happens to be a member of the board of the Finkbeiner Foundation: Professor Ernst Haslinger. He was dean of the law faculty and vice president of the Goethe University, and was later called to Karlsruhe to serve on the federal Supreme Court."

"That doesn't have to mean anything," said Pia. "But why are you so interested in State Attorney Frey?"

"Because I find his fascination with the case odd." Christian stopped. "I've been doing crime-scene investigation for ten years now, but I've never seen a chief state attorney show up in person for a house search. If anything, they send some underling."

"I suppose he has more than a professional interest in the case," replied Pia. "He and Rothemund were once the best of friends."

"So why did he show up on that evening in Eddersheim when we discovered the dead girl in the river?"

"He'd been visiting friends nearby for a barbecue." Pia tried to remember what explanation Frey had given for putting in an appearance that evening. She had wondered about that, too.

"I believe the part about the barbecue," said Christian. "But not the part about being in the vicinity."

"What are you getting at?" Pia asked.

"I don't really know," Christian admitted. He picked a blade of grass and absentmindedly wrapped it around his finger. "But there seem to be way too many coincidences."

They walked on.

"And what's bothering you?" he asked after a while.

Pia pondered whether to tell him about the Erik Lessing case and Frank Behnke's involvement in it. She had to talk about it with someone. Kai was out, because he had been too directly involved in the events at the time. Cem, she didn't know well enough; Bodenstein and Kathrin were not neutral observers. Actually, Christian had developed more and more into the only colleague she really trusted. Finally, she got up the nerve and told him her suspicions.

"Oh my God," he said when she was done. "That explains a lot. Especially Frank's behavior."

"Who would have given the order to eliminate Lessing?" Pia asked. "It couldn't have been Engel, who was the head of the department; it must have come from much higher up. The president of police? The Interior Ministry? The National Criminal Police? And today, Behnke is still enjoying special protection. Considering everything he's done, normally suspension would be too lenient a punishment. He would have been thrown out of the civil service for good."

"We have to ask ourselves who would have benefited from getting rid of Lessing," Christian deliberated. "What had he found out? It must have been something really explosive, something that could be a serious threat to one of the bigwigs."

"Bribery," Pia suggested. "Drug dealing. Human trafficking."

"I'm sure that was his official undercover mission," replied Christian. "No, it had to be something personal. Something that could ruin someone's career."

"We should ask Prinzler about it," said Pia, casting a glance at her watch. "In exactly one hour. Are you going with me to Preungesheim?"

"I know that you didn't want me to come here, but I just had to see you." Wolfgang looked around with embarrassment, turning the bouquet in his hands.

"Just put it on the table. The nurses will find a vase later." Hanna would have preferred to tell him to take the flowers away. White lilies! She hated that intense fragrance, which reminded her of funeral parlors and cemeteries. Flowers belonged in the garden, not in a small room that was badly ventilated.

Last night, she'd written Wolfgang a text message, asking him not to come to the hospital. It was unpleasant for her to be seen in this condition by any man who was not a doctor. She couldn't imagine how she looked. She'd touched her face, felt the swelling and the stitches on her forehead, the left eyebrow, and chin. She wondered if the makeup artists would be skillful enough to conjure up a face suitable for television out of this disastrous battlefield.

The last time she'd looked in the mirror was in her dressing room at the TV studio that evening. Back then, her face had been flawless and beautiful, except for a few wrinkles. Now she didn't want to see it; she knew she wouldn't be able to stand the sight. She saw the appalled expression on her visitor's face.

"Sit down for a moment," she told Wolfgang.

He shoved a chair over to her bed and awkwardly took her hand. All the tubes running in and out of her body bothered him. Hanna could see him trying to avoid looking at them.

"How are you feeling?"

"Good would be a lie," she croaked.

The conversation was strained, faltering. Wolfgang looked pale and bleary-eyed and seemed nervous. He had purple shadows under his eyes that she'd never seen there before. At some point he ran out of topics to talk about and fell silent. Hanna said nothing more, either. What could she tell him anyway? How shitty it was to live with a colostomy bag? How great her fear was of being disfigured and traumatized for the rest of her life? In the past, she would have confided in him, but now things were different. Now she wished someone else were sitting beside her and holding her hand.

"Oh, Hanna," Wolfgang said with a sigh. "I'm so sorry that you had to go through all of this. I wish there was something I could do for you. Do you have any idea who did it?"

Hanna swallowed, fighting back the rising horror: the memory of pain and terror and the fear of death.

"No," she whispered. "Did you know that Leonie Verges, my therapist, was murdered?"

"Meike told me," he said with a nod. "It's all so horrible."

"I just don't understand it. In my case, the police have two suspects." Talking was tiring her out. "But I'm sure it wasn't either one of them. Why would they do it? I used to work with them. Instead, I think it must be because of the story I was working on. . . ."

Suddenly, she had a suspicion—an appalling suspicion.

"You haven't spoken to anyone about it, have you, Wolfgang?"

She tried to sit up but couldn't. Powerless, she sank back.

Wolfgang hesitated. For an instant, his eyes shifted away.

"No. That is, only to my father," he admitted, embarrassed. "He was not enthusiastic—and that's putting it mildly. We had a big argument about it. He said that sometimes there are more important things than ratings. I can't believe that he, of all people, would say that."

He laughed out loud, but it was a forced laugh.

"He didn't want his TV station to broadcast such unverified slander. He was really upset by those names. He's terribly afraid of a lawsuit or bad PR. I'm . . . I'm really sorry, Hanna. Really I am."

"All right." Hanna nodded weakly.

She'd known Wolfgang's father for thirty years, and could vividly picture his reaction. She knew Wolfgang equally well. She should have known that he would tell his authoritarian father about what she was working on. Wolfgang had a hell of a lot of respect for his father, and was at his beck and call for better or worse. He still lived in his parents' villa, and he held the position of CEO only because of his father's intervention. Even though Wolfgang did his job well and conscientiously, he lacked courage and the ability to assert himself. All his life, he'd been the son of the great media mogul Hartmut Matern, and in their friendship Hanna had always been the more successful, cleverer, and stronger one. Hanna knew that this didn't bother him, but she wasn't sure how he was handling the fact that even now, in his mid-forties, he risked being chewed out by his father in front of the whole crew whenever he made a mistake or ventured to make a decision on his own. Wolfgang never talked about this. In general, he never liked to talk about himself. If Hanna really thought about it, she knew hardly anything about him, because everything had always revolved around her: her show, her success, her men. In her boundless egotism, it had never occurred to her to think about Wolfgang, but now she was filled with regret, as she was about so much else she had done or not done in her life.

Her throat hurt from talking, and her eyelids had grown heavy.

"I think you'd better go now," she murmured, turning her head away. "Talking is a real strain for me."

"Yes, of course." Wolfgang let go of her hand and got up.

Hanna's eyes closed, and her spirit retreated from the intolerable glare of reality back to the twilight realm of a world in between, in which she was healthy and happy and . . . loved.

"Good-bye, Hanna," she heard Wolfgang say, as if from a great distance. "Maybe someday you can forgive me."

• • •

"Louisa? Louisa!"

Emma had searched the whole apartment. She'd only been in the bathroom a few minutes, and now the little girl was gone.

"Louisa! Grandpa and Grandma are waiting for us. And Grandma baked a carrot cake especially for you."

No reaction. Had she run away?

Emma went to the front door. No, the key was in the keyhole, and the door was locked. She always did this now, because one time she'd accidentally locked herself out. Louisa had run around the apartment screaming in panic until Mr. Grasser appeared and opened the old-fashioned door using a picklock.

It just couldn't be true. Emma needed to pull herself together and think calmly. But what she most wanted to do was scream. She always had to be so considerate of others—but sometimes she wondered if anyone was ever considerate of her.

"Louisa?"

She went into Louisa's bedroom. The wardrobe wasn't closed all the way. She opened the door and gave a start of surprise when she spied her daughter cowering under the clothes and jackets hanging inside. She had her thumb in her mouth and was staring into space.

"Oh, sweetie!" Emma squatted down. "What are you doing in here?"

No answer. The girl sucked harder on her thumb, at the same time rubbing her forefinger over her nose, which was already quite red.

"Don't you want to go downstairs and see Grandma and Grandpa? Don't you want any carrot cake with whipped cream?"

Vigorous head shaking.

"Wouldn't you at least like to come out of the wardrobe?"

More head shaking.

Emma felt helpless, at a complete loss. What was happening to her daughter? Should Louisa be seeing a child psychologist? What fears were tormenting her?

"You know what? I'm going to call Grandma and tell her we're not coming. And then I'll sit down and read you a story. Okay?"

Louisa nodded timidly without looking at her.

With an effort, Emma got up and went to the telephone. Anger was now mixed with her concern. If she found out that Florian had actually done something to Louisa, then God help him!

She called her mother-in-law and said they couldn't come to tea because Louisa wasn't feeling well. She quickly cut short Renate's disappointed laments; she had no desire to make excuses.

Louisa was still sitting in the wardrobe when she came back.

"What book do you want me to read to you?" Emma asked.

"Franz Hahn and Johnny Mauser," Louisa mumbled without taking her thumb out of her mouth. Emma looked for the book on the shelf, moved the beanbag chair over next to the bed, and sat down.

It was extremely uncomfortable to sit on the floor in her condition. First her left leg went to sleep, then her right. But she bravely kept reading, because it was doing Louisa good. She stopped sucking her thumb, and then she crept out of the wardrobe and cuddled up in Emma's arm so she could look at the book, too. She was laughing and enjoying the pictures, which she knew by heart. When Emma closed the book, Louisa sighed and closed her eyes.

"Mama?"

"Yes, my sweet?" Emma tenderly caressed her daughter's cheek. She was so small and innocent, her soft skin so translucent that Emma could see the veins in her temples.

"I don't ever want to go away from you, Mama. I'm so scared of the bad wolf."

Emma caught her breath.

"You mustn't be afraid." She had to make an effort to keep her voice calm and sound firm. "No wolf is ever going to come here."

"Yes, he does," Louisa whispered sleepily. "Every time you're away. But it's a secret. I can't tell you because then he'll eat me up."

• • •

In the morning, they had taken Bernd Prinzler before the judge and then transferred him from the holding cell at the police station, where he'd spent the night, to the remand prison in Preungesheim. It took almost half an hour before they brought him to the visitors' room where Pia and Christian were waiting. The two guards who accompanied him were taller than Pia, but Prinzler was more than a head taller than they were. Pia was prepared for a difficult conversation. The man had years of prison experience, and the atmosphere of the prison wouldn't intimidate him in the least—not like someone who had spent his first night in a jail cell and was feeling alarmed about being locked up. Men like Prinzler usually didn't say a word; at most, they might refer all questions to their lawyers.

"Hello, Mr. Prinzler," said Pia. "My name is Pia Kirchhoff, and this is my colleague Chief Detective Inspector Kröger. K-11 Hofheim."

There was no visible emotion on Prinzler's face, but in his brown eyes Pia saw an expression of concern and tension that surprised her.

"Please have a seat." She turned to the two guards. "Thank you. Would you mind waiting outside?"

Prinzler sat down on the chair with his legs apart, crossed his tattooed arms, and fixed his steady gaze on Pia.

"What do you guys want with me?" he asked as

the key turned in the lock from outside. "What's this all about anyway?" His voice was deep and rough.

"We're investigating the murder of Leonie Verges," said Pia. "A witness saw you and a second man coming out of Ms. Verges's house on the evening that her body was discovered. What were you doing there?"

"When we got to the house, she was already dead," he replied. "I called one one zero from my cell and reported the body."

After this promising beginning, he refused to answer any more of the questions that Pia and Christian took turns asking.

"Why were you at Ms. Verges's house?"

"How did you happen to know her?"

"Your car was observed multiple times at Ms. Verges's house. What were you doing there?"

"Who was the man who accompanied you?"

"When was the last time you spoke to Kilian Rothemund?"

"What were you doing on the night of the twenty-fourth of June?"

Finally, he deigned to open his mouth.

"Why do you want to know that?"

"That night, the TV host Hanna Herzmann was attacked, beaten, and brutally raped."

Pia noticed a flicker in Prinzler's eyes. His jaw muscles were tensing, and his neck muscles were noticeably taut.

"I have no need to rape women. And I've never beaten one, either. On the twenty-fourth I was at a bikers' convention. There are about five hundred people who can testify to that."

He still hadn't denied that he knew Hanna Herzmann.

"On the evening mentioned, why did you accompany Kilian Rothemund to Ms. Herzmann's house?"

Pia hadn't expected Bernd Prinzler to be a chatterbox, but her patience, which is the highest virtue an investigator can have, was being sorely tested. Time was running out.

"Listen, Mr. Prinzler," said Pia, taking an unconventional tack. "My colleague and I do not consider you a suspect in either case. I think you're trying to cover up for someone or protect him. I can understand that. But we're looking for a dangerous psychopath who abused, violated, and drowned a young girl before the Main spit her out like a piece of garbage. You have children yourself, and something like this could happen to them."

Prinzler's eyes showed surprise, and respect.

Pia went on. "Hanna Herzmann was bestially violated with the handle of an umbrella and so severely injured that she almost bled to death. Then they locked her in the trunk of her car, and she was very lucky to have survived. Leonie Verges was tied to a chair. Somebody watched her die of thirst; a video camera recorded and transmitted her agonizing death. I would be very grateful if you could somehow help us find and arrest the perpetrator or perpetrators and bring them to justice."

"If you help me get out of here," replied Prinzler, "then I can help you, too."

"If it were up to us, you could go right now." Pia gave a rueful shrug. "But there are higher powers involved."

"It doesn't bother me to hang around here for a few days," he said. "There are no warrants for my arrest. My lawyer will appeal, and I'll even get paid for the days I was here."

His face with the neatly trimmed beard seemed almost carved out of stone, but the expression in his eyes belied his inscrutable façade. This man had countless hearings and interrogations behind him; he was used to a rough way of speaking and certainly had no scruples. Yet he was worried— very worried. The person he was trying to protect must be someone close to his heart. Pia decided to take a shot in the dark.

"If you're worried about your family, I can arrange for them to have police protection," she said.

The thought of police protection for his family seemed to amuse Prinzler; a tiny smile twitched at the corners of his mouth but vanished immediately.

"I'd rather you see about getting me out of here today." He gave her an urgent and stern look. "I have a permanent residence, so I'm not going to split."

"Then answer our questions," Christian told him.

Prinzler ignored him. It showed his great self-confidence that he would let down his guard and practically beg a cop bitch to help him. Men of his caliber normally had nothing but contempt for the police.

"Someone saw you at the site where Ms. Herzmann was found in the trunk of her car. Tomorrow there will be a lineup with the witness."

"I already told you where I was that night." Prinzler was avoiding the insults, macho behavior, and biker slang that were doubtless his normal modus operandi. He was an intelligent man who had retired after fourteen years spent handling the daily business of the Road Kings. He now lived in a paradise, far from the strip clubs and dives of the red-light district that had once been his home. Why? What had caused him to change his life like that? Pia guessed he was in his mid-fifties. At the time, he must have been somewhere in his late thirties—not an age at which somebody like Bernd Prinzler would simply retire. And although he seemed to have left his criminal days behind, he was still doing everything he could to remain invisible. Who was he hiding from? And once again, a big "Why?"

Time passed, and for a moment no one said a word.

Pia broke the silence. "Why did Erik Lessing have to die? What did he know?"

Prinzler had his poker face well under control, but he couldn't help his eyebrows from reflexively rising.

"That's exactly what this is all about," he said roughly.

"What do you mean by that?" Pia asked. She didn't avoid his gaze.

"Think about it," replied Prinzler. "That's all I'm saying without my lawyer present."

She was pissed off—totally pissed off—and insulted.

What was the idea of that asshole, giving her the brush-off like that? Tears of rage were burning in Meike's eyes as she went down the stairs, her back rigid.

After visiting Hanna, she had driven out to see Wolfgang in Oberursel. She didn't know why he had become so important to her or why she had the feeling that he was lying to her. Where did the distrust come from? When he told her on the phone that she couldn't stay overnight at his place because his father had visitors, she hadn't believed him.

But the driveway and the neatly raked gravel forecourt were both jammed with parked cars—big fancy ones from Karlsruhe, Munich, Stuttgart, Hamburg, Berlin, even from abroad. Okay, so Wolfgang hadn't lied. She stood there for a while, trying to decide whether she should simply drive off or ring the bell. Wolfgang knew that she was sitting home alone. If there was a party at his house, he could have at least invited her. Hanna always received an invitation to every occasion.

Meike looked at the big old house that she loved so much. The high mullioned windows, the dark green shutters, the half-hipped roof covered with reddish beaver-tail tiles, the eight front steps leading up to the dark green double door, on which a brass lion's head knocker was mounted. The lavender bushes in front of the house gave off an intense fragrance on this warm evening, reminding Meike of vacations in southern France. Hanna had brought back the lavender from Provence for Wolfgang's mother many years ago.

She had often come here with Hanna, and in her memory the house seemed like the epitome of security and safety. But now Aunt Christine was dead, and Hanna was in the hospital looking more dead than alive. And Meike had nobody waiting for her, nobody she could turn to in order to feel safe and protected. Yet it was true that Wolfgang had developed into the most important person in her life, a sort of father figure, for whom she felt the deepest trust. Her stepfathers had come and gone, viewing her as nothing more than a troublesome but unavoidable appendage to Hanna, and her own father had married a jealous shrew.

Meike cast a last look at the house; then she turned around to leave. At that moment, a black Maybach drove up the driveway and stopped right in front of the steps. A slim white-haired man got out, and his eyes met hers. She smiled and waved and registered with astonishment the expression of displeasure that passed over the suntanned face of Peter Weissbecker. Peter was an old acquaintance of Hanna, an actor and master of ceremonies who was a legend on German television. Meike had known him all her life. Of course she found it a bit silly to call him Uncle Pitti now that she was twenty-four, but that's what she'd always called him.

"Little Meike! How wonderful to see you," he said with feigned enthusiasm. "Tell me, is your mother here, too?" He gave her a clumsy hug.

"No, Mama is in the hospital," she said, linking arms with him.

"Oh no, I'm so sorry. Is it something serious?"

She walked up the steps with him. The front door swung open and there stood Wolfgang's father. She could see from his expression that he, too, was not happy to see her. At least he made no pretense about his displeasure, unlike Uncle Pitti, the professional stage actor.

"What are you doing here?" Hartmut Matern reproached Meike.

A slap wouldn't have hurt more than this surly greeting.

"Hello, Uncle Hartmut. I happened to be in the neighborhood," Meike lied. "I just wanted to stop by and say hello."

"This evening is not a good time," said Hartmut. "I have guests, as you can see."

Meike stared at him, dumbfounded. He had never before spoken to her with such rudeness. Wolfgang came up behind him. He seemed nervous and tense. His father and Uncle Pitti went inside the house, leaving her standing there like a stranger without saying good-bye or even sending a greeting to Hanna. Meike was deeply hurt.

"What's going on here?" she asked. "Some sort of stag party? Or was Mama invited, too?"

Wolfgang grabbed her by the arm and ushered her down the stairs.

"Meike, please. Today is a very bad time." He spoke quietly, as if he didn't want anyone else to hear. "It's sort of . . . sort of a shareholders' meeting. To discuss business."

It was a smooth attempt to lie, but so obvious that it hurt her more than the humiliating feeling of being more or less thrown out.

"Why don't you answer the phone when I call?" Meike hated the tone of her own voice. She wanted to be cool, but she sounded like a hysterical, jealous bitch.

"In the past week, I've had so much to do. Please, Meike, don't make a scene," he implored her.

"I most certainly will not make a *scene*," she snorted in fury. "I just thought you meant what you said, that I could come here anytime."

Wolfgang hemmed and hawed, stammering something about a crisis meeting and restructuring. What a lame excuse.

Meike yanked her arm away from his grasp. She was hugely disappointed.

"All right, I get it. It was all just talk to ease your guilty conscience. Actually, I don't give a shit. Have fun tonight."

"Meike, wait! Please. It's not like that."

She kept walking, hoping that he would follow her and apologize or something, but when she melodramatically turned around to forgive him, he'd gone back inside the house and closed the door. Never before had she felt so alone and shut out. It was devastating to realize that these people had never felt any real affection or friendliness for her. They had merely accepted her because she was the ugly, irritating daughter of the famous Hanna Herzmann.

Meike trudged along the driveway, fighting back tears of rage. Before she went out to the street, she shot a few photos of the parked cars with her iPhone. If this was a shareholders' meeting, then she was Lady Gaga. Something was going on here, and she was going to find out what it was. Fucking idiots!

"Good God!" Pia tilted her head back and gazed up at the façade of a gray apartment block on the Hattersheimer Schillerring. "I had no idea he lived here now."

"Why? Where did he live before?" asked Christian Kröger. He was standing at the street door, squinting at the long list of tenants.

"In an old building in Sachsenhausen," Pia recalled. "Not far from the apartment where Henning and I used to live."

That was the address the computer had spit out as Frank Behnke's current place of residence. She had told her boss she was going home, but she and Christian had met twenty minutes later in the parking lot of the Real Market in Hattersheim. It caused her no great pangs of conscience to keep secrets from Bodenstein. Whatever role he might have played in this story, she was sure that he had not been directly involved. So in that respect, it was none of his business if she decided to question a few people behind his back.

"Okay, I found him," said Christian. "What should I say?"

"Just tell him your name," Pia suggested. "You've never had any trouble with him."

Her colleague pressed the doorbell, and seconds later someone croaked "Hello?" and Christian answered. The door opener buzzed, and they went into the foyer, which may have been old but was kept up better than the ugly concrete block would suggest from the outside. The elevator was vintage 1976, according to the manufacturer's nameplate, and the sounds that it emitted on the trip to the seventeenth floor did not arouse confidence. The hall smelled of food and cleaning products; the walls were painted in a hideous ocher color, which made the windowless corridor look drearier than it was.

Pia, who remembered all too well Behnke's profound abhorrence of these kinds of housing projects and their inhabitants, felt a hint of sympathy at the thought that he was now living among them.

A door opened and Behnke appeared in the doorway. He was wearing gray sweatpants and a stained T-shirt; he was unshaven and bare-foot.

"If you'd told me that she was coming along, I wouldn't have let you in," he said to Christian. His breath smelled strongly of booze. "What do you want?"

Pia ignored the unfriendly greeting. "Hello, Frank. Are you going to let us in?"

"Please come in. It's an honor to welcome you to my luxury penthouse," he said sarcastically.

"Unfortunately, I'm all out of champagne, and my butler has already gone home."

Pia entered the apartment and was shocked. It consisted of a single room of about 375 square feet, with a tiny open kitchen and a sleeping alcove separated off by a curtain. She saw a worn couch, a coffee table, and a cheap pine sideboard with a small TV sitting on top. It was on, but the sound was turned off. In the corner was a clothes rack with shirts, ties, and suits. A few pairs of shoes stood underneath, along with a vacuum cleaner. Every free surface was covered with something, and with three adults in the room, the place felt jam-packed. With each step, they ran into some piece of furniture. The only thing that was really beautiful was the distant view of the Taunus from the balcony, but that was no consolation. What a depressing way to live.

"Are you two the new dream team?" Behnke asked spitefully.

Pia saw pure hatred glittering in his watery, red-rimmed eyes. In the past, Frank had shown misanthropic tendencies, but it was clear that lately he had come to loathe all humanity without exception.

"I'm sure this isn't a courtesy call. So, tell me what you want, and then leave me in peace."

"We're here because we want to hear from you about the whole Erik Lessing case." Pia knew that it made no sense to beat around the bush, so she got straight to the point.

"Erik who? Never heard of him," Behnke declared without batting an eye. "Is that all? Then you can leave now."

"In our current investigations, the names of two people have come up—people who also played a role in the Lessing incident," Pia went on, unfazed. "We think that there may be a connection."

"I don't know what you're talking about." Behnke crossed his arms. "And I don't give a shit."

"We know that you shot three men in a brothel in Frankfurt. And not in self-defense, but on someone's express orders. They used you and didn't tell you the truth in advance. You've never gotten over the fact that you shot a colleague to death."

Behnke first turned red, then pale. He balled his hands into fists.

"They ruined your life, but that didn't mean shit to them," Pia said. "If we find out who was behind it, we can bring them to justice."

"Get out of here," Frank snarled between clenched teeth. "Beat it and don't let me see you here again."

"You were a soldier before you joined the police force," said Christian, taking over. "You were trained as a sharpshooter and were a member of a special unit. You were really good. They chose you for this action because they knew that you'd obey and wouldn't ask questions. Who gave you the order? And above all, why?"

Frank Behnke looked from Pia to Christian.

"What the hell is the meaning of this?" he said furiously. "What do you want from me? Don't you think my life is shitty enough already?"

"Frank! We're not here to hassle you," Kröger protested. "But people are dying. A girl was brutally raped and murdered. Then they just tossed her into the Main. A little while ago, we spoke to the man who owned the car in which the weapon was found after Lessing died. This man and his lawyer from back then are both involved in at least two current cases."

"And you think you can simply drop by here for a little chat? 'Hey, let's go ask Frank. He'll probably tell us everything.'" Behnke gave a scornful laugh. "Are you totally insane? This fucking shit has ruined my whole life! Take a look around and see what's become of me. I'm not about to get sucked into something like that again. And definitely not for the sake of the old man and his . . . his golden princess!"

Bright red splotches had appeared on Behnke's neck, and sweat was beading on his brow. His whole body was shaking. Pia knew him well enough to see that it would take only a tiny spark for him to explode.

"Come on, Christian, let's go," she said quietly. There was no point. Behnke was consumed by bitterness, hatred, and revenge. He wasn't going to help them, not even if they lay bleeding right in front of him. He was the type of person who was always looking for a scapegoat for his personal misery, and in his eyes, Pia was the reason that Bodenstein had turned his back on him.

Christian wasn't about to give up so easily. "It's not about Bodenstein, Pia, or me. It's about people issuing contracts for murder and then walking away scot-free."

"You have no idea what they're capable of. Not the faintest idea." Frank turned and went over to the kitchenette. He grabbed a bottle of clear liquid and filled a glass to the brim.

"Who are 'they'?" Pia asked.

Frank stared at her, then brought the glass to his mouth and drank the contents all in one gulp. His eyes wandered over the tiny room, and with a fury that frightened Pia, he threw the glass against the wall, but it didn't break.

"There! Look at that!" Frank gave a bitter laugh. "I'm totally worthless. I can't even make a glass break. Fucking piece of shit!"

He was far drunker than Pia had guessed. When he tried to pick up the glass, he lost his balance and stumbled against a bookshelf, which collapsed with a crash. Laughing, he rolled on the floor, but his laughter rapidly turned into a desperate sobbing. The man had changed from a sports fanatic in top condition, who ate only organic food and had never touched a cigarette, into a drunk. What had happened in March 1997 in Frankfurt had destroyed him, because he had never figured out how to process what he'd done. His honor was shattered, and his life was one big heap of rubble.

"I can't do anything anymore," he gasped, pounding his fist on the floor. "Not a damn thing! I'm finished, because I'm a fucking zero!"

Pia and Christian exchanged a worried look.

"Frank, come on, get up." Christian bent over and held out his hand.

"I can't even get a woman anymore," Frank babbled on. "What would a woman want with somebody like me? My ex takes all my money, and I'm left with just enough to pay for this shithole!"

Those last words had come out in a howl. He straightened up, ignoring Christian's outstretched hand, and got to his feet without assistance.

"You know what?" he said to Pia, blowing breath reeking of schnapps in her face. "I couldn't stand you from the very first day. Wife of the rich Dr. Kirchhoff, who with her millions in stock rushed off to buy a farm and turned the heads of all the guys with her big tits. Shit! You were so fucking . . . efficient and so . . . so goddamned clever—you just couldn't work hard enough.

Compared to you, the rest of us looked like lazy pigs. You made sure to kiss the old man's ass whenever you could."

The alcohol made him slur his words. His hatred, bottled up for so long, had finally found an escape valve. Pia let the insults roll off her back without replying to any of them.

"Yeah, I shot three people! I didn't know what was going on. I didn't know there was an undercover guy. We went into the place because some informant ratted them out, said there was a big deal going down. Maybe I should have suspected something when they palmed off a different weapon on me. It was all rigged. When we got into the courtyard, one of the bikers fired first. What should I have done, let him gun me down? I fired back, and I was a better shot than that jerk. Double tap to the head, a third round to the throat. It was a gigantic mess. Before I knew what was happening, I was sitting in a car. And that was that. I don't remember anything else."

Pia believed him. They'd set a trap not only for the undercover agent Erik Lessing but for Behnke, too. He was the sacrificed pawn in a dirty game between powerful men for whom a human life had absolutely no value.

"Who was with you in the courtyard?" Christian asked.

Behnke snorted. He staggered past Pia and dropped onto the couch. They looked down at him. Despite all the curses he'd hurled at them, they felt no anger, only the deepest sympathy.

"You want to know who was with me in the courtyard?" he blurted out with eyes half-closed. "Really? You want to know who said 'Shit, my service weapon is in the car'? I'll tell you. Yeah, I'll tell you all right. Because I don't give a shit. She really took me for a ride, that ice-cold bitch. And afterward, she threatened me. If I ever said a word about it, then I'd never be happy again in my life."

He uttered a sound, somewhere between a laugh and a sob, and slapped the arm of the couch hard. "And I never was happy again. In thirty seconds, I'd fucked up my whole life. I shot a colleague! And you know why? Because that fucking bitch ordered me to do it."

"Who, Frank?" Christian asked, although he and Pia already knew.

"Engel." Frank Behnke straightened halfway up, his face distorted with bitterness and hate. "Commissioner Nicola Engel."

The time was 11:48 P.M. For more than twenty-four hours, he hadn't seen a soul or heard a sound other than a nerve-racking squeaking coming from the vent behind a barred opening near the ceiling of the cell. It was probably the only source of fresh air, because there was no window, not even a light shaft. The only light source was a dusty twenty-five-watt bulb on the ceiling, for which there was no switch. The cell smelled unused, musty and damp, like a typical basement.

Kilian Rothemund lay on the narrow plank bed, his arms behind his head, and stared at the rusty metal door, which was more solid than it looked. When he was arrested, he hadn't felt afraid, but gradually the fear had crept up on him. He wasn't in the custody of the Dutch police; that much was clear. But where was he? Who were the black-clad masked men who had apprehended him on the train platform? Why was he being held prisoner in this hole? How had they even known that he was in Amsterdam? Had Leonie given something away before they bound her and taped her mouth shut?

The last thing he'd had to eat were two pieces of pastry, and since then his stomach had been growling miserably. He drank the lukewarm water only in sips because he had no idea how long it would have to last. They had taken away his belt and shoelaces, even though in this room with the smooth, high walls there was nothing he could hang himself from. At least they'd left him his watch.

Rothemund closed his eyes and allowed his thoughts to leave the moldy-smelling prison and fly to more pleasant realms. Hanna! The second their eyes had met for the first time, something had happened, something he'd never before experienced. He had seen her on TV, of course, but in person she was completely different. That evening, she hadn't worn any makeup and her hair had been pulled back into a simple knot, yet she possessed a radiance that fascinated him.

Leonie couldn't stand Hanna. Bernd's suggestion that they present Michaela's terrible story to the public with Hanna Herzmann's help had not pleased her at all. Leonie said Hanna was arrogant and egotistical, without a single spark of empathy.

None of that was true.

Kilian hadn't kept anything from Hanna. He'd been open and honest with her, even at the risk that she might not believe him. But she had believed him. A deep trust had been quick to develop between them. The tone and detail of their e-mails had changed, and out of initial fascination had grown affection. Kilian had never talked on the phone with anyone for an hour and a half, but with Hanna, it happened often. He knew after only two weeks that it was more than infatuation. Hanna made him feel like a human being again. Her firm conviction that everything would be all right, that with her support he would find his way back to a normal life, fully rehabilitated, had given him a strength that he thought he'd lost forever. Chiara would no longer have to visit him in secret at the trailer park, and maybe he would soon be able to see his children again with official permission.

He heaved a big sigh. His longing for Hanna's voice, her carefree laughter, her warm, soft body next to his was mixed with deep concern. How he wished he could be with her now to offer her solace. Especially now. Because of her, everything had seemed to be taking a turn for the better, but then fate once again struck without mercy. Was it his fault that they had attacked her? Worry, anxiety, and helplessness transformed into despair. Suddenly, he heard something. He sat up and listened. Footsteps were approaching. A key turned in the lock. He got up from the bed, balled his hands into fists, and girded himself for whatever was coming. His despair vanished. It didn't matter what they did to him; he would survive it, because he wanted to see his children again. And Hanna.

"Don't you like it?"

Christoph was sitting across from her at the kitchen table and watching as she pushed her food back and forth on her plate. The ratatouille with rice was delicious, but Pia felt like her stomach was tied in knots.

"Yes, I do. But for some reason, I just don't have any appetite." Pia put down her knife and fork and sighed heavily.

The visit to Frank Behnke had given her a shock from which she hadn't yet recovered. She knew that what she had learned would stay with her forever. She and Frank had not been friends. During the time they were both in K-11 in Hofheim, he'd always been uncooperative and grouchy, leaving the major part of the work to her and their other colleagues. He had insulted everybody and butted heads with anyone who tried to be nice to him. Like everyone else, she had decided after a while that he was simply an asshole. Even worse now was the realization that she'd been so unfair to him, because basically he was a victim. They had used him and then dropped him, ruining his mind and his conscience and destroying his whole life. Although Frank had so often hurled curses and insults at her, Pia felt unaccountably sad now that she knew how this human tragedy had played out for years almost right before her eyes.

"Do you want to talk about it?" Christoph asked. There was a concerned expression in his dark eyes. He'd known her long enough and well enough to tell when she was merely preoccupied and needed a little rest after a stressful day and when she was truly upset about certain events. Lack of appetite was a serious reason for concern, because Pia could eat in almost any situation.

"Not at the moment." She propped her elbows on the table and massaged the bridge of her nose. "Besides, I have no idea where to start. Good Lord, it's all such a mess."

But the full scope of what she had learned

today in that depressing apartment was something she hadn't comprehended until now. She and Christian had agreed for the time being not to mention to anyone what Frank had revealed, but it was obvious that they had to do something, now that they knew what had really happened back then.

Christoph didn't say anything, didn't try to pressure her. He never did. He got up, briefly put a hand on her shoulder, and began clearing the table.

"Leave it. I can do it," Pia said with a yawn, but he just grinned.

"You know what, sweetie," he told her, "the best thing would be for you to get in the shower, and then we'll have a glass of wine together."

"Good idea." Pia gave him a wan smile. She got up, went to him, and threw her arms around his waist.

"What did I ever do to deserve you?" she murmured. "I'm sorry that I haven't paid much attention to you and Lilly lately. I really left you in the lurch."

He took her face in his hands and kissed her tenderly on the lips.

"Well, that much is definitely true. I've been feeling totally neglected."

"Is there anything I can do to make it up to you?" Pia returned his kiss and slid her hands down his back. Since Lilly was there, they hadn't been making love. But the girl really wasn't to blame, because for days Pia had been coming home late and jumping out of bed early in the morning to dash off to work.

"I'm sure I can think of something," Christoph whispered in her ear, squeezing her tight. She felt his desire. The smell of his skin, the touch of his hands, his warm, slim body so close to hers ignited a spark of desire deep inside her.

"Are you thinking what I'm thinking?" Pia pressed her cheek against his. Her secret fear that daily routine might damage the physical side of their relationship remained unfounded after three and a half years. The very opposite had occurred.

"What are you thinking of?" asked Christoph with a teasing undertone.

"Of . . . sex," Pia replied.

"What a coincidence." He kissed her neck, then her lips. "That's exactly what I had in mind."

Pia pulled out of his embrace and went upstairs to the bathroom. She undressed, dropped her sweaty clothes on the floor, and stepped into the shower. The hot water washed the sticky sweat from her skin and banished all thought of Frank's shabby apartment and his desperation, as well as the troubling notion that Bodenstein had been keeping murky secrets from her.

Christoph was already in bed when she went into the bedroom a little later. Soft music was coming from the speakers, and on the nightstand stood two glasses and a bottle of white wine. Pia slipped under the covers and into his arms. Through the wide-open French doors to the balcony, a damp, cool breeze swirled in with the fragrance of freshly mown grass and roses. The lamp with the paper shade cast a golden light on their moving limbs, and Pia savored the excitement and the wonderful feelings of lust that Christoph's caresses awoke in her. Suddenly, the door opened. A tiny figure with tangled blond hair appeared in the doorway. Christoph and Pia sprang apart in shock.

"I had a bad dream, Grandpa," said Lilly in a whiny voice. "Can I sleep with you?"

"Damn," Christoph muttered, quickly pulling the covers over them.

"Grandpa," said Pia, giggling as she rested her forehead on his back.

"Not right now, Lilly," Christoph told his granddaughter. "Go back to bed. In a few minutes, I'll come and tuck you in."

"You don't have any clothes on," Lilly stated calmly. "Are you going to make a baby?"

Christoph was speechless.

"Mama and Daddy try it almost every night, and sometimes in the daytime, too," said Lilly wisely as she sat down on the edge of the bed. "But so far, I don't have any sisters or brothers. Grandpa, if Pia has a baby, will he be my grandson?"

Pia pressed her hand to her lips, fighting back a fit of laughter.

"No." Christoph sighed. "But to be honest, right now I can't concentrate on possible family ties."

"Don't worry, Grandpa. You're pretty old anyway." Lilly cocked her head to one side. "But I can play with the baby, can't I?"

"Right now, you have to go back to bed," said Christoph. Lilly yawned and nodded, but then she recalled her nightmare.

"But I'm afraid to go downstairs by myself," she told him. "Can you come with me? Please, Grandpa. I promise to fall asleep right away."

"You managed to come upstairs by yourself," said Christoph, but he was already defeated.

"Go on," Pia chortled. "I'll have a glass of wine in the meantime."

"Traitor," Christoph complained. "You're torpedoing all my attempts at child rearing. Lilly, wait outside the door. I'll be right there."

"Okay." The little girl slid down off the edge of the bed. "Good night, Pia."

"Good night, Lilly," said Pia. When the girl was gone, she exploded with laughter. She laughed until the tears ran down her face.

Christoph stood up and slipped on undershorts and a T-shirt.

"That kid!" He shook his head in feigned desperation. "I think I'm going to have to speak to Anna about raising kids."

Pia turned over on her back and grinned.

"Lover man, oh, where can you be?" Pia sang, laughing.

"Don't think you're getting off so easy," said Christoph with a grin. "I'll be right back. And don't you dare fall asleep!"

Friday, July 2, 2010

They had blindfolded him and his hands were cuffed behind his back. No one said a word during the drive, which lasted about half an hour. The car wasn't a minivan like the one they had transported him in from the Amsterdam main station to the building with the cellar room. This was a sedan, a limousine. Not a BMW or Mercedes—the suspension was too soft for that; instead, something British. Maybe a Jaguar or Bentley. Kilian Rothemund inhaled the faint aroma of leather and wood; he heard the silky soft purr of the twelve-cylinder engine and felt the gentle tilt of the chassis on every curve. The removal of visual input sharpened all his other senses, and Kilian concentrated on what he could hear, smell, and feel. Besides him, there were at least three other men in the car—two in front and another next to him on the backseat. He could smell an expensive aftershave, but also the body odor of a man who hadn't washed in a while. That was the one sitting next to him. He wore a cheap fake-leather jacket and had smoked recently. Of course, none of this helped him with the question of where they were taking him and what they wanted from him, but concentrating on external conditions helped Kilian suppress his anxiety.

After they'd been driving for a while at high speed on a highway with no noticeable bumps, the driver slowed down and made a sharp right turn. Autobahn exit, Kilian assumed. The blinker was ticking. The man in the passenger seat coughed.

"On the left up ahead," he said in a low voice. German, with no accent. A little later, the car rolled over cobblestone pavement and came to a halt. The doors opened, and Kilian felt his arm gripped hard as he was yanked out of the car. Gravel crunched loudly under his shoes, and the air was mild. The scent of damp soil mixed with country smells. Frogs croaked in the distance.

It was a weird feeling to walk without being able to see.

"Watch the step," somebody said beside him, but he stumbled anyway and banged his shoulder against a rough brick wall.

"Where are you taking me?" Kilian asked. He didn't expect an answer, and he got none. More stairs, going down now. It smelled sweet, like apples and cider. A cellar, judging by the intensity of the smell, maybe even with a cider press. Another set of stairs, this time going up.

A door opened in front of him, the hinges

squeaking lightly. No more cellar smell. A parquet floor. And books. The smell of old books—leather, paper, dust. A library?

"Ah, you're all here," someone said quietly. Chair legs scraped on the floor.

"Sit down."

This order was for him. Kilian sat down on a chair, and his arms were yanked behind him, his ankles fastened to the chair legs. Someone tore the blindfold off his eyes. Harsh light bombarded his retinas; his eyes teared up, and he blinked.

"What were you doing in Amsterdam?" asked a man whose voice he hadn't heard before. This question set off all the alarm bells in Kilian's brain and confirmed his worst fears. He was in the hands of the people who had ruined his life nine years ago. They had shown no mercy the last time, and they weren't about to do so today, either. It was pointless to ask where they'd gotten the information that he had gone to Holland. It made no difference to the outcome.

"Visiting friends," he replied.

"We know these so-called friends you visited," said the man. "Now cut the crap. What did you talk to them about?"

Kilian perceived the men behind the light only as silhouettes; he could see no faces, not even outlines.

"About sailing," said Kilian.

The punch came with no warning and hit him in

537

the middle of his face. His nose cracked and he tasted blood.

"I don't like asking questions twice," said the man. "So, what did you talk about?"

Kilian said nothing. He was waiting with muscles tensed for the next blow, the next pain. Instead, somebody turned the chair he was sitting on to the left. There was a TV hanging on the wall.

He jumped when he suddenly saw Hanna's face. They had gagged her. Blood was running over her forehead and her eyes were wide in panicky terror. The camera pulled back a little. Hanna was naked and bound, kneeling on bare concrete. These motherfuckers had filmed her being beaten and raped. It tore Kilian's heart open. He turned his head away and closed his eyes; he couldn't watch the woman he loved suffering the torments of hell and fear of death.

"Look at it!" Somebody grabbed his hair, jerked his head up, but he squeezed his eyes shut. They couldn't force him to watch, but he had to listen to the desperate sounds Hanna was making, hear the sneering voice of her torturer, who was giving a running commentary of his disgusting actions. His stomach convulsed and he retched up a flood of bitter gall.

"You fucks!" he yelled. "You filthy, rotten pigs! What have you done?"

He was pummeled by fists and couldn't defend

himself. It sounded like a gunshot inside his head when his cheekbone snapped; his skin burst open and blood ran down his chin, mixed with the tears he couldn't hold back.

"Do you want the same thing to happen to your daughter?" hissed a voice close to his ear. "Yeah, you want that? Here, look, there she is, your innocent little daughter. That's her, right?"

Kilian opened his eyes. The video was poor quality, probably taken with a hidden camera, but it was clearly Chiara standing in front of the goal at the hockey club, talking to a young man who had turned his back to the camera. She gave a coquettish laugh, her long blond hair falling over her bare shoulders as she looked up at the man. He gasped for breath. His throat was now choked, his nose stopped up with blood and tears. Fear crept like ice through every vein in his body.

"A really sweet kid, little Chiara. Nice small titties and a tight ass," said the voice behind him. "A video starring her would probably be a big hit."

Laughter.

"If you don't open your mouth soon, your little girl is going to experience the same thing this afternoon as that TV bitch."

Kilian broke down. He had held out through every pain, every torment, and every torture, but the thought of these people doing the same thing to his daughter that they'd done to Hanna was absolutely intolerable. He opened his mouth and started talking.

"Come, Lomax!"

She opened the front door. The dog jumped out of his basket like greased lightning and dashed past her out the door. She crossed the courtyard and went into the garden. Droplets of dew glittered on the grass in the light of the rising sun. The brindled Staffordshire bull terrier was frolicking all over the lawn, peeing on every other rosebush, growling each time as he kicked up dirt with his hind legs. He was the king of the yard, the boss. The other dogs respected him without protest.

Just like other men respect Bernd, Michaela thought. Since the day before yesterday, she hadn't heard a word from her husband. In the past, that had happened often, but for many years he hadn't had anything to do with the cops. Even when she wasn't alone on the big estate and didn't need to fear break-ins, she worried when he was gone. Since yesterday, the kids had been away, too, ten days of vacation on the Baltic coast with the sports club. That was for the best, after the cops had scared her youngest almost to death with their stupid raid. Not letting him go with his friends and pals on the team would have been sending the wrong signal.

Still, Michaela missed them both. It was quiet in the house without Bernd and the kids. Natasha liked keeping her company, but she was much less talkative than Ludmilla, who had been their previous au pair. Michaela ended her grand tour up front at the workshop. Three of the boys were still there.

"Morning," Freddy, the foreman, greeted her. "Want some coffee, boss?"

"Morning. Yes, sure," Michaela said. She sat down on the wooden bench in front of the barn and leaned back against the wall, which was already warm from the sun. Lomax settled down next to her feet with a sigh and laid his snout on his front paws. Only seconds later, Freddy brought her a mug of steaming coffee.

"Shot of milk, two sugars," he said with a grin. "Everything okay otherwise? Heard anything from the boss?"

"No, afraid not." Michaela nodded in thanks and sipped at the coffee. "But otherwise, everything's fine."

The boys were always so attentive. Sometimes it was almost too much, because they wanted to do everything for her, even the shopping. She reached for the *Bild* tabloid, which one of the men had brought and left lying on the table. She wasn't that interested in what was going on in the world; all the disasters, wars, and crises just depressed her. She preferred books. Lomax rolled over on his side with a contented rumble, enjoying the warmth of the sun.

Suddenly, Michaela gave a start. The photo of a man jumped out at her and she had to swallow hard. Before she could stop herself, she had read the first few lines, and then she kept reading, as if compelled.

The former industrialist and founder of Sonnenkinder, the shelter for mothers and children, Dr. Josef Finkbeiner, turns eighty years old today. To celebrate the occasion, Finkbeiner, who has already received the Federal Service Cross First Class and the Certificate of Honor from the State of Hessen for his magnanimous charitable works, was honored by his family and numerous guests in the garden of his villa. A further occasion for celebration is the fortieth anniversary of the founding of the Sonnenkinder Association.

The type swam before her eyes as her fingers clutched the handle of the coffee mug. She turned alternately hot and cold. Josef Finkbeiner! Something in her head, something that she and Leonie had laboriously patched together, burst into a thousand pieces. All at once she was again six years old. She was sitting at a big oval table; in front of her lay an open book, and she wished she could read what it said. She could still see the pictures, as if she'd held the book in her hands only yesterday, but it was forty years ago.

Michaela Prinzler stared at the photo of the white-haired man, smiling kindly and benevolently into the camera. Oh, how much she had loved him! He'd been the warm sun in her childhood universe. The happiest memories of her childhood, and there weren't very many, had been inextricably bound to him. For many years, she hadn't understood what was wrong with her, why in her life there were hours, sometimes even days and weeks, that were missing. They were simply not in her memory any longer. Leonie had discovered that she was not alone in her body. There was not only Michaela. There were others, too, and they all had their own names, their own memories, feelings, preferences, and dislikes. For a long time, Michaela hadn't wanted to accept this; it sounded totally crazy, and yet it explained the strange and frightening blackouts. Ever since she was a little girl, she'd had to share her time with Tanya, Sandra, Stella, Dorothee, Carina, Nina, Babsi, and many other identities.

"Cut it out, Michaela," she said out loud to herself. It was dangerous to sink into reminiscences, because she might suddenly slip into one of the other identities, and then she would black out again. Swiftly, she turned the pages of the newspaper, and on the very next page, another familiar face caught her eye.

"Kilian!" she muttered in amazement. Why did he have his picture in *Bild*? She quickly scanned the short caption and shuddered. No! That's not right. It can't be true! But Bernd had told her that Leonie was on vacation. She had wondered about that because right now, at this phase of their plan, it was no time to be traveling. But Leonie had done so much for her, she really deserved a vacation. The newspapers said she was dead. And there was a manhunt for Kilian in connection with her death and the attack on the TV host Johanna H.

Michaela felt numb, and her hands were shaking so hard that she could barely hold her coffee cup. Lomax sensed her tenseness; he jumped up and tried to lick her hand.

What was reality? What was she imagining? Had time once again been swallowed up without her noticing? Maybe the kids weren't on a vacation trip, but had long ago grown up, married, and moved out. And Bernd? Where was he? What day was it? How old was she? Michaela folded up the paper, stuck it in the pocket of her vest, and stood up. She was dizzy. Where the heck was that fairy-tale book she'd just been looking at? Her mother was going to scold her if she'd left it somewhere, because that was a book from her own childhood. Crap! It was here a minute ago. Or was it? She looked around. Where was she anyway? Who were these men?

Michaela clutched her head. No, no, no, it couldn't start again now; she had to stop it. She had to call Leonie; she couldn't lose hold of her Michaela life. If she did, it would be a disaster.

Pia rushed up the stairs. She always took two at a time. Half the night, she'd lain awake thinking about what she could do to regain her trust in Bodenstein. No way could she let this whole matter rest and act as if she didn't know anything. Torn between loyalty to her boss and her sense of duty, she fell into a restless sleep full of nightmares around dawn and then ended up oversleeping. Today she had half a day off anyway, because she had to go to a reception in Falkenstein at eleven. Emma had invited her.

It was twenty after eight when she tore open the door of the conference room and muttered "Good morning" along with an apology. She sat down on the empty chair between Cem and Kathrin and got a disapproving glance from Commissioner Engel, who had made it a habit to take part in the morning meetings of K-11.

"Our inquiries to the psychologists registered in Höchst and Unterliederbach and to the psychiatry department at the Höchst Hospital have produced nothing so far," said Kai Ostermann. "Nobody claims to have seen the girl. And no one recognized her from the police sketch, either."

"Why are you all dressed up today?" Kathrin whispered.

"Because I have to go to a birthday reception,"

Pia whispered back. She felt like she was in disguise in her bright blue summer dress with the rather deep décolletage, the thin knit jacket, and the sling-back pumps, which were so new that they rubbed painfully on the instep of her right foot. Every colleague she'd met on the way upstairs had given her an appreciative look, and one had even whistled at her in fun. Maybe she ought to be happy about that, but she couldn't get Behnke's caustic remark about her breasts out of her head. She hated being reduced to physical attributes.

"Are the artist's sketches ready?" she asked her colleague. Kathrin nodded and shoved two computer printouts across the table. The man had a beard, but it was clearly not Bernd Prinzler. His face was narrower, the beard fuller, and he had deeper-set eyes and a broader nose. The woman had a dark pageboy and a pretty but forgettable face. No features that particularly stood out. Pia was disappointed. She had expected more.

"Today we'll keep trying the psychotherapeutic practices that primarily treat children and young people," Kai went on. "According to our witness, the couple spoke perfect standard High German, but the girl had a strong accent. They called the girl 'our daughter,' so we may be dealing with an adopted child. That's why we're checking all the adoption agencies."

Bernd Prinzler was going to show up around

nine from Preungesheim. In the opinion of Dr. Engel, Bodenstein, and Cem, he was their prime suspect in the Hanna Herzmann case, next to Kilian Rothemund. Pia had no comment. She was only half-listening to what they were talking about. It was an utterly miserable feeling not to be able to trust two people on the team anymore. She secretly asked herself whether Nicola Engel was taking part in their meetings solely out of interest, or whether she wanted to prevent the investigations from heading in a direction that would be personally dangerous for herself.

"Okay, so let's get going," said Bodenstein. "Pia, I'd like to have you attend the lineup and sit in on the questioning of Prinzler."

"I have to leave no later than twenty to eleven," she reminded her boss. "I'm taking a half day of vacation today."

"Vacation? In the middle of ongoing investigations?" Dr. Engel raised her eyebrows. "Who approved that?"

"I did." Bodenstein shoved his chair back and stood up. "We'll probably be done by then. So, downstairs in ten."

"Check." Pia grabbed her bag, which she had brought along instead of her usual backpack, and went to her office. Kai followed her.

"Why don't you wear a dress more often?" he remarked.

"Don't start," Pia grumbled.

"Start what?" Kai asked innocently. "I think your legs are a feast for the eyes."

"Oh right, my *legs!*"

"Yes, your legs. Since I have only one, I've become a leg connoisseur." He grinned and sat down behind his desk. "What did you think I meant?"

"I . . . I didn't think anything," Pia hastened to say, turning on her computer. Why was she so touchy?

She entered her password and checked her e-mail. Nothing special. The police server had the advantage of filtering out annoying spam and advertisements. Just as she was about to close the e-mail program, a new message popped up with the subject line *Lilly.* The sender was unfamiliar. She clicked on the e-mail, which had an attachment.

Little girls keep disappearing and are never found again. It would be a shame if that happened to this sweet little thing just because her mama keeps sticking her nose into things that are none of her business.

Attached was a photo that showed Lilly and Pia along with the dogs in one of the paddocks at Birkenhof. It was a little blurry, as though it had been taken from a great distance. Pia stared at the message for a couple of seconds, uncompre-hending. Only gradually did it dawn on her what this e-mail meant, and she felt a chill. It was an unmistakable threat. They thought Lilly was her daughter and were threatening to do something to her if Pia didn't stop . . . Well, what was she supposed to stop doing? What things had she stuck her nose into?

"Now don't get all huffy just because I pay you a compliment," said Kai. "But you really do have great—"

"Come over here and take a look at this," Pia said, interrupting her colleague.

"What is it?" He went over to her desk. "You're as white as a sheet."

"Here, look!" Pia rolled her chair away, grabbed her bag, and took out her cell. Her stomach was queasy, and her hands were shaking like crazy. She had to call Christoph right away and warn him. He couldn't let Lilly out of his sight for even a millisecond.

"This is a threat that has to be taken seriously," Kai agreed with a frown, looking at the sender's address: MaxMurks@hotmail.com—obviously a fake address. "The boss needs to see this."

A little later, Bodenstein, Christian, Cem, and Kathrin were standing around Pia's desk, looking somber. Pia had called Christoph, who'd grasped the seriousness of the situation at once and assured her that he would keep an eye on Lilly and impress on her to stay near him.

"You must have really stepped on some big shot's toes," Cem said.

"Yeah, but who?" Pia was still bewildered. Someone knew where she lived and had taken pictures of her and Lilly. The thought that somebody was sneaking around her house awakened deep fears that she thought she'd put aside long ago. "I don't understand. We don't know anything."

"That's obvious," Bodenstein said, scrutinizing her. "Think hard. Whom have you talked to lately?"

Pia swallowed. Should she tell her boss that she had spoken with Behnke about Erik Lessing? Was the threat coming from that direction? Could Frank be behind it? Her eyes met Christian's, and he shook his head almost imperceptibly.

There was a knock on the door. A female officer from the watch told them that the men were here for the lineup and waiting downstairs.

"We'll be right there," said Bodenstein. "You can't do anything more than you've done, Pia. Kai will inform our colleagues in Königstein, and then all Christoph will have to do is call them if he notices anything suspicious."

Pia nodded. It didn't reassure her in the least, but her boss was right. For the moment, that was all she could do.

The weather god was merciful and granted her father-in-law for his eightieth birthday a cobalt blue sky scattered with puffy white clouds.

Nothing would disrupt the reception and the party outdoors. Emma looked out the bathroom window onto the garden below as she dried her hair. Yesterday, Helmut Grasser and his diligent helpers had set up a speaker's podium, chairs, cocktail tables, and a little stage for the various presentations. This morning, they'd installed the PA system and done a sound check. Everyone was very busy down there. The jazz band that Josef had received as a birthday present from Nicky, Sarah, Ralf, and Corinna had already been warming up for an hour, and the Sonnenkinder choir had also rehearsed. With the music playing in the background, Emma had been through a real struggle with her daughter, who had fought vigorously against wearing the pink-checked dress with the white collar, which she usually loved. Patience and a stern approach had been fruitless; no argument had worked. Louisa had insisted stubbornly on wearing jeans and a long-sleeved white T-shirt. The little girl had become more and more defiant, until she'd finally broken out in hysterical shrieking that had even drowned out the tootling from the jazz band. But Emma had refused to give up, and finally she'd gotten the howling child into the dress. Now Louisa was sitting in her room sulking, and Emma had used the opportunity to take a quick shower and wash her hair.

It was high time to go downstairs. A catering

service had provided canapés, finger food, glasses, dishes, flatware, and the drinks for the reception. Lunch for a smaller circle of invited guests was being prepared by the estate's own cooks. The serving staff, which Corinna had also booked through the caterers, stood around, looking bored. It would probably be another forty-five minutes before the first official guests arrived, but Renate and Josef wanted to drink a toast with "their" children in honor of his birthday and this family reunion.

Emma sighed deeply and wished she could fast-forward time till evening. She used to love parties like this, but today she was dreading seeing Florian, and she was in no mood for small talk with the guests, who were of no importance to her. She went to the bedroom to squeeze into the lemon yellow maternity dress, which was the only garment from her wardrobe that still fit, although it, too, was tight. The phone rang. Renate.

"Emma, where are you? Most people are already here, except for Florian, you, and Louisa."

"We'll be right down," Emma told her mother-in-law. "Five minutes."

She hung up, glanced one more time in the mirror, not looking too closely, and walked down the hall to Louisa's room. Empty! That darned kid! She wasn't in the living room, either. Emma went in the kitchen.

"Louisa? Louisa! Come on, we have to go downstairs. Grandma already called and . . ." The words stuck in her throat. She clapped her hands over her mouth and stared at her little daughter in shock. Louisa was sitting on the floor in the middle of the kitchen, wearing only panties, with the kitchen shears in her hand. Her lovely blond hair, which they'd washed last night, lay in curls all around her on the floor.

"Oh my God, Louisa! What have you done?" Emma whispered, beside herself.

Louisa started sobbing and flung the shears down, making them clatter on the floor underneath the table. Her sobs increased to a desperate howl. Emma squatted down and reached out her hand, running it over the stubbly bristles sticking out in all directions from Louisa's head. The girl flinched under her touch and turned her face away, but then she snuggled into Emma's arms. Her body was shaking with violent sobs, and the tears flowed in torrents down her little face.

"Why did you cut off your beautiful hair?" Emma asked softly. She rocked the girl in her arms and cuddled her head to her cheek. It hadn't been done on a whim, nor out of protest or anger. It broke her heart to see her daughter so unhappy and frightened and not be able to help her. "Tell me, why did you do that, sweetie?"

"Because I want to be *ugly*," Louisa murmured, and stuck her thumb in her mouth.

She had turned off the alarm clock at eight and slept until ten. She had no job anymore and nobody who was waiting for her. After she'd been to Oberursel, Meike decided not to go back to Sachsenhausen, but to drive to Langenhain. After she got up, she spent half an hour in the Jacuzzi on the terrace and then tried out a few creams and peelings from the countless little bottles and jars she found in her mother's bathroom. Hanna spent a fortune on this junk, but for her it seemed to work. Meike found her attempts anything but satisfactory. She looked like shit and had bad skin. Her mood sank toward zero.

"You ugly cow!" she said to her reflection, and made a face.

Downstairs, the front door opened. She raised her head in alarm and listened. Who could that be? The cleaning lady always came on Tuesdays, and no way would she voluntarily work overtime. Did some neighbor have a key? Meike crept down the hall, heart pounding as she pressed her body against the wall, and looked down into the entry hall. There were two men in the house! One had his back turned, but the other, a thin man with a beard and ponytail, ambled right into the kitchen as if he owned the place. Burglars in broad daylight!

Meike slunk back into Hanna's bedroom, where she had slept, and looked around. Shit! Where was her cell? She rummaged through the bed, but then she remembered that she'd been listening to music in the Jacuzzi with the earbuds. Her phone was probably still there.

Instead of finding her cell, she stuck the Taser, which she always carried with her since Hanna's attack, in the back pocket of her jeans. All she could do was slip downstairs and take off through the front door if she didn't want to be caught upstairs by these guys. The two were banging around loudly on the ground floor. They were standing in the kitchen, and suddenly she heard the coffee grinder of the espresso machine. These guys really had balls.

Meike crouched at the top of the stairs and listened, holding her breath. To make her escape through the front door, she would have to wait for the optimal moment. Then one of the men came out of the kitchen with his cell pressed to his ear. Meike couldn't believe her eyes.

"Wolfgang?" she said incredulously, and stood up.

The man jumped in fright and dropped the phone. He stared at her as if she were a ghost.

"W . . . w . . . what are you doing here?" he stammered. "Why aren't you in Frankfurt?"

Meike came down the stairs.

"I stayed here overnight. Why are you here?" she replied coolly. She hadn't forgotten the way he'd treated her yesterday. "And who's your pal?

Why do you think you can walk right in and even fix yourselves an espresso?"

She propped her hand on her hip and regarded Wolfgang with feigned indignation. "Does Mama know about this?"

All color had drained from Wolfgang's face and now he was deathly pale.

"Please, Meike." He raised his hands beseechingly, and his Adam's apple bobbed up and down. Sweat glistened on his brow. "Get out of here and just forget you ever saw us. . . ."

He stopped when the ponytail guy appeared in the kitchen doorway behind him.

"Well, well," said the man, "what do we have here?"

"Do you like your coffee?" Meike asked sharply.

"It's all right," said the bearded, muscular man, whose suntan indicated that he spent a lot of time outdoors. His eyes flashed mockingly. "In my opinion, the Saeco makes a better cup of coffee, but this is acceptable."

Meike gave him a dirty look. The gall of this guy. Who was he anyway? And what was Wolfgang doing on a Friday morning in her mother's house? She walked down the last two steps.

"Please, Meike!" Wolfgang stepped between her and the man. "Just go. You didn't see us here. . . ."

"It's too late for that now," said the other man, shoving him aside. "Go check the mail, Wolfi."

Meike suspiciously looked back and forth between him and Wolfgang, but Wolfgang avoided her eyes and turned away. Incredible! He just left her standing there.

"Wolfgang, why did—"

The punch came out of nowhere, hitting her right in the face. She staggered back and barely managed to catch hold of the banister. She touched her face and looked down in disbelief at the blood on her hand. A wave of heat pulsed through her body.

"Are you crazy, you asshole?" she screamed. She didn't know what made her madder: this outrageous jerk who had really hurt her, or Wolfgang, who had turned away like a coward as he took out his cell and left her to her fate. Hatred, disappointment, and adrenaline boiled over, and instead of running to the front door and yelling for help, she pounced on the bearded man with a furious shriek.

"Oh yeah? Your mama didn't fight back like this. She was really boring compared to you." He had his hands full fending her off, but in the end, Meike didn't have a chance. He was a full-grown man and she only half his size. Still, he grunted with the effort as he toppled her to the floor and then jammed his knee into her spine and brutally tied her wrists together behind her back.

"You're a regular little wildcat, aren't you?" he hissed.

"And you're a shit-eating jerk-off!" Meike gasped between clenched teeth as she tried to kick him.

"Get up. Let's go." The bearded guy pulled her to her feet and dragged her down the basement stairs.

"Wolfgang!" she shrieked. "Shit, do something! *Wolfgang!*"

"Shut your trap," the man panted, slapping her a couple of times. Meike spit in his face and kicked at him, striking a particularly sensitive spot. That made him blow his top. He shoved her into the furnace room, then began beating her until she dropped to the floor.

Finally, he seemed to think it was enough. He straightened up, breathing hard, and wiped his brow with his forearm. His ponytail had come undone and his hair fell in his face. Meike was doubled up, coughing, on the bare concrete floor.

Upstairs, the doorbell rang.

"The mailman is here," said the man. "Don't go away. You've still got a date."

"With you, or what?" Meike croaked. He leaned over her, grabbed her by the hair, and forced her to look at him.

"No, baby. Not with me." His grin was diabolical. "You've got a date with the Grim Reaper."

The witness shook his head.

"Nope," he said firmly. "It's not any of these guys."

"Really?" Bodenstein asked to make sure. "Take your time."

"No." Andreas Hasselbach was quite sure. "I saw him only briefly, but it wasn't any of these men."

Five men were standing on the other side of the one-way mirror, each holding a sign with a number on it. Prinzler was number three, but the witness didn't look at him any longer or more intently than at the other four. Pia saw the disappointment on her boss's face, but she knew at once that the man wasn't there, because all of them except for Prinzler were police colleagues.

"What about this guy?" She handed Hasselbach the printout of the artist's sketch that was done with the assistance of the eyewitness from Höchst. All it took was one glance.

"That's the guy!" he shouted, excited and without hesitation.

"Thank you," Pia said with a nod. "You've been very helpful."

Now all she had to do was find this man. Maybe the public could help them again. Her colleagues returned to their desks, the witness was ushered out, and Prinzler was taken to the nearby interview room. Bodenstein and Pia sat down across from him, while Cem leaned against the wall.

"Why are you keeping me here?" Prinzler was pissed off. "There are no charges against me. This is sheer police brutality. I want to call my wife."

"Just talk to us first," Bodenstein suggested. "Tell us how you knew Leonie Verges and Hanna Herzmann and why you visited them. Then you can call your wife and leave."

Prinzler gave Bodenstein an appraising look.

"I'm not saying a thing without my lawyer present. You'll just use anything I say against me."

Bodenstein bombarded the man with the same questions that Pia and Kröger had already asked him yesterday, and received the same answers.

"I want to call my wife," Prinzler replied to each question. It seemed really important to him, even when he tried to act calm. He seemed extremely worried about his wife. But why?

Pia glanced at her watch. In an hour, she had to be in Falkenstein. Then she wasn't coming back here today. She shoved the artist's drawing in front of Prinzler.

"Who is this man?"

"Is that the guy you're looking for? That's why you had the lineup?"

"Right. Do you know him?"

"Yeah. That's Helmut Grasser," he replied brusquely. "If you'd asked me in the beginning, I could have saved you this whole song and dance."

Fury rose up inside Pia, like blood oozing out of a cut on the skin. Time was running out, and this guy, who might hold the key to solving their cases, was holding things up. And she couldn't find anywhere to insert a crowbar. Bernd Prinzler was like a concrete wall with no cracks or crevices, an impregnable wall of stubborn determination.

"Where do you know him from? Where can we find him?"

He shrugged.

Pia felt her blood really start to boil. Was she going to have to physically drag every scrap of information out of this guy?

Cem left the room.

"Take a look at this." Pia put in front of Prinzler a printout of the e-mail she'd received that morning. "Someone was taking pictures of me and my partner's granddaughter yesterday."

He didn't even look at it.

"I don't have my reading glasses with me," he said.

"Then I'll read it to you." Pia snatched the page. " 'Little girls keep disappearing and are never found again. It would be a shame if that happened to this sweet little thing just because her mama keeps sticking her nose into things that are none of her business.' "

"I have nothing to do with that." Prinzler kept

his gaze fixed on Pia's face. "I've been in jail since Wednesday, remember?"

"But you know what this is about!" She had to control herself to keep from yelling at the man. "Who writes e-mails like this? And why? What was Hanna Herzmann researching? Why did Leonie Verges have to die? Who else has to die before you finally open your mouth? Your wife? Should we bring her down here? Maybe she'll talk to us if you won't."

Prinzler rubbed his chin in thought.

"Let's make a deal. You let me phone her," he replied at last. "And once I know that she's okay, then I'll tell you everything I know."

It was no deal; it was extortion. But it was a tiny breach in the impenetrable defensive wall that Prinzler had built around himself. A chance. Pia glanced over at Bodenstein. He nodded. Pia took out her cell and laid it on the table in front of Prinzler.

"Okay, go ahead," she told him. "Call her up."

The car slowed down and swerved to the left. Kilian noticed someone leaning over him, and then the door opened. He felt the wind rushing past and the centrifugal force pulling him sideways. Shocked, he braced his knees against the front seat, trying instinctively to hold on somehow, but his hands were bound behind his back. A violent shove, and he tipped sideways and fell. A flash of fear as he felt momentarily weightless before his brain grasped what had happened. Damn, they'd shoved him out of the moving car! He slammed to the ground, landing on his right shoulder, and his collarbone cracked with a loud snap. The pain took his breath away. Tires screeched and skidded over the asphalt, brakes squealed, and the horn of a truck blasted right next to him. Kilian desperately tried to roll off the road, hitting his head on the sharp edge of a guardrail. Was he safe now? Where was the road? Gravel scratched his cheek and he smelled grass.

A car door slammed and quick footsteps approached. Kilian pulled up his legs and squirmed farther toward the grass.

"Hey! Hello!" Somebody touched his arm and the pain exploded like white-hot fire in his brain.

Excited voices all began talking at once.

"Call an ambulance!"

". . . just fell right out of the car."

"Is he still alive?"

"I almost ran him over!"

Hands on his head. The pressure of the blindfold loosened. Kilian blinked at the bright light, saw a man with a mustache in a checked shirt. He looked shocked.

"How are you feeling, man? Can you move? Are you in pain?"

Kilian stared at him and nodded slowly.

"My shoulder," he whispered with an effort. "I think something's broken."

"The ambulance will be here soon," the man assured him. "Oh man, what the hell happened?"

Kilian's field of vision broadened. He raised his head and saw that he was lying under a guardrail at the edge of a two-lane highway. A big truck with its blinkers on was half on, half off the oncoming lane, another directly behind it.

"They just tossed him out of the car!" exclaimed the man, who was probably the truck driver. His face was as white as chalk. "I just missed running over you by a hair."

"Where am I?" Kilian licked his dry lips and tried to sit up.

"On the L56, right near Selfkant."

"In Germany?"

"Yeah. What happened?"

Another man came over holding a cell phone in his hand.

"No reception," he said, and he, too, bent over Kilian in concern. "Hey, man, what's going on? What happened to you?"

"I have to get to Frankfurt. And I have to make a call." Kilian could only imagine how he looked. "Please call an ambulance or the police."

"Hey, you look half-dead," said the younger of the two men. Kilian could think only of Chiara. He had to reach her before something happened to her. The two men helped him sit up and then propped him against the guardrail so they could free him from his bonds. With their help, he managed to get to his feet.

"Could you give me a ride?" he asked. "I really have to get to Frankfurt urgently."

The two truck drivers weren't too crazy about getting in trouble with their shipping contractors for stopping and giving statements to the police. They asked no questions, just gave him a bottle of water and a rag to wipe the dried blood off his face and hands.

"I'm heading for Mönchengladbach," said the one with the mustache. "Maybe I can find another trucker on the radio who can take you from there to Frankfurt."

"Thank you." Kilian nodded. He barely managed to climb into the cab of the truck. He felt consumed with pain, and the skin was stretched taut on his face. From the side mirror, a swollen, grotesque face stared back at him. It bore no resemblance to him whatsoever.

The guy with the mustache started the engine of the huge semi and maneuvered it back onto the right side of the road. Kilian shuddered. The tires of the big thirty-ton truck would have crushed his bones like a walnut. That's probably just what his abductors were hoping.

The garden was full of guests dressed in their summer best. Everyone was in a festive mood.

The jazz band played and waiters squeezed through the throng with trays of champagne glasses and finger food. Emma was looking for her in-laws. From the invitations, she knew every single name on the guest list, but personally she knew hardly anyone. Louisa was holding on to her hand and staying close, acting as shy as if she were a stranger at the party. It had taken all of Emma's skill to conjure up an acceptable short hairdo for Louisa after she had hacked off her curls. Wearing jeans and a white long-sleeved shirt, she looked like a little boy.

"Ah, there are Grandma and Grandpa," said Emma. Her in-laws were standing on the big terrace, Josef in a light-colored linen suit, Renate in an apricot-colored dress that went wonderfully with her tanned skin and white hair. They were greeting the guests as they arrived. Renate's face was radiant, and she seemed happy and relaxed.

Emma congratulated her father-in-law on his birthday.

"So, where's my little princess?" Josef bent down to Louisa, but she hid behind her mother. "Don't you want to give your grandpa a little kiss on his birthday?"

"No!" Louisa shook her head vigorously. The people standing nearby laughed in amusement.

"What happened to Louisa's beautiful hair?" Renate asked in consternation. "And where's the pretty pink dress?"

"We like the short hairdo better," Emma hastened to say. "Don't we, Louisa? It makes washing hair a lot quicker."

"But what . . ." Renate began, but Emma silenced her with a pleading look.

"Papa!" Louisa shouted at that moment. She tore out of Emma's grasp and ran over to Florian. Emma's heart skipped a beat at the sight of her husband. Like his father, Florian wore a light-colored suit and looked simply fantastic. He picked up Louisa and held her high. Then she flung her little arms around his neck and pressed her cheek to his.

"Hello," Florian said to Emma. He didn't comment on Louisa's new hairdo or the jeans. "How are you doing?"

"Hello," Emma replied coolly. "Fine. You?"

Even though her anger and the feeling of humiliation that his infidelity had caused momentarily disappeared, the distance between them remained. He seemed like a stranger to her.

Renate and Josef greeted their son. He kissed his mother dutifully on both cheeks and held out his hand to his father with a strained smile. Before Emma could even exchange a few words with her husband, Renate took her by the arm and started introducing her to all the guests. Emma smiled politely and shook hands, matching names to faces, although she immediately forgot them. She kept looking around for Florian. He was talking to all sorts of people, but she could see from his body language how ill at ease he felt.

Deferring to her condition, Emma declined to toast with champagne. Finally, she managed to shake off her mother-in-law and go over to Florian, who had fled to a cocktail table at the edge of the garden. Louisa was playing tag with a couple of other kids.

"Great party," he remarked.

"Yes, it is," she replied. She felt his uneasiness like an echo of her own. "I wish it were over."

"Me, too. What happened to our little girl?"

Emma told him about it, also mentioning the hand puppet Louisa had cut up, and the fact that she'd said she was afraid of the bad wolf.

"She said *what?*" Florian's voice suddenly sounded brittle, and their eyes met for the first time. Emma was startled when she saw the intense emotion in his eyes, which he tried to hide behind a stoic expression. His hand was gripping the stem of the champagne glass so hard that his knuckles were white.

"Florian, I . . . I'm sorry, but . . . but I—" Emma broke off.

"I know," he said in a strained voice. "You thought that I did something to Louisa. That I *abused* her. . . ."

He made a sound and shook his head hard, as if he wanted to drive off a thought, an unwelcome memory.

"What is it?" she asked cautiously.

"She's afraid of the bad wolf," he muttered gloomily. "I simply don't believe it."

Emma couldn't make heads or tails of his odd behavior. Her eyes scanned the area, looking for Louisa among the laughing and happily celebrating crowd. She saw Corinna, who was pacing back and forth at the rear of the garden, by the woods. She was talking on her cell. Ralf stood nearby with his hands in his pockets, looking just as tense and angry as his wife. How rude of those two to make a blatant display of their lack of interest.

The mayor and the district executive had already arrived, and finally the prime minister of the state of Hessen appeared. So now the list of dignitaries was complete.

"All my father's old pals have paraded in. Or more precisely, they've rolled in," said Florian with barely concealed contempt. "I'm sure my mother introduced you to all of them, didn't she?"

"She introduced me to nearly five thousand people," replied Emma. "I can't remember a single name."

"The old bald guy standing next to my mother is my godfather," Florian explained. "Hartmut Matern, the big guru of German commercial television. Next to him is Dr. Richard Mehring, former chief justice of the federal constitutional court. And the little fat guy with the bow tie was once the president of the Goethe University in Frankfurt, Professor Ernst Haslinger. Oh yeah, and the tall man with the silver mane I'm sure you know from TV: Peter Weissbecker. Officially, he's been fifty-four for the past twenty years."

Emma was surprised at Florian's sarcasm.

"And there's Nicky," he noted bitterly. "It would have broken my father's heart if he hadn't come."

"I thought Nicky was your friend," said Emma, astounded.

"Sure, all of them are my very best friends," said Florian with a mocking laugh. "All the children from neglected asocial families, the orphans, the disadvantaged, all the kids who were suddenly my sisters and brothers and took up my parents' attention."

Emma saw how Nicky was looking around, as if searching for someone. Corinna had finished her phone call and hurried over to him, with Ralf following. She didn't seem to hold a grudge against her brother because he'd slapped her. The three were discussing something; then Nicky straightened his tie, put on a smile, and went over to Josef and Renate. Corinna and Ralf followed him, also smiling as if everything was just fine.

"They always told me that I should show some consideration, because the poor children needed love and warmth and security, which I already had," Florian went on. "How often I wished I were an orphan with drug-addicted alcoholic parents. How I wanted to act lazy, difficult, and impudent, or do poorly in school, but I could never permit myself to do that."

At that moment, Emma understood her husband's real problem. He had suffered throughout his whole childhood and youth because other children got more attention from his parents than he did. Florian took another glass of champagne from the tray of a passing waiter and drank it straight down, while his parents' foster children stood in a semicircle and sang "Happy Birthday" to Josef. The old man was beaming, and Renate dabbed away tears of emotion from her cheeks.

"Oh, Emmi," Florian said, heaving a deep sigh. "I'm so sorry about what happened these past few weeks. Let's go look for a house and get out of here."

"Why didn't you tell me about all this before?" Emma was fighting back tears. "Why did you let it go so far?"

"Because—" he broke off, looked at her, searching for the right words. "I thought I could hold out until the baby was born. But suddenly . . . I don't know . . . you were so happy here all of a sudden. And so I thought you wanted to stay here."

"But . . . but . . . why did you . . ." Emma couldn't finish and say "cheat on me." What he'd done would always be between them, and she wasn't sure if she could ever forgive him.

"There is no other woman, and I'm not having an affair. I . . . I was . . ." He took a deep breath and then forced himself to go on. "I was in Frankfurt in the . . . red-light district for the first and last time in my life. I . . . I didn't want to go there. It was . . . I . . . was standing waiting for the light to change, and all of a sudden this woman was standing next to me. I know it was unforgivable, what I did. I can't tell you how much I regret hurting you like this. There's no excuse for it. I can only hope that one day you'll forgive me."

Emma saw tears shining in his eyes. She took his hand and squeezed it without saying a word. Maybe everything would be all right after all.

Thanks to Miriam's grandmother, Pia had some experience when it came to social occasions like this birthday reception, but she still didn't feel good among these dolled-up strangers who all seemed to know one another: ladies of a more sedate age, marinated in perfume and sporting dark crocodile tans that betrayed decades on golf courses and yachts, women who preferred to wear hats and liberated their expensive jewelry from the bank vault for the sole purpose of showing it off. Shrill cries of greeting were mixed with cackling like in a henhouse. Pia pushed through the crowd, looking for Emma and asking herself what she was actually doing here. She was up to her neck in work, worried sick about Lilly, and yet here she was, wasting her time because she'd made a foolish promise in a sentimental moment to an old classmate she hadn't seen in twenty-five years. Actually, Pia was hoping she'd have a chance to talk to Emma about the appointment with the therapist at the Frankfurt Girls House that she'd set up for her. Pia had never been the maternal type, but she'd changed a bit because of Lilly. Ever since Emma had mentioned her fear that her little daughter might have been abused, Pia kept thinking that the Mermaid from the river may have been the victim of the same thing as a child. Was it really a coincidence that Kilian Rothemund, the convicted child molester, lived only a mile or so from where the girl's body had been found? Was Prinzler possibly covering up for his former lawyer out of a misplaced sense of solidarity? Or was he even in cahoots with Rothemund? Prinzler had been unable to reach his wife or his lawyer and was still not talking, although they had allowed him the phone call he had requested.

A kid bumped into her.

"Scuse me," he said, and ran on, followed by three other kids.

"No worries." Pia had already noticed that there was an unusually large number of children at this reception, until she recalled that it was not only the eightieth birthday of Emma's father-in-law, Josef Finkbeiner, but also the fortieth anniversary of the founding of the Sonnenkinder Association for single mothers.

Pia kept looking around as she occasionally checked her cell phone, which she had put on vibrate. She'd told her boss that she wanted to be informed and was reachable at any time in case Prinzler finally decided to talk. She hoped that he would, so that she'd have an excuse to get out of here.

At a cocktail table near the entrance stood the prime minister's bodyguards, four men in black suits with sunglasses and earpieces. They were munching on wasabi peanuts and pretzel sticks and looking bored. Their boss was just congratulating the guest of honor, who was receiving birthday wishes and gifts up on the big terrace with his wife. Pia recognized Chief State Attorney Markus Maria Frey, who was standing next to Josef. She was surprised to see him there until she recalled what Christian Kröger had told her: that Frey had been a foster son of the Finkbeiners, and he'd studied law under a scholarship from his foster father's foundation.

A woman stepped up to the microphone at the lectern, which had been set up next to a stage in front of the impressive backdrop of almost faded rhododendrons. She asked everyone present to take a seat. Obediently, all the guests headed for the rows of chairs, and Pia spied Emma and a dark-haired man with a child in his arms who sat down in the second row. Should she go up and say hello? No, better not. Emma might offer her a seat, and then she wouldn't be able to get away unnoticed.

Instead, Pia found a seat in the last row on the left side of the center aisle and sat down as the children's choir opened the official portion of the celebration with a moving rendition of "How Lovely That You Were Born." Around fifty little girls and boys in pink and bright blue T-shirts sang at the top of their lungs, producing smiles on the faces of all the guests. Pia caught herself grinning, too, but then she thought of Lilly and the weird threat she'd received. She began fidgeting. Her subconscious had been trying to tell her something for quite a while, but she'd been so busy that it couldn't find a free synapse. Thunderous applause rewarded the children, who now marched two by two down the center aisle. And at that moment, something went *click* in Pia's brain. Like a flash flood after a heavy thunderstorm, the information suddenly flowed through her brain. Everything fell into place of its own accord and made perfect sense. Her heart did a somersault. The pink scraps of fabric from the Mermaid's stomach! The letters that she had deciphered from the photos: S-O-N-I-D.

"Wait a second, please!" she said to two little

girls, and took her cell phone out of her pocket. "May I take a picture of you?"

The two beamed and nodded. Pia clicked a photo of the two of them from the front, a second from the back, and sent the pictures straight off to Kai, Christian, and Bodenstein. SONnenkInDer. Damn, that was it. That's exactly what it was!

The truck stopped at a red light.

"Thanks," said Kilian to the driver, who had taken a big detour just for him. Instead of driving straight on the A3 to the airport, he had turned off the autobahn at Niedernhausen to drive through Fischbach and Kelkheim to Bad Soden. He told Kilian he had plenty of time and could just as well take the A66 via Frankfurter Kreuz. Kilian was deeply grateful for this unexpected helpfulness. People he thought he knew had turned away from him in the past few years, betrayed him, and left him in the lurch, humiliated—but this stranger, who at the request of the man who'd saved him had offered him a ride toward Frankfurt, offered to help him, no questions asked.

"You're welcome," said the driver with a grin, but then he turned serious. "But get yourself to a doctor, pal. You look terrible."

"I will," Kilian assured him. "Thanks again."

He climbed down the steps and closed the door. The truck rolled off, put on its blinker, and joined the line of traffic heading toward Frankfurt.

Kilian took a deep breath and looked both ways before he crossed the street. It was nine years ago that he'd last set foot in Bad Soden. He'd never been here without a car, so he'd underestimated what a long uphill climb it was up Alleestrasse to the Dachberg. His throat was parched, and each step was causing him hellish pain. Only now that his adrenaline level had gradually dropped did he feel the results of the punches and kicks, plus the fall from the car. They had really beaten the shit out of him, and he had sung like a nightingale, out of fear for his daughter. But despite the pain and the fear of death, he'd retained enough presence of mind not to tell them where he had actually sent the package with the recordings and transcripts of his conversations with the two men from Amsterdam. He hoped they would be waiting patiently in front of Hanna's house for the mail until they turned blue in the face.

It took him forty-five minutes to reach the house on Oranienstrasse that had once been his. He stood silently across the street from it. How high the boxwood hedge had grown! Even the cherry laurel and the rhododendron next to the front door had grown huge. A feeling of nostalgia tore at his heart, and he asked himself how he had managed to survive these past years. He had been a man who needed order in his life, rituals, fixed anchor points. They had robbed him of every-thing; nothing was left except life itself, and that hadn't been worth much anymore. Resolutely, he crossed the street, opened the gate, and climbed up the steps to the front door. He rang the doorbell, noting the unfamiliar name on the doorplate. After their lightning divorce, Britta had immediately looked for a new breadwinner; he knew that from Chiara, who despised her stepfather with all her heart. What a feeling it must be for a man to slip so easily into the life of his predecessor.

Footsteps were approaching on the other side of the door, and Kilian prepared himself for the confrontation. And then Britta stood before him for the first time since that day when he'd been taken away by the police. She looked old. Old and bitter. The new husband was not making her happy.

Kilian saw shock and horror in her eyes and quickly stuck his foot in the door before she could slam it in his face.

"Where is Chiara?" he asked.

"Get lost!" she replied. "You know that you're not allowed to see her."

"Where is she?" he repeated.

"Why do you want to know?"

"Is she home? Please, Britta. If she's not here, then call her up and tell her to come home at once."

"What's the meaning of this? What business is it of yours where the kids are? And just look at you!"

Kilian skipped the explanation. His ex-wife wouldn't understand anyway; she never had. For her, he was the enemy. It was hopeless to expect even a scrap of sympathy.

"Are you planning to drag her into your filthy, disgusting world?" Britta hissed, full of hate. "Haven't you brought enough misfortune down on all of us? Fuck off! Get out of here!"

"I want to see Chiara," he insisted.

"No! Now take your foot out of my door or I'll call the cops!" Her voice had turned shrill. She was scared—not of him, but of what the neighbors would say. Even in the past, that had always been more important to her than the truth.

"Yes, please, do that." Kilian removed his foot. "I'm staying right here. If necessary, all day long."

She slammed the door, and he sat down on the top step. Better for the police to pick him up right here so he wouldn't have to try walking down through the town again. The police were his only chance to protect Chiara.

It had taken less than three minutes to free her hands from her bonds. The guy who'd tied her up hadn't taken a lot of trouble. Meike rubbed her sore wrists. The heavy iron door of the furnace room swallowed every sound, so she couldn't hear what was going on upstairs in the house or if the guy was coming back. The tiny barred window behind the furnace was more a ventilation shaft than a window. Even for a person as thin as she was, it wouldn't provide a way to escape.

Meike was still stunned by Wolfgang's cowardly behavior. Even though she'd screamed for help and begged, he had simply turned around and left as the bearded guy struck her down. The knowledge that she'd misjudged him for all these years hurt far more than all the punches the guy had delivered. For the first time since she'd known Wolfgang, Meike saw him for what he was: not the understanding, protective, fatherly friend whom she had idolized, but, rather, a wimp, a spineless coward, a scaredy-cat who in his mid-forties still lived with his papa and didn't have the guts to stand up to him. What a monumental disappointment.

Meike touched her face. The nosebleed had stopped. She looked around the furnace room for some object she could use to defend herself. But unfortunately, the room had been cleaned out, thanks to Georg, Hanna's second husband, who was an incredible neat freak. Besides the furnace, there were only a few shelves on the wall. A rolled-up clothesline, a bag of clothespins, two dusty rolls of blue garbage bags, a stack of old T-shirts and underwear that Georg had used to polish his shoes and his car. Nothing that would serve as a weapon. Shit!

But the thought of stepfather number two reminded Meike of the Taser. She dug in her back pocket and felt instantly more optimistic. It was still there. In the heat of the fray, Wolfgang's pal had forgotten to search her for possible weapons. He probably didn't think she had any. Firmly determined not to give in to her fate without a fight, Meike took up position next to the door. He was going to come back to kill her; that threat had been unmistakable.

She didn't have to wait long. Only a few minutes later, the key turned in the lock with a scraping sound and the door swung open with a creak. Like a beast of prey, Meike hurled herself at the man, using the element of surprise to her advantage. She pressed the Taser to his chest. A shock of 500,000 volts whipped through his body, jerked him off his feet, and flung him against the wall. He collapsed and gaped at Meike like a baffled sheep. She had no idea how long the paralysis would last, so she didn't hesitate. Just letting him lie here was much too humane; he had to suffer, really suffer. Meike put the Taser in her back pocket and took the clothesline from the shelf.

It wasn't easy to tie up the limp body with the nylon cord. The guy weighed a ton, but Meike was furious and determined to take her revenge, so she mobilized powers she hadn't dreamed she possessed. She rolled the paralyzed man back and forth until she had him tied up like a package.

"Now the Grim Reaper is nothing but a Mini Reaper." Meike straightened up and swept her sweat-soaked hair out of her face. With malicious satisfaction, she saw the fear in his eyes. She hoped this bastard felt the same fear of death that her mother must have felt when he attacked and beat her so bestially.

He moved the fingers of one hand and muttered some incomprehensible gibberish.

Meike couldn't resist the temptation to give him another shock, and this time she picked a spot that would really hurt him. Feeling no sympathy, she watched his eyes roll up. Drool ran out of the corner of his mouth, and a convulsive twitching shook his body. A dark spot widened on the front of his light-colored jeans.

Content, she stood back to regard her handiwork.

"All right. Now I'm going to Munich. No one is going to find you here. By the time my mother gets out of the hospital and happens to come down here, you'll be nothing but a skeleton."

In farewell, she gave him a kick in the side, left the room, and locked the door behind her. Maybe she would tell the police what was down in the furnace room. Or maybe not.

Bodenstein waited patiently. He had his hands clasped on the table, watching the man across from him with an almost rapt calm, saying nothing. Bernd Prinzler was trying hard to appear composed, but Bodenstein noticed the nervous play of his jaw muscles and the drops of sweat on his brow.

This bone-hard giant, who feared neither death nor the devil, and certainly not the police, was very worried. He would never admit it, but under those mountains of muscles and tattooed skin beat a soft heart.

"I rescued her from the streets," he said unexpectedly. "She was walking the strip for some little pimp. I happened to see him beating her and stepped in between them. That was seventeen years ago. She hadn't even turned thirty, and she was at the end of her rope." He cleared his throat, took a deep breath, and gave a shrug. "Naturally, I didn't have the faintest idea what was wrong with her. I just liked her."

Bodenstein was careful not to interrupt him with a question.

"I got her out of there and we moved to the country and got married. Our youngest had just turned one when she tried to kill herself. She jumped off a bridge and broke both legs. She was sent to the nuthouse, and that's where Leonie met her. Leonie Verges. Until then, my wife didn't really know what was wrong with her."

He paused, wrestling with himself for a moment, before he went on.

"Michaela suffered abuse even as a baby at the hands of her old man and his perverted pals. She went through total shit. In order to cope with it all, she split inside. So there was not only Michaela but also dozens of other personalities with their own names, but she didn't know about them. I can't explain it as well as a psychologist, but Michaela would spend years as another person, and that's why she couldn't remember a lot of things."

Prinzler rubbed his beard absentmindedly.

"Michaela went to therapy with Leonie for years, and what came out of it was genuinely awful. You can't even imagine that people could do things like that to a child. Her old man was important, and his pals were, too. Real Mr. Cleans, the upper crust of society." He snorted with contempt. "But in reality, they were all lousy, deviant pigs, abusing children. Even their own. When the children got older, they had to go. Most of them landed on the strip, turning into drunks or dope addicts. These fucking pigs are real clever; they always keep an eye on the kids. And if they fuck up, they get sent out of the country or bumped off. Most of them are never missed. Michaela always called them the 'lost kids.' Orphans, for example. Who cares about them? This child-molesting organization is worse than the Mafia. They're not afraid to do anything, and there's no way out for the kids. Michaela's family kept trying to get in touch with her, but when they came to me, I pretended I didn't know her. At some point, I got the idea of faking her death—with a funeral and the works. After that, nobody bothered us anymore."

Bodenstein, who had expected a completely different story, listened quietly and with growing bewilderment.

"A few years ago," Prinzler went on, "a dead girl was found in the Main. It was a big deal in the papers. Michaela somehow found out about it, although I always tried to hide things like that from her. She found out about it anyway and totally flipped out. She was dead certain that the same guys were behind it who'd done all that harm to her. We thought about what we could do. Michaela definitely wanted to tell her story to the public, but I considered that dangerous as hell. These guys are everywhere and have gigantic influence. If we did go public, the accusations would have to be absolutely airtight, with evidence, names, places, witnesses and everything. I talked to my lawyer about it, and he thought we could pull it off."

"You're talking about Kilian Rothemund?" Bodenstein asked.

"Yeah, that's right," Prinzler said with a nod. "But Kilian made some sort of mistake, and they really screwed him. All that evidence that he was a child molester was faked. He had zero chance of fighting back. They ruined his whole life because he was a threat to them."

"Why didn't you do anything else about it back then?" Bodenstein asked. "What about the evidence that your wife had?"

"Who could we trust?" Prinzler replied. "They were everywhere; some were even cops. Who's going to believe a biker and a woman who's been in the loony bin half her life? We decided not to do anything else, and went underground. I know all about what people are capable of doing if they have a lot to lose. Shortly before I retired, an undercover cop and two of our boys were shot in one of our locales. Then the same thing happened."

"What happened?" Bodenstein asked.

Prinzler stared at him, eyes narrowed.

"You know. Your colleague asked me about it yesterday. About the undercover guy and why his own side had him wasted."

Bodenstein didn't follow up on the comment, because then he'd have to admit to Prinzler that he didn't know what he was talking about or what his colleague had done. Rage was rising up in him. The nerve of Pia, withholding investigative results from him. He feverishly attempted to reconstruct the chronology of what happened yesterday. When had Pia spoken to Prinzler at the Preungesheim jail? Before or after she talked to him in his office and asked him about Erik

Lessing? What had she found out? And why had she even followed that line of questioning?

In order not to reveal his ignorance to Prinzler, he merely asked him to go on.

"At any rate," Prinzler said, "my wife began writing down her story with Leonie's help. It was a good exercise, Leonie thought. That was the point of it. But then another dead girl was found in the river. I always stayed in contact with Kilian. Together with Leonie, we decided to see it through this time. But not with the cops or the state attorney's office. We wanted to go straight to the public. We had plenty of evidence, even statements from insiders who corroborated what my wife had experienced."

Bodenstein could hardly believe his ears. Pia's suspicions had been right: All three of their cases were connected.

"We discussed the best way to spin it so that nobody could thwart our plans. At some point, Leonie told us about Hanna Herzmann, and then I had the idea of getting her on board. She was instantly a hundred percent behind the idea, and she checked over Michaela's notebooks together with Kilian. But then—"

There was a knock on the door of the interview room. Kai stuck his head in and signaled to Bodenstein that he had something important to tell him. Bodenstein excused himself, got up, and stepped out to the hallway.

"Boss, Kilian Rothemund has given himself up," Kai announced even before Bodenstein had closed the door behind him. "Our colleagues are bringing him here."

"Very good." Bodenstein went to the water-cooler and got a cup of water. Kai followed him.

"I also have information about Helmut Grasser. He lives in Falkenstein, at Reichenbachweg One thirty-two B."

"Then send somebody over there to bring him down here for questioning."

"I will in a sec." Kai held out his phone to him. "Have you seen the photos that Pia just sent over?"

"No. What's that?" Bodenstein squinted. Without his reading glasses, he could see only colored splotches on the display.

"Two little girls in pink T-shirts with the logo *Sonnenkinder*," Kai replied excitedly. "They look like the scraps of fabric in the stomach of our Mermaid, don't you think? Pink cotton with white type? The cloth could be from one of the T-shirts."

"And how does that help us now?" Bodenstein's thoughts were somewhere else entirely. Had mistakes been made in the cases of the Mermaid and Hanna Herzmann? Had he overlooked something important? Should they have figured out earlier that behind the brutal attack and the murder of the therapist there was a child-molestation ring? Could that be true?

"Pia was at a party in Falkenstein. Celebrating the eightieth birthday of the founder of the Sonnenkinder Association. She suspects that this charitable organization has something to do with our Mermaid."

"Aha." Bodenstein drank the rest of his water and filled the cup again. What if Prinzler were lying only to get himself and the criminal organization that he belonged to out of the line of fire? What he'd said so far sounded logical, but it could also be a pack of lies.

"The address of the Sonnenkinder Association is Reichenbachweg One thirty-four."

Ostermann looked at him expectantly, but Bodenstein didn't immediately grasp what he was getting at.

"Helmut Grasser, who was seen by the witness on the evening that Hanna Herzmann was raped, has something to do with this association," Kai explained to help him connect the dots.

Before Bodenstein could reply, a uniformed colleague came out of the watch room.

"Ah, there you are," he said. "We just got an emergency call. Rotkehlchenweg-Eight in Langenhain. The address is from one of your cases, right?"

What now?

"What sort of emergency?" Bodenstein said, a bit annoyed. He hadn't even had a chance to sort out his thoughts.

"Breaking and entering, assault and battery." The officer frowned. "It sounded a little confused, but the caller said we should hurry. She had overpowered the perp in the furnace room and tied him up."

"Then send somebody over to check it out." Bodenstein flicked the paper cup into the wastebasket next to the cooler. "Kai, come with me. I think I'm beginning to figure out the connections."

Ostermann nodded and followed him.

"Can I go now?" Prinzler asked. "I've told you everything."

"No, you haven't told us all of it yet," said Bodenstein. "Have you ever heard of the Sonnenkinder Association?"

Prinzler's expression darkened.

"Yes, of course. My wife's old man founded the thing," he replied. His tone turned sarcastic. "Smart idea, wasn't it? An inexhaustible supply for perverse child molesters."

Pia felt her cell vibrate and took it out of her pocket.

She read Bodenstein's name on the display and took the call.

"Where are you?" her boss asked, and he didn't sound pleased.

"At Josef Finkbeiner's birthday reception," she said in a low voice. "I told you that I—"

"Rothemund turned himself in and Prinzler talked," said Bodenstein, interrupting her. "This Finkbeiner is the father of Prinzler's wife!"

Pia held her hand over her left ear to hear him, because people were talking all around her.

". . . and he's . . . head of . . . ring molesting children! . . . wanted Hanna Herzmann . . . but . . . somehow leaked out. . . . Stay there. . . . send . . . colleagues . . . come myself . . . nothing . . ."

"I didn't get all that," she said. "Oliver? I . . ."

". . . got a gun! Watch out!" A woman suddenly screamed.

Almost in the same instant, two shots rang out, and Pia looked up in surprise.

"What was that?" Bodenstein shouted in her ear, then she heard nothing more, because a commotion broke out. Two more shots rang out. People jumped up from their chairs, screaming hysterically, or threw themselves to the ground. The prime minister's four bodyguards awoke from their lethargy and pushed their way through the throng of people fleeing in panic.

"Oh shit!" For a couple of seconds, Pia felt paralyzed with shock. What was all this? An attack on the prime minister? A crazy man running amok? She resisted the reflex to take cover, straightened up, and watched in disbelief as the slim dark-haired woman in the pink dress who had been standing behind her holding a bouquet was knocked down by a man.

Pia stuck her cell in her pocket and tried to move forward. Unpleasant memories of the mass panic in the Dattenbach Hall in Ehlhalten last year flashed through her mind as she was borne roughly along by screaming people, but she fought her way across tipped-over chairs toward the speaker's podium.

"Somebody call a doctor! Get a doctor, quick!" several voices were shouting.

Shaking all over, Pia tried to get an overview of the chaos. In a few seconds, the peaceful scene in the festively decorated garden had turned into a battlefield. All around her, sobbing, shocked people were holding on to one another, while the musicians in the jazz band stood on the bandstand as if frozen, still holding their instruments. Men, women, and children were calling one another in panic.

One of the victims was slumped in his chair, legs and arms crossed, as if he were still listening to a speech, but half of his head was gone—a gruesome sight. The other man had tipped over sideways; he must have landed right in the lap of the person sitting next to him. What a horror! Pia gazed around helplessly. Chief State Attorney Markus Maria Frey stood in the midst of the confusion, rigid with shock, his face white as a sheet, a pistol in his hand. At his feet lay the dark-haired woman in the pink dress. A white-haired woman had thrown herself over a man lying on the ground; Pia couldn't tell whether he was dead or just wounded. The woman was shrieking like a crazy person as a younger, weeping brunette tried to pull her away from him. Pia spied Emma in the second row. Her friend sat there motionless, eyes wide with terror. Her sun yellow dress, her face, her arms, and her hair were spattered all over with blood, and for a moment Pia feared that she was dead. Next to Emma stood a little girl, who was staring vacantly at the dead people sitting right in front of her. It was the sight of the girl that catapulted Pia back to reality. Resolutely, she shoved a chair aside, grabbed Emma by the arm, and pulled her up. Then she snatched up the girl and carried her away. Emma staggered behind her in a daze.

"What happened here?" Pia asked, her knees still weak from fright. She cautiously put down the girl.

"The woman . . . the woman . . ." Emma stammered. "Suddenly . . . suddenly she was standing there and . . . she was shooting. . . . There was . . . blood everywhere. . . . I saw a man's head explode in front of me like . . . like a . . . watermelon."

Only then did she emerge from her shocked state enough to look at her daughter, whose back was also covered in blood. "Oh my God, Louisa! Oh God!"

"Sit down." Pia was worried. Emma's baby was due any day. "Where's your husband?"

"I . . . I don't know. . . ." Emma plopped onto a chair and drew her daughter into her arms. "He . . . he was sitting next to me and had Louisa on his lap. . . ."

In the distance, sirens were approaching, and a helicopter circled above the treetops. Soon after, two patrol cars came racing toward the scene.

Pia never liked to question the relatives of murder victims while they were still under the influence of events, but she knew from experience that it was actually the best time to talk to them, while memories were still fresh and uncorrupted.

"Do you know the woman?" she asked.

"No," said Emma, shaking her head. "I've never seen her before."

"What exactly did she do?"

"She . . . she was suddenly standing there, as if she'd popped up out of the ground," Emma said, her voice still shaky. "She stopped in front of my father-in-law and said something."

"Can you remember what she said?" Pia pulled out her notebook and fished in her bag for a ballpoint. This was routine for her, and it made her feel a bit more steady.

Emma thought hard, mechanically stroking the back of her daughter, who had snuggled up to her and was sucking her thumb.

"Yes." She raised her head and looked at Pia. " 'Aren't you happy to see your little princess again?' That's exactly what she said and then

594

she . . . fired. First at my father-in-law and then at the two men sitting next to him. They were old friends of his."

"Do you know who those two were? Do you know their names?"

"Yes. Hartmut Matern was my husband's godfather, and the other man was Dr. Richard Mehring."

Pia nodded and took notes.

"Can I go back upstairs in the house?" Emma asked. "I have to get Louisa and myself out of these clothes."

"Yes, of course. I know where to find you if I have any more questions."

Medics shoved the gurney with Emma's father-in-law into an ambulance that was parked only a few yards away. The white-haired woman that Pia had noticed was now being supported by two younger women. She was weeping, her hand pressed to her mouth.

"Who's that?" Pia asked.

"Renate, my mother-in-law. And my sisters-in-law, Sarah and Corinna. Corinna is the administrative manager of Sonnenkinder." Tears came to Emma's eyes. "What a disaster. My poor mother-in-law. She was so looking forward to this day."

The doors of the ambulance closed and the blue light on the roof began to flash. Louisa took her thumb out of her mouth.

"Mama?"

"Yes, sweetie?"

"Is the bad wolf dead now?" the child asked. "He can't do anything to me anymore, can he?"

Pia met her friend's astonished look; then she recognized an expression of confused understanding in Emma's eyes.

"No," Emma whispered through her tears as she rocked her daughter in her arms. "The bad wolf will never do anything to you again. I promise you."

Pia took her police ID out of her bag and returned to the scene of all the horror. State Attorney Frey was still standing there like stone with the gun in his hand, his shirt and trousers covered in blood. He stared as if hypnotized at the woman lying right in front of him. Pia touched Frey's arm, and he awoke from his daze.

"Ms. Kirchhoff," he said in a hoarse whisper. "What . . . what are you doing here?"

"Come with me," Pia said firmly, and took his arm. Uniformed officers stormed into the garden. Pia showed them her ID and instructed them to cordon off a wide area around the garden, grounds, and street to make sure that no rubberneckers and especially no reporters sneaked inside. Then she put on a pair of latex gloves and got out an evidence bag. Carefully, she took the pistol from the state attorney's hand, removed the clip, and stuck both in the plastic bag.

"Who is the woman?" asked Pia. "Do you know her?"

"No, I've never seen her before," said State Attorney Frey, shaking his head. "I was standing at the podium and saw her coming up the center aisle holding a bouquet of flowers. And suddenly . . . suddenly she had a pistol in her hand and . . . and . . ."

His voice failed, and he ran his fingers through his hair, pausing for a moment with his head lowered. Then he looked up.

"She shot my father." He sounded incredulous, as if he hadn't yet fully comprehended what had just occurred. "For a moment, I was paralyzed. I . . . I couldn't stop her from shooting two more people!"

"Your father isn't dead," said Pia. "But you put yourself in mortal danger when you disarmed the woman."

"I didn't even think about it," Frey murmured. "Suddenly, I was standing behind her and I grabbed her arm, the one holding the gun. . . . Somehow . . . I must have fired a shot. Is she . . . is she . . . dead?"

"I don't know," said Pia.

Distraught children were crying and looking for their parents. Ambulances and EMTs arrived, along with more police. Pia's cell was buzzing and vibrating nonstop, but she didn't pay any attention.

"I have to go to my family." State Attorney Frey straightened his shoulders. "I have to look for my wife. And my mother needs me now. Oh God, she saw it all."

He looked at Pia.

"Thank you, Ms. Kirchhoff," he said in a quavering voice. "If you need me, I am at your service anytime."

"All right. Now go see about your family," Pia said, giving his arm a sympathetic pat. She watched him go and did not envy what he now had to do. Then she finally answered her cell phone.

"Pia, damn it, where are you?" Bodenstein yelled in her ear. "Why aren't you picking up your cell?"

"There's been a shooting here," she replied. "At least two dead and two seriously injured."

"We're already on our way." Bodenstein sounded somewhat calmer. "Are you all right?"

"Yeah, yeah, nothing happened to me," she assured her boss. She turned around and went a few steps. From a distance, the whole scene seemed as unreal as a movie set. She sat down on the edge of a fountain, wedged her cell between her ear and shoulder, and looked in her bag for cigarettes.

"Listen," Bodenstein said. "Prinzler finally talked. Hanna Herzmann was researching the topic of child abuse. As a child, Prinzler's wife was abused by her own father and wanted to go public with the truth after she saw the story about our Mermaid on TV. Leonie Verges was her therapist and had been for years. Through Leonie, contact was made with Hanna Herzmann, Rothemund, and Prinzler. It's all connected. And the whole thing goes even further back, as we thought. There's a child-molestation ring that operates internationally, and Josef Finkbeiner plays a central role in it. But if what Prinzler said is true, then there are also a number of other influential people involved who won't stop at murder to prevent exposure. Pia, it's probable that the murder of the undercover agent years ago in Frankfurt also has something to do with this!"

His words echoed in her ears as if he'd shouted them. She stuck a cigarette between her lips and flicked her lighter, but her fingers were shaking so hard that she could hardly get it lit.

"Pia? Pia! Are you still there?"

"Yeah, I heard you," she said softly. She slipped off her shoes and dug her toes into the summer-warm gravel. The water splashed in the fountain; a blackbird hopped across the grass in front of her and then flew off. Quiet. Peace. And twenty minutes ago, two people had been executed in cold blood not a hundred yards away.

"We'll be there in ten minutes," she heard Bodenstein say; then he ended the call. Pia tipped her head back and looked up at the deep blue sky with little white clouds sailing across.

She was overwhelmed by the realization that once again, against all odds, she'd been right. The tension inside her released, and she began to sob.

In his years on the force, Bodenstein had seen innumerable scenes of murder and manslaughter, and he secretly classified them according to a personal system. What he saw now undoubtedly belonged to the worst type, in the five-star category. A woman had executed two men and seriously wounded another in front of two hundred grown-ups and children. Maybe it would have been even worse if someone hadn't risked his life to overpower the assassin and disarm her. Bodenstein had known Chief State Attorney Markus Maria Frey for many years, and he never would have believed him capable of taking such fearless action. But in dangerous situations, some people surpass their normal capabilities, especially if it is a matter of their own family. Kröger had informed Bodenstein of Frey's family relationships on the drive to Falkenstein, and Pia had tersely related what had happened. By now, she had recovered from her initial shock. What she had to do now was tend to her job, and she was enough of a professional to do that even though she was just as stunned as the other guests.

"Where was the prime minister when the shots were fired?" Bodenstein asked.

"As far as I know, he, the district executive, and the mayor were sitting on the other side of the aisle. In front on the right sat Josef Finkbeiner and his wife, next to them the two dead men." She glanced at her notebook. "Hartmut Matern and Richard Mehring, old friends of Finkbeiner. In the row behind them sat Finkbeiner's son Florian with his daughter on his lap, next to him his wife, Emma, my classmate, who invited me to the party."

"*The* Hartmut Matern?" Bodenstein raised his eyebrows.

"Yes, that's the one. . . ." Pia looked at her boss. "His son Wolfgang is a friend of Hanna Herzmann. Isn't that a funny coincidence?"

"No, I'm afraid none of this is a coincidence," replied Bodenstein. "As I already told you on the phone, everything is connected. I hope that Rothemund will confirm this for us later on."

Dr. Josef Finkbeiner, hit by two shots in the chest and neck, had already been taken away in the ambulance. Covers had been draped over the two dead men, still sitting on their chairs. Bodenstein had transferred leadership of the team to Cem Altunay, because he thought it was more important for him to talk to Rothemund. A medical examiner arrived, as well as the crisis intervention team that Altunay had requested.

Two psychologists took care of Finkbeiner's relatives, who had been sitting right behind the murder victims. Christian Kröger and his team had already begun securing evidence, cordoning off and photographing the crime scene and the two bodies. Some distance away, a medic was attending to the unconscious assassin, who had taken a round in the abdomen. Next to her head knelt a dark-haired man in a light-colored suit. He was crying and stroking the woman's face.

"Please," said the medic impatiently, "let us do our work."

"I'm a doctor," insisted the man. "And this is my sister."

Bodenstein and Pia exchanged a surprised look.

"Come with us." Bodenstein bent down over the man and placed a hand on his shoulder. "Let the medics do their work."

The man swayed as he got up. He followed Bodenstein and Pia, but only reluctantly, to one of the cocktail tables. He was pressing a blood-smeared ladies' handkerchief to his chest.

"May I ask who you are?" Bodenstein asked after introducing himself.

"Florian Finkbeiner," replied the man in a shaky voice.

"Are you related to . . ." Bodenstein began.

"Yes, Josef Finkbeiner is my father. *Our* father." Suddenly, tears came to his eyes. "The woman . . . that's my twin sister, Michaela. I . . . I haven't seen her in more than thirty years, not since we were fourteen. I thought she was dead—that's what my parents always told me. I . . . I was abroad for many years, but last year I visited Michaela's grave. When she suddenly stood there today, it was . . . a shock."

His voice failed, and he began sobbing. And Bodenstein understood. All at once, the pieces of the puzzle fell into place and the whole picture made sense.

The woman who had shot the two men to death and seriously wounded Josef Finkbeiner was the wife of Bernd Prinzler. She had been abused by her father as a little girl, suffered great torment, and was finally driven into prostitution. Prinzler had been telling the truth.

"Why did your sister shoot your father? And why the two other men?" Pia asked.

As Bodenstein had expected, Florian had absolutely no idea of the torture his twin sister had endured.

"That's not true," he whispered, appalled, when Bodenstein confronted him with what he knew. "My sister was always troubled, that's true. She often ran away from home, drank alcohol, and took drugs. My parents also told me that she'd spent years in a psychiatric clinic. But I was never happy, either. It's not easy for kids when their parents care more about strangers' children than their own. But my father never would have . . .

touched my sister. He loved her more than anything."

"I'm afraid you're fooling yourself," said Pia. "When they loaded your father into the ambulance, your little daughter asked your wife whether the bad wolf was dead now, so he couldn't do anything to her again."

If possible, Florian Finkbeiner's face turned a shade paler. He shook his head in disbelief.

"Do you remember when the doctor at the hospital said that your daughter may have been abused?" Pia asked. "Emma was afraid that you might have done something to the girl. But it wasn't you. It was your father."

Florian Finkbeiner stared at her and swallowed hard. His fingers were still gripping his sister's handbag.

"Michaela used to say she was scared of the bad wolf. I never understood that it was a cry for help. I thought she was just making things up," he whispered hoarsely. "It was also my idea for my wife and Louisa to live here until the baby was born. As long as I live, I'll never forgive myself for that."

"Would you please give us the handbag?" Pia asked, and Finkbeiner handed it to her.

State Attorney Frey was heading in their direction, accompanied by a dark-haired woman. She stopped to talk to somebody, but Frey came over to their table. He wanted to put his arm around Finkbeiner's shoulder, but Florian shrank away from him.

"All of you knew that Michaela was still alive," he accused his adopted brother. "You always know everything, you and Ralf and Corinna."

"No. We didn't know," the state attorney protested. "We even went to her funeral. I'm utterly shocked."

"I don't believe a word of it," Finkbeiner snorted, full of hate. "You always sucked up to my parents, kissing their ass, just to push us out and win their favor. We never had a chance against the likes of you. And now you've shot my sister! I hope you'll roast in hell for that!"

He spit at Frey's feet and left. Frey sighed. There were tears in his eyes.

"I don't blame Florian," he said softly. "It's a shock for all of us, but it must be especially bad for him. It's true that he always had to take us into consideration."

Bodenstein's cell rang. It was Kai Ostermann, who reported that they had actually found a man in the basement of Hanna Herzmann's house.

"You wouldn't believe it, boss," said Ostermann. "The man is Helmut Grasser. He's here at the station now. He didn't want to go to the hospital."

Bodenstein turned away to give Ostermann further instructions.

"Pia, we're leaving," he said then. "We've got Grasser."

"Who?" Frey asked, and Bodenstein, who at first wanted to ignore him, remembered that he was the prosecutor in three of their cases.

"The man's name is Helmut Grasser," he replied. "On the night Hanna Herzmann was attacked, a witness saw him not far from the scene where she was found the next day. You must know him, don't you? He lives here on the grounds."

He caught Pia's glance, which changed from bafflement to anger. She was about to reproach her boss for not keeping her informed, but there had been no time for that. And besides, she was keeping secrets from him, too.

"I've known Helmut for ages," said Frey. "He's the caretaker and handyman here. Is he a suspect?"

"Until proven otherwise, yes," Bodenstein said with a nod. "First we're going to talk to him, and then we'll see."

"I'd like to be there when you question him," said Frey.

"Do you really want to do that? Maybe today you should—"

"No, it's no problem," Frey said, interrupting. "There's nothing more for me to do here anyway. If you don't mind, I'll go change clothes and then go down to Hofheim."

"Of course."

"I'll see you soon."

Pia and Bodenstein watched him go, heading

through the grounds with his cell pressed to his ear.

"Only moments ago he was still in shock, and now he's as cold as a dog's nose," Pia said, slightly taken aback.

"Maybe he's trying to escape into some sort of routine," Bodenstein suggested.

"I didn't recognize Mrs. Prinzler, either. She looked totally different. And then everything happened so fast. . . ."

"Come on, let's go. First up is Rothemund. I'm really anxious to hear what he's going to tell us."

Kai Ostermann had put Helmut Grasser and Kilian Rothemund in interview rooms 2 and 3 on the ground floor of the Regional Criminal Unit. Bodenstein first went to see Bernd Prinzler, who was still waiting in room number 1. Silently and with a stony expression, he listened to Bodenstein and Pia's account of the events in Falkenstein. Whatever was going on inside him, he had his emotions in an iron grip and showed neither anger nor concern.

"That wouldn't have happened if you hadn't kept me in custody here," he reproached Bodenstein. "Fucking shit!"

"Wrong," said Bodenstein. "If you'd told us right away what this was all about, we would have let you go home long ago. Why did your wife do this? And where did she get the gun?"

"I have no idea," Prinzler growled as he balled his hands into fists. "Are you finally going to let me go?"

"Yes, you can go." Bodenstein nodded. "Your wife, by the way, was taken to the hospital in Bad Soden. If you like, we can have someone drive you there."

"Thanks, but no thanks." Prinzler stood up. "I've had enough cops chauffeuring me around in my life."

He left the room, accompanied by a uniformed officer, who escorted him to the exit. Bodenstein and Pia followed, but at the door of the interview room, they found Dr. Nicola Engel.

"Why are you letting him go?" she asked. "What happened in Falkenstein?"

"He told us everything, and he has a permanent residence," said Bodenstein. Before he could continue, Pia interrupted him. She couldn't stop thinking about what Behnke had said about Nicola Engel's involvement in the Erik Lessing case. She could also see that her boss mistrusted Engel. If there actually was a connection between the old case and the current ones, then it was better not to tell her every detail.

So Pia asked her boss, "First Rothemund, then Grasser?"

"Yes, Rothemund first," Bodenstein agreed.

The commissioner's cell phone rang and she stepped away to take the call. Pia was racking her brain, trying to think of how to get rid of Engel so that she wouldn't be listening in on the interview with Rothemund via the loudspeaker behind the one-way mirror. There was no time for a detailed explanation, so she had to trust that Bodenstein wouldn't object.

"I'd prefer to question Rothemund in your office," she said.

"Good idea," replied Bodenstein, to her relief. "The fluorescent lights give me a headache after half an hour anyway. Have him taken upstairs. I have to go to the little boys' room first."

"Er, Oliver?" Pia saw that Engel had finished her call. "I'd rather do the first interview with Rothemund without the commissioner being present. Can you fix it?"

She saw the question in his eyes, but he nodded.

"Chief State Attorney Frey is here," Engel announced. "How shall we proceed?"

"Ms. Kirchhoff and I will first speak with Rothemund and Grasser alone," Bodenstein replied. "Frey can join us later."

Pia gave him a sharp look; then she went to interview room 3 to make sure they'd taken Kilian Rothemund up to the second floor.

"I'd also like to be there," Pia heard Engel say. She couldn't make out Bodenstein's answer, but she hoped that he'd managed to dissuade her. When she came back, the commissioner was gone, but State Attorney Frey was coming down the hall. He was wearing a light gray suit, a white shirt, and a tie, and his hair was still damp and slicked straight back. Outwardly, he seemed as controlled and composed as always, but his normally piercing eyes were clouded and full of sadness.

"Hello, Dr. Frey," she greeted him. "How are you?"

"Hello, Ms. Kirchhoff." He extended his hand with the hint of a smile on his face. "Not so good. I don't think I've really come to grips yet with what happened or how in the world it could have occurred."

If Pia hadn't seen with her own eyes the state he'd been in only two hours ago, she wouldn't have believed it possible that he'd experienced something so horrible. His professionalism won her genuine admiration.

"I'd like to thank you once again," he said. "It was amazing, what you did."

"Don't mention it." Pia asked herself why she had previously considered him such a self-righteous bureaucrat. She really hadn't liked him.

Bodenstein emerged from the men's room. At the same moment, the door of the interview room down the hall opened, and an officer escorted Kilian Rothemund in handcuffs to the back stairs leading to the second floor. Frey watched him go. Pia noticed his expression change for a split second. His body stiffened and he raised his chin.

"That was not Helmut Grasser," he said.

"No," said Bodenstein. "That's Kilian Rothemund. He turned himself in today. My colleague and I will speak with him first; then we'll talk to Grasser."

Frey eyed the man with whom he'd once been friends, and yet he'd sent him to prison for years. Then he nodded.

"I'd like to be present during the interview," he said.

"No, Ms. Kirchhoff and I will speak with the gentlemen first," Bodenstein replied firmly. "You may take a seat in the waiting room in the meantime."

Chief State Attorney Frey wasn't used to having his requests refused. His displeasure was unmistakable. He frowned and opened his mouth to object, but then he changed his mind and shrugged.

"All right," he said. "I'll go have a cup of coffee. See you later."

Emma and Florian were sitting in the empty waiting room of the surgical outpatient department at the Bad Soden Hospital, holding hands and waiting. Louisa had gone to sleep on Florian's lap. For over an hour, Michaela had been in the operating room. The bullet had penetrated obliquely below her breast and lodged in her pelvis. Josef had been taken by helicopter to the university clinic in Frankfurt, and Emma was glad of that. The mere thought of her innocent little daughter being under the same roof with that despicable bastard would have been intolerable. She gave Florian a sidelong glance. This whole situation must be much worse for him, she realized.

He'd always had a difficult relationship with his father, which had led him to withdraw and feel unloved. That was one of the main reasons why he'd chosen a profession that took him far away from home. It must be horrible to realize now that his own father is a child molester, a pedophile, who had abused their own daughter. Haltingly, Florian had told her about Michaela, about how much he had envied his sister because she was loved by their father, and because she had a close friendship with Nicky. As a child, Florian had both loved and hated Nicky, who had been taken into the Finkbeiner family when he was eight, after several foster families had given up on him and taken him back to the orphanage. Even as a kid, Nicky had been a talented manipulator, highly intelligent, ambitious, and with a narcissistic tendency. Florian had been glad to have a playmate of the same age, but Nicky had preferred Michaela and had completely monopolized her.

Michaela had always had her head in the clouds and was untruthful and aggressive, but Florian had idolized his twin sister, who was only ten minutes younger than he was. So it was all the more painful for him to lose his only ally within the family to Nicky. Their parents always forgave Nicky and Michaela everything, whereas he was rebuked and punished. At the age of ten, the two had started smoking, and at eleven, Michaela was the first to run away from home. At thirteen, she was smoking joints; at fourteen, shooting up heroin. And then she was gone, first to juvenile prison, then to the locked psychiatric ward. Nicky, on the other hand, had turned into an exemplary pupil and had passed the university entrance exam at the top of his class. He never talked about Michaela anymore, but instead had developed a close friendship with Corinna, Florian's favorite sister after Michaela.

His memories of his twin sister were anything but happy, and now that they knew the story behind her disappearance, Emma could understand why he'd never mentioned Michaela.

They heard loud voices outside in the hallway. Someone said the name Michaela Prinzler, and Florian and Emma tried to listen. Then a man came into the waiting room. He was so big that he almost filled the whole doorway; his arms were covered in tattoos, and he looked scary.

"Are you Michaela's brother?" he asked Florian in a strangely hoarse voice.

"Yes, I am," said Florian. "Who are you?"

"I'm her husband. Bernd Prinzler."

Emma stared at the tattooed giant, speechless.

Prinzler took a seat on one of the plastic chairs across from them and rubbed his face with both hands. Then he leaned his elbow on his knee and gave Florian a penetrating look.

"What happened?" he asked.

Florian cleared his throat and began telling this stranger the whole story.

"I thought my sister died many years ago. That's what my parents told me," he said, concluding his account.

"Exactly what we wanted them to believe," replied Prinzler. "We faked Michaela's funeral so that she wouldn't be hounded by these monsters anymore."

"What monsters?" Florian asked.

"Her old man and his pedophile pals. It's a Mafia. Once they get their hooks into someone, they'll never let the person out of their sight. They know about every move the girls make. And they're better organized than any secret service."

"What . . . what does this mean?" Florian asked.

Emma would have preferred not to hear it, but Bernd Prinzler told them with brutal frankness about the hierarchy and the means used to operate the child-molesting ring. The disgusting details were unbearable.

Emma shuddered. Was this gruesome nightmare ever going to end? Would Louisa someday be able to forget what had been done to her? Emma wondered why she hadn't noticed anything sooner. Were there any signs that she should have seen? She tried to remember how her father-in-law had behaved toward Louisa, tried to find some proof that would show her that he hadn't molested her daughter. He'd never been anything but friendly toward her.

A doctor in blue scrubs came into the waiting room. Prinzler and Florian jumped up.

"How is my wife?" Prinzler asked.

"How is my sister?" asked Florian at the same time.

The doctor looked from one man to the other.

"She came through the operation fine, and her condition is stable," he replied, almost dislocating his neck as he peered up at Prinzler. "We've taken her to the ICU for observation, but we were able to remove the bullet and repair the damage to her intestines."

Suddenly, a searing pain shot through Emma's abdomen. She gasped for air, and at the same moment her water broke, soaking her panties.

"Florian," she said quietly. "I think the baby's coming."

"What happened to you?" asked Pia, appalled, when Kilian Rothemund turned around to face her. She thought about the photos they'd used during the search. His handsome face was now badly swollen; the left half was one big purple bruise all the way to his eye. His nose seemed to be broken, and his right arm looked like it had been caught in a meat grinder. Kilian Rothemund belonged in a hospital.

"When I tried to board the train yesterday in Amsterdam, they were waiting for me," he replied.

"Who was?" Pia sat down across from him at the interview table in Bodenstein's office. Bodenstein gave Rothemund a signal to hold his answer for a moment. He turned on the tape recorder, placed it on the table, and gave a few details about the case.

"It wasn't the Dutch police who caught me," said Rothemund with a grimace as the tape ran. "And it wasn't the police who tortured me last night and shoved me out of a moving car this morning. It was the thugs from the pedophile Mafia; evidently, I'd become a threat to them. They forced me to watch a video of Hanna Herzmann being raped, and they threatened me by saying the same would happen to my daughter if I didn't tell them where I'd sent the information that I got from two insiders."

"Did you tell them?" Bodenstein asked.

"No." Rothemund cautiously rubbed his unshaven chin. "I still had enough presence of mind to prevent them from getting their hands on that material. Because I knew that Hanna was in the hospital, I claimed that I'd sent the package of tape recordings to her."

"That was clever of you," Pia said. "There was actually somebody waiting for the mail at Hanna Herzmann's house. Unfortunately, her daughter, Meike, was also in the house when it arrived."

"Good God!" Rothemund was startled.

"But Meike managed to overpower the man and lock him in the basement. He's here at the station now."

Kilian Rothemund breathed a sigh of relief.

"Who was it? Helmut Grasser?" he asked.

"Exactly. How do you know him?"

"He's Finkbeiner's man who does the dirty work. He was once one of the Sonnenkinder kids himself. And he's mentally ill."

"Where's your daughter now? Is she safe?" Pia asked.

"Yes. My ex-wife called her. She just got home when the police arrived to take me in." Rothemund nodded. "I was able to talk to her briefly, and she promised not to leave the house for now."

"We're providing police protection for her," said Pia.

Bodenstein cleared his throat.

"Now let's take things in order," he said. "We've already learned quite a bit from Bernd Prinzler about the life story of his wife. Today she showed up at the birthday party for Josef Finkbeiner. There she shot two men to death and critically wounded her father."

"Good Lord!" Rothemund gasped. This news

had a dramatic effect on him, and he struggled to maintain his composure. "Who did she kill?"

"Dr. Hartmut Matern and Dr. Richard Mehring, former chief justice of the federal constitutional court."

"Those two are in the inner circle of the pedophile ring," Kilian Rothemund stated. "They pull the strings, together with three other men, and have done so for over forty years. Until now, they've been committing their crimes unchecked. I have a long list of names and also plenty of proof that this list is accurate. Michaela Prinzler recounted her long years as a victim in minute detail, and she also wrote it all down. In recent weeks, Ms. Herzmann and I were able to gather a lot of evidence and statements from former victims and perpetrators to substantiate Michaela's story. I've spent the past few years extremely involved with this topic, as you can imagine."

No matter how damaged his face was, his extraordinary bright blue eyes possessed an alert intensity that made it hard for Pia to look at him. She had to force herself not to look away.

"Nine years ago, when Bernd Prinzler came to me and asked me to help his wife, I was fascinated by the topic," Rothemund went on after a brief pause. "I had completely under-estimated the determination and dangerous intent of these men. They destroyed me. I lost every-thing: my family, my reputation, my job. I went to prison and was convicted of child molestation and possession of child pornography. Photos and videos were found on my computer. It was all a skillfully set trap and I fell into it blindly."

"How could that happen?" Pia asked.

"I was a blue-eyed boy in the true sense of the word." He smiled a little, but the smile vanished a moment later. "I trusted the wrong people and I felt too safe. They put knockout drops in my drink. Twenty-four hours later, I woke up in my car after a total blackout. While I was unconscious, they put me in a bed with naked children and took pictures. This is the usual way they keep difficult people in check. I know of two employees of the Youth Welfare Department who had the same thing happen to them. Also a teacher who wanted to report his suspicions that a pupil was being abused, and at least three others. Nobody has a chance, because these men have connections in government ministries, business, politics, and even the police. They provide cover for one another, and not only in Germany. It's an international operation, and there's a lot of money at stake."

He pensively studied his injured right hand, turning it back and forth.

"When the girl was found dead in the river a few weeks ago, Michaela finally wanted to talk. Bernd called me up and I immediately agreed to work with them. I had nothing more to lose, but there was a small chance I might be able to redeem myself if we could prove everything in public. Through Michaela's therapist, Leonie, we were put in contact with Hanna Herzmann. She was excited about the possibility of getting such an explosive topic for her show. And although we warned her, she obviously underestimated the danger of these men. Just as I did. She told her old childhood friend Wolfgang Matern about it. He's the CEO of Herzmann Productions." Rothemund sighed. "Hanna didn't have the slightest idea that Wolfgang Matern's father, Hartmut, was involved in the abuse. Naturally, I knew that he owned the TV station, so I purposely didn't include his name on the list. I didn't want to put Hanna into a conflict-of-interest situation. Besides, at first I wasn't sure whether she could be trusted. Unfortunately, I didn't know that she was such close friends with Wolfgang Matern and would tell him all the details."

"You mean that Wolfgang Matern attacked Hanna Herzmann?" Pia asked him.

"No, certainly not in person. I think that Helmut Grasser was the one who assaulted her. And who killed Leonie. You can't intimidate women with compromising photos or videos. These criminals use different tactics with women than with men."

Pia remembered the car with the local license plates that Leonie Verges's neighbor had seen several times in the vicinity of her house. It was registered to the Sonnenkinder Association.

"This Sonnenkinder group," Bodenstein said, "does it really do anything for mothers and children, or is it purely a front organization?"

"Oh, no, they do quite a lot," replied Kilian Rothemund. "It's actually an excellent program. They support the education of young mothers and provide scholarships for children and teenagers. But there are also children who officially don't exist. Young mothers disappear right after they give birth and leave their babies behind because they think the children will be in good hands. Finkbeiner also likes to bring in orphans from the Far East and Eastern Europe. They aren't reported here; they simply don't exist, and no one misses them. They are fodder for the pedophiles. Michaela knew all about it, and she called them the 'lost kids.' It's simply incomprehensible what is done to them. When the kids get too old and are no longer attractive to the pedophiles, they're passed on to pimps or simply disposed of."

Pia thought of the artist's renderings that they'd had done with the help of the witness from Höchst. She excused herself, went to her office, and returned with the printouts.

"Do you know these two?" she asked Rothemund.

A fleeting glance was enough.

"The man is Helmut Grasser," he said. "And the woman is Corinna Wiesner, also an adopted child of the Finkbeiners, just like her husband, Ralf Wiesner, the director of Finkbeiner Holding Company. He and Corinna are probably the most loyal soldiers in Finkbeiner's underground army. Officially, she is administrative director of the Sonnenkinder Association, but in reality she's the leader of the 'secret police' of the ring. She knows about everything, and she's ice-cold and absolutely ruthless."

Helmut Grasser talked for fifteen minutes, his words spilling out like a waterfall. Thankful at last to have such an attentive audience, he told them about a sad, loveless childhood in various foster families, and a mentally ill mother who had rejected him as the unwanted product of a rape. She was only sixteen when he was born. The Youth Welfare authorities had eventually contacted the Finkbeiners, and there he had experienced for the first time in his life something like affection and care, and yet he would always remain a second-class child. Because his mother was alive, the Finkbeiners had not adopted him or taken him as a foster child. He had grown up in the orphanage at the Sonnenkinder Association, and he'd done everything he could to win acceptance because he so wanted to belong to the family. But the Finkbeiner children, who were younger than he was, had looked down on him. They shamelessly exploited his efforts to gain their favor and constantly made fun of him.

Grasser was not married. He lived with his mother in one of the houses on the Finkbeiner estate in Falkenstein, right next door to the people he'd worshiped for thirty years. And they had never stopped exploiting his devotion for their own purposes.

"Okay," Bodenstein finally interjected. "What about Hanna Herzmann and Leonie Verges?"

"I was supposed to scare the Herzmann woman so that she'd stop sniffing around," Grasser admitted. "The whole thing got a bit out of hand."

"'A bit out of hand'?" Bodenstein said, raising his voice. "You bestially tortured a woman and almost killed her! And then you left her in the car trunk, and with that you became an accomplice to attempted murder!"

"I only did what they asked me to do," he said defensively, and in his deep brown eyes lurked a trace of self-pity. According to his logic, he didn't view himself as a perpetrator, but a victim. "I didn't have a choice."

"Everyone always has a choice," Bodenstein shot back. "Who demanded that you do such a thing?"

Grasser was intelligent enough to acknowledge his dependence on the Finkbeiners and to recognize the constant humiliations he had endured. But he was too weak-willed to free himself from them. He justified his actions to himself by saying that he was only following orders. After being ridiculed all his life, he sought revenge for his hurt pride by attacking those weaker than himself.

"Who demanded that you do that?" Bodenstein repeated.

Grasser realized that lying would do no good, so he seized the opportunity to pay back his oppressors at last.

"Corinna Wiesner. She's my immediate boss. I do what she tells me, and I don't ask questions."

Pia's phone started buzzing. She glanced quickly at the display. It was Hans Georg's number, the farmer from Liederbach who always pressed the hay for her horses. He probably wanted to tell her that he'd finished mowing. It could wait.

"Did Corinna also order you to film your attack on Hanna Herzmann? And did she order you to let Leonie Verges die of thirst and to film that, too?" Bodenstein asked caustically.

"Not directly," Grasser said evasively. "She didn't tell me exactly what to do."

"Then what are you talking about?" Bodenstein leaned forward. "You just said you would do what people tell you to do!"

"Well . . ." Grasser shrugged. "I was just told that this and that had to be done. But how I did it was up to me."

"What does that mean, specifically?"

"I came up with the idea of pretending to be

cops." Grasser seemed almost proud of himself. "I ordered all the stuff on the Internet; it's a great con. And it works every time. Sometimes we do it just for fun, making some money."

"What about taking the videos?" Pia asked.

"There are plenty of people who are into that stuff," he said.

"What stuff?"

"You know, watching somebody die. The real thing, not faked." Grasser was completely unmoved. "For a video like the one showing the TV bitch, you could get a cool two grand."

Kröger had already told them about the so-called snuff movies. Pia herself had never seen one, but she knew that online in IRC chats, Usenet forums, in closed user groups, videos were offered that apparently showed genuine murders in full-length features, often as the perverse climax of the worst hard-core pornographic scenes, but there were also executions, torture, murders of babies and children in the context of child pornography.

Grasser described the details of his sickening deeds with such relish that Pia felt ill. He seemed to her like a horny gorilla pounding on his chest with his fists.

"Just stick to the facts," she said, interrupting his description of the attack on Hanna Herzmann. "What about the girl? How did she end up in the river?"

"Don't rush me. One thing at a time," said Grasser, enjoying being the center of attention for once. His life had otherwise been spent playing a minor role.

Pia pretended she was getting a phone call and left the interview room. The way this jerk was gaping at her, steadily undressing her with his eyes, was just too much to take after all she'd been through today.

Outside, she leaned against the wall, closed her eyes, and breathed calmly in and out so as not to hyperventilate. How could there be such revolting, sick people in the world?

"Hey, is everything all right?" said Christian Kröger, coming out of the listening room between the interview rooms. It had a one-way mirror and was used to observe interrogation sessions. Pia opened her eyes and looked into his worried face.

"I couldn't stand looking at that asshole one second longer," she blurted out. "A team of horses couldn't get me back in there."

"Let me take over." Christian patted her arm sympathetically. "The others are in the listening room. Go in there and join them."

Pia exhaled deeply.

"Thanks," she said.

"Have you eaten anything today?" Christian asked.

"No. I'll grab something later." Pia managed a smile. "I hope this whole thing will be over soon."

She went in to join Kai, Cem, and Kathrin and sat down on a chair. Helmut Grasser let loose a couple of obscene remarks from his vast storehouse as Christian came into the interview room and took up a position behind Grasser's chair.

"Get to the point, you sick little fuck," he said. "Otherwise, you're going to get another electro-shock treatment."

The smug grin on Grasser's face vanished.

"Did you hear that? He's threatening to torture me!" he complained.

"I didn't hear a thing." Bodenstein didn't bat an eye. "We were discussing the girl. Please continue."

Grasser gave Kröger a dark look.

"Oksana, that stupid slut," he said, "she kept running away. I was always the one who had to do the dirty work, and I got shit if the little bitches made trouble. Somehow she made it downtown, so we had to pretend we were her parents."

"Who is 'we'?" Bodenstein asked.

"Corinna and me," said Grasser.

"Where did the girl run away from?"

"From the palace."

"Can you be more specific?"

Helmut Grasser gave him a surly look, but then he began talking again. The catacombs of the Palais Ettringhausen in Höchst, which belonged to the Finkbeiner Foundation, housed the cellars where the abuse took place and the videos were shot. They sold like hotcakes all over the world. The children were normally kept in Falkenstein, but some of them were always in Höchst, to "be available."

Just this expression made cold shivers run down Pia's back.

Oksana, Grasser explained, was actually too old for the needs of the pedophile men, but for some reason, the boss was crazy about her. One evening, she provoked his wrath by refusing to do what he ordered.

"As long as they're small, they're easy to intimidate," Grasser said as blithely as if he were talking about animals. "When they're older, they get devious and sly, those little beasts. Then you sometimes have to take more drastic measures."

Pia turned away and buried her face in her hands.

"I can't take any more of this," she muttered.

"Me, neither," said Cem dully. "I have two daughters. I don't dare think about them."

"Oksana was tough; these Russian girls often are. Something in their genes," Helmut Grasser's voice said through the loudspeakers. "The boss had beaten her until she could hardly breathe; then he held her under in the Jacuzzi. A little too long, I guess. It was an accident."

He shrugged.

"And then what?" Bodenstein's face remained impassive.

"Once in a while, one of them doesn't survive. It happens. I was supposed to get rid of her that same evening," replicd Grasser. "But I was a little behind schedule, so I tossed her in the river."

"Unbelievable. Because he was a little behind schedule!" Kathrin muttered.

"It's lucky that he was," Cem said cynically. "Otherwise, no one would ever have known what was happening."

"My God," was all Pia said. Cem was right. Yet the discovery of the dead girl had been the trigger for a whole series of tragedies that they hadn't been able to prevent. If the witncss had called in earlier, if she'd seen the photo of Oksana in the paper and not first on *Germany's Most Wanted*, then perhaps Hanna Herzmann wouldn't have been attacked, Leonie Verges might still be alive, and Michaela Prinzler might not have shot two pcople to death.

Could have, would have, if only.

"Would you please answer your cell?" said Kathrin, because Pia's phone kept humming and buzzing.

"Later. It's not that important," Pia replied, leaning forward because Bodenstein had shoved a photo across the table toward Grasser.

"What is this?" he asked. "We found it in the girl's stomach."

"Hmm. Looks like a piece of a T-shirt. The boss likes the girls to wear these pink shirts, especially

629

when they're a bit older. It makes them look younger."

"We found the fabric in the child's *stomach,*" Bodenstein repeated.

"Maybe she ate it. We always kept her hungry, or she'd get too insolent."

Cem gasped for air.

"All this can't really be true, can it?" Pia was stunned. "No human being could do these things."

"Yes, they can." Kai nodded. "Unfortunately. Just think about the guards in the concentration camps. They would go home in the evening and behave like completely normal family men after driving people into the gas chambers all day long."

"I'd like to do the same thing to these guys," Cem grumbled. "But someone like Grasser probably won't even be sent to prison. He'll end up in the loony bin, because he had a difficult childhood. I don't even want to think about it."

Again, Pia's cell buzzed. She turned it off

"Did you do all this by yourself, or did you have help?" Christian was asking on the other side of the mirror.

"Occasionally, I take somebody with me," Grasser said. "With the TV bitch, the boss even came along. I took Andi with me to deal with Leonie; usually, he's only allowed to drive the kids around."

"So, the boss himself was there," Kröger repeated. "Isn't he a little old for . . . field work?"

"'Field work.'" Grasser chortled in amusement. "I like that. But what do you mean 'old'? He isn't much older than you are."

"We're talking about Josef Finkbeiner, aren't we?" Bodenstein asked.

"Oh, no, Josef doesn't do it anymore." Grasser dismissed the idea with a wave of his hand. "He might paw a kid once in a while, whatever he can get his fingers on. No, Nicky is the boss."

"Nicky?" Bodenstein and Kröger asked simultaneously. "Who's that?"

Grasser looked at them in surprise, then grinned and leaned back.

"You already arrested him," he said. "I just saw him walk past in the hallway."

"Who is Nicky?" Bodenstein asked angrily, having lost his patience. He slammed his palm on the table.

"Well, you guys aren't very smart, are you?" Helmut Grasser shook his head, not the least bit intimidated. "Nicky's real name is Markus Maria Frey."

"We need arrest warrants at once for Frey and Corinna Wiesner," said Bodenstein. "I want an immediate all-points bulletin sent out. He can't have gotten too far."

"I'll take care of it," said Kai Ostermann with a nod.

When they confirmed that Chief State Attorney Frey had flown the coop, Bodenstein had called all members of K-11 to the waiting room behind the watch room. They were joined by a few colleagues from other departments as well as those officers who were already off duty but had been summoned back to work.

"Who saw Frey last?" Bodenstein asked.

"He left the building at four thirty-six, supposedly because he wanted to get his cell phone from his car," said the officer who had been on watch at the door.

"Okay," said Bodenstein, checking his watch. "It's six forty-two now. That means he has a good two-hour head start."

He clapped his hands.

"Let's go, people. Let's get to work!" he shouted. "There's no time to waste. Frey will try to get rid of any evidence. I want a search warrant for the Palais Ettringhausen and for all locations of the Sonnenkinder Association, as well as for the private residences of Grasser, Wiesner, and Frey. For the search in Höchst, we'll need the Special Assignment Unit, a hundred men, and, in the event Frey goes on the run, a helicopter. Our colleagues from the River Police have to be informed, too."

Pia was sitting on a chair by the wall,

completely stunned. The voices around her were only a distant rumble in her ears.

Why hadn't she noticed how skillfully Chief State Attorney Frey had manipulated and duped her? Why had she fallen for it? Gradually, it had dawned on her what she had done. Stupidly naïve, she had told him about Rothemund going to Amsterdam, and reported each step of their investigative work to him—all because he'd been so friendly to Lilly.

Lilly! Good God! Pia flinched, as if somebody had poured scalding water on her. The threatening e-mail that she'd gotten this morning must have come from Frey. He naturally assumed that Lilly was her daughter, because she'd never mentioned Christoph to him.

"K-9 team, medics," Bodenstein's voice penetrated her consciousness. "In one hour, we'll meet in Höchst. Surround the building and seal it off. Kai, inform the traffic police and our colleagues in Frankfurt."

"Pia?" Rüdiger Dreyer, the detective on duty from the swing shift, stuck his head in the door.

Pia looked up.

"Yes, what is it?"

"We just got an emergency call," her colleague said, and came closer. His worried expression set off all the alarm bells in Pia's head. "Something has happened at Birkenhof."

"Oh God, no!" Pia whispered, putting her hands

over her mouth. Not Lilly! If anything had happened to the girl, she was the only one to blame. It was deathly quiet in the big room. Everyone was looking at Pia. She took out her cell. Twenty-three calls missed, five texts, all from Hans Georg, mostly variations on *CALL ME BACK RIGHT AWAY. IT'S URGENT.* And she'd thought he wanted to tell her something about the hay harvest.

"Come on," said Christian Kröger, patting her on the shoulder. "I'll drive you there."

Yes, thanks, Pia wanted to say, but then she noticed her colleagues scrutinizing her. She couldn't show any weakness, not in a situation like this, when every officer was needed. She was the chief detective inspector and had to act professionally. She couldn't run around like a chicken with her head cut off. Under no circumstances should her private life take precedence over the apprehension of a dangerous criminal— especially someone that she herself had supplied with crucial information.

"Thanks, I can manage on my own," she said in a firm voice, and straightened her shoulders. "I'll see you later at Höchst."

"You are definitely not driving over there by yourself." Christian caught up with her in the parking lot and took the car keys out of her hand. "Don't argue! I'm driving you."

Pia nodded mutely. She was shaking all over with fear and worry. If she had to face a disciplinary hearing because she'd given the state attorney too much information, then that was a fair punishment for her stupidity. But she would never forgive herself if something had happened to Lilly and she was to blame.

Kröger unlocked her car and opened the passenger door for her. Pia turned to him.

"It's all my fault," she whispered.

"What's your fault?" He nudged her gently into the car, then reached over and fastened her seat belt as if she were a child.

"I gave Frey too much information. Why in the world did I do that?"

"Because he was the state attorney on the case," Kröger said. "If you hadn't told him, he would have found out everything from the files."

"No, that's not true," Pia said, shaking her head. "I told him that Kilian Rothemund was on his way to Amsterdam. Then Frey must have activated his connections in Holland."

Kröger got in, started the engine, and backed out of the parking spot.

"Pia," he said. "You did nothing wrong. You couldn't have known what sort of game Frey was playing. If a state attorney asks me for information, I give it to him."

"You're just saying that now." Pia sighed. "When Frey showed up to watch the search of

Rothemund's trailer, you didn't tell him every-thing you knew. His excessive interest in the case should have warned me something was fishy."

She stopped talking. Kröger drove up the Strawberry Mile, paying no attention to the speed limit, heading for the autobahn.

"Turn left and take the dirt road; it's faster," said Pia before they reached the bridge. He braked, signaled, and turned sharp left across the oncoming lane. A driver flashed his brights and honked.

"If Erik Lessing had to die because he'd found out from Bernd Prinzler about this pedophile Mafia," said Kröger after a while, "then I have to ask myself what Engel knew at the time. And what she knows today. What if she has something to do with it?"

"I don't dare think about that," replied Pia in a gloomy voice. "At any rate, Bodenstein had no idea what the whole thing was about back then. And Frank didn't know, either. If we don't root out all the men behind it, then Kilian Rothemund will be in danger for the rest of his life, along with his kids."

Kröger slowed down to cross the farm road that led from Zeilsheim to the B519 toward Kelkheim. On the other side, he followed the paved road that ran parallel to the A66 autobahn. Dusk was already falling, and yet there were still many skaters and joggers on the road who couldn't hear their car coming because of the noise from the autobahn, so they didn't move out of the way. Kröger was impatiently drumming his fingers on the steering wheel, and Pia could see the tension in his face. He was just as worried as she was. A few minutes later, they reached Birkenhof. In front of the gate stood Hans Georg's green tractor and two patrol cars with blue lights flashing. A medic's vehicle and an ambulance were parked under the walnut tree in the courtyard. Pia's blood froze in her veins at the sight. Until now, she'd been worried about Lilly and hadn't even thought that something might have happened to Christoph.

In the backlight of the setting sun, she saw something dark lying on the gravel drive between the paddocks and the riding area. Kröger saw it, too, and slammed on the brakes so hard that the gravel sprayed from the tires. Pia jumped out of the car before it even came to a stop.

"Oh my God!"

All strength drained from her body, and she felt sick. Tears filled her eyes.

"What is it?" Kröger asked behind her, and then he saw for himself. He put his arm around her shoulder and pulled her away, preventing her from looking any longer. The dead dog lay in a big pool of blood, and not five yards away lay a second dog's body.

"Pia!"

A big gray-haired man in green overalls came hurrying toward her. It was Hans Georg, but she saw him through a haze. The sight of the two dogs that had been shot made her fear the worst. The anxiety inside her had turned to panic, overwhelming her.

"Where's Christoph? What happened here?" she yelled shrilly. She tried to pull out of Kröger's grasp, but he held her tight and led her onto the grass strip so she wouldn't have to step over the dead dogs.

"I tried to call you a zillion times," said the farmer, but Pia wasn't listening.

"Where are Christoph and Lilly? Where are they?" she shrieked hysterically, pushing against Kröger's chest. He let her go.

"In the house," said Hans Georg, but he sounded stressed. "Wait, Pia!"

She ducked around him as he stepped into her path and tried to stop her. Like a condemned criminal on her way to the scaffold, filled with dread, she headed for the front door with a fixed expression. Fears she had long thought repressed surged up inside her, and her heart was pounding so hard that it hurt. She was wet with sweat yet freezing at the same time.

"Ms. Kirchhoff!" A uniformed officer came out of the house. She didn't react as she stared at the puddle of blood on the steps, and the blood on the wall and door. Was she now going to encounter the nightmare of all police officers who find their loved ones dead?

"Come with me," said her colleague. Christian Kröger was right behind her. Her house was full of total strangers. In the kitchen, she saw the reddish orange vests of the EMTs, open medical kits, tubes, cables, clothing smeared with blood. And in the middle of the floor lay Christoph in his underpants, with the electrodes of an EKG stuck to his chest.

"Your wife is here now," she heard someone say, and they made room for her. Christoph was alive! Pia felt faint with relief. She squeezed past the others and knelt down next to him, cautiously touching his shoulder. He had a laceration on his head, which had already been treated by a medic.

"What happened?" she whispered. "Where's Lilly?"

Christoph opened his eyes, giving her a dazed look.

"Pia," he murmured. "He took her. He . . . he was standing by the gate and . . . and he waved. Lilly . . . she said she knew him . . . from the zoo and . . . and from visiting Miriam's grandmother. I . . . I didn't think anything of it . . . so I opened the gate. . . ."

Pia's heart skipped a couple of beats. Of course Lilly knew Chief State Attorney Frey. She took Christoph's hand.

"Lilly ran up to him . . . and suddenly he had a

gun in his hand. He shoved her into his car; then the dogs went after him . . . and he . . . shot them." He broke off and briefly closed his eyes. He was breathing hard.

"I saw them." Pia was fighting back tears. "What about you?"

"I . . . I took off after him. He tried to shoot at me, but . . . but the clip must have been empty. And then . . . then Hans Georg was there all of a sudden. . . ."

"Concussion," the EMT interjected. "He took at least three blows to the head. We're taking him to the hospital."

Pia heard Kröger on the phone, talking in a low voice about Lilly and Frey.

"I want to go to the hospital with you," she said to Christoph, stroking his cheek. He grabbed her hand.

"No," he implored her desperately. "You have to find Lilly. Please, Pia, promise me you'll find her. Nothing must happen to her."

He was as worried as she was about the little girl. In order to protect Lilly, he had gone after an armed man who had shot her dogs, showing that he would shoot without hesitation. If the clip hadn't been empty, then Frey might have shot Christoph, too.

Pia leaned over him and kissed his cheek.

"I not only promise that I'll find her," she said gruffly. "I *swear* I will."

• • •

"I'm going with you to Höchst," she announced as the ambulance drove off. "I'm just going to change real quick."

She was still wearing her summer dress and the sling-back heels that she'd put on that morning to attend the birthday reception. It seemed like ages ago.

"I'll take the other two dogs back to my place; they can sit beside me on the tractor," said Hans Georg. "And I'll see to the horses."

"Thank you." Pia nodded to him, then ran up the stairs. In the bedroom, she tore off her dress, slipped into a T-shirt and jeans, and took her service weapon out of the safe in the wardrobe. With trembling fingers, she strapped on her shoulder holster and stuck in the P30. Socks, running shoes, a gray hoodie—she was already feeling more like herself.

Five minutes later, she got in the car with Christian.

"Are you okay?" he asked as they drove through Unterliederbach.

"Yes," replied Pia curtly. Her fear had been transformed to cold rage. Just as they stopped on Kasinostrasse at a barricade, her cell rang. A crowd of onlookers had shown up, eager for a break from the monotony of their daily lives. The police could never make people understand how dangerous a situation could be, so the

641

cordon had to block off as wide an area as possible.

"We're here," said Pia to Bodenstein. "Where are you?"

She showed her ID to the officer manning the cordon, and he moved the barricade a little to the side to let them drive in.

"On the street, right in front of the Palais," her boss replied. "The SAU stormed the building and we were able to apprehend a few of the Sonnenkinder people just as they were trying to escape with some children."

"What about Lilly?" Pia asked. Kröger had already told Bodenstein that Lilly was in Frey's hands.

"We're still searching for the entrance to the catacombs. Frey must be here. His car is parked out front."

Pia and Kröger ran across the Bolongarostrasse, which was deserted in the glow of the street-lights. No cars, no bicyclists, and no pedestrians were allowed inside the blocked-off zone. In the distance, a tram rattled by; otherwise, it was very quiet. Bodenstein, Kathrin, and Cem were waiting in the courtyard of the Palais Ettringhausen, which was right next to the Bolongaro Palace. With them were the squad leaders of the SAU and the SWAT team, and the courtyard was teeming with police. Solemn, shocked expressions were evident everywhere. Nobody was cracking jokes.

In the glare of a searchlight, they saw a dark blue VW bus with the Sonnenkinder logo on the side.

"Is Corinna Wiesner here?" Pia asked.

"No," Bodenstein said, shaking his head. She could see what a toll the tension of the past few hours had taken on him. He had dark rings under his eyes, and a bluish shadow covered his cheeks and chin. "They must be down in the cellar. We apprehended two women who were about to drive off with six kids inside the vehicle."

"How many people are still down there?" Pia asked.

"According to the two women, only the Wiesners and Frey," Bodenstein replied. "And four more children."

"And Lilly," Pia added gloomily. "That shithead knocked out Christoph and shot my dogs. If I get hold of him, I'm—"

"You're staying up here, Pia," Bodenstein said, interrupting her. "The SAU has taken over the operation."

"No," Pia objected vehemently. "I'm going down there to bring Lilly out. And I swear to you, I'm not taking any prisoners."

Bodenstein grimaced.

"You will do nothing," he said. "Not in this state of mind."

Pia fell silent. There was no point in arguing with Bodenstein. She'd have to wait for the right opportunity.

"Is that the blueprint of the cellar?" She nodded toward a car, where she could see a building plan spread out on the hood; it showed all the rooms in the cellar.

"Yes. But you're not going down there," Bodenstein repeated.

"Understood." Pia studied the plan, which a colleague illuminated with his pocket flashlight. She was twitching with impatience. Somewhere down there was Lilly, in the hands of a maniac, and they were just standing here babbling.

"We've got officers covering all the exits. Not even a mouse could get out unseen," the team leader of the SAU explained.

"The whole place belongs to Finkbeiner Holding," Bodenstein told Pia. "This is their headquarters. The tenants also include tax consultants and a legal firm. On the ground floor, there are two doctors' offices and a municipal agency dealing with young people. The perfect camouflage."

Two ambulances quietly rolled into the court-yard to take the children who were still in the VW bus to the hospital.

"That's why these upper-crust pedophiles can come and go even in broad daylight without anyone noticing," said Cem. The radio in Bodenstein's hand crackled and hissed. The hundred men from the SWAT team had already cleared the area all the way down to the Nidda River.

Pia took that moment while Bodenstein wasn't looking to dash across the courtyard and slip into the Palais through the main entrance. Two colleagues from the SAU wanted to stop her, but after she told them to go to hell, they reluctantly showed her the way to an unobtrusive wooden door underneath the curving flight of stairs. It opened into a room where cleaning supplies and equipment, toilet paper, and other items were stored, but another door inside led down to the catacombs.

"I knew you wouldn't listen to me," said Bodenstein behind her. He sounded out of breath. "That was an order, not a request."

"Then turn me in for disciplinary action. I don't care." Pia drew her weapon. Christian and Cem had also joined them and were now following her down the worn steps. The corridor at the bottom was so narrow that their shoulders almost touched the concrete walls on either side. Every few yards, a neon light provided dim illumination. Pia shuddered. What must the children have felt when they were brought here and led along this corridor? Had they screamed and struggled, or had they resigned themselves to their cruel fate? How could a child's soul ever cope with this?

There was a sharp turn and then they ascended a couple of short flights of stairs, whereupon the corridor became wider and higher. It smelled musty and damp. Pia suppressed any thought of how many tons of earth were above her head.

"Let me go first," Christian whispered behind her.

"No." Pia marched on with determination. Every cell in her body was so full to the brim with adrenaline that she no longer felt a thing, neither fear nor anger. How often had men slunk along this passageway, driven by their disgusting obsession? How perverse and sick must a grown man be, especially someone who might even have children himself, to do violence to a child in order to quell his lust?

Suddenly, Pia heard voices, and she stopped so abruptly that Bodenstein ran into her.

"They're up ahead," Pia whispered.

"You stay here and let us do this," Bodenstein ordered her in a low voice. "If you follow us, it will have serious consequences."

Bla, bla, bla, thought Pia, and nodded. She let her boss, Cem, and Christian go past her, then waited thirty seconds before she followed them into a long, low room, and what she saw there took her breath away. Many years ago, she'd been on a raid of a Frankfurt S and M club that had looked similar, except that the members of the club were adults and satisfied their strange desires of their own free will. This place was specifically designed for the abuse of children. This was where Oksana, the Mermaid, had been tormented and tortured. At the sight of the rack, the chains, the handcuffs, the cages, and the other horrendous implements, Pia felt all the horror and fear that had eaten into the concrete walls like acid.

"Hands up!" Pia heard Bodenstein shout, making her flinch. "Get over by the wall! Go, go!"

Under different conditions, Pia would have stayed back, as her boss had ordered her to do. But right now, she had to keep going. Her worry about Lilly was greater than any sense of reason. She stepped through the doorway and entered another big room, in which there were barred cells to the left and right. Her gaze swept over a group of four children, not much older than eight or nine, who stood lethargically in front of one of the cells without moving. Christian and Cem had their weapons aimed at a man and a woman, and Pia recognized the dark-haired woman who that morning had attempted to pull Renate Finkbeiner away from her wounded husband. So that was Corinna Wiesner, the woman who had pretended to be Oksana's mother. But where was Frey?

"Lilly!" Pia shouted as loudly as she could. "Where are you?"

Hanna had been scared to see him again. Everything inside her had resisted allowing him to see her lying so helpless and ugly in a hospital bed. But when he entered her room so unexpectedly and took her in his arms without hesitation, kissing her gently, all her fears evaporated. For quite a while, they just sat there looking at each other. At their first meeting in Leonie's kitchen, Hanna had first noticed his eyes, those extraordinarily bright blue eyes, which exerted a strong magnetic attraction on her. Back then, his eyes had been full of bitterness and despair, but today they shone with warmth and confidence. It took a moment before she noticed how his face looked and the fact that his right arm was in a sling.

"What happened?" she asked softly. Talking was still difficult for her.

"It's a long story," replied Kilian, pressing her right hand tenderly with his left. "But maybe it's finally over."

"Will you tell me about it?" Hanna asked. "There's so much I can't remember."

"There'll be plenty of time for that later." His fingers twined with hers. "First you have to get well."

She heaved a deep sigh. Until this moment, she had dreaded the day when she would leave the protective walls of the hospital and have to look life in the face again. Now this fear vanished, as well. Kilian was here. He didn't care how she looked. Even if she never regained her flawless beauty 100 percent, he would stand by her.

"Do you still have our e-mails?" Hanna asked.

"Yes. Every one." He smiled, even though it was difficult with the bruises. "I've read them over and over."

Hanna returned his smile.

In the past few days, she had also been rereading his e-mails on her new iPhone, and she knew them almost by heart. He had lost everything from his former life and had done time in prison, an innocent man who had been abandoned by all. But neither the humiliating social ostracism nor the loss of status, possessions, and family had succeeded in breaking him. On the contrary. Hanna, too, had been ripped out of her world of superficialities and propelled by fate into the deepest abysses of hell. Yet they would both manage to survive and work their way back up to the light. But she would never again take for granted what life had given her.

"Meike was here earlier," Hanna croaked. "She left an envelope for me. I didn't understand everything that she told me. Look in the drawer of the nightstand."

Kilian released her hand and opened the drawer.

"Here's the envelope," he said.

"Please open it," Hanna replied. The painkillers made her feel so woozy that she had a hard time keeping her eyes open. Kilian's expression changed as he looked at the pages inside the envelope, and he frowned.

"What is it?" she asked.

"They're photos of . . . cars." He said it casually, but Hanna still noticed his sudden tension, despite her dazed state.

"May I see them?" Hanna held out her hand, and Kilian gave her the photos, which had been printed by a color ink-jet printer.

"This is in front of the Matern villa in Oberursel," Hanna said in surprise. "What . . . what does this mean? Why did Meike give me these?"

"I don't know." Kilian gently took the pages from her hands, folded them up, and shoved them back in the envelope. "I'm sorry, Hanna, I have to go now. The police allowed me to visit you briefly because I turned myself in, but I'm spending the night at state expense."

"Then at least I won't have to worry about you," Hanna murmured. Fatigue was making her eyelids feel like lead.

"Will you come and visit me tomorrow?"

"Of course." He bent over her. His lips touched hers, and he stroked her cheek. "As soon as they lift the arrest order against me and I'm free again, I'll come back to you."

After she left the hospital, Meike drove around aimlessly for a couple of hours. She felt terribly alone. She would never again set foot in the house in Langenhain, not after everything that had occurred there, so she'd decided to drive to Sachsenhausen to her friend's apartment. Hanna still wasn't doing much better; the painkillers fogged her mind and made a rational conversation with her impossible. There were so many things Meike wanted to talk to her mother about. She hoped at least that she'd received the envelope with the photos and passed them on to the cops.

Meike drove along the river on Deutschherrnufer and turned down Seehofstrasse. Since so many people were away on summer vacation, she found a parking place not far from the apartment building. She maneuvered the Mini into the spot, grabbed her backpack, and got out. The slam of the car door echoed loudly in the silent neighborhood, and Meike looked around. Her body was still sore from the fight and she was dead tired, yet her mind was still on high alert. What she had experienced today would haunt her forever—she knew that. Her flight from the attack dog in the woods had been bad enough, but it was nothing compared to what had happened at her mother's house. She shuddered. The guy would have killed her without hesitation; she had seen it in his eyes, which had held absolutely no sympathy. She didn't want to think about what might have happened if she hadn't had the Taser.

Meike crossed the street as she fished the door key out of her backpack. Out of the corner of her eye she saw a movement between the parked cars. Fear surged inside her. Her pulse quickened, she broke out in a sweat, and she ran the last few yards to the front door.

"Shit," she whispered. Her fingers were shaking

so hard that she couldn't get the key in the lock. Finally, she managed to do it and shoved the door open. She was startled when something dark darted past her. The cat from the old lady's apartment on the ground floor!

Meike slammed the door behind her, leaned against it in relief, and waited until her heart had calmed down a bit. In front of her was the small courtyard and the door of the house in back, where the apartment was located; then she would finally be safe. She longed for a hot shower and twenty-four hours of uninterrupted sleep. Tomorrow she would decide whether she'd better stay here for a while and then ask her father and his wife to take her in.

She stepped away from the door. The motion detector clicked, the light in the entry went on, and a moment later she was inside the house and trudging up the creaking staircase. Made it! She unlocked the door of the apartment and suddenly heard a voice behind her.

"There you are, finally. I've been waiting all evening for you."

The blood froze in her veins; the fine hairs on the back of her neck stood on end. Very slowly, she turned around and looked straight into the bloodshot eyes of Wolfgang Matern.

"Pia! I am here!" The bright little voice was shrill with fear.

At that second, the lioness awoke inside Pia. She would rather die than leave the child to this monster.

"Stay where you are!" Bodenstein barked at her, but Pia ignored him. She turned around and ran back in the direction where Lilly's voice was coming from. At the fork in the corridor, she turned right, trying to call up the layout in her memory, but in vain. The cellar was an underground labyrinth of passages, drainage canals, old air-raid bunkers, and countless rooms. The part she had seen so far seemed to have been expanded fairly recently, with concrete floors and modern fluorescent lights and light switches. But now she entered an area that seemed as old as the Palais itself. The corridor was alarmingly low and dim, the walls and ceilings were made of brick, and the floor was dirt. The only light sources were old-fashioned latticed ceiling lamps, which did little to penetrate the gloom. The deeper Pia went, the stronger became the musty smell of dampness and rat droppings. Suddenly, a black hole yawned in front of her, and it was only at the last second that she saw the steps, which led down into another narrow, dark tunnel. Water dripped from the ceiling, and the steps were so slippery that she had to hold on to the rusty handrail to keep from falling. Pia stopped, listening in the dark.

"Lilly!" she yelled, but she got no answer. The only sound she heard was her own gasping breath.

Was she still going the right way? Fear and despair threatened to overwhelm her, and she had to force herself not to turn back. The passage was straight ahead now; there were no more forks in the path or other rooms, and Pia realized that she must be underneath the park of Palais Ettringhausen, in the secret passage that led down to the Nidda River. At the same time, she figured out Frey's plan: He wanted to escape with Lilly. Maybe there was a boat waiting for him at the river. She had to hurry! She heard footsteps behind her, and she risked a look back over her shoulder.

"Wait for us, Pia!" Christian called. But instead of waiting, she ran even faster. Frey had a head start, and she had to catch up with him. The corridor abruptly widened and ended at a huge grated gate, one side of which was standing open. Pia stepped out, and suddenly there he was, this ruthless beast in human form.

"Hello, Ms. Kirchhoff." Markus Maria Frey was somewhat out of breath, but still he smiled. In the pale light of the full moon, she could see his face and his eyes. And she saw the empty smile of an insane person, a sick mind. She hoped he would be tormented by it for the rest of his life. Frey was backing up but didn't let Pia out of his sight. With one hand, he had a tight grip on Lilly's upper arm; with the other, he was pressing a pistol into the girl's neck.

"Put down your weapon at once! And stay where you are. Or I'll be forced to shoot the little girl."

This was exactly the spot where Helmut Grasser must have thrown Oksana into the river. He had run through the passage, carrying the dead child in his arms, and then stopped to check that nobody was walking on the path along the riverbank, which ran past a few yards below. Frey had now reached the path, and between him and the river lay only the narrow embankment.

"Give up!" said Pia in a commanding voice. "You haven't got a chance. This place is crawling with police."

A thousand thoughts raced through her head. Frey was less than thirty feet away from her, and she was an excellent shot. All she had to do was pull the trigger. But what if he reflexively fired his gun, which he surely would have reloaded?

"Take it easy, Lilly," she said, lowering her weapon. "Nothing is going to happen to you."

"Pia, the man wasn't nice to me at all," the girl complained. Her eyes were huge with fear, and her voice quavered. "He shot Robbie and Simba and he hurt Grandpa!"

Christian and Bodenstein appeared behind Pia; above them on the wall enclosing the park, floodlights went on, bathing the whole scene in a ghostly bright light. Pia heard her boss talking on the phone in a low voice, trying to get the River

Police to come here from their position downstream, where the river flowed into the Main. From the left and right, the black-clad figures of their colleagues from the SAU approached, keeping out of the light.

"State Attorney Frey!" Bodenstein called. "Let the girl go!"

"What's he up to?" Christian whispered. "He can't get away from here; he must realize that."

Pia could no longer think clearly. All she could see was Lilly, whose blond hair shone like gold in the garish light. What terror this little soul must have had to endure! How could a man who had children of her age do something like this?

Frey stood motionless for almost a minute atop the embankment, but now all of a sudden he was moving. Everything happened at a furious pace. He grabbed Lilly around the waist and jumped into the inky water of the river.

"No! Lilly!" Pia roared, full of panic. She wanted to take off running, but Bodenstein caught her arm and yanked her back. She saw Christian take a few steps forward and then jump into the water, too. Within seconds, pandemonium broke out on the riverbank promenade, which until then had been totally deserted. Police officers stormed in from all directions, an ambulance appeared, and from the direction of the Main, the brightly lit boat of the River Police turned into the Nidda. Bodenstein held Pia tightly in his arms.

"There she is!" he shouted. "Kröger has the girl!"

Overcome with relief, Pia's knees buckled. If her boss hadn't been holding her, she would have collapsed. Colleagues from the SWAT team helped Christian out of the water, and someone picked up Lilly and wrapped her in a blanket. Only two minutes later, Pia was able to hold the child in her arms. She no longer cared what happened to Frey. As far as she was concerned, he could drown in the river like a rat.

Saturday, July 3, 2010

For Ostermann, it was an easy task to find the owner of a vehicle by tracing the license plate number, at least for cars registered in Germany. He was not too surprised when he read the names, which were gradually correlated with the photos. An hour and a half earlier, two patrol officers had shown up with Kilian Rothemund, who had given him an envelope with photos of parked cars. Meike Herzmann had taken the pictures of the cars on Thursday evening in front of the house of the media mogul Hartmut Matern in Oberursel. Rothemund had no idea why she had done that, but he had an interesting theory about why all those cars were there, which was corroborated by each name that came up.

The night before Finkbeiner's birthday, the

leading figures in the child-molestation ring had gathered at the Matern villa—all respected, influential men who had achieved much in their lives and belonged to the upper crust of society. Two of them were now dead, executed by one of their former victims, and the third was still fighting for his life. Rothemund had phoned Prinzler and asked him to bring over as quickly as possible the recorder and the transcripts of conversations that he'd mailed from Holland to Prinzler's post office box.

Bodenstein, Cem, and Kathrin met at three in the morning at the station. The horror at what they had seen and experienced in the catacombs under the Palais Ettringhausen was written on their faces. Eleven of the "lost kids," as Michaela Prinzler had called them, had been liberated from Höchst and placed in the care of the child-protection agency. Three additional little girls had been discovered in a basement in Falkenstein. None of them knew her own last name, nor were there any birth certificates. They simply did not officially exist. Corinna Wiesner's two assistants were already in custody in Preungesheim, and Helmut Grasser was expected to be brought before the judge for arraignment in the morning.

Markus Maria Frey had disappeared. The police had searched the river, and at dawn divers would be called in, but they had good reason to believe that they would find only his corpse.

"Come on, have a cup of coffee first." Dr. Nicola Engel, who had been holding the fort in her office, sat down across from Bodenstein in the conference room of K-11. "Or better yet, go home and come back to work tomorrow."

"No." Bodenstein shook his head. He had talked to Corinna Wiesner, astonished to discover that there were still people who were able to shock him. That woman, so beautiful and friendly at first glance, and a mother of four herself, was in reality a merciless, heartless control freak. Her fascination with her own importance and her power over other people had become an addiction. But for her—unlike Grasser—the driving force for what she'd done was not power over weaker individuals; she was utterly indifferent to the young victims. Instead, she liked dominating powerful men who could not control their perverted desires. With her keen intellect and her organizational abilities, Corinna Wiesner had governed this association of child molesters with absolute efficiency, although in the end, both she and Frey had made mistakes.

Their first disastrous mistake was that they'd lost sight of Michaela Prinzler. Even so, they had safeguarded their gruesome secret for years by establishing connections in all the right places, and by using extortion and intimidation. Frey had made the second mistake when he lost control of Oksana.

Corinna Wiesner did not deny her responsibility for the atrocities. She had absolutely no moral scruples, having firmly convinced herself that there was nothing wrong with what she was doing. She showed no emotion, and she had a ready excuse for every accusation that Bodenstein leveled against her.

Helmut Grasser had told the police how furious Corinna had been when she learned that Frey had drowned Oksana. In her wrath, she had threatened to cancel the birthday festivities. And when she heard from her sister-in-law Emma that Louisa had apparently been abused, she had reproached old Finkbeiner for endangering the whole group with his behavior. A fierce argument had erupted among Finkbeiner, Frey, and Corinna, and it escalated to the point where Frey had even struck his sister.

"I'm not finished yet," Bodenstein told his boss. "The way things stand, we now have all the names of the inner circle of the child-molestation ring, as confirmed by Corinna Wiesner. Tonight, I want to apply for arrest warrants."

That was a bluff, because Corinna Wiesner hadn't said a word when he confronted her with the names, and he was doubtful that they would get anything more out of her. Ralf Wiesner hadn't said a word. If they were unlucky, they might never be able to prove that the people who were at Matern's villa on Thursday evening had anything to do with the child-abuse Mafia.

The commissioner raised her eyebrows.

"Arrest warrants? For whom?" she asked.

Bodenstein shoved over to her the list that Ostermann had prepared.

"A few names from abroad are still missing, but we've already contacted our colleagues in Holland, Belgium, Austria, France, and Switzerland. Tomorrow we'll have IDs on all the individuals who were at the meeting on Thursday evening at Matern's villa."

"I see." Dr. Engel scanned the list.

"We have a complete confession from Helmut Grasser, and I'm hoping that Corinna and Ralf Wiesner and their assistants will confirm everything in the days to come." Bodenstein rubbed both hands over his face, then looked up. "Frey killed the girl, and Grasser tossed her body in the river. He and Frey attacked Hanna Herzmann and almost killed her, and the murder of Leonie Verges can be chalked up to Grasser."

"Very good. You've solved all three cases," the commissioner said with a nod. "Congratulations, Chief Detective Inspector."

"Thank you. We'll also be able to prove that Kilian Rothemund was wrongly accused and convicted. Back in the summer of 2001, when he learned the names of the child molesters from Michaela Prinzler, he turned to Frey, of all people, and asked him for his help. Frey saw the names and was alarmed. He realized that this would be extremely perilous for the whole organization, so he lured his old friend Kilian into a trap. But he and Corinna Wiesner didn't manage to get hold of Michaela. Prinzler protected his wife by faking her death, staging a funeral, obituaries, and a gravestone. That's how he took her out of the line of fire." Bodenstein paused briefly. "Markus Frey did not have a good childhood. He went through several families before he ended up with the Finkbeiners. He was dependent on old Finkbeiner, just like his foster siblings. I suspect that he was also abused and at some point he decided to turn the tables. Perhaps he found satisfaction in wielding power over weaker individuals."

"His wife, Sarah, is from India, and she looks like a child herself," Kathrin Fachinger remarked. "Why didn't we figure out much earlier that Nicky is actually Markus Frey? We knew that he had a close connection to the Finkbeiners."

"I didn't figure it out, either," replied Bodenstein. "I learned from Corinna Wiesner that his real name was Dominik. But Renate didn't like that name, so she renamed him Markus. But his nickname, Nicky, stuck. He added his middle name, Maria, later, because he thought Markus Frey sounded too plain."

"Whew," Kai Ostermann said. "And then he even bought himself a doctorate. How pathetic."

"Be that as it may. The system functioned perfectly. Girls who were too old were sold to pimps, turned into addicts, or landed in mental hospitals. Corinna Wiesner had it all under control. Michaela was the only one to escape." Bodenstein paused as he studied the face of the woman he'd loved many years ago and thought that he knew. "Apart from the fact that we've solved our current cases, there's something else we've managed to prove. Thanks to Rothemund and Prinzler, I know why undercover agent Erik Lessing had to die."

"Really?" Nicola Engel didn't seem to be disturbed by this news, and it gave Bodenstein the meager hope that she might not have known the truth. Maybe she had simply been following orders from above. That didn't change the fact that she had covered up a crime. But Nicola Engel was an ambitious woman, and maybe that explained why she'd done it.

There was a knock, and in the doorway stood Pia and Christian Kröger, who had changed out of his wet clothes. They stepped inside.

"How's the girl doing?" the commissioner asked.

"So far so good," said Pia. "She's asleep in my office. Ostermann is with her."

"Well then . . . nothing remains but to congratulate all of you." Dr. Engel smiled. "It was really good work."

She stood up.

"Just a moment, please," said Bodenstein, holding her back.

"What is it? I'm tired. It's been a long day," said the commissioner. "And you should all be getting home."

"Erik Lessing, who once went undercover to infiltrate the Frankfurt Road Kings, had befriended Bernd Prinzler. Through him, he learned of the existence of a child-abuse ring that included the deputy police president of Frankfurt at the time, as well as a state secretary from the Interior Ministry, a judge from the state supreme court, and a whole list of state attorneys, judges, politicians, and industrialists. Lessing wanted to make this information public, and that's why he had to die."

"That's utter nonsense," Nicola Engel countered.

"Lessing's superior always knew his where-abouts," Bodenstein went on, ignoring her protest. "A raid was organized under the table. Not using the SAU, as is usual for raids on the underworld, especially when the Road Kings are involved. No, they were looking for the perfect officer to follow orders, somebody who also happened to be a crack shot, and an ambitious chief detective inspector who they knew had no moral scruples. Namely you, Dr. Engel."

Engel's expression froze.

"Be careful what you say, Oliver," she admonished him, forgetting to use his surname, which she usually did when others were present.

"You accompanied Behnke to the brothel,

having planted a different weapon on him in advance, one that wasn't registered and would later be found in Prinzler's car, making it look like the whole thing was just another shoot-out in the underworld. And you ordered Behnke to commit a triple murder."

Bodenstein wouldn't have been surprised if Nicola Engel lost her composure when confronted with such serious accusations, but she remained completely unfazed, just like Corinna Wiesner earlier.

"That's a very entertaining story." She shook her head. "Who wrote it? Behnke? That drunken, vengeful dimwit?"

"He told us what happened," Kröger confirmed. "And we didn't get the impression he was lying."

Dr. Nicola Engel gave him a contemptuous stare, then turned to look first at Pia and then at Bodenstein.

"Making unjustified accusations like this will cost all three of you your jobs, I can promise you that," she said calmly. For a moment, no one spoke.

"Wrong." Bodenstein got up from his chair. "You're the only one in this room who's going to lose her job, Dr. Engel. I hereby arrest you on suspicion of inciting three counts of homicide. Unfortunately, I can't let you leave, because I'm afraid that you might attempt to destroy evidence."

• • •

Morning was dawning outside the windows by the time Wolfgang Matern finished speaking. He'd been talking for almost an hour and a half, hesitantly at first, then more and more rapidly, almost as if under duress. Meike had been listening to him, stunned and upset. He had admitted to her that he was the one who had betrayed Hanna. He was her oldest and best friend, whom she had trusted without reservation, and yet he was responsible for the most devastating experience of her life.

"There was nothing else I could do," he'd replied tersely when Meike asked him why he'd done it. "When she gave me the exposé to read and I saw the names in it, I knew it would spell disaster."

"But not for you!" Meike sat facing him in an easy chair, her arms wrapped around her knees. "You had nothing to do with the whole mess. Nothing at all. You could have finally freed yourself from your father and this . . . this shit."

"Yes." He sighed heavily and rubbed his tired eyes. "Yes, I could have. But I didn't think anything like that would ever happen. I . . . I thought I could talk Hanna out of it, but before I even had a chance to speak to her, my father alerted the Finkbeiners, and they sent their bloodhounds after her."

Wolfgang avoided looking at Meike.

"I visited Hanna in the hospital. It was so horrible to see her like that," he said in a hoarse whisper. "Meike, you can't imagine how tormented I feel because I am to blame. I thought about killing myself, but I was too cowardly even for that."

Meike saw not a man sitting in front of her, but a shadow.

"When did you find out what your father was doing?" she asked.

"I always knew," he admitted. "At least since I was sixteen or seventeen. At first, I didn't really understand it. I thought they were meeting with young girls, with prostitutes. My mother always looked the other way. She must have known what my father was up to."

"Maybe that's why she killed herself." Gradually, Meike was making the connections and realizing what dramas must have played out behind the walls of the beautiful villa in Oberursel.

"Of course that's why she did it," Wolfgang confirmed. He was slumped on the sofa, looking sick. "She did leave behind a farewell note. I was the one who found it and I . . . I hid it. Nobody but me has ever read it."

"You mean you protected your father, that perverted pig who drove your mother to her death, even then?" Meike blurted out. "Why? Why did you do it?"

For the first time in an hour, Wolfgang looked at

her. His face was blank, his expression so dazed and hopeless that Meike was startled.

"Because . . . because he was still my father," he whispered. "I wanted to admire him, not see evil in him. He was . . . he was exactly how I always wanted to be, so strong, so self-assured. I was always trying to win his recognition and hoped that someday he would like me and respect me. But . . . but he never did. And now . . . now he's dead, and I can no longer tell him that I . . . despise him!"

He buried his face in his hands and began to sob.

"I can never make it right again," he said, crying like a little boy. Meike felt no sympathy for him after everything he'd done and allowed to happen.

"Yes, you can," she said.

"How? How can I?" He raised his head in despair, the tears flowing down his unshaven face. "How can I make up for all this?"

"You can go with me to the police and tell them everything you just told me, so that they can catch these guys," Meike replied. "That's the least you can do."

"But what'll happen to me then? Won't I be implicated?" He sounded whiny and self-pitying. Meike grimaced as she stared at this wretched weakling, this coward steeped in denial. How could she ever have loved and admired this man?

"You've got to take a chance," she said. "Otherwise, you'll never be happy for the rest of your life."

Christian Kröger placed the sleeping child carefully on the backseat of Pia's car. Lilly was sound asleep, exhausted from the most terrifying episode of her young life. Once, she woke up briefly and, groggy with sleep, asked Pia whether Robbie and Simba were in dog heaven now, and then she wanted to know what happened to the kids who were in the cellar. Before Pia could answer, she was asleep again, and now she lay there wrapped in a soft fleece blanket, a tiny snoring angel.

"I hope she won't be traumatized for the rest of her life," said Pia. Christian closed the car door as quietly as he could.

"I don't think she will," he replied. "She's a robust little thing."

Pia sighed and looked at him.

"Thank you, Christian. You saved her life."

"Well . . ." He shrugged in embarrassment and grinned. "I never would have thought that I'd voluntarily jump into a river, especially at night."

"For Lilly, I would have jumped into the Grand Canyon," said Pia. "I feel like she's my own kid."

"Every woman has a maternal instinct," Christian Kröger said. "That's why it's inconceivable to me how a woman like Corinna Wiesner could do something like that and let it go on for years."

"She's sick. Just like Helmut Grasser and all the rest of these pedophiles."

Pia leaned against her car and lit a cigarette. It was over. They had solved all three cases and a couple of old ones, too, and yet she felt no sense of relief nor any real pride in a job well done. Kilian Rothemund would have his conviction overturned, and Hanna Herzmann might someday be healthy again. Michaela Prinzler had survived the surgery, and Emma had brought a baby boy into the world. Pia thought about Louisa. She had loving parents and was young enough that she might be able to forget what had happened to her. Many other children weren't so lucky. They would have to live with the memory of all the atrocities they'd suffered, they might have mental breakdowns, and the anguish would haunt them like a shadow for the rest of their lives.

"Go home and try to get some sleep," said Christian.

"Yes, I'm going to do that." Pia took a drag on her cigarette. "I should be happy that we were able to break up a really big child-abuse ring. But I'm not. Child abuse will never end."

"Unfortunately, you're right," said Christian with a nod. "And we'll also never be able to stop people from killing each other."

The sky reddened in the east. Soon the sun would come up, as it had for billions of years every morning, in spite of all the tragedies played out on earth.

"I hope that pig is on the bottom of the Nidda River, being eaten by the fish for all the things he did." Pia dropped the cigarette and ground it out with her foot. "Now I have to go see Christoph in the hospital and take him a few things."

She and Kröger looked at each other; then she gave her colleague a hug. "Thank you for everything," she murmured.

"You're welcome."

Pia was just about to get in the car, when a red Mini turned into the parking lot. Meike Herzmann and Wolfgang Matern!

"What are they doing here?"

"You go home." Kröger gently shoved her into the car. "I'll take care of this. See you on Monday."

Pia was too exhausted to argue. She fastened her seat belt, started the engine, and drove off. The streets were empty so early in the morning, and she reached Birkenhof in only ten minutes. In front of the gate stood a taxi with its motor running. Pia set the hand brake and got out. Her heart skipped a beat, but this time not from fear. She felt joy and relief. Christoph sat in the passenger seat. He was a little pale, and he had a bandage on his head, but otherwise he looked all right. When he caught sight of her, he got out of the taxi. She gave him a big hug.

"Lilly is doing fine," she said quietly. "She's asleep on the backseat."

"Thank God," Christoph murmured. He took her face in both hands and looked at her. "And how are you doing?"

"That's what I should be asking you," replied Pia. "So they really let you out of the hospital this morning?"

"The bed was so uncomfortable." Christoph smiled wryly. "And I don't need to lie around in a hospital just because of a little concussion."

The taxi driver rolled down the window on the passenger side.

"It's great that you're all back together," he griped, "but could somebody please pay me?"

Pia got her wallet out of her backpack and handed him a twenty-euro note.

"Keep the change," she said; then she opened the gate and got back in her car. Christoph sat in the passenger seat and Pia drove off. The bodies of their dogs and the blood spots on the driveway were gone, no doubt thanks to Hans Georg.

Lilly stirred on the backseat. "Are we already home?" She mumbled.

"What do you mean, 'already'?" Pia stopped in front of the house. "It's four-thirty in the morning."

"Pretty early all right," said Lilly. Then she noticed Christoph, and her eyes grew wide.

"Grandpa is wearing a turban! That's really funny-looking." She giggled.

Pia looked at Christoph. It did look pretty funny. The tension of the past few hours fell away, and she started to laugh.

"Don't mock the afflicted," Christoph commented drily. "Okay, out of the car, you silly girls. I really need a cup of coffee."

"Me, too." Lilly heaved a huge sigh. "And I won't tell Mommy and Daddy."

"About what?" Pia and Christoph turned around at the same time to look at her.

"That you let me drink coffee, of course," replied Lilly with a grin.

Epilogue

"*Välkommen till Sverige*, Mr. de la Rosa." The young Swedish officer at passport control gave the man a friendly smile and handed back his Argentine diplomatic passport. "*Jag hoppas att ni hade en trevlig flygning.*"

"Yes, the flight was fine, thank you." Markus Maria Frey nodded, smiled, and left the secure area of Arlanda Airport in Stockholm. She was waiting outside in the departure hall, and he recognized her at once, although it had been a few years since they'd seen each other. The years had been kind to her, and she was even more beautiful than he remembered.

"Nicky!" She was beaming as she kissed him first on one cheek, then on the other. "How wonderful to see you. Welcome to Sweden."

"Hello, Linda. Nice of you to pick me up," he replied. "And how is Magnus?"

"He's waiting outside in the car." She put her hand through his arm. "I'm glad you're here. That whole business in Germany has been causing our friends great concern."

"A tempest in a teapot." Markus Maria Frey, now Hector de la Rosa, according to his passport, dismissed the matter with a wave of his hand. "Things will calm down eventually."

A family stood in front of him on the escalator. The father was struggling with several pieces of luggage, and the mother seemed frazzled. The boy looked sullen. The girl, no older than five or six, was hopping about and didn't notice the end of the escalator approaching. Before she could fall over and hurt herself, Frey quickly reached out and grabbed her, setting her back on her feet.

"*Kan du inte akta dig?*" the mother chided her daughter.

"Don't worry; she's all right," Frey said with a smile, stroking the girl's hair and then walking on. What a sweet little girl, he thought, even if she's crying now. Children really make life worthwhile.

Acknowledgments

As I was doing research for *Bad Wolf*, I came across the book *Our Father Who Art in Hell* [*Vater Unser in der Hölle*], by Ulla Fröhling (Bastei Lübbe Verlag). I was shocked, shaken, and deeply moved by the protagonist's terrible fate, and I could see that the story that I originally wanted to write only scratched the surface of what is really concealed beneath the term "child abuse." I have done a lot of research and reading on this topic.

I am a supporter of the project 101 Guardian Angels Wanted, sponsored by the FeM Girls House in Frankfurt. I spoke with a therapist at this organization, which cares for traumatized girls, and I learned that cases such as those Ulla Fröhling describes in her book are, unfortunately, not unique. Women and children repeatedly endure this kind of suffering behind closed doors, and on a daily basis within families and in circles of friends and acquaintances. I realized how crucial it is to examine the topic of child abuse, and how immense the fear and distress of these abused girls are.

I offer my thanks to Ulla Fröhling for her courageous and important book. I hope that with this novel I can make a small contribution to continuing the discussion of this taboo topic.

Many wonderful people have supported me during the writing of this book, encouraging me and showing me the right path whenever I got stuck. Here I have to mention especially Susanne Hecker and my dear writer colleague Steffi von Wolff.

I thank my parents, Dr. Bernward and Carola Löwenberg, and my wonderful sisters, Claudia Cohen and Camilla Altvater, as well as my niece, Caroline Cohen, for their support, and for patiently reading drafts of the manuscript and offering very helpful suggestions. They are the best family anyone could wish for.

A big thank-you to Margrit Osterwold and once again to Steffi. You made Hamburg into a second home for me.

I thank Catrin Runge, Gaby Pohl, Simone Schreiber, Ewald Jacobi, Vanessa Müller-Raidt, Iska Peller, Frank Wagner, Susanne Trouet, Andrea Wildgruber, Anke Demmig, Anne Pfenninger, Beate Caglar, Claudia Gnass, and Claudia Herrmann. *Amicus certus in re incerta cernitur.* Thank you for your friendship.

Special thanks to Detective Superintendent Andrea Rupp for giving the book a careful early reading and for offering helpful remarks with regard to the work of the Criminal Police.

A big thank-you goes out to the wonderful staff at Ullstein Verlag for their trust and support. In particular, I'd like to thank my excellent editors,

Marion Vazquez and Kristine Kress, who with tact and encouragement have made a book emerge from an initial idea.

Many thanks to Steven T. Murray and his wife, Tiina, for yet another fantastic and sensitive translation! Thanks also to my U.S. publisher, St. Martin's Press, and to PanMacmillan in the UK, and to my editors at both publishers, Daniela Rapp and Trisha Jackson.

I also thank all my readers for liking my books. That makes me happy.

And finally, I thank from the bottom of my heart a very special person. Matthias, I have arrived. So it should be; so it shall remain.

Nele Neuhaus, August 2012

Center Point Large Print
600 Brooks Road / PO Box 1
Thorndike ME 04986-0001 USA

(207) 568-3717

US & Canada:
1 800 929-9108
www.centerpointlargeprint.com